SNOW WHITE

MATT PHELAN

CANDLEWICK PRESS

First edition 2016

Library of Congress Catalog Card Number 2015940364
ISBN 978-0-7636-7233-1

17 18 19 20 21 CCP 10 9 8 7 6 5

Printed in Shenzhen, Guangdong, China

FSC www.fsc.org MIX Paper from responsible sources FSC® C008047

This book was typeset in Futura.
The illustrations were done in pencil, ink, and
watercolor with digital adjustments.

Candlewick Press
99 Dover Street
Somerville, Massachusetts 02144

visit us at www.candlewick.com

For Rebecca Sherman

A DROP OF BLOOD

QUEEN OF THE FOLLIES

A YOUNG GIRL SENT AWAY TO SCHOOL

THE TICKER TAPE

SNOW RETURNS

MR. HUNT HAS A DRINK

HOOVERVILLE

LATE NIGHT AT THE BUTCHER'S

LOST IN THE ALLEYS

SEVEN SMALL MEN

THE WINDOW AT MACY'S

INSANE WITH JEALOUSY

AN APPLE FOR A PRETTY THING

NAMES

UP IN LIGHTS

THE GLASS COFFIN

DETECTIVE PRINCE OVERSTEPS HIS BOUNDS

AND THEY LIVED . . .

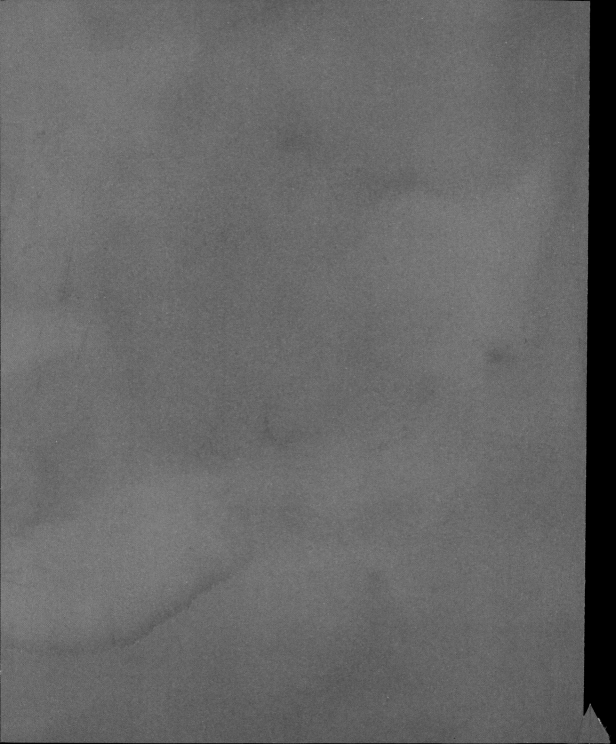

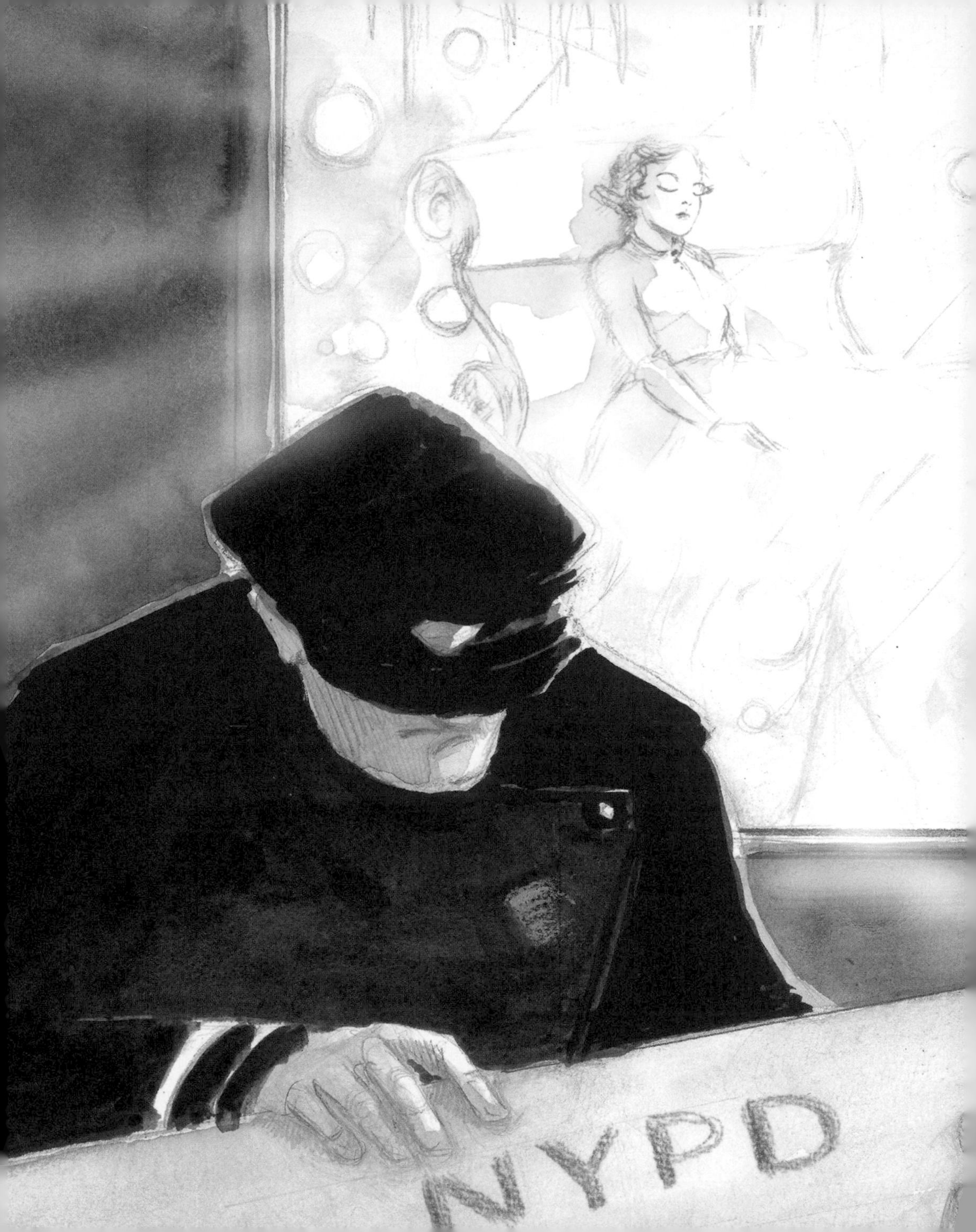
NYPD

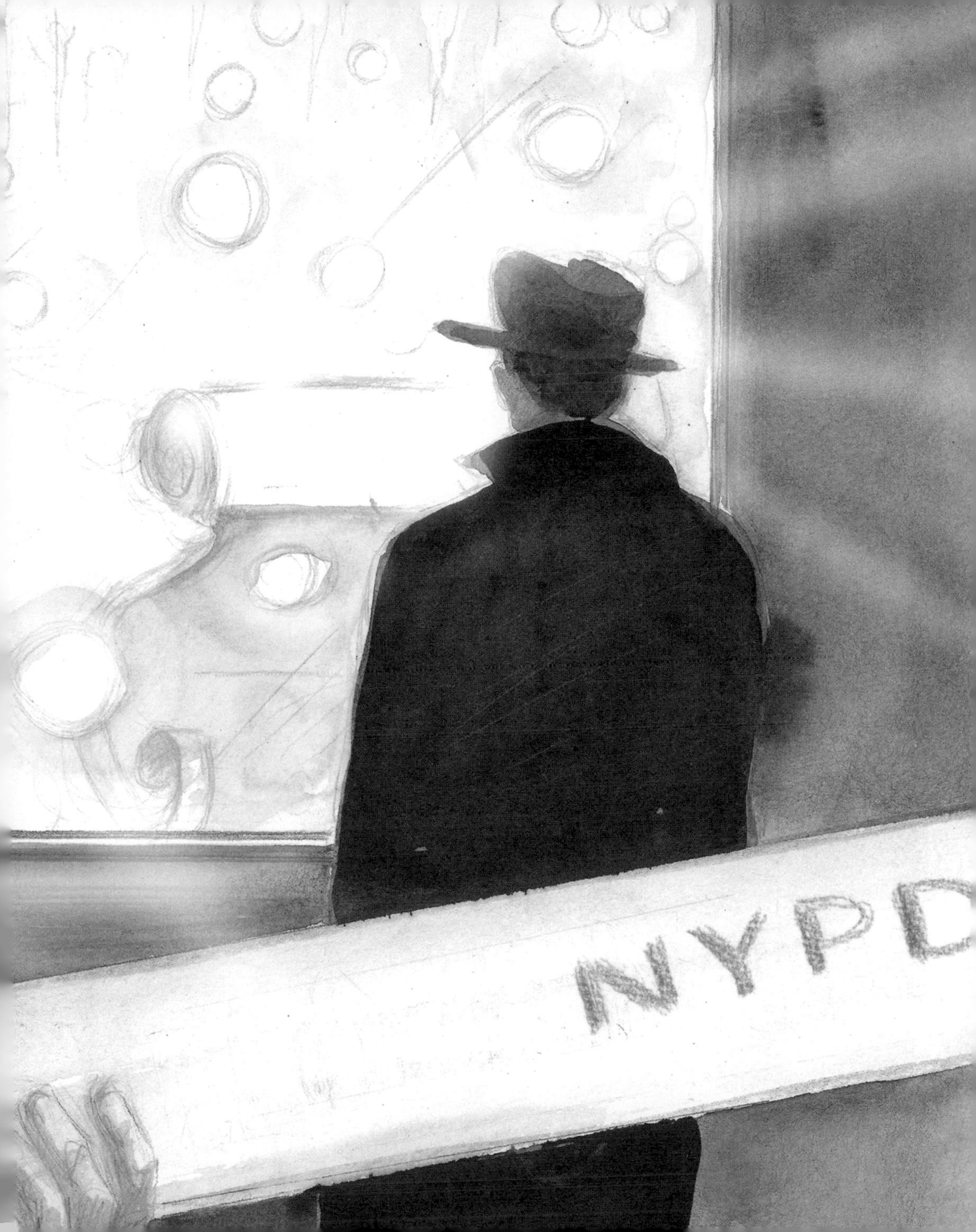
NYPD

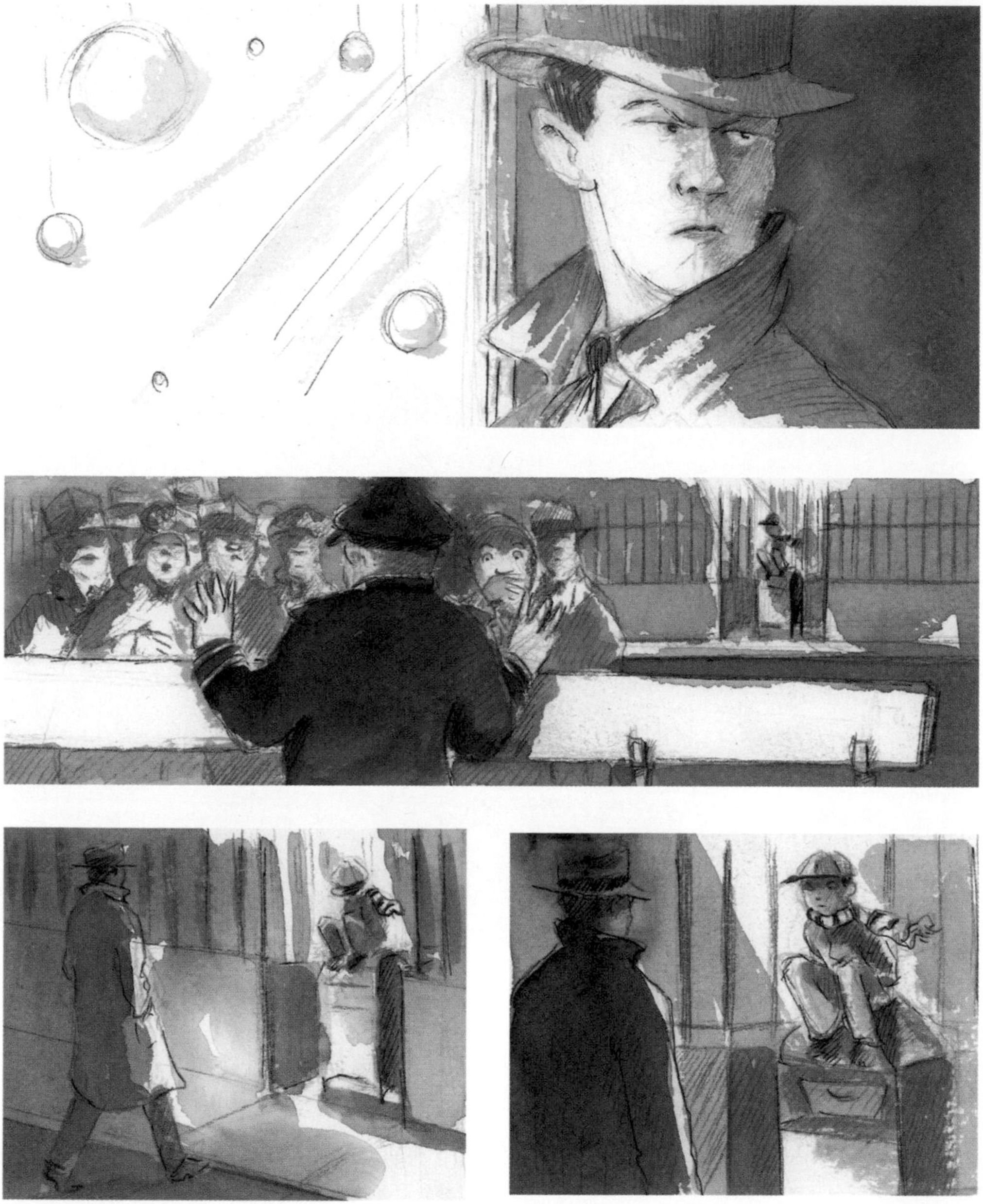

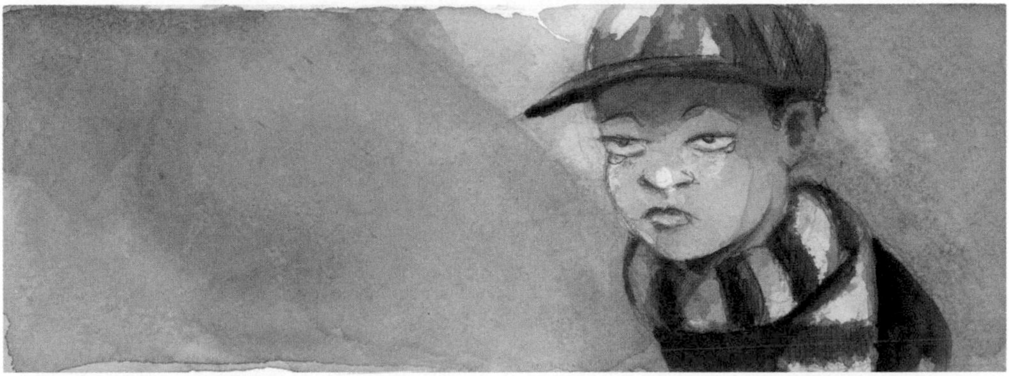

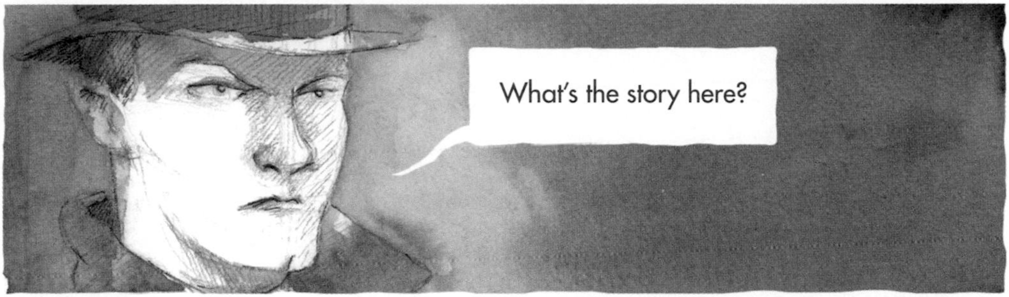
What's the story here?

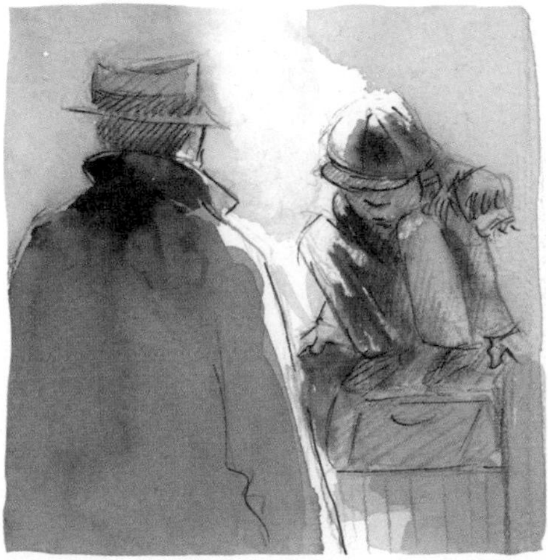

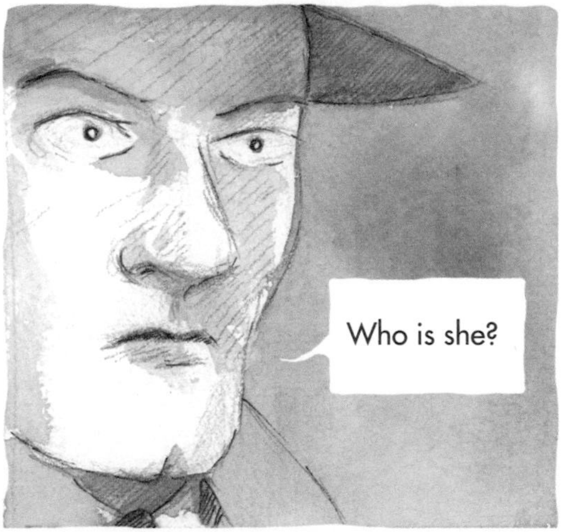
Who is she?

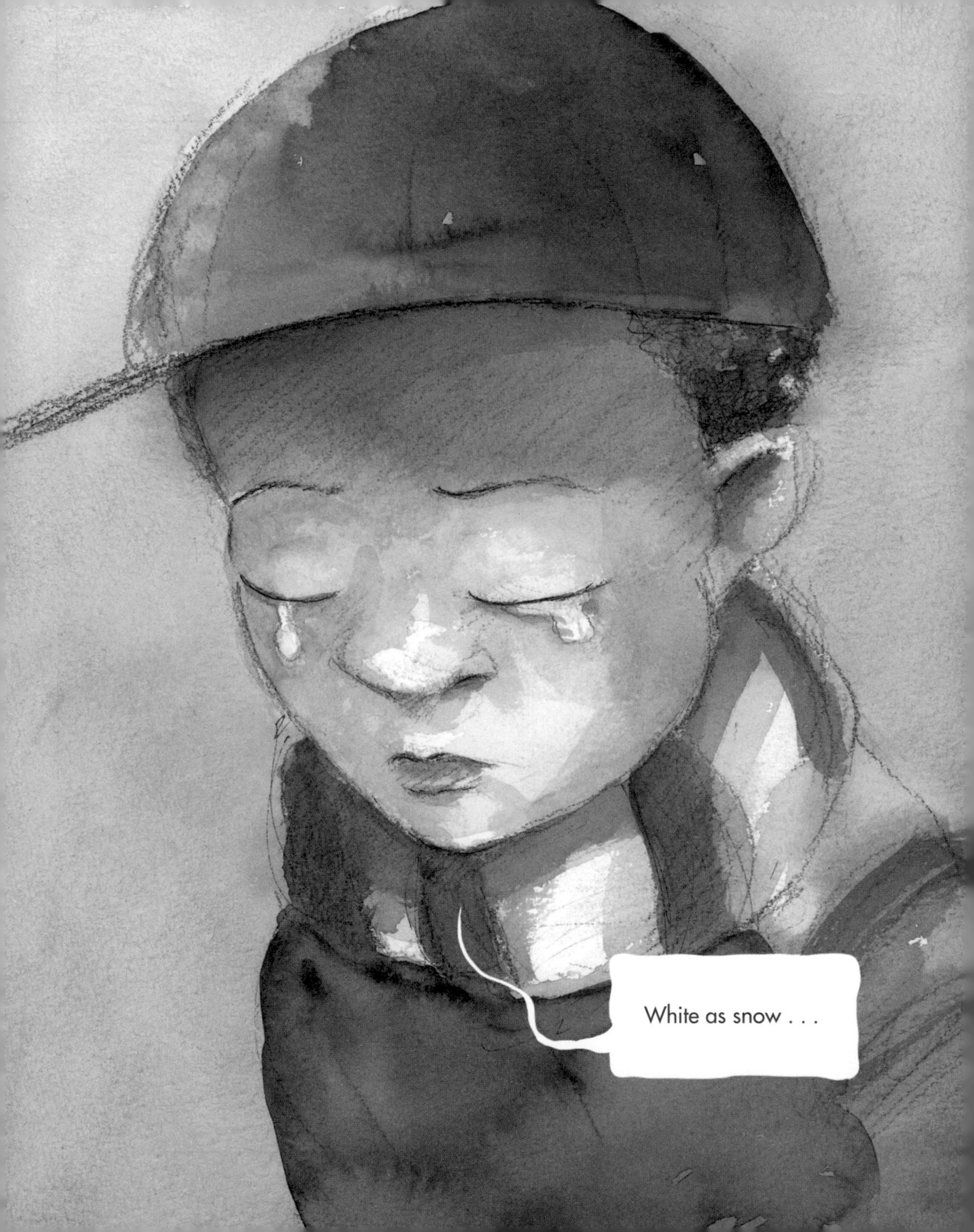
White as snow . . .

A DROP
OF BLOOD

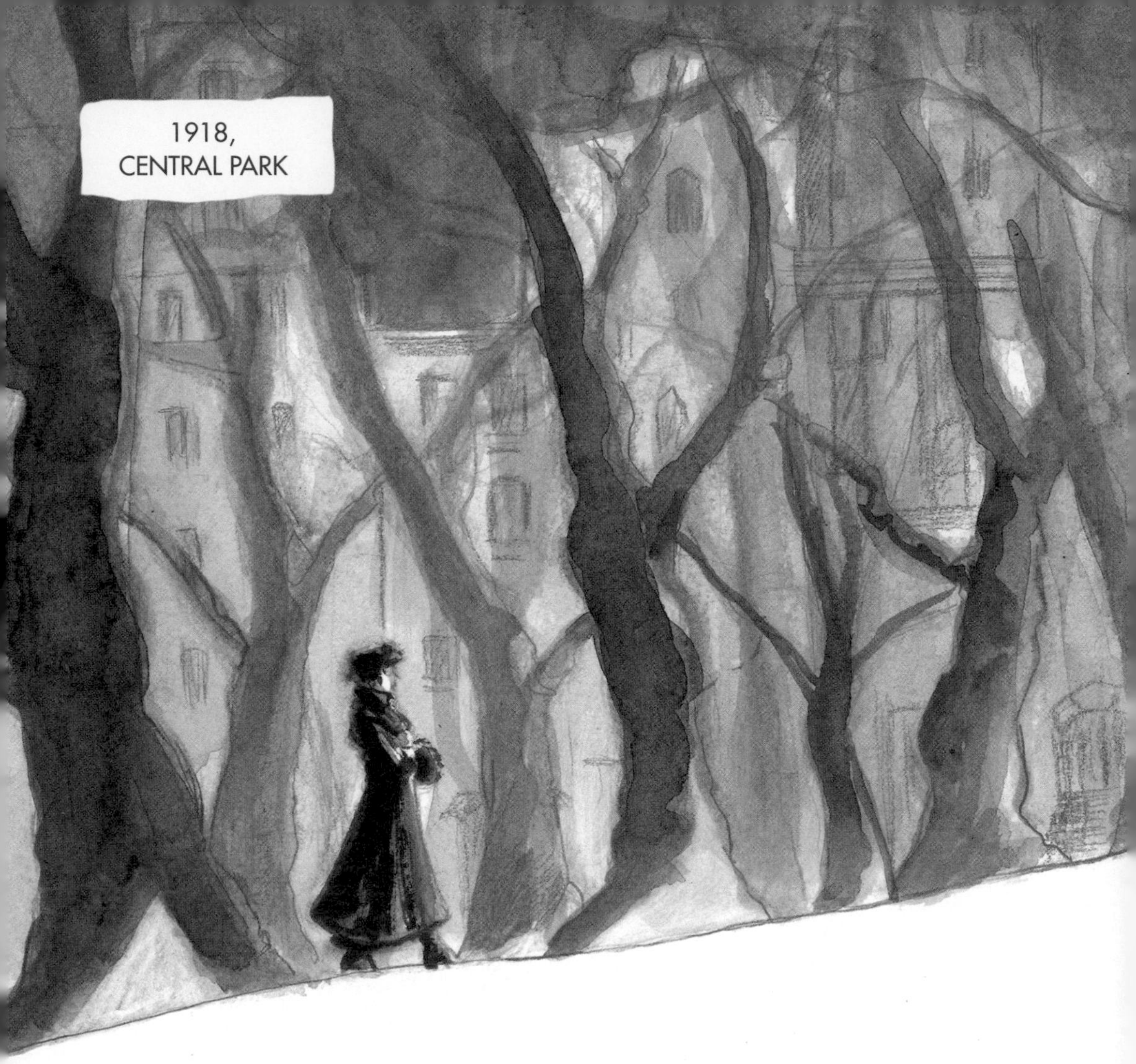
1918,
CENTRAL PARK

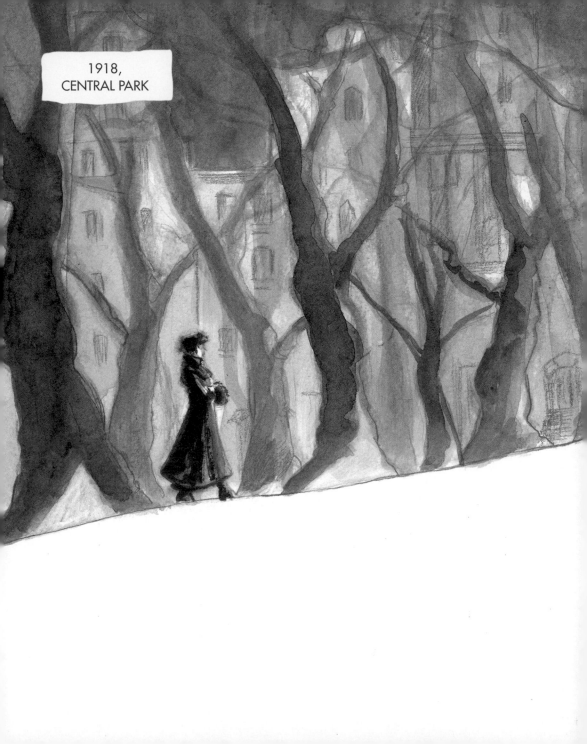

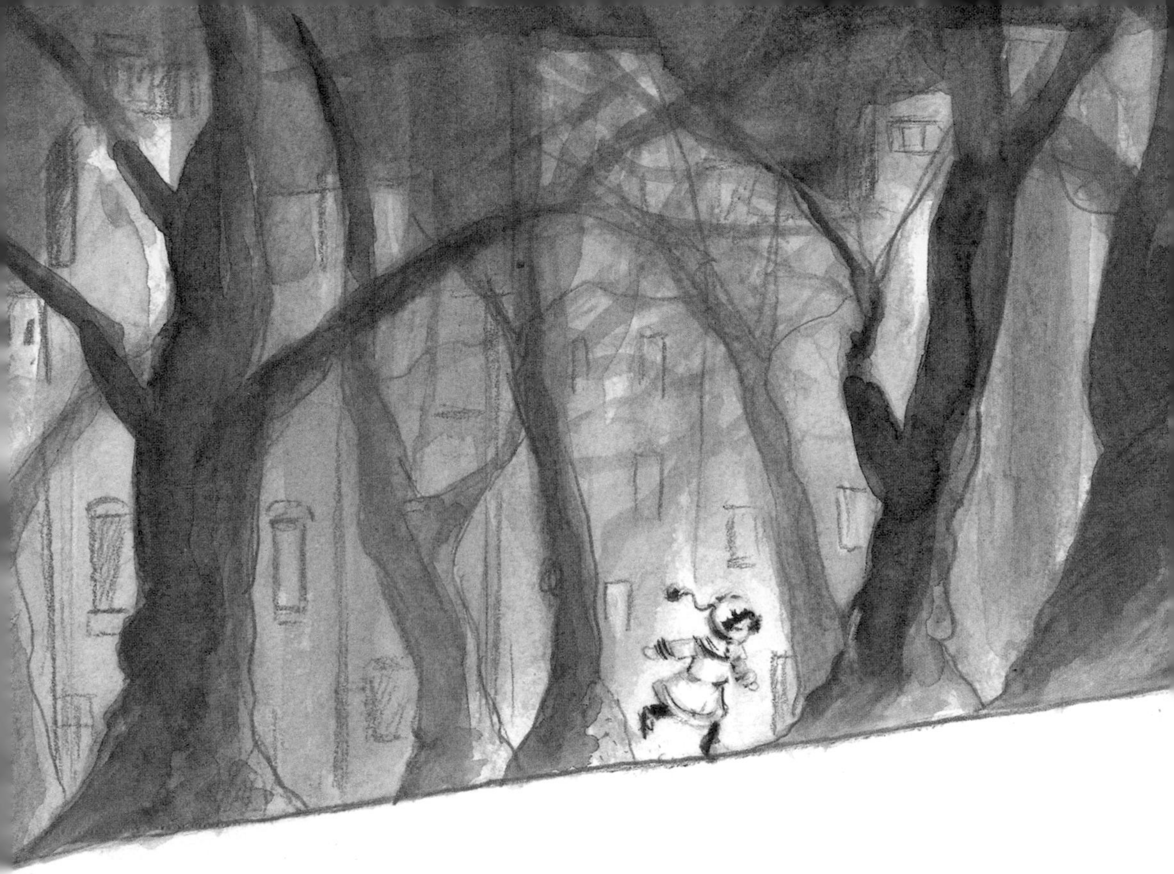

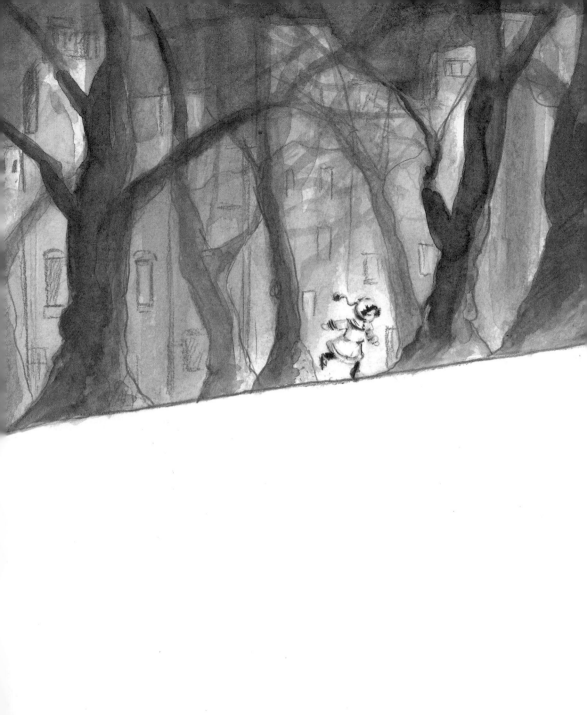

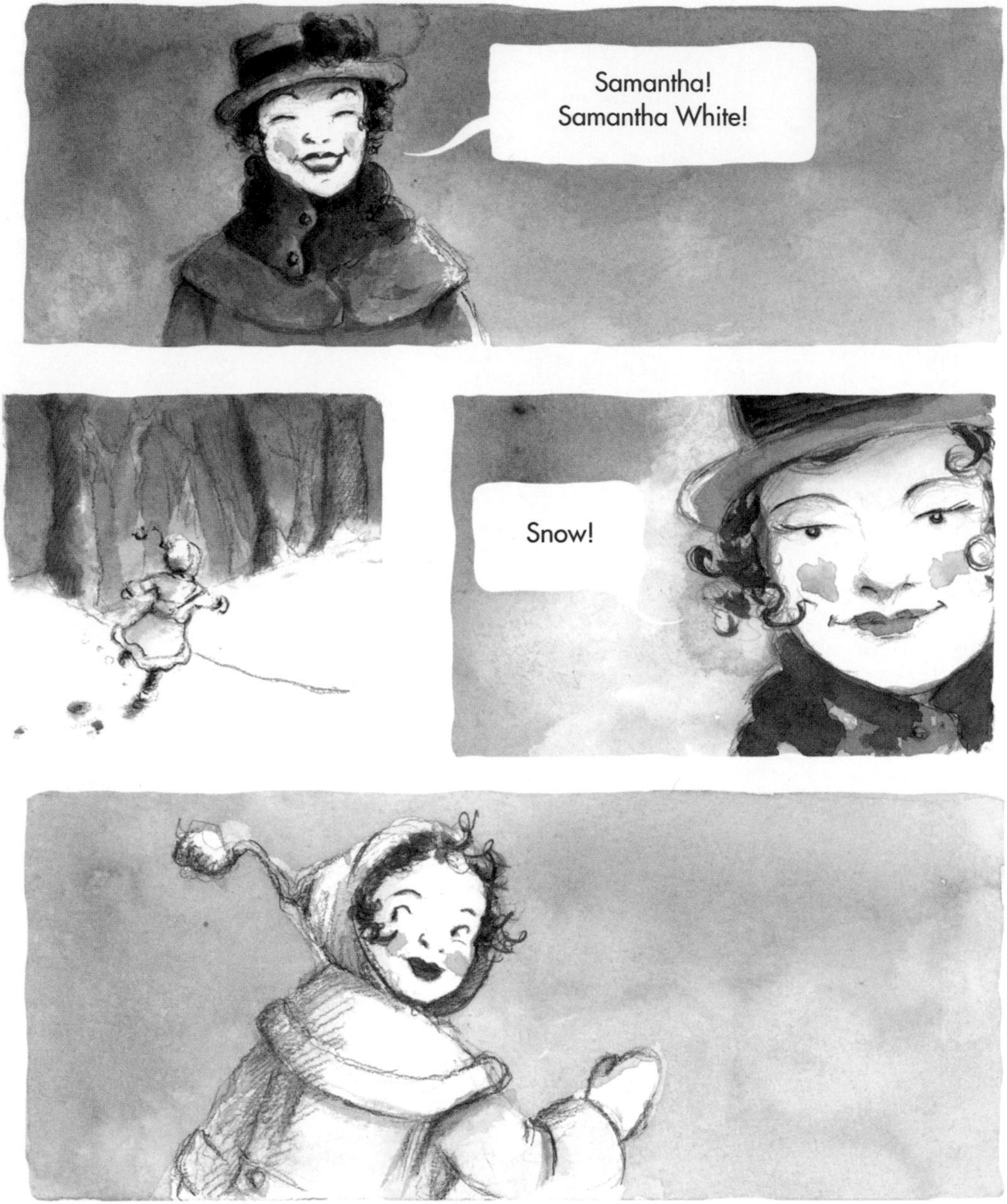
Samantha!
Samantha White!
Snow!

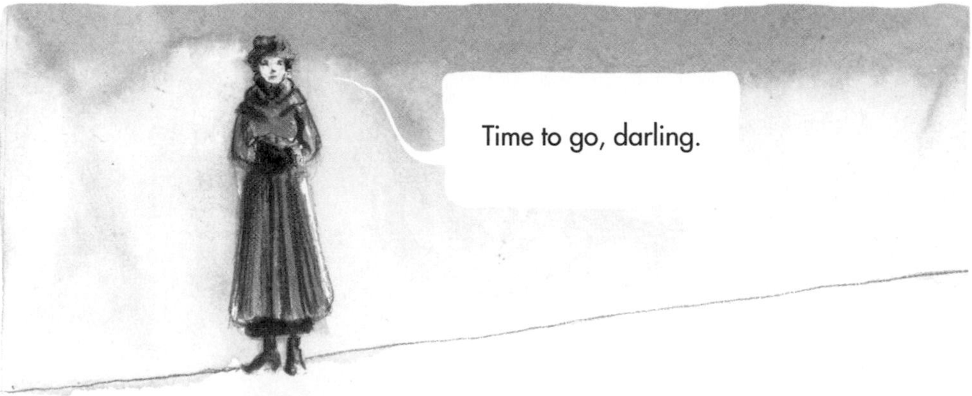
Time to go, darling.

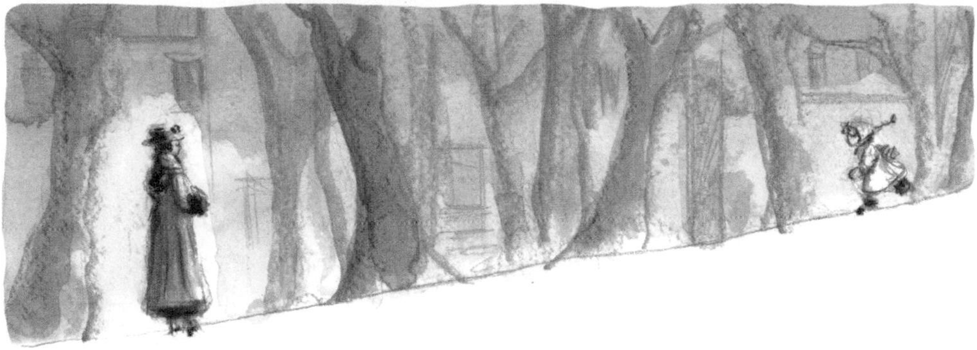

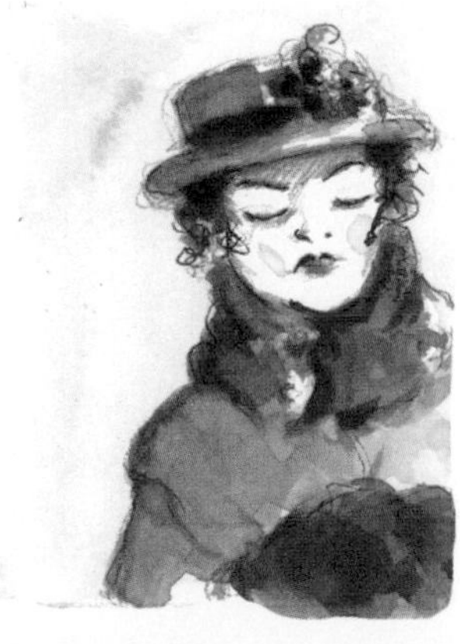

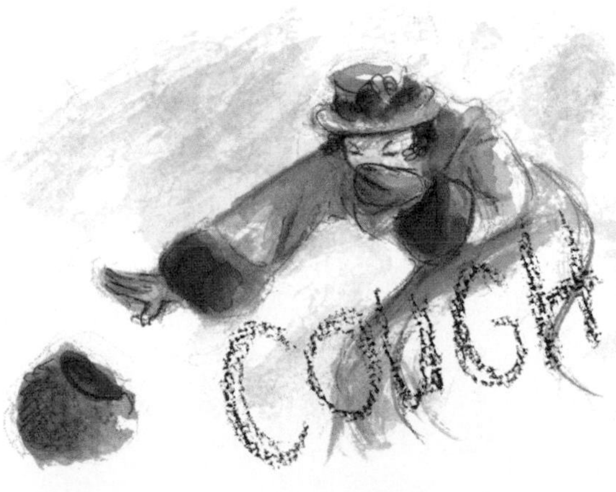
COUGH

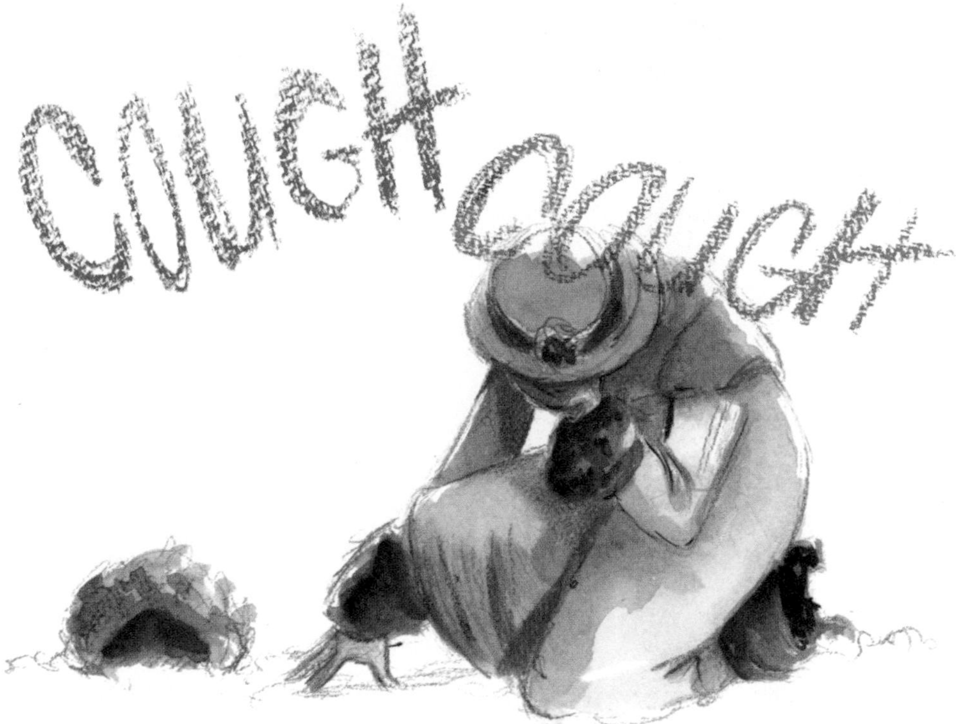
COUGH
COUGH

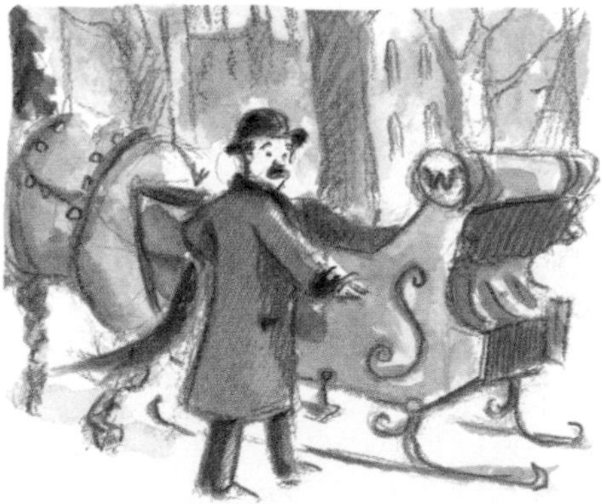

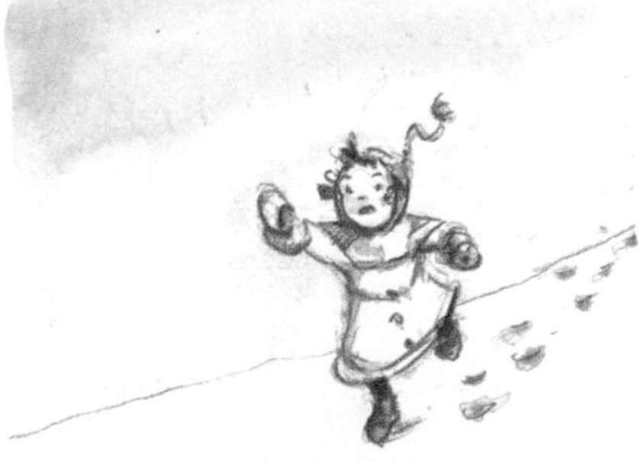

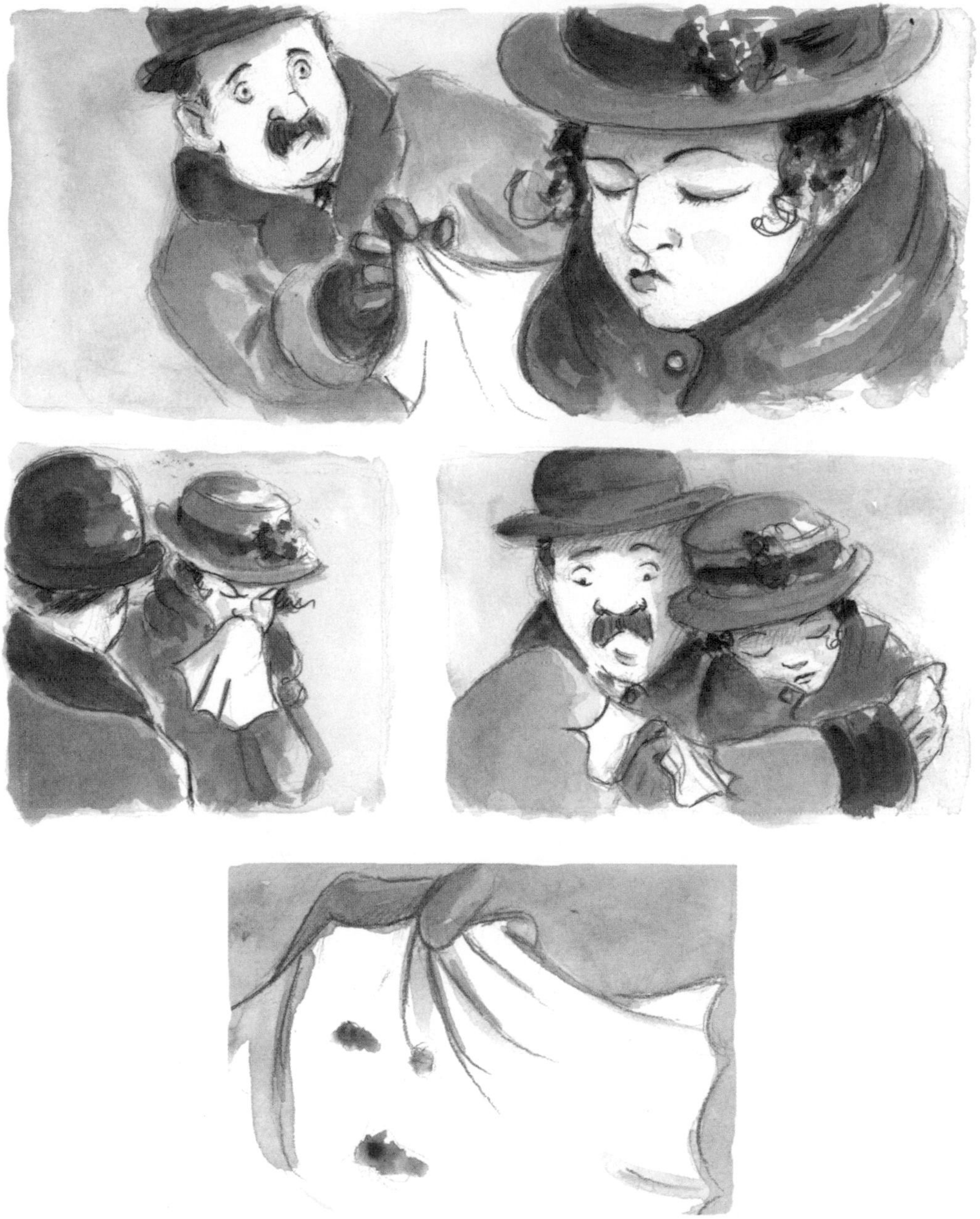

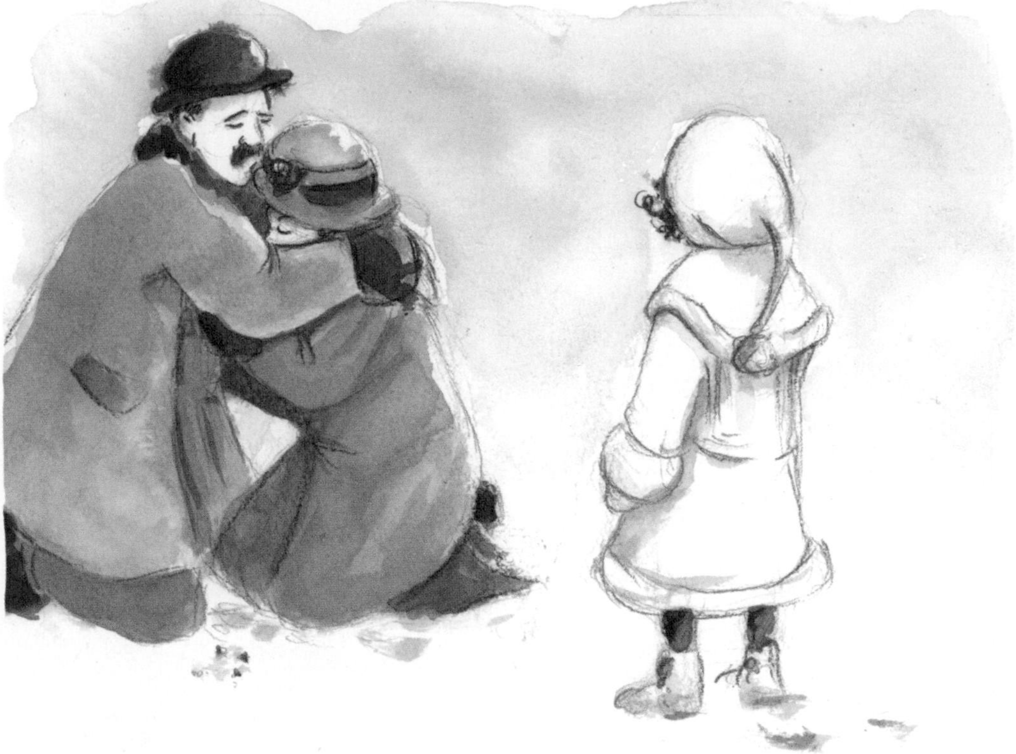

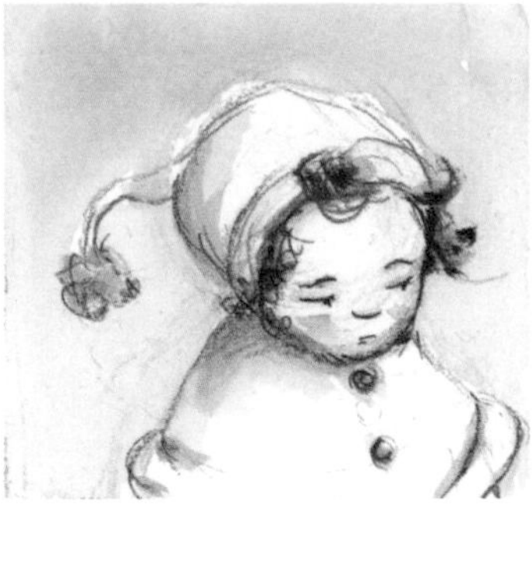

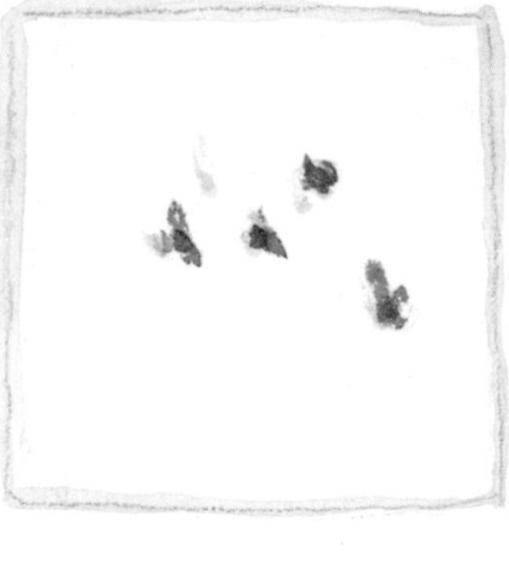

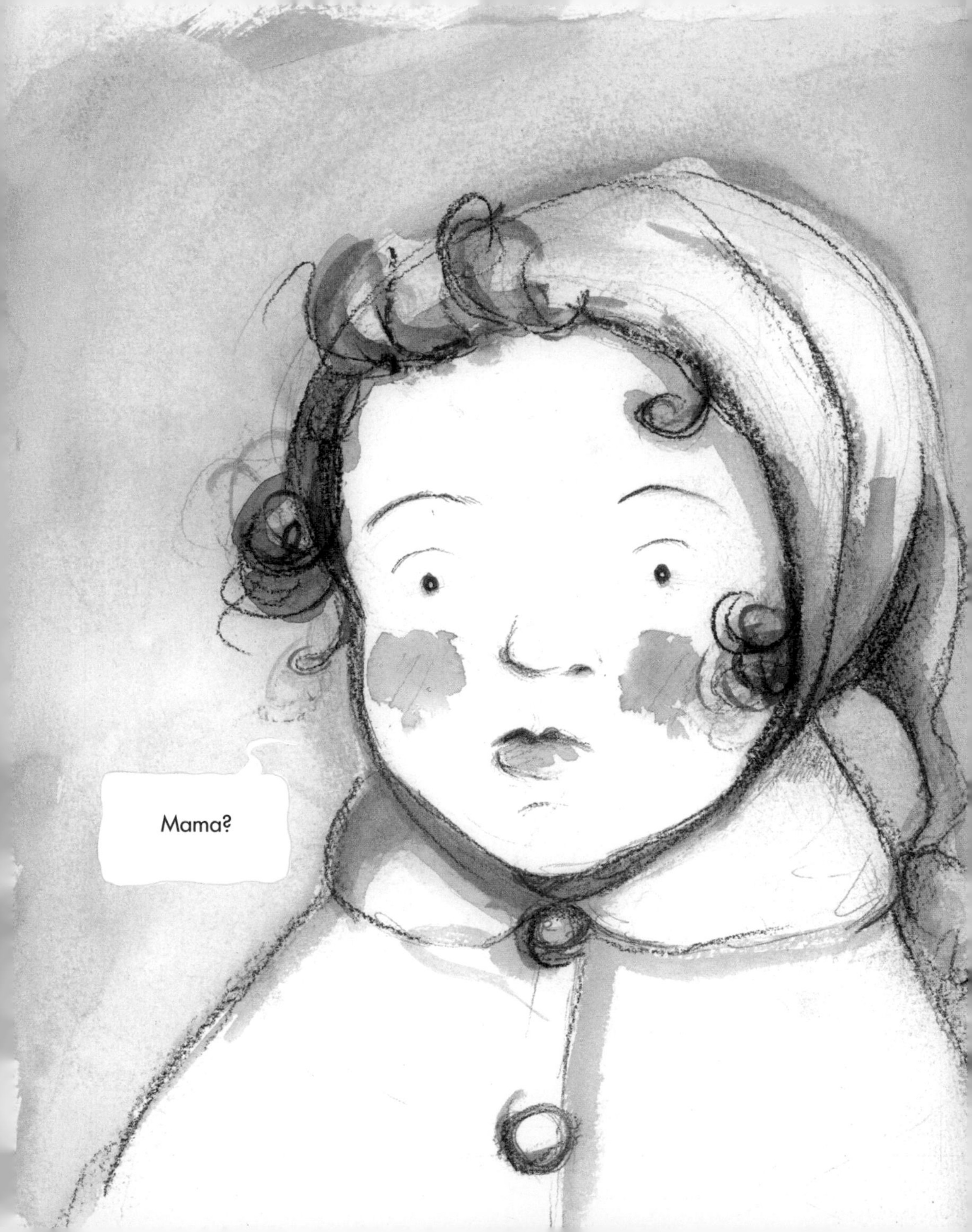
Mama?

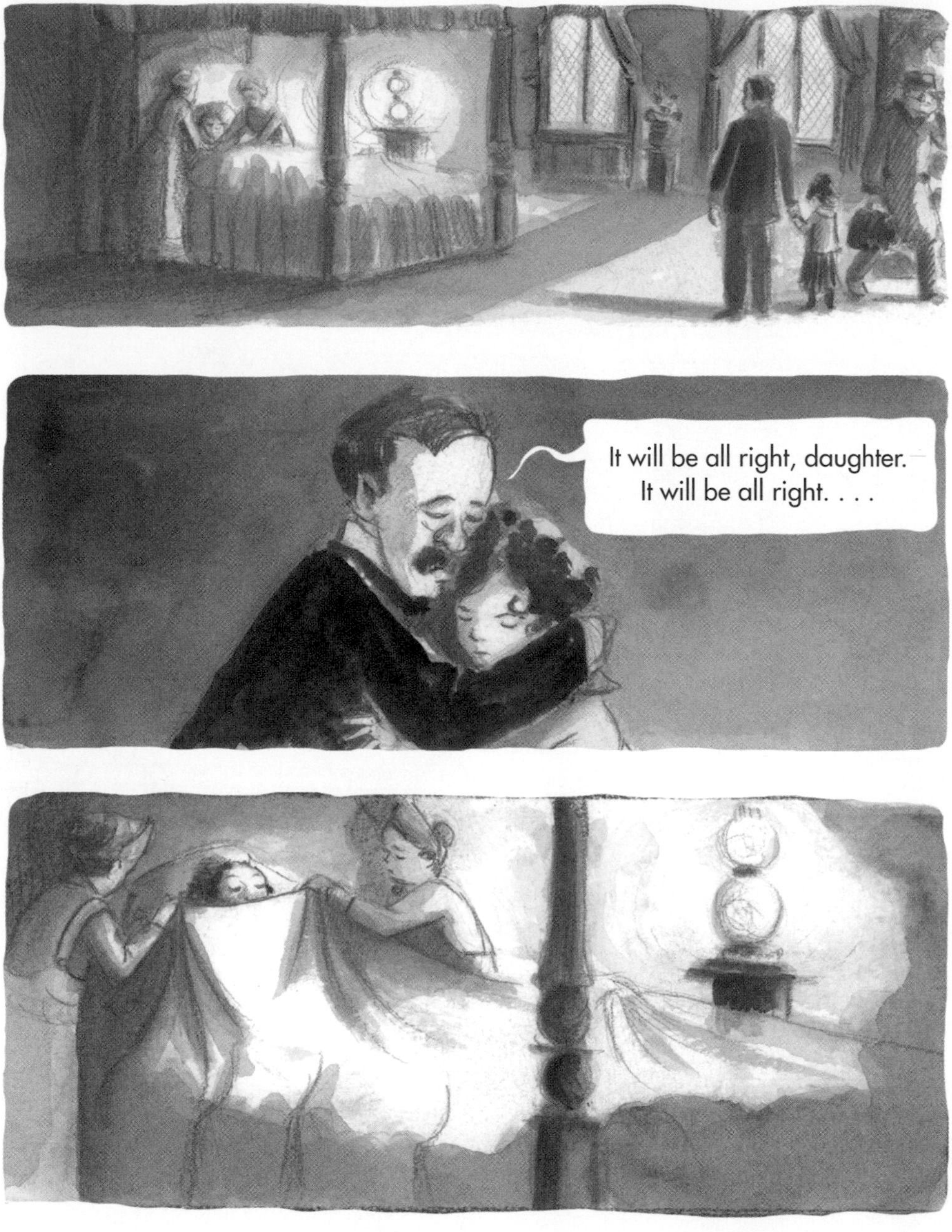
It will be all right, daughter.
It will be all right. . . .

QUEEN

OF THE

FOLLIES

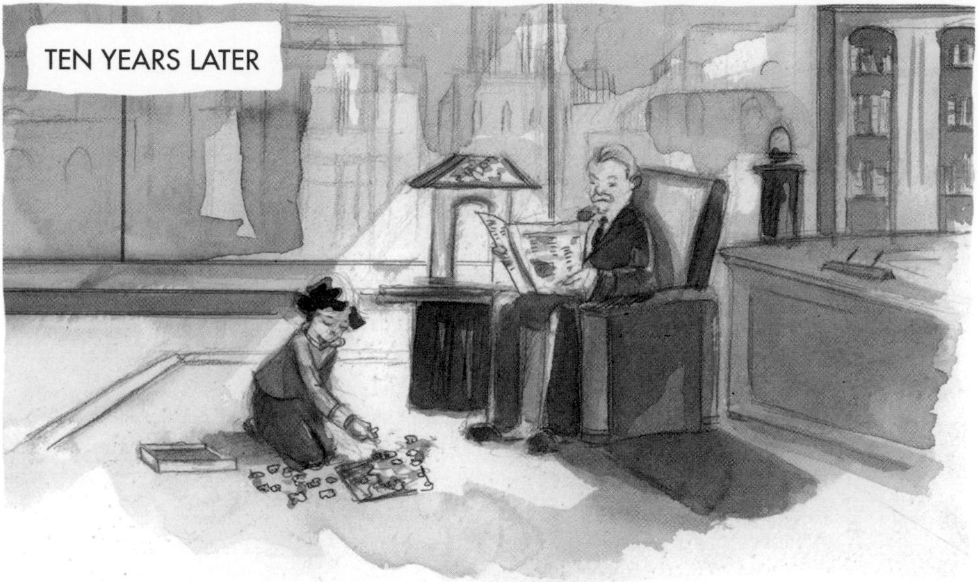
TEN YEARS LATER

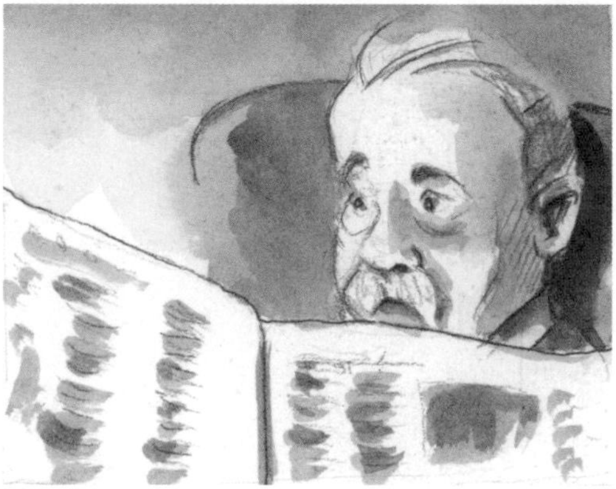

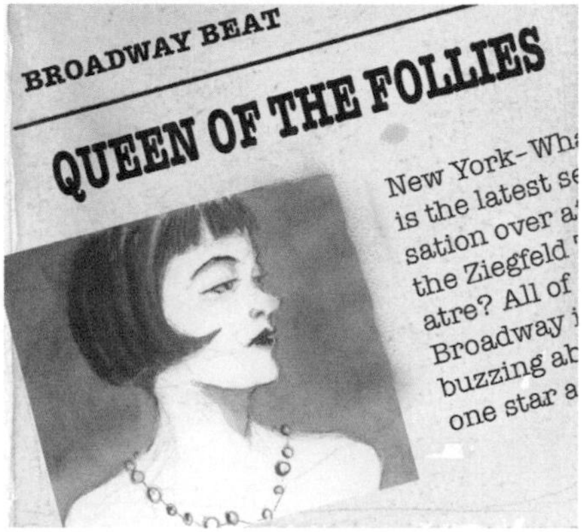
BROADWAY BEAT
QUEEN OF THE FOLLIES
New York- Wh
is the latest s
sation over a
the Ziegfeld
atre? All of
Broadway
buzzing ab
one star a

Her rise has been as stunning as it is meteoric.

Once upon a time, she was a simple, anonymous chorus girl. Today, she is Broadway royalty.

This Saturday at the Ziegfeld Theatre, 1341 Sixth Avenue.

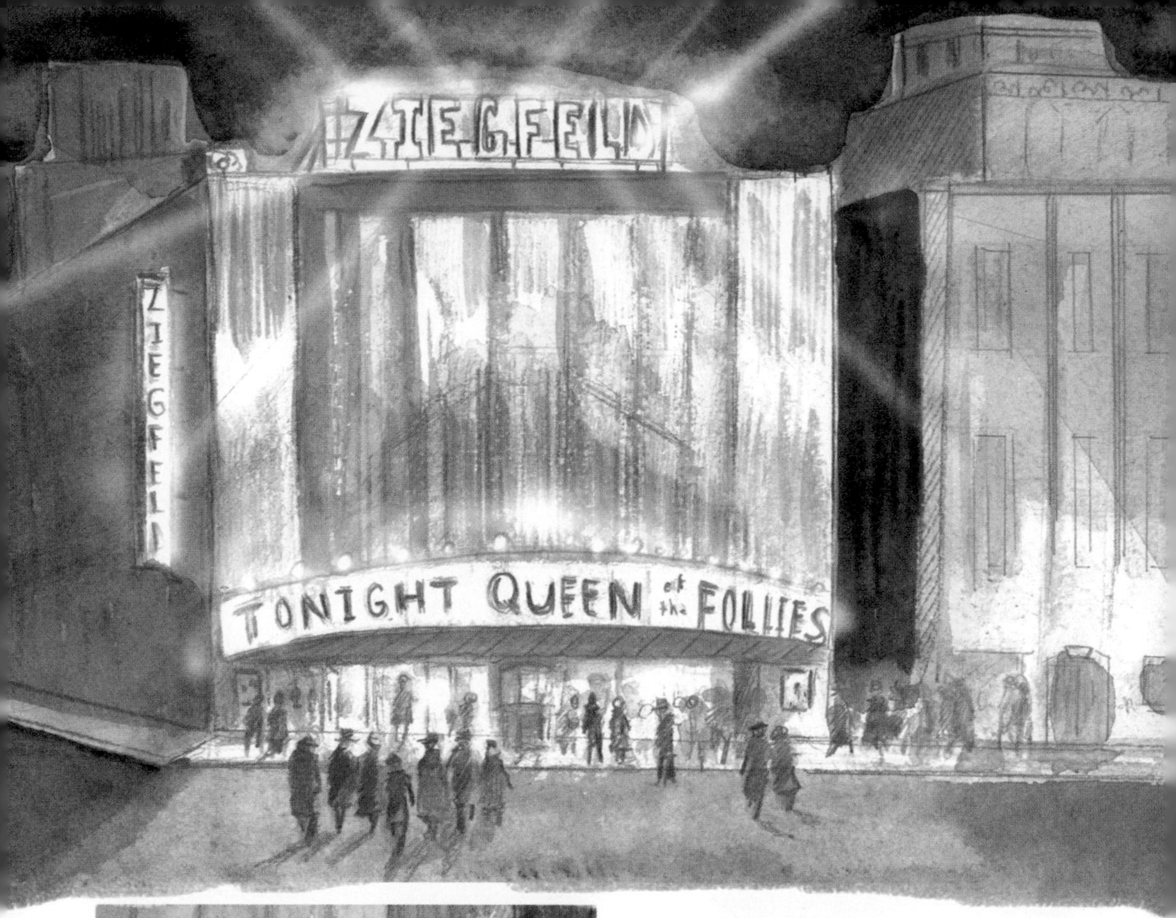
ZIEGFELD
ZIEGFELD
TONIGHT QUEEN of the FOLLIES

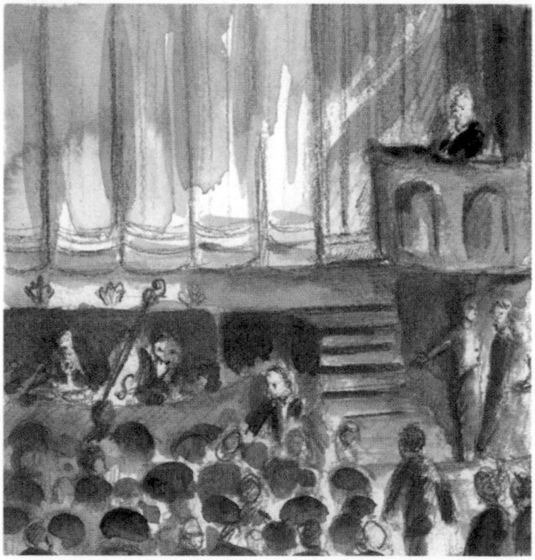

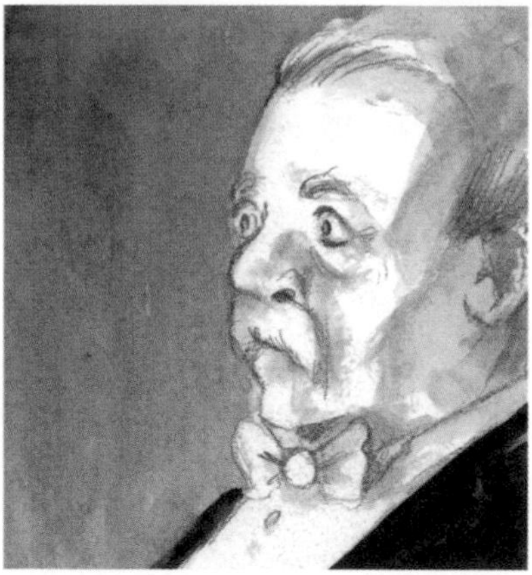

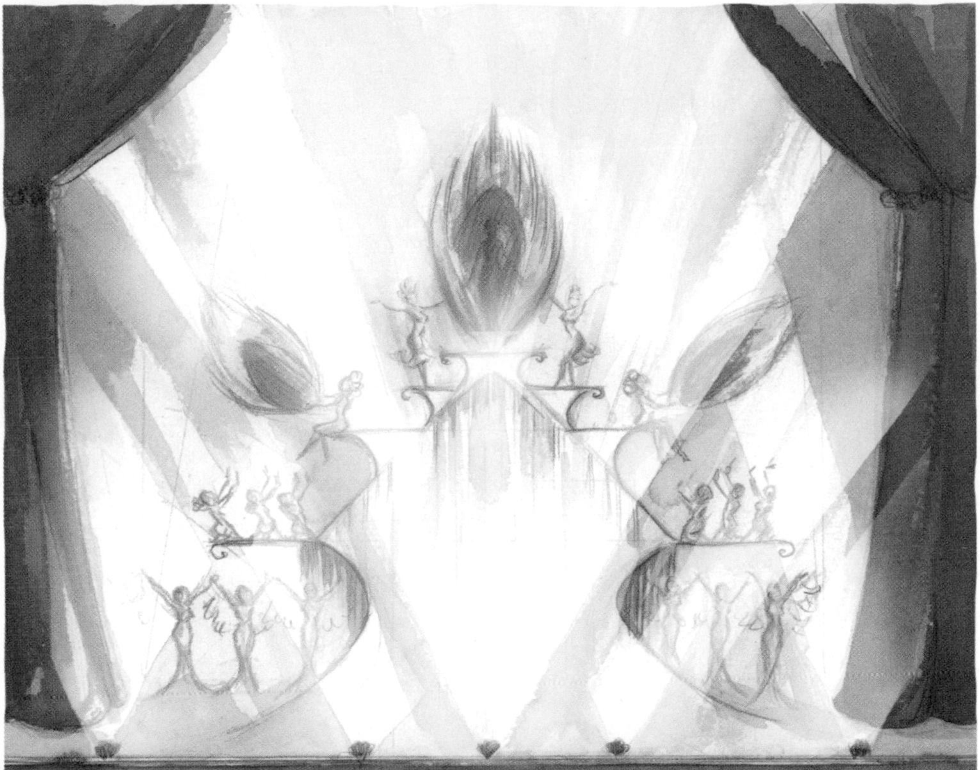

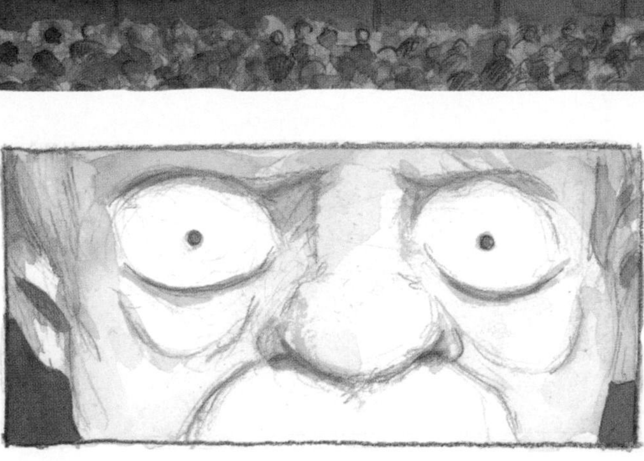

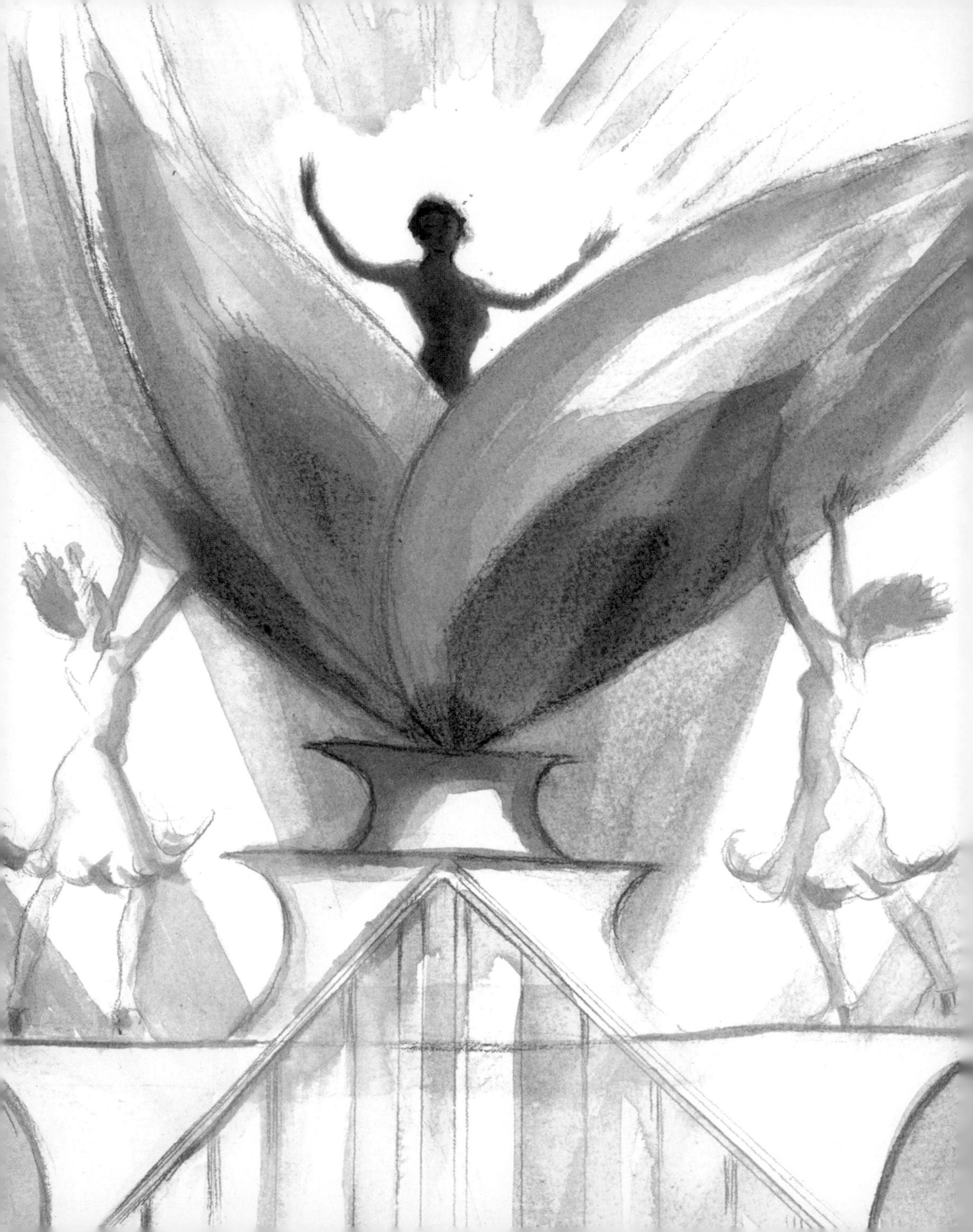

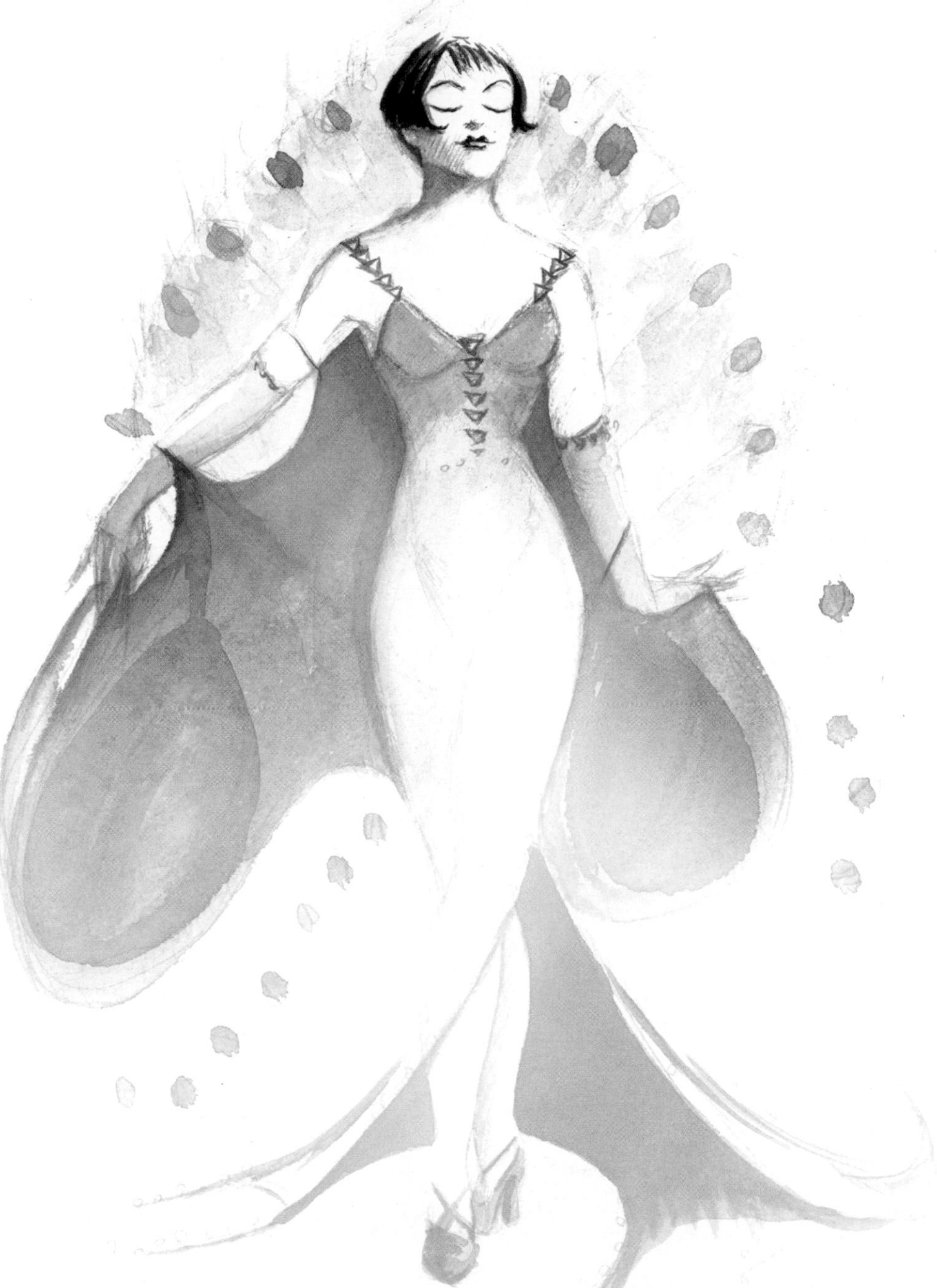

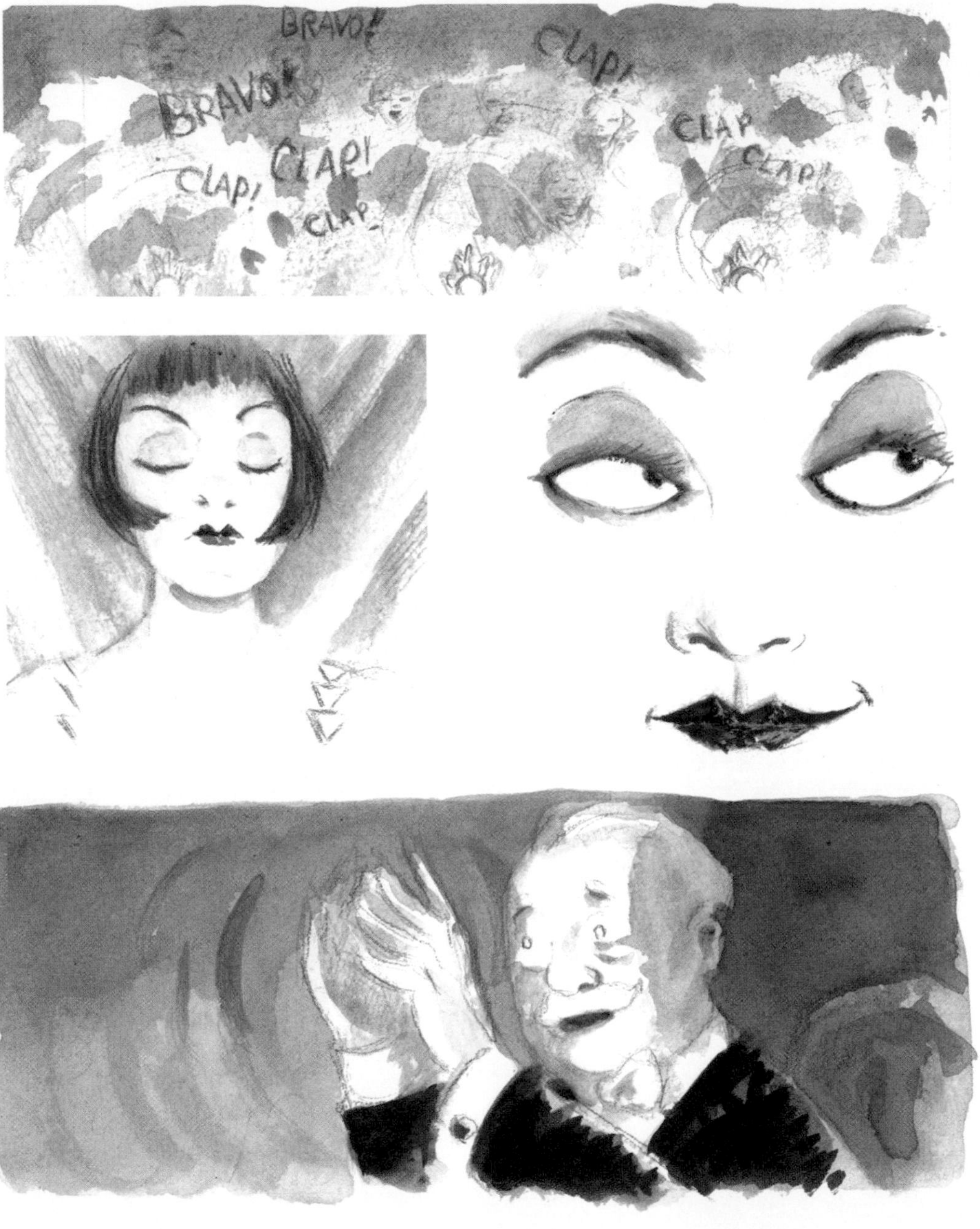
BRAVO!
CLAP!
BRAVO!
CLAP!
CLAP!
CLAP
CLAP
CLAP!

A
YOUNG GIRL
SENT AWAY TO
SCHOOL

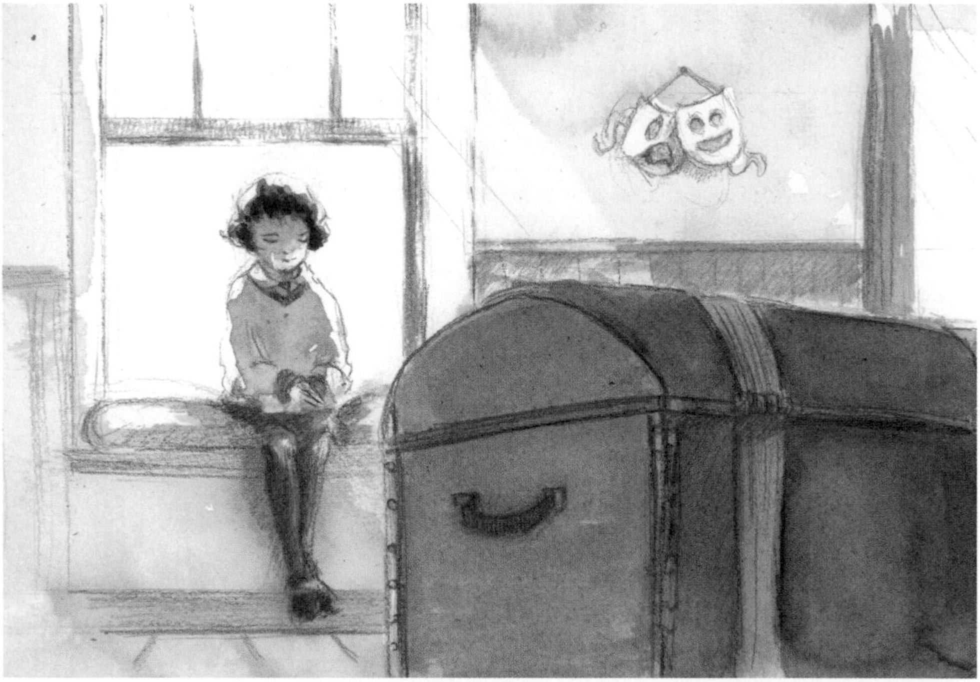

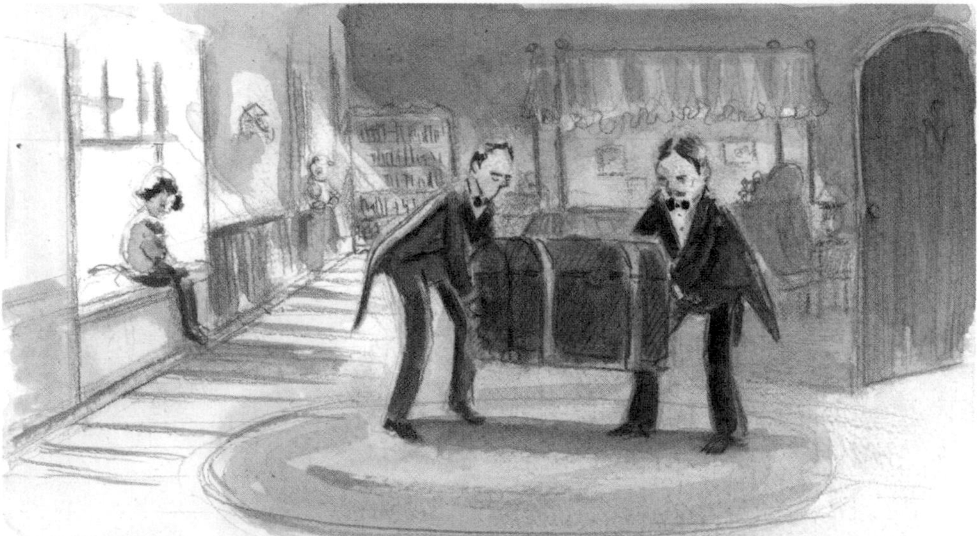

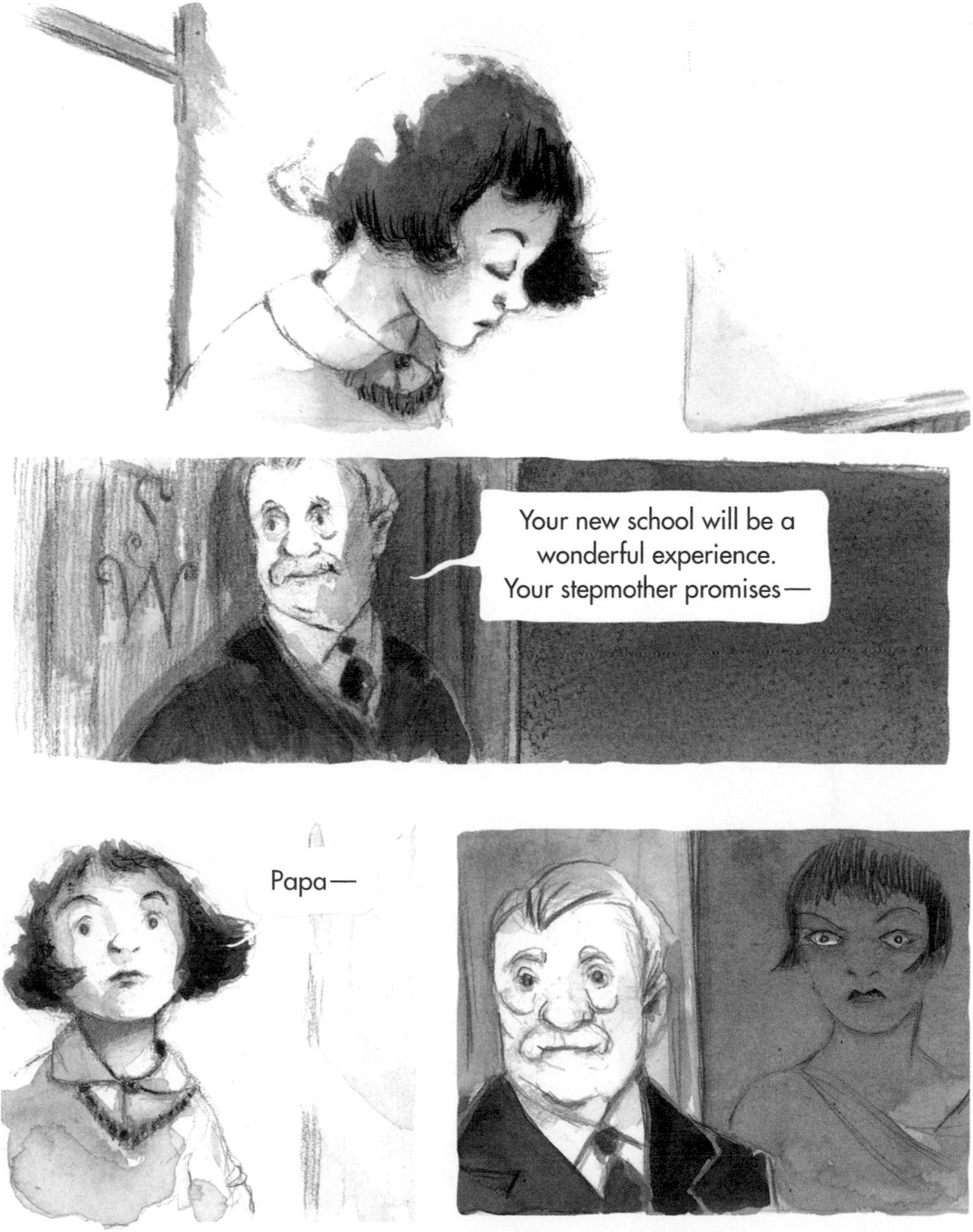
Your new school will be a wonderful experience. Your stepmother promises—
Papa—

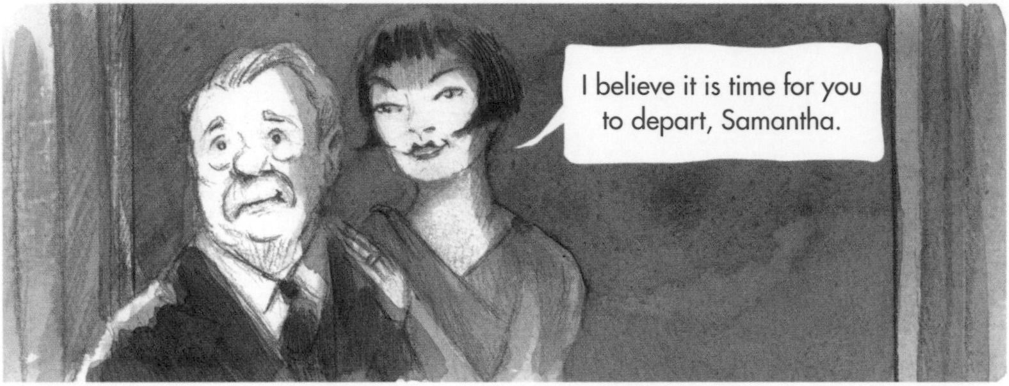
I believe it is time for you to depart, Samantha.

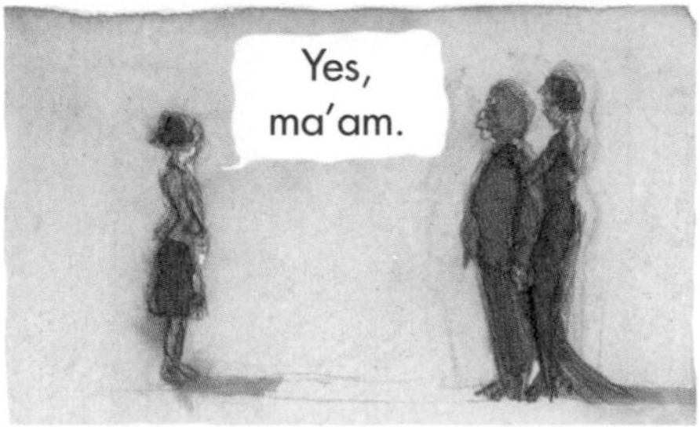
Yes, ma'am.

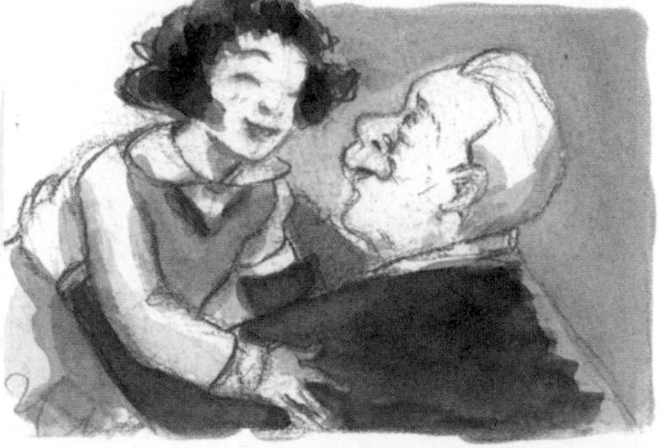

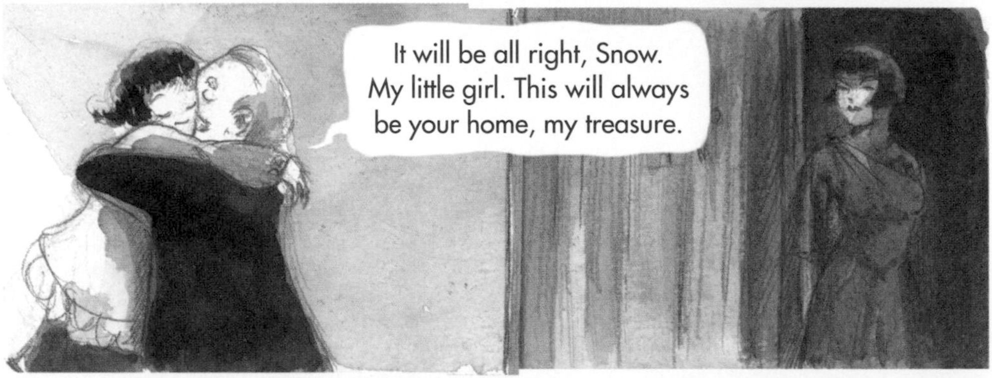
It will be all right, Snow. My little girl. This will always be your home, my treasure.

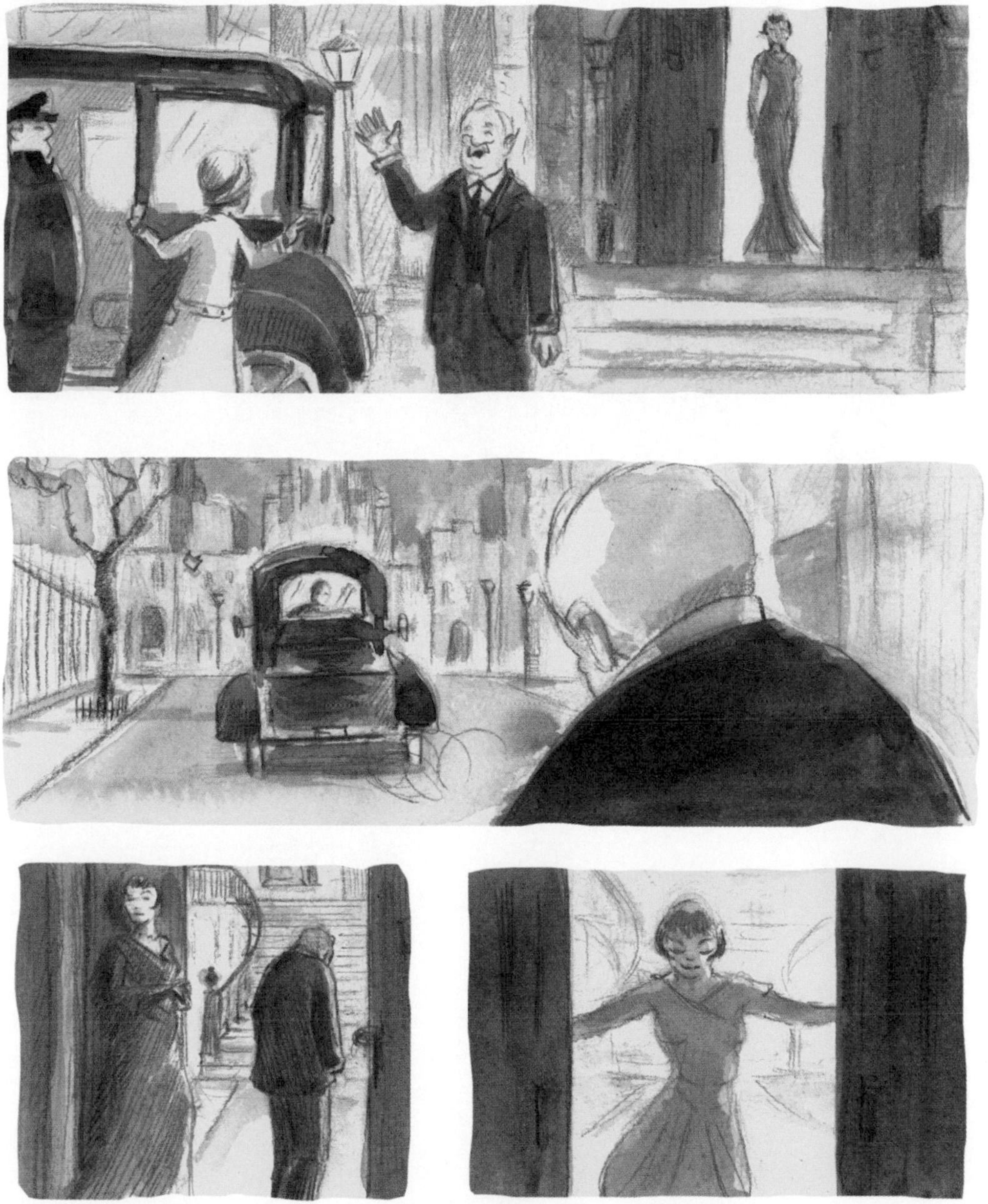

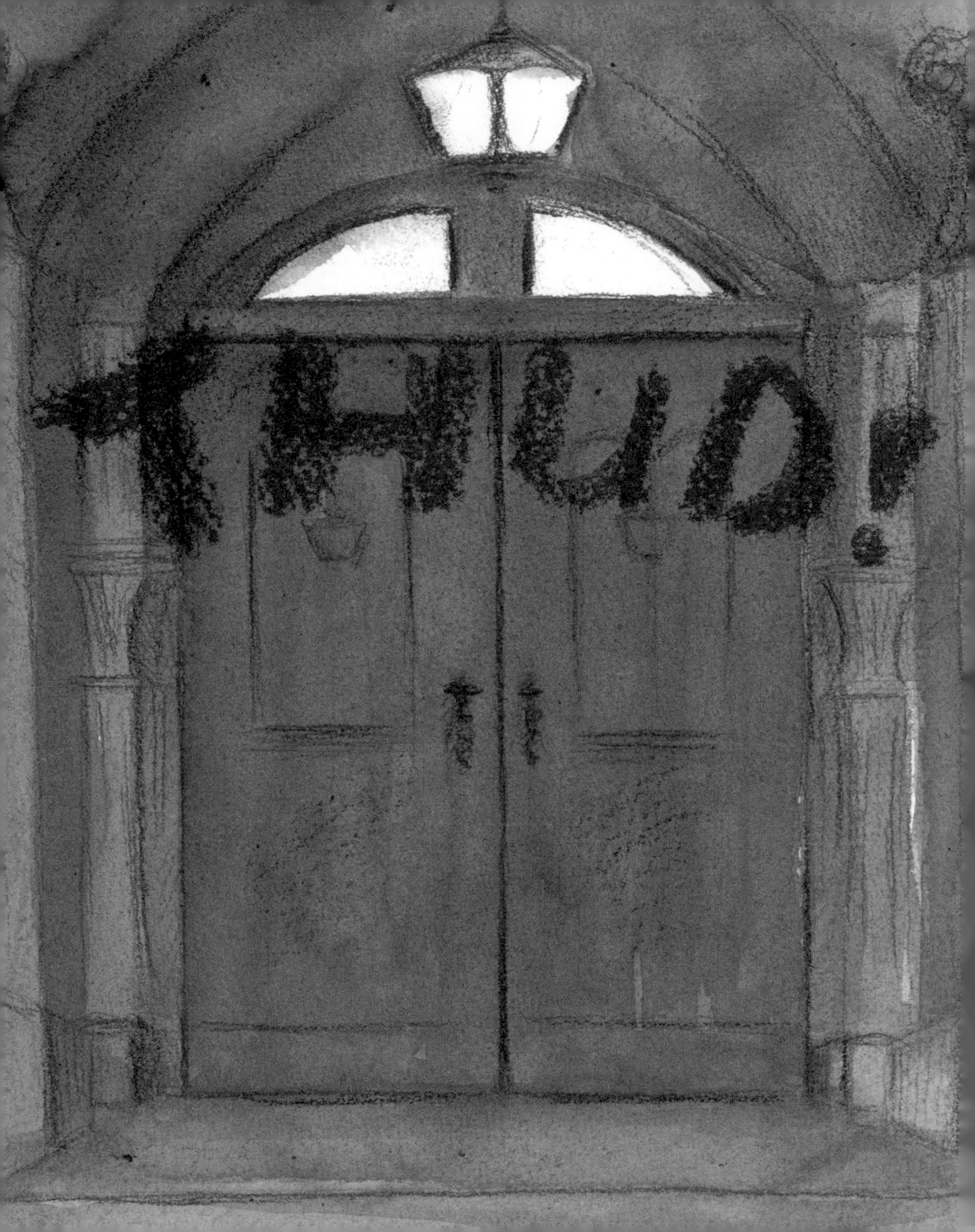
THUD!

THE
TICKER TAPE

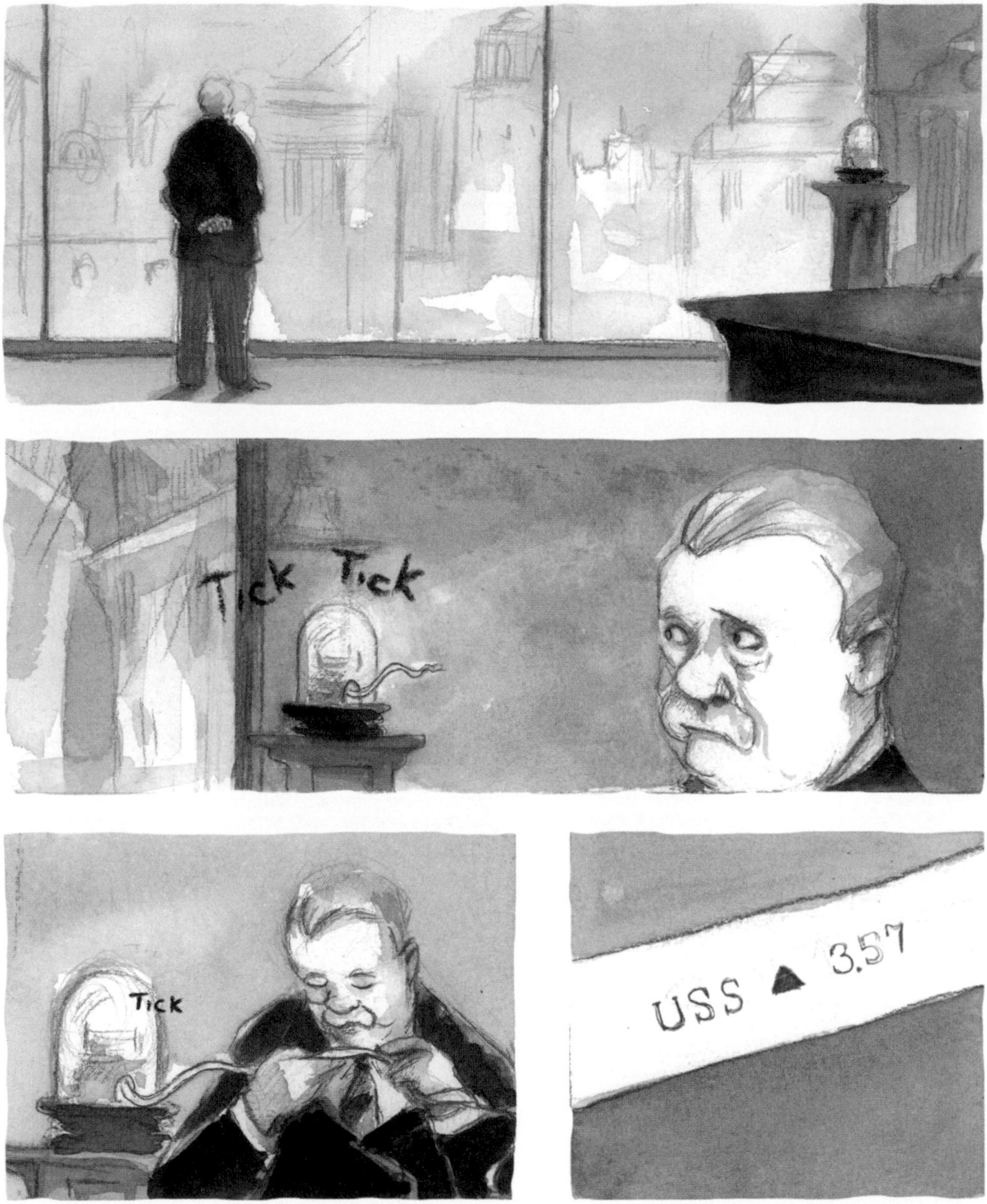
Tick Tick
Tick
USS ▲ 3.57

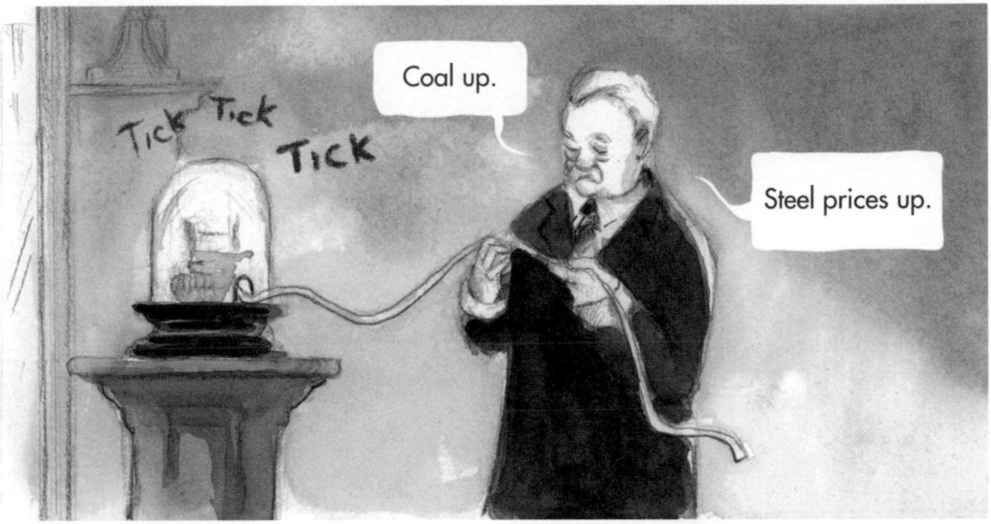
TICK TICK
TICK
Coal up.
Steel prices up.

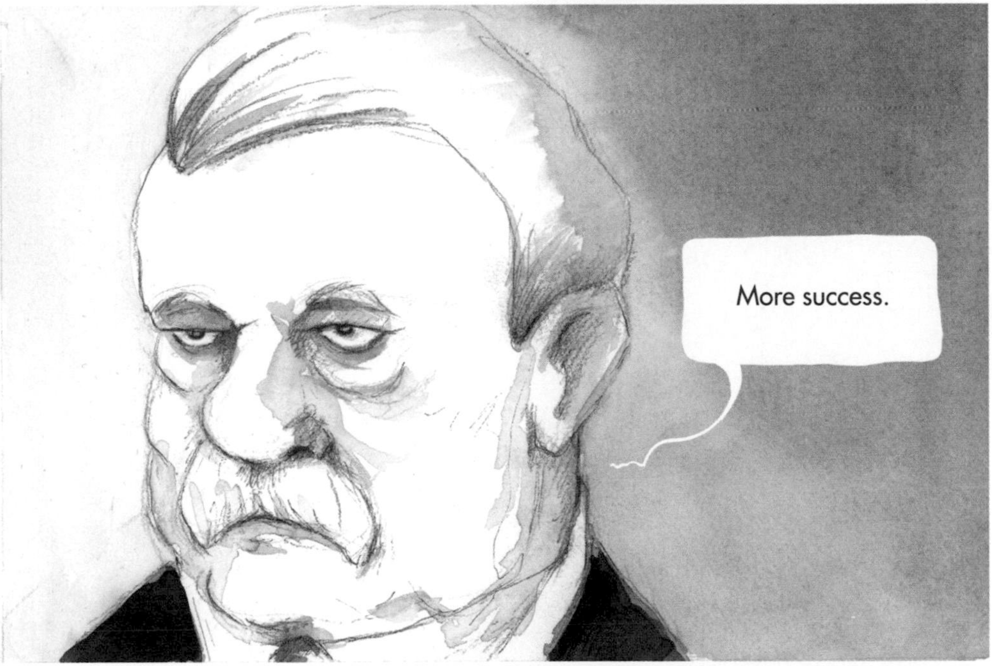
More success.

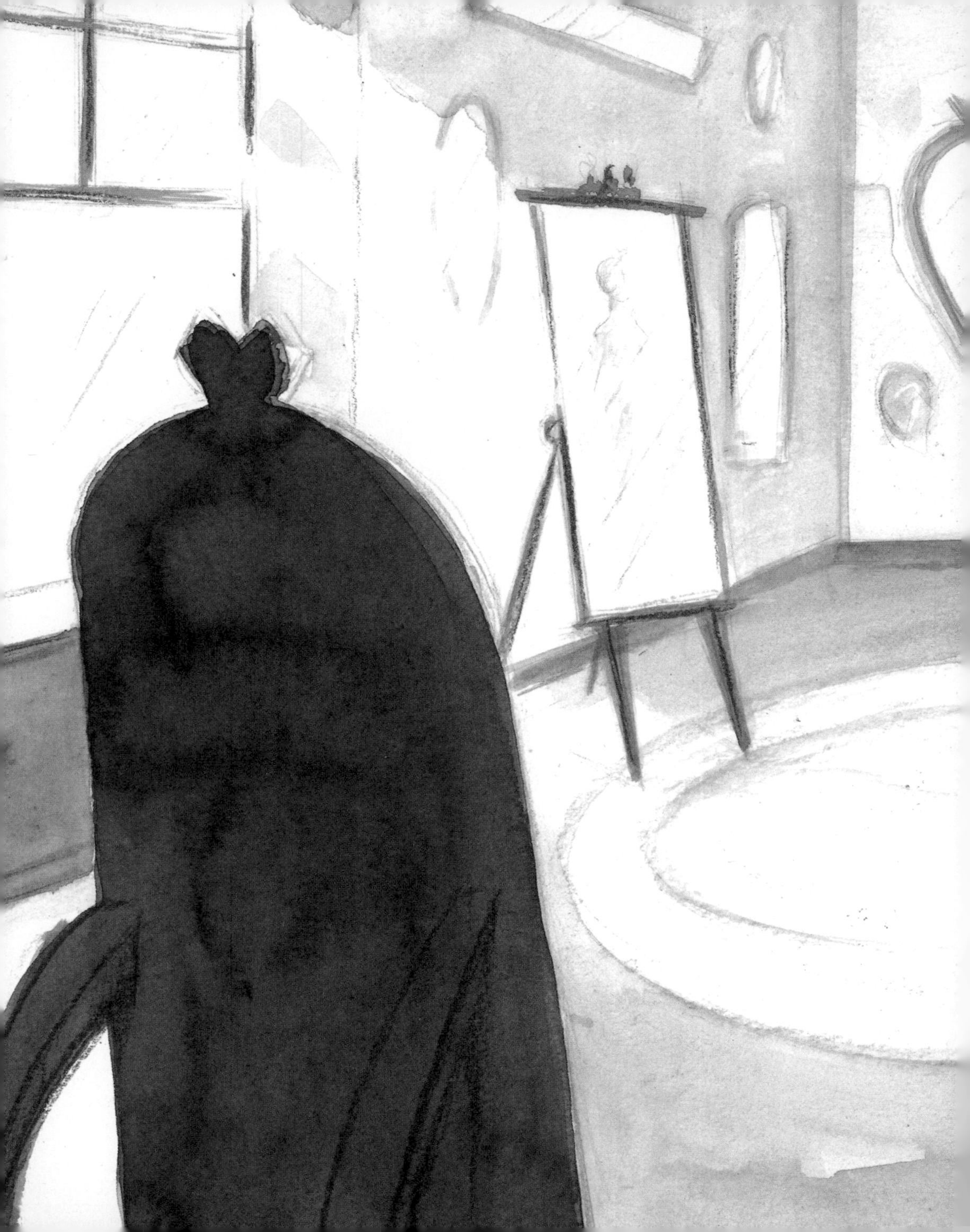

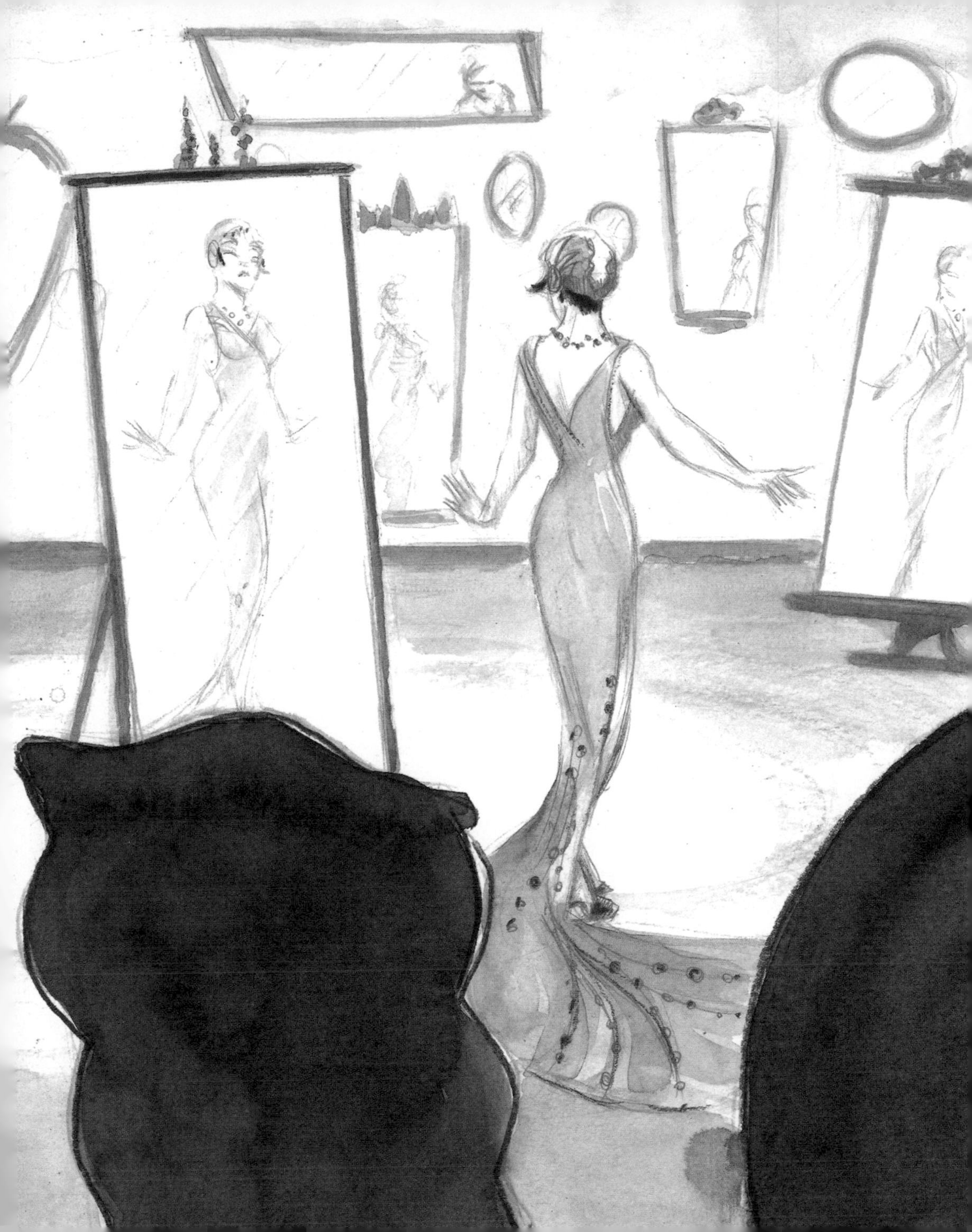

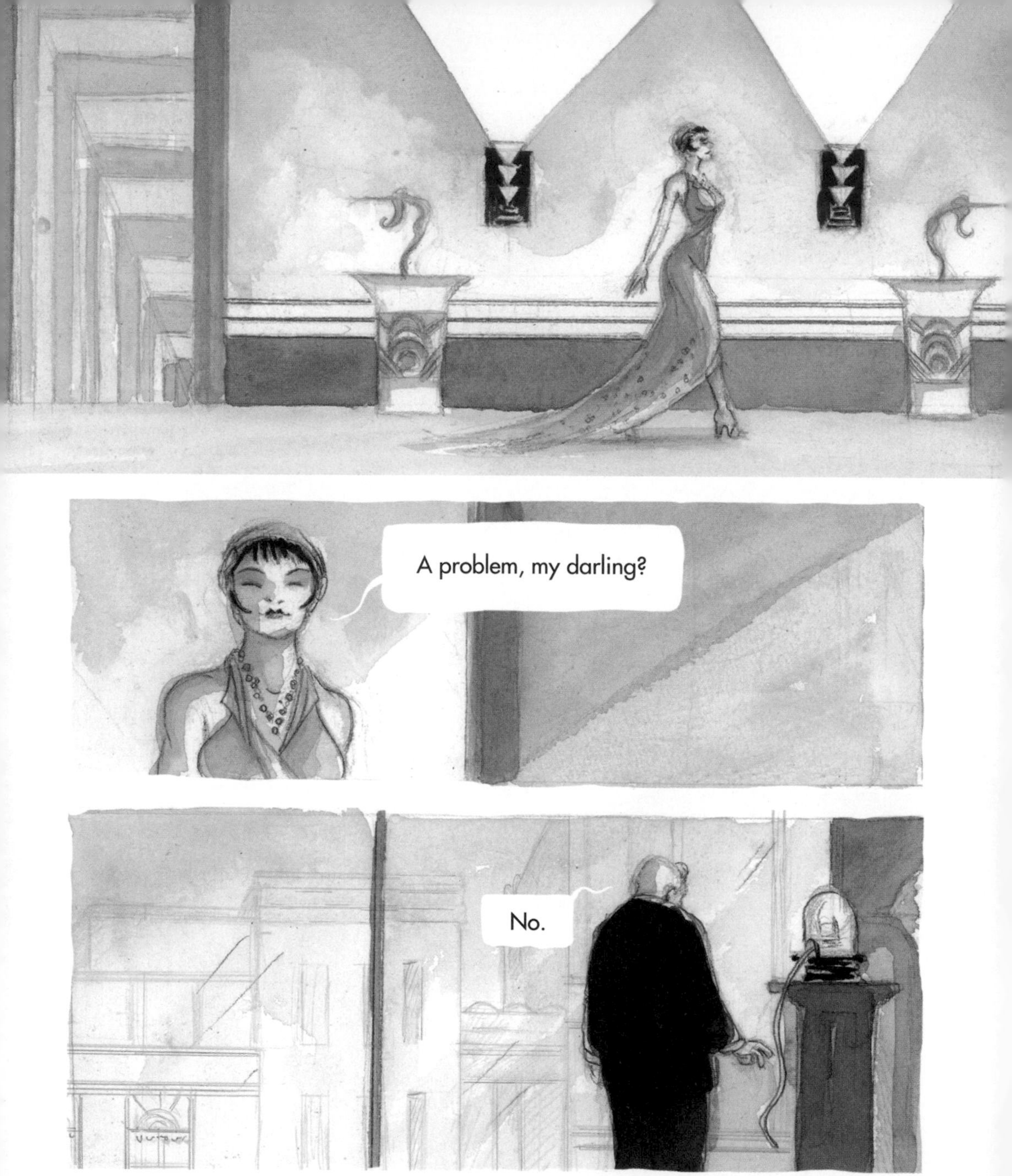
A problem, my darling?
No.

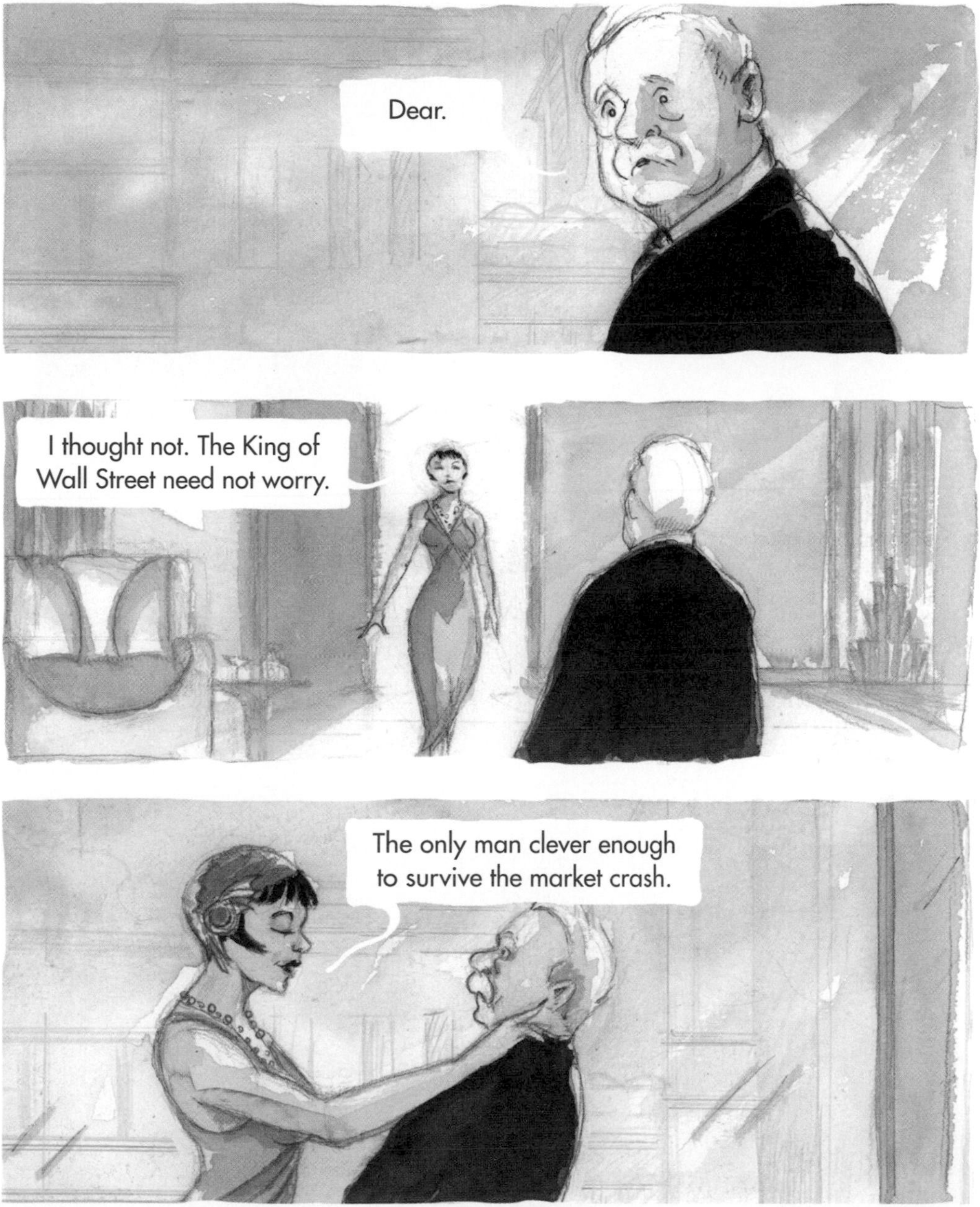
Dear.
I thought not. The King of Wall Street need not worry.
The only man clever enough to survive the market crash.

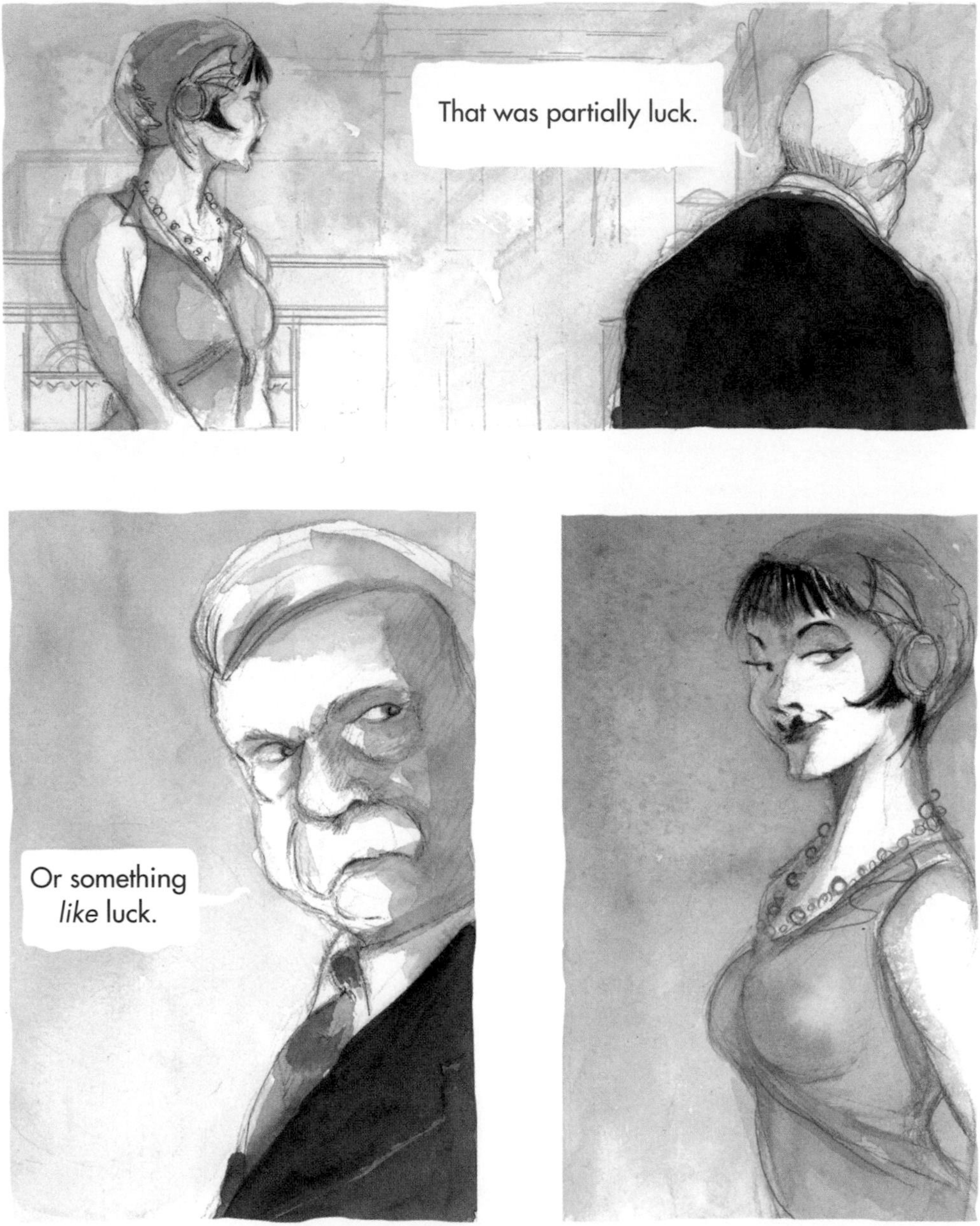
That was partially luck.
Or something *like* luck.

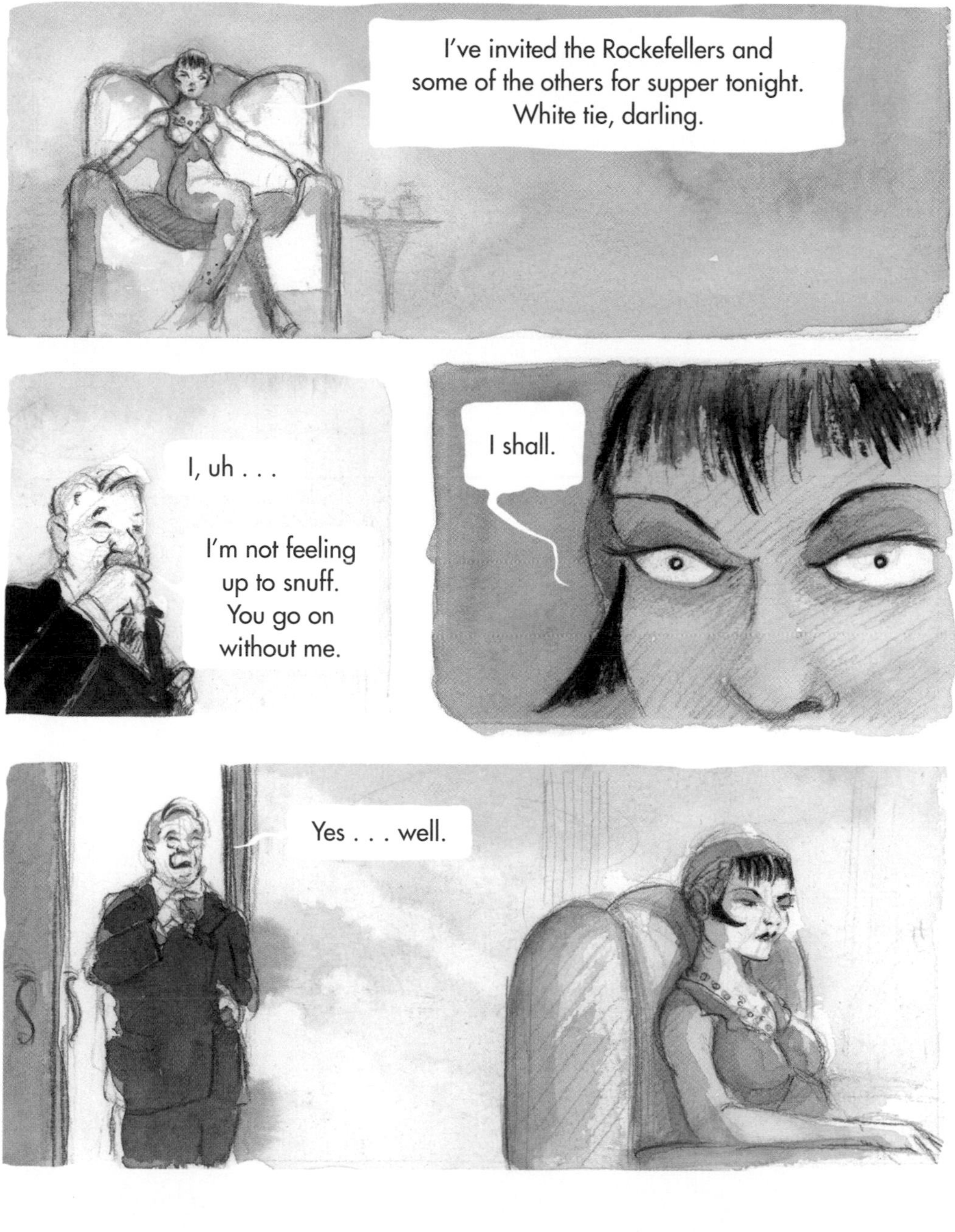
I've invited the Rockefellers and some of the others for supper tonight. White tie, darling.
I, uh . . .
I'm not feeling up to snuff. You go on without me.
I shall.
Yes . . . well.

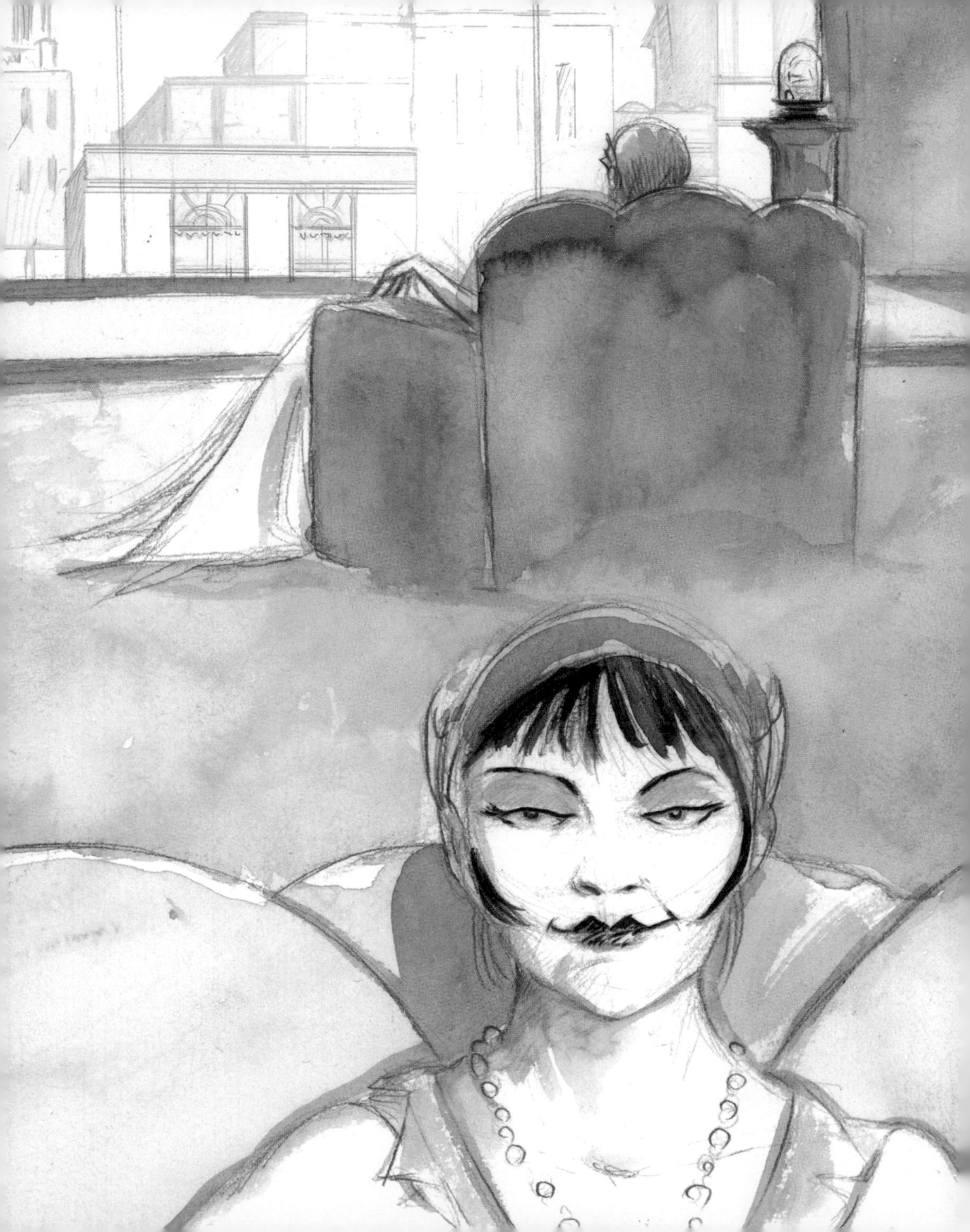

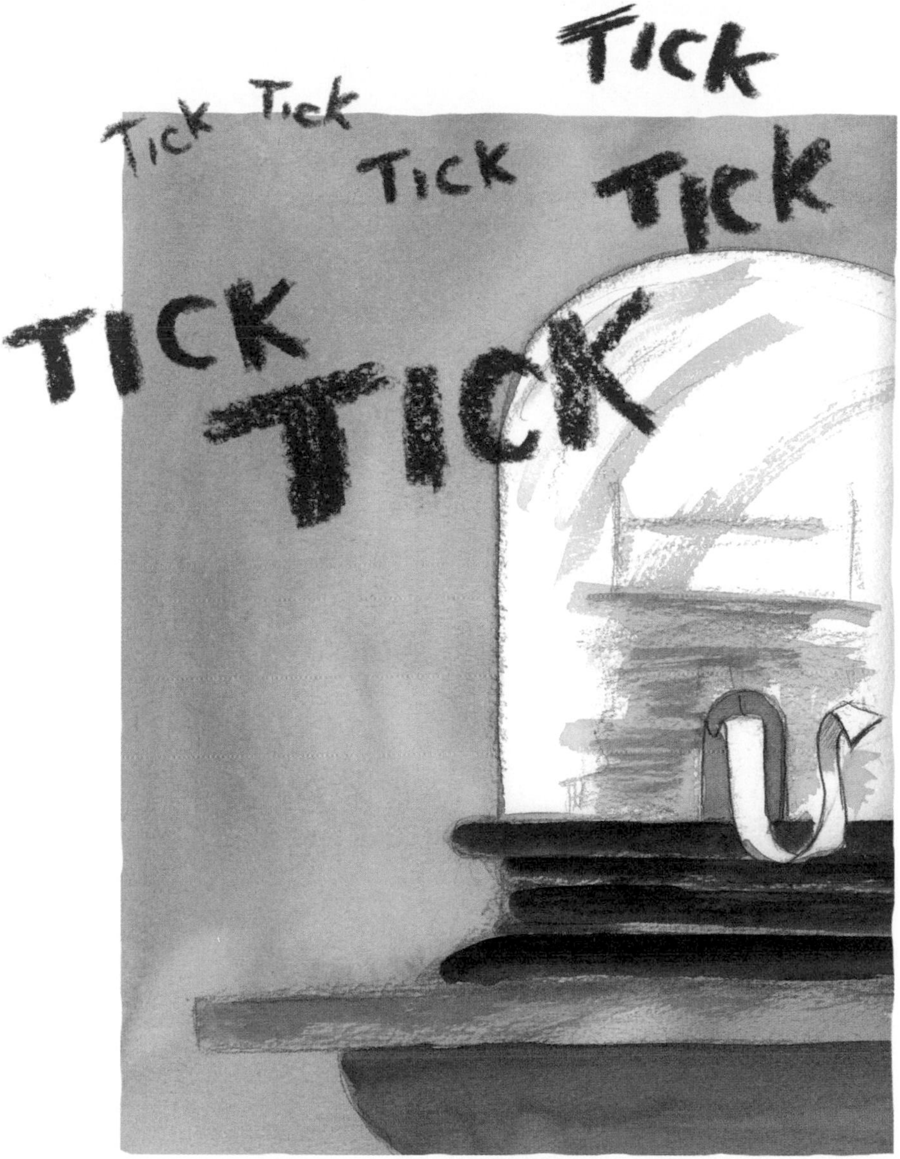
TICK
TICK TICK
TICK
TICK
TICK
TICK

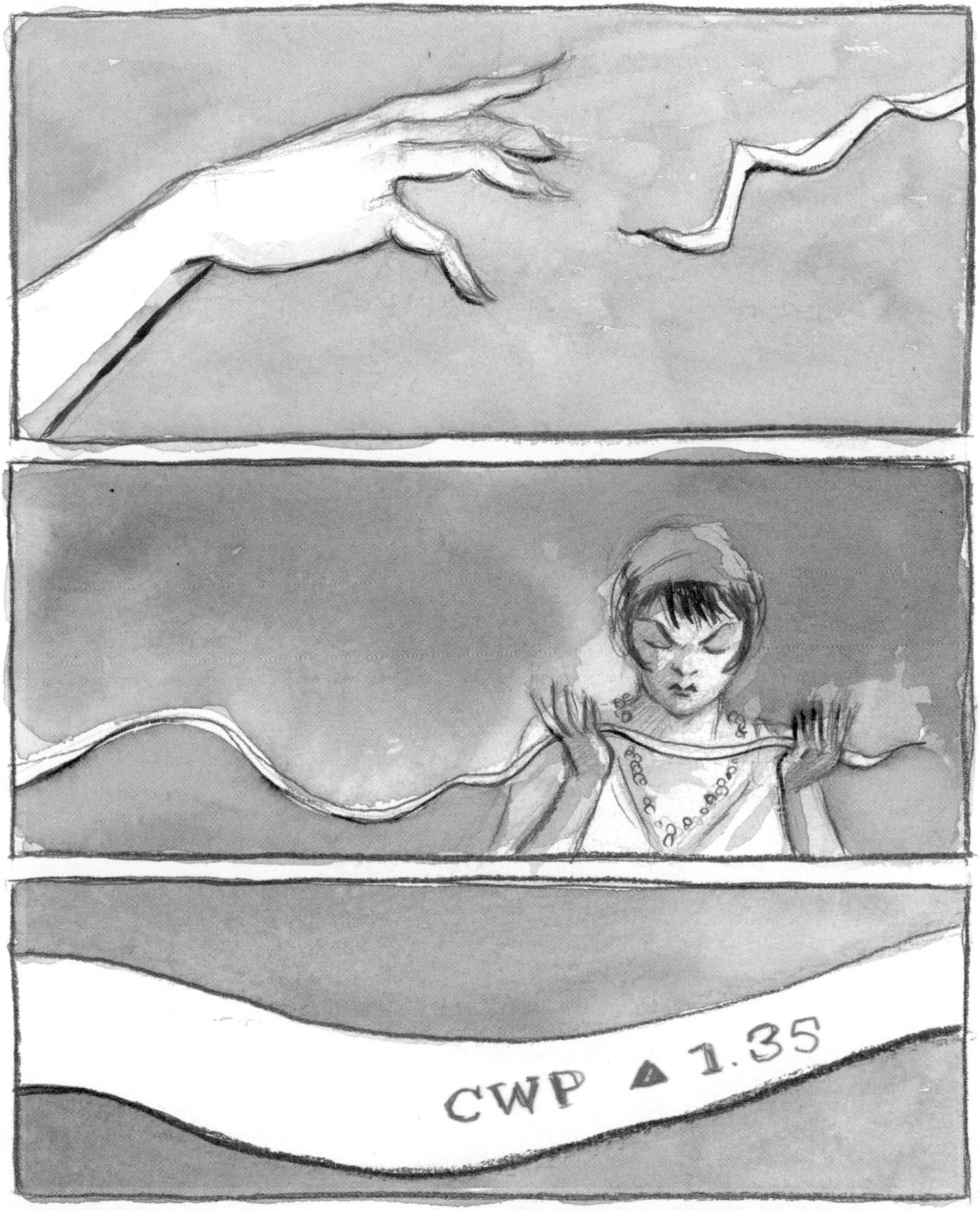
CWP ▲ 1.35

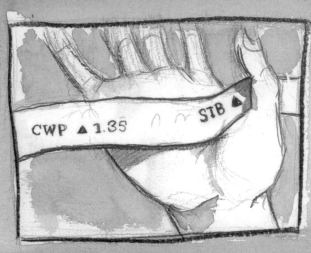

CWP ▲ 1.35   STB ▲

STB ▲ 2.15   ATW ▼ 1.15

ATW ▼ 1.15   USS ▲

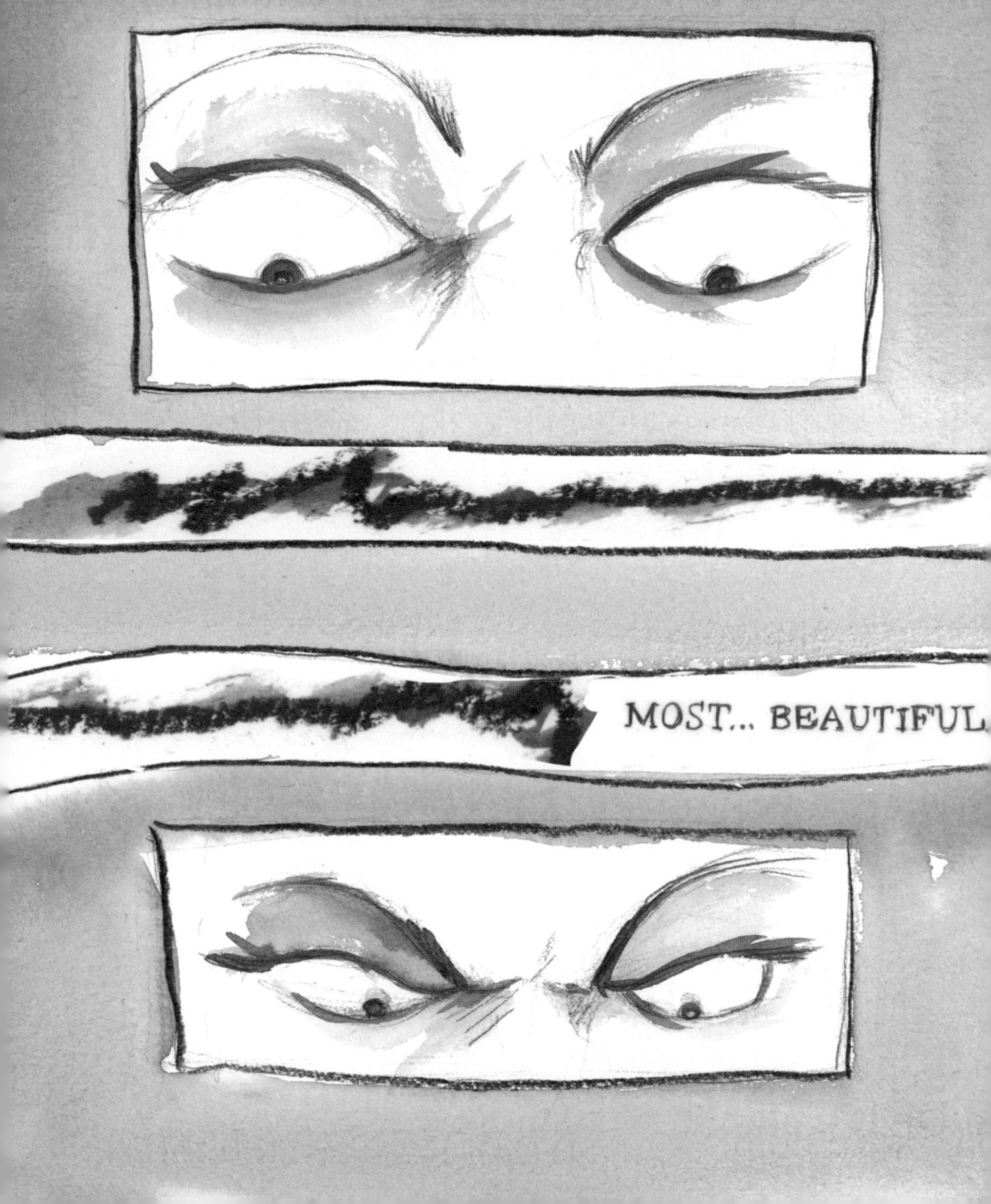
MOST... BEAUTIFUL

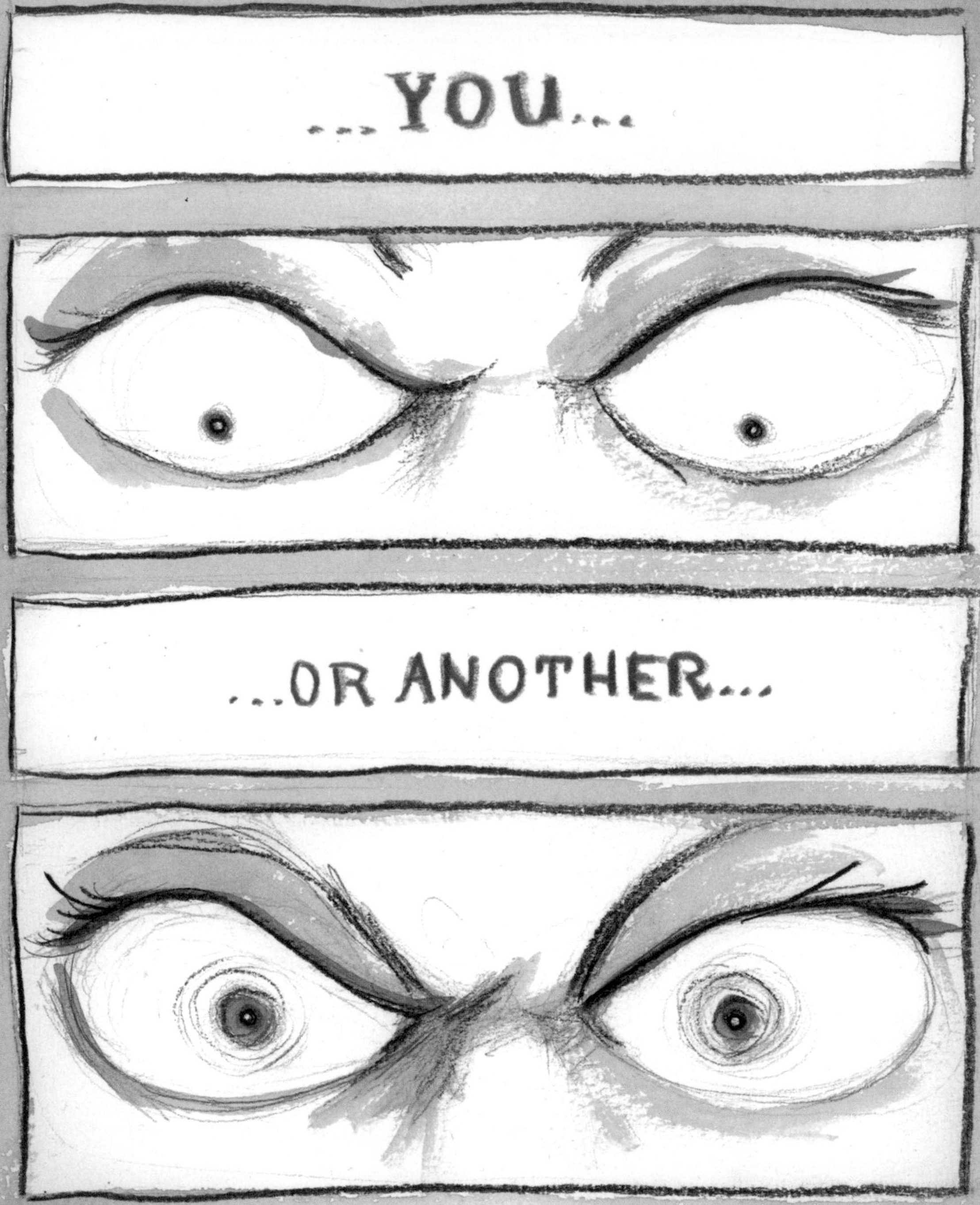
...YOU...
...OR ANOTHER...

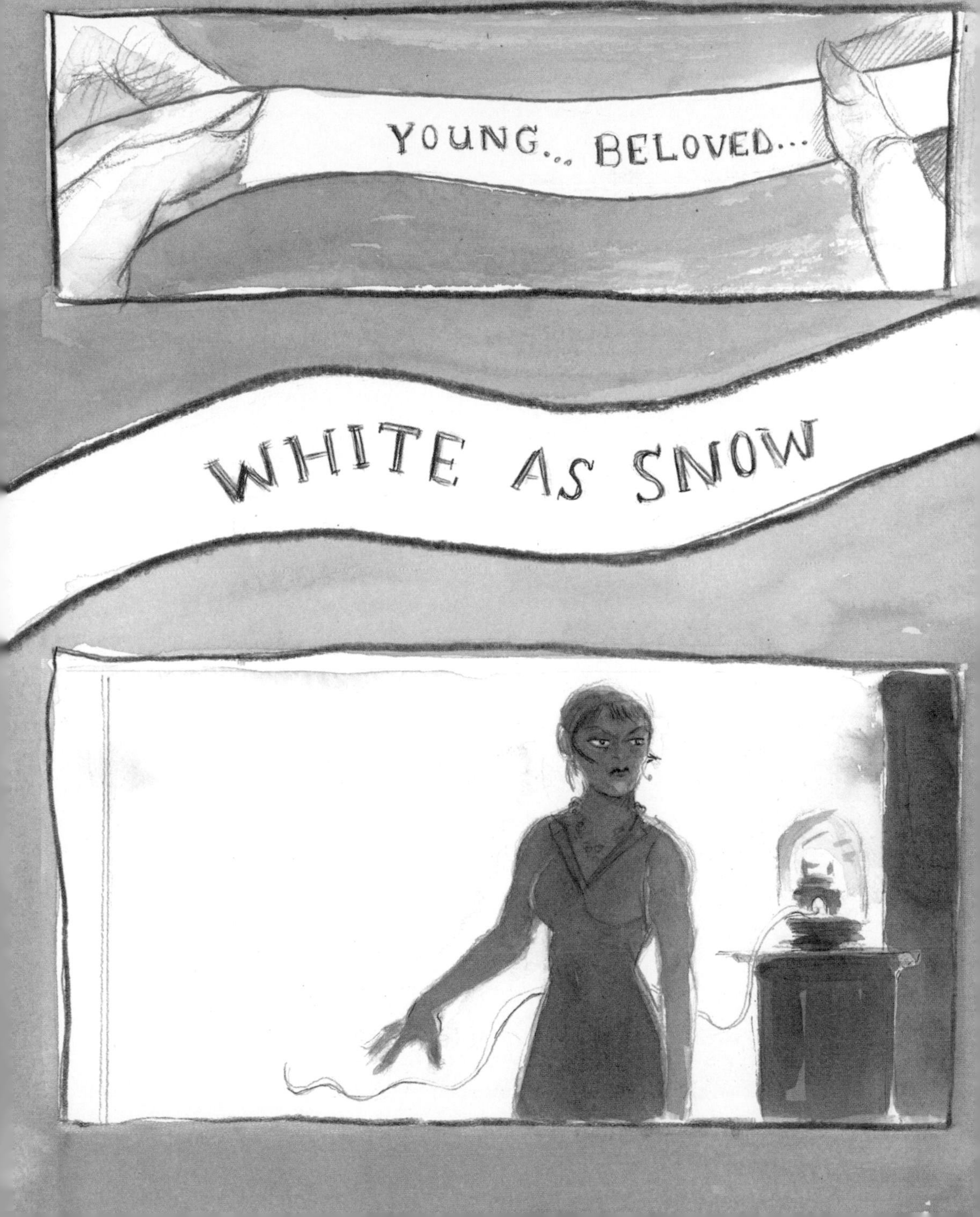
YOUNG... BELOVED...
WHITE AS SNOW

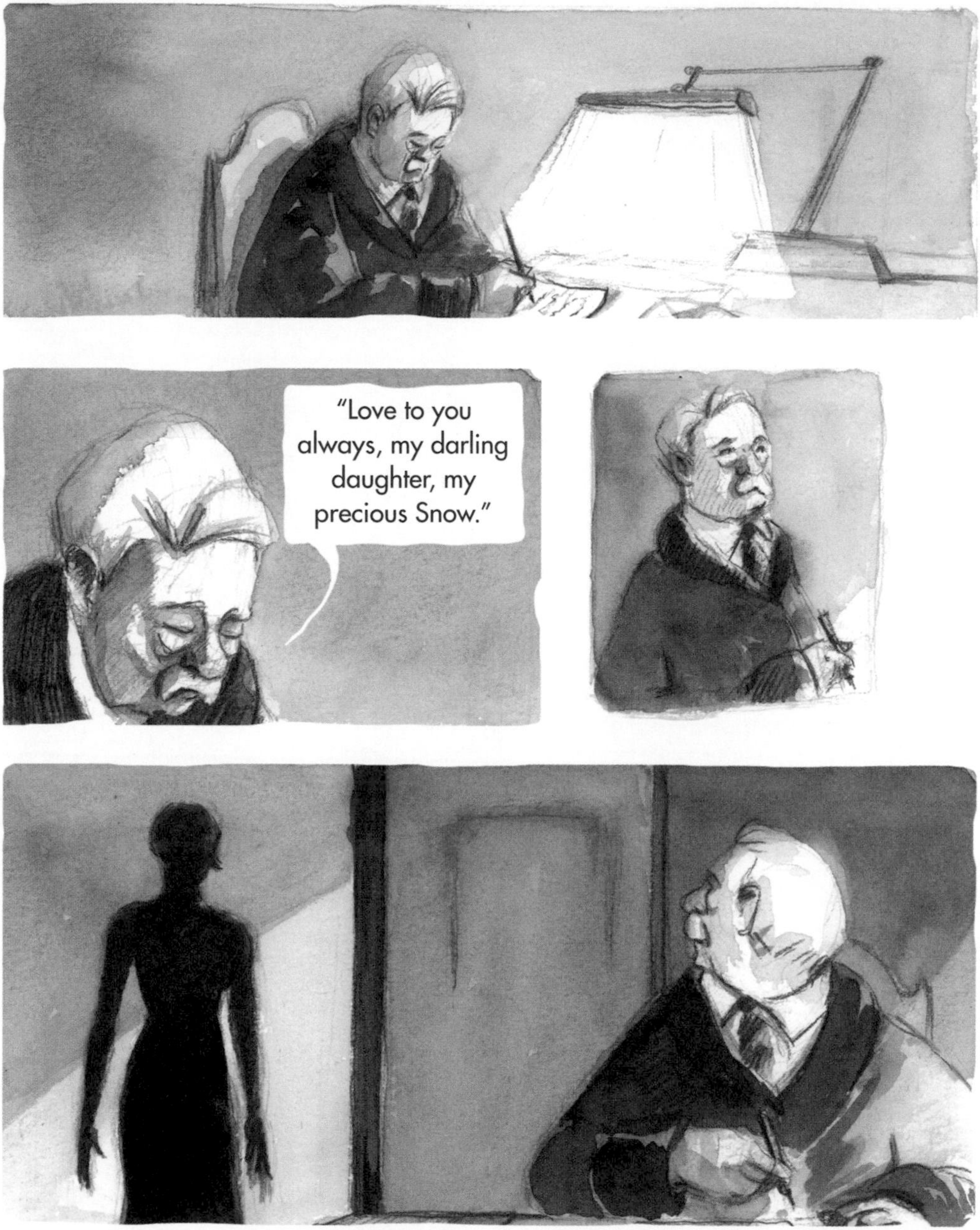
"Love to you always, my darling daughter, my precious Snow."

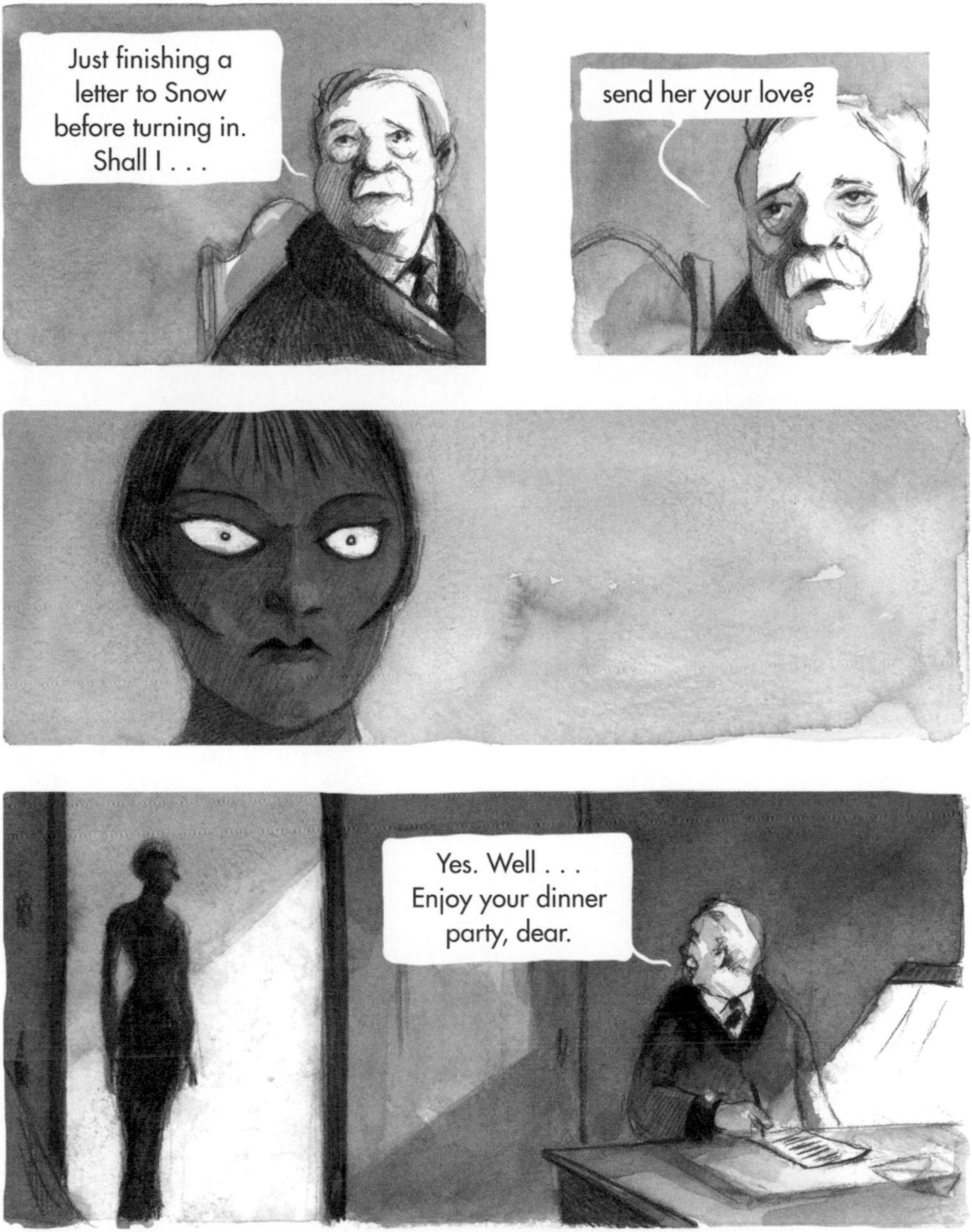
Just finishing a letter to Snow before turning in. Shall I . . .
send her your love?
Yes. Well . . . Enjoy your dinner party, dear.

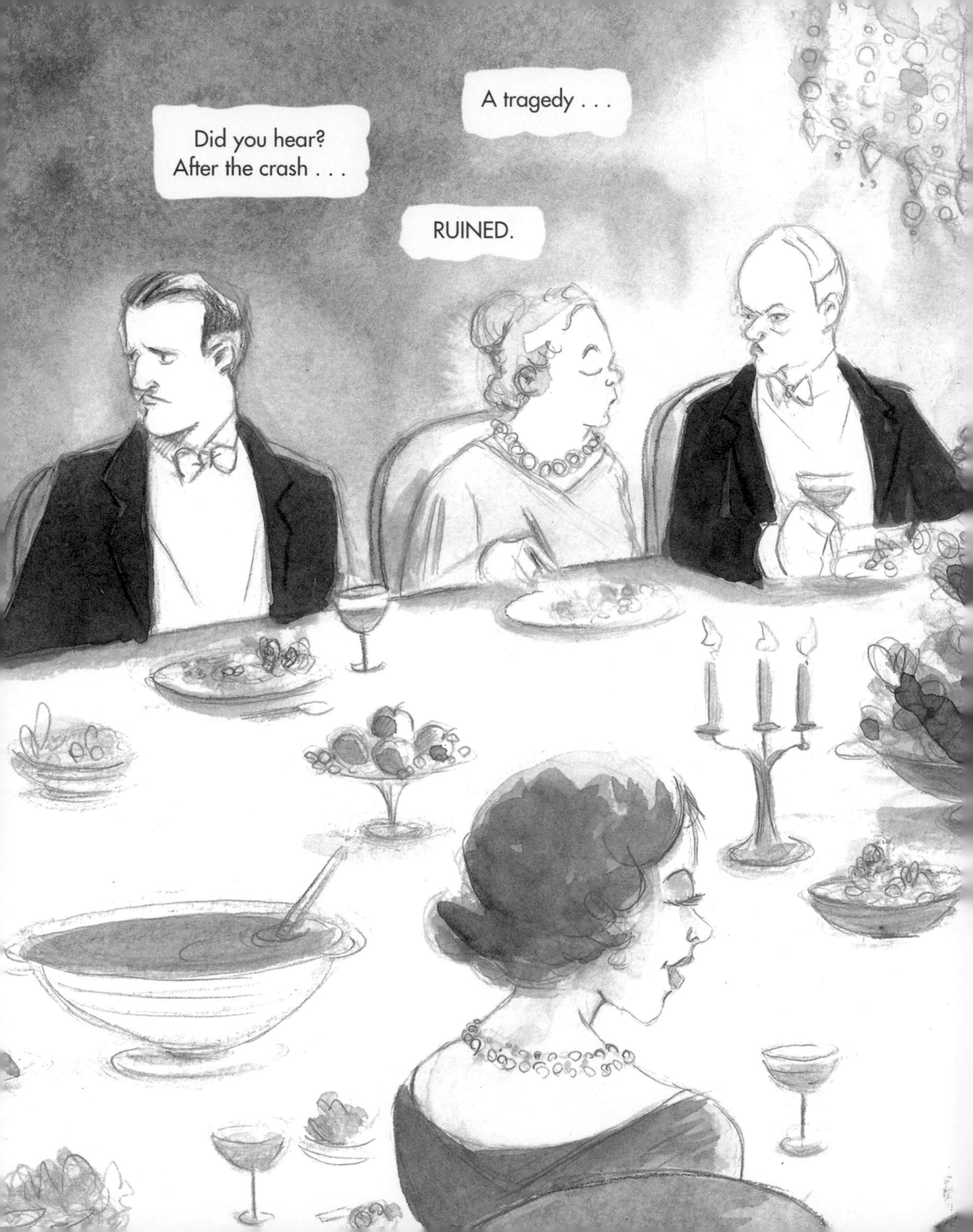
Did you hear?
After the crash . . .
A tragedy . . .
RUINED.

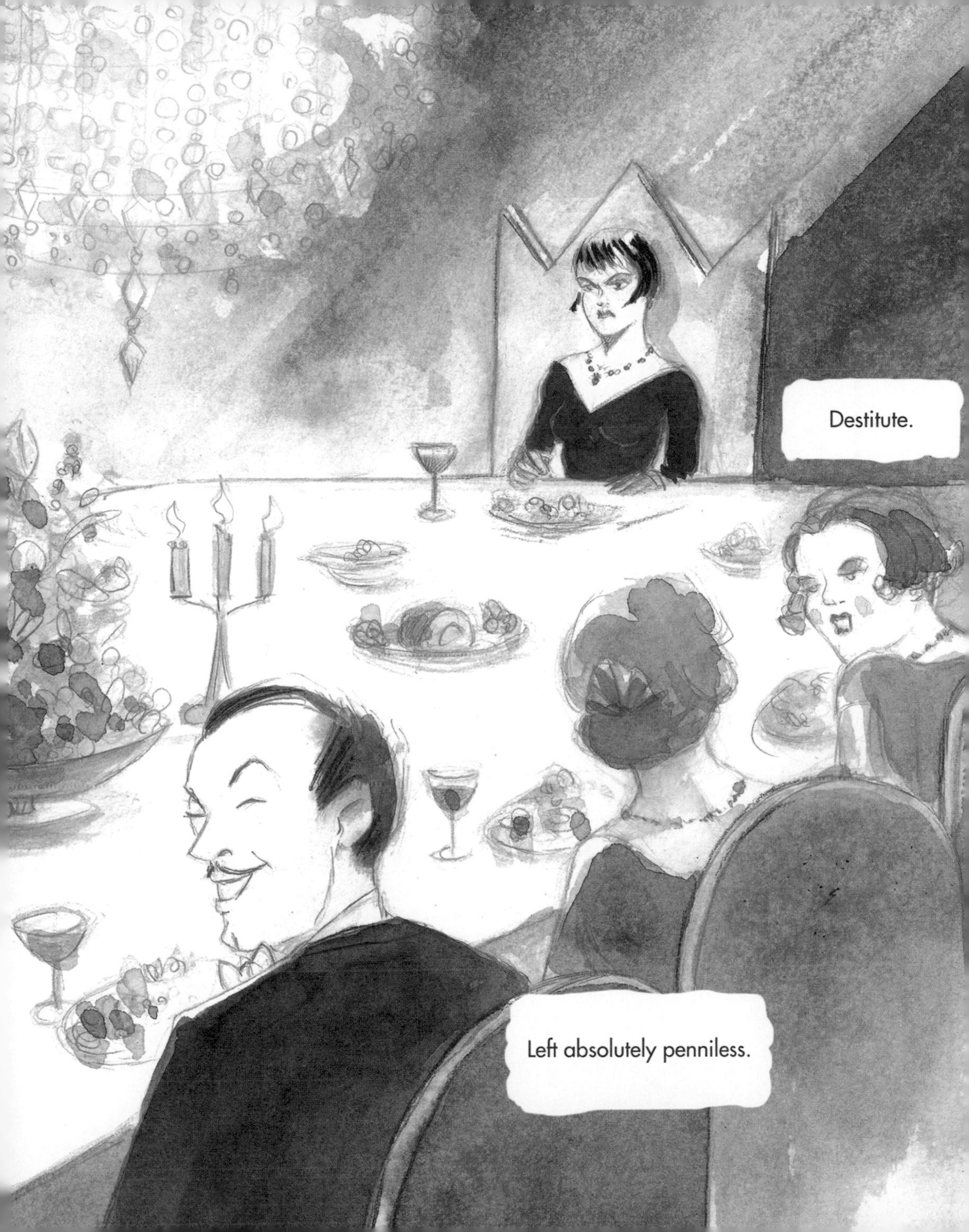
Destitute.
Left absolutely penniless.

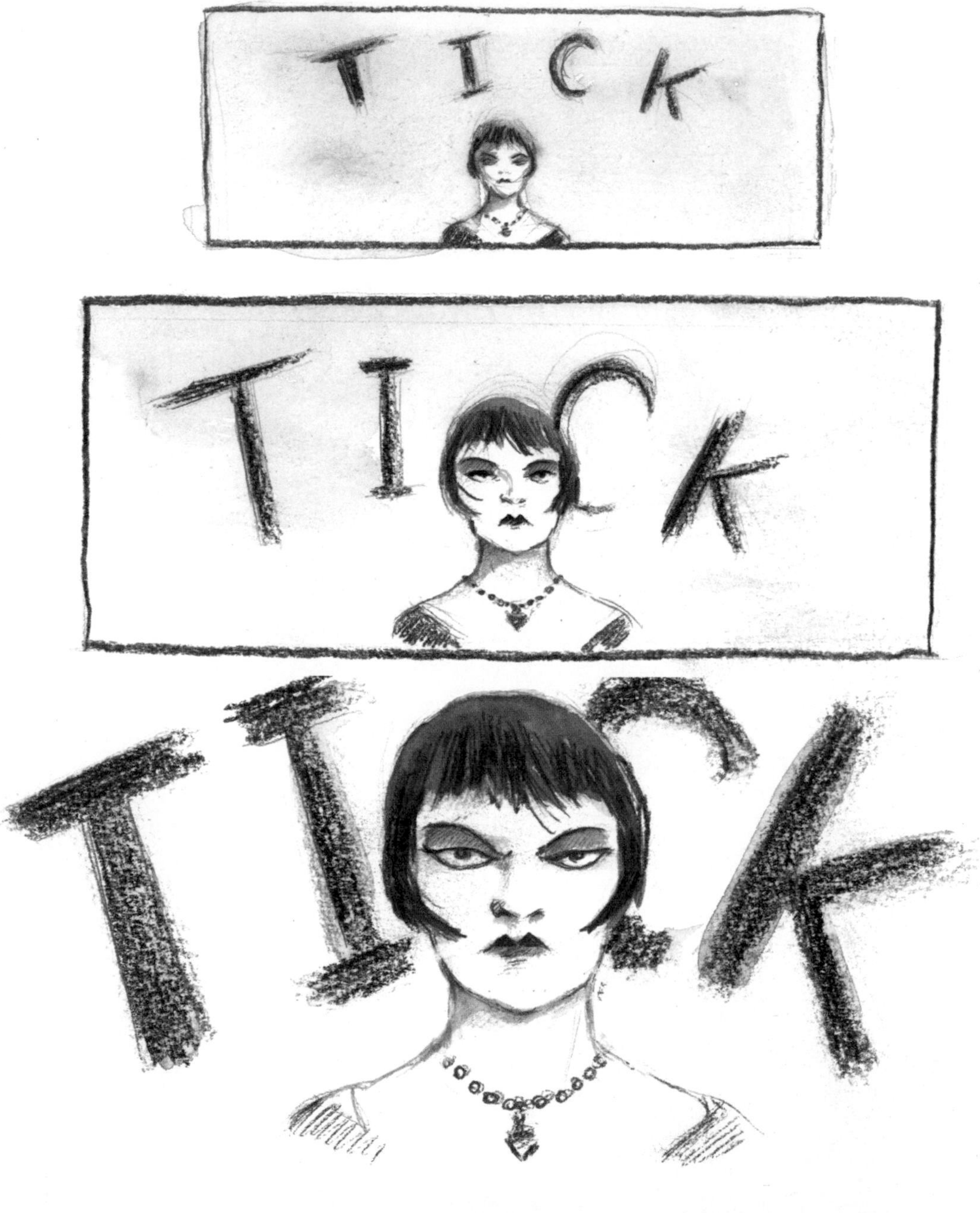
TICK
TICK
TICK

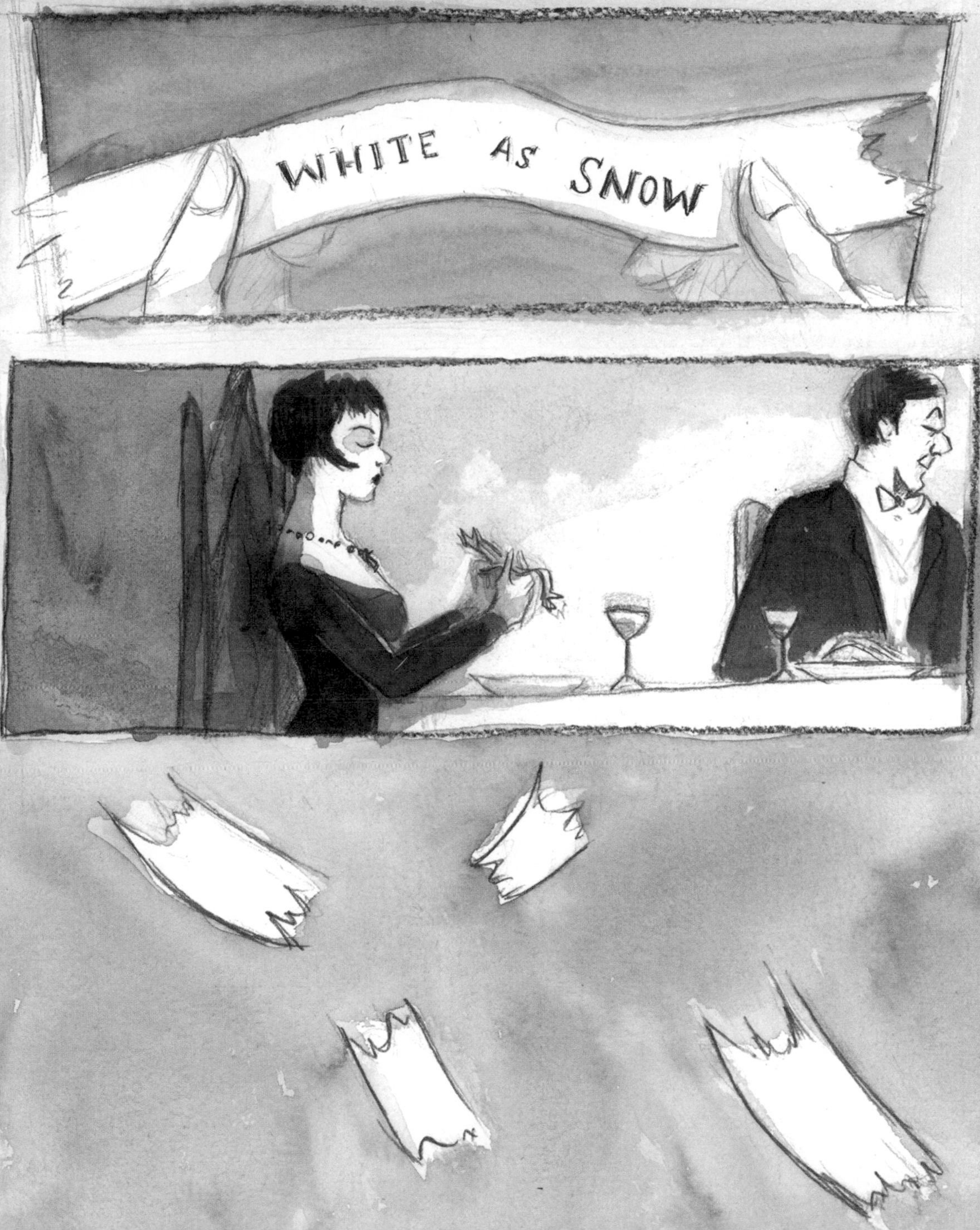
WHITE AS SNOW

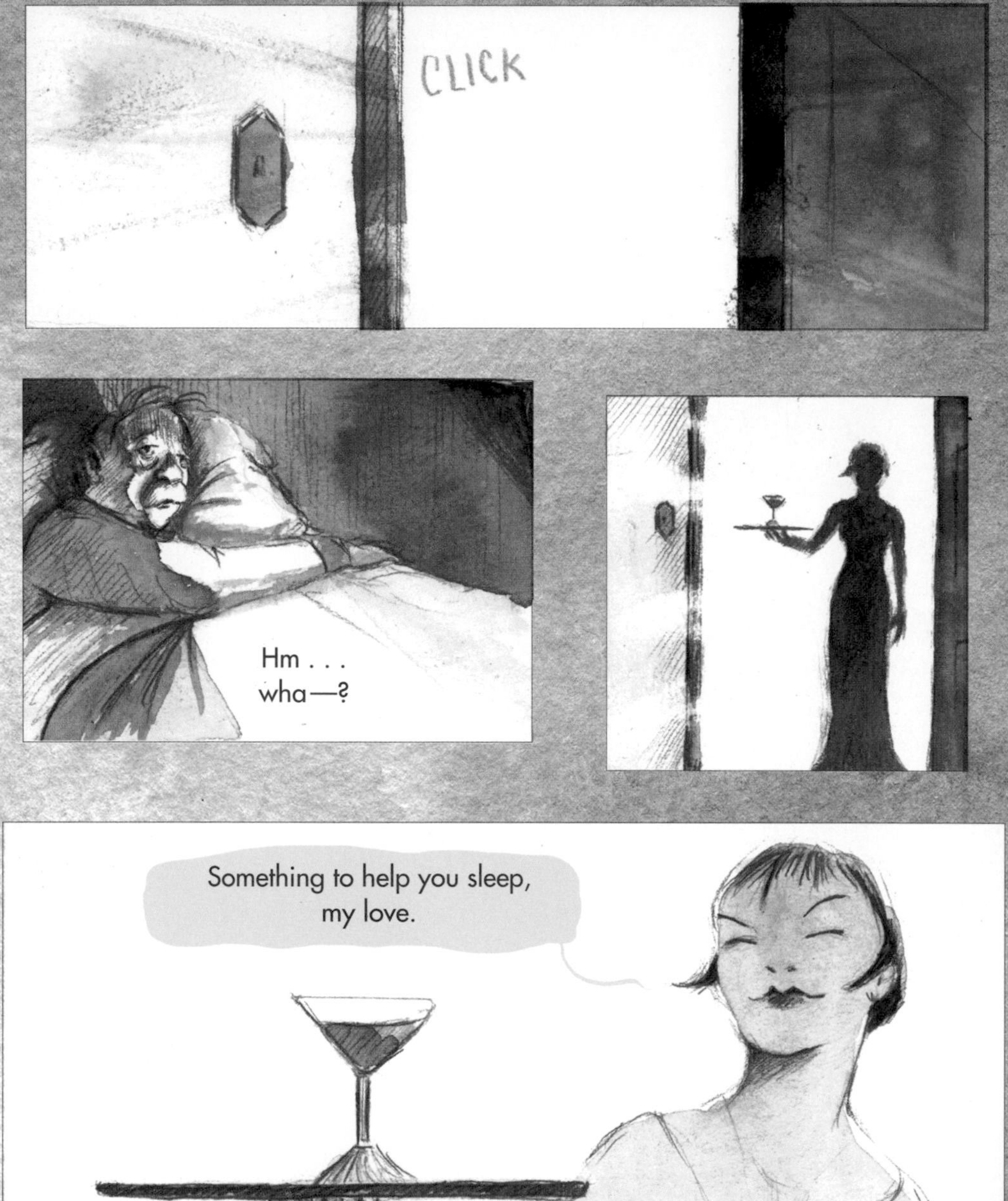
CLICK
Hm . . . wha—?
Something to help you sleep, my love.

SNOW
RETURNS

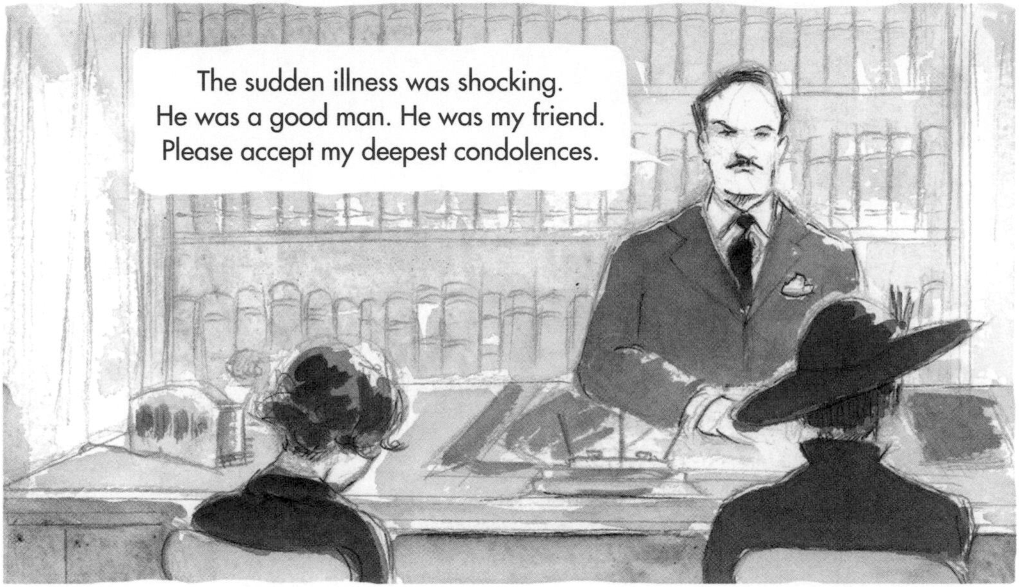
The sudden illness was shocking. He was a good man. He was my friend. Please accept my deepest condolences.

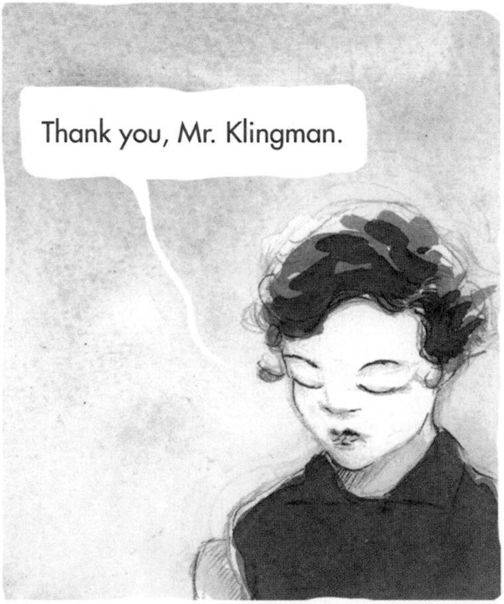
Thank you, Mr. Klingman.

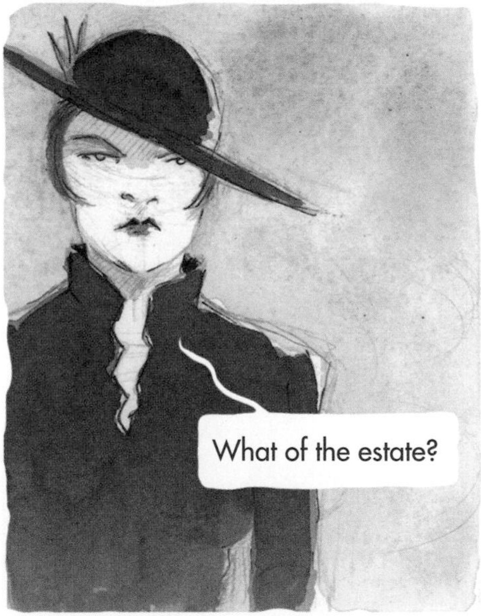
What of the estate?

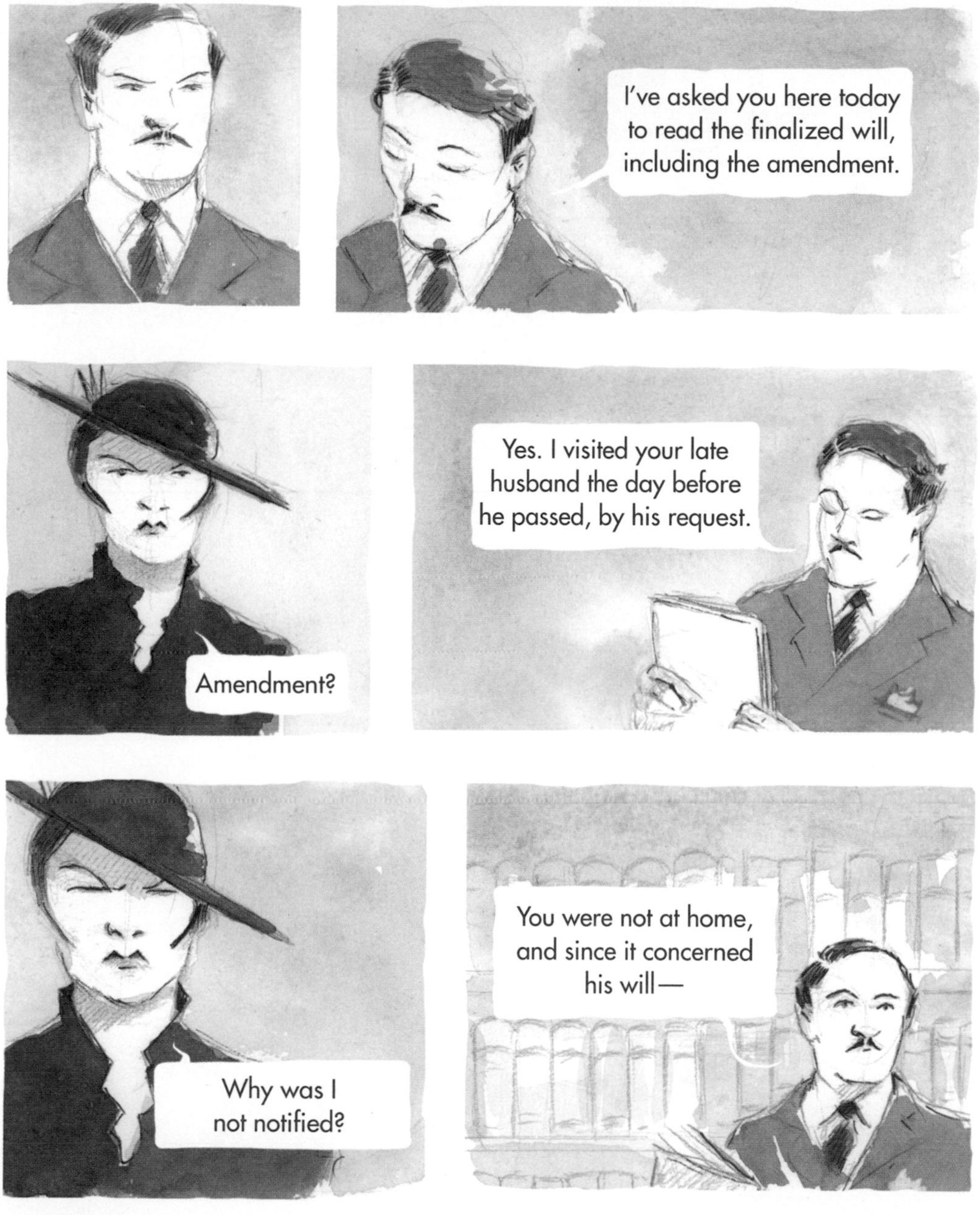
I've asked you here today to read the finalized will, including the amendment.
Amendment?
Yes. I visited your late husband the day before he passed, by his request.
Why was I not notified?
You were not at home, and since it concerned his will—

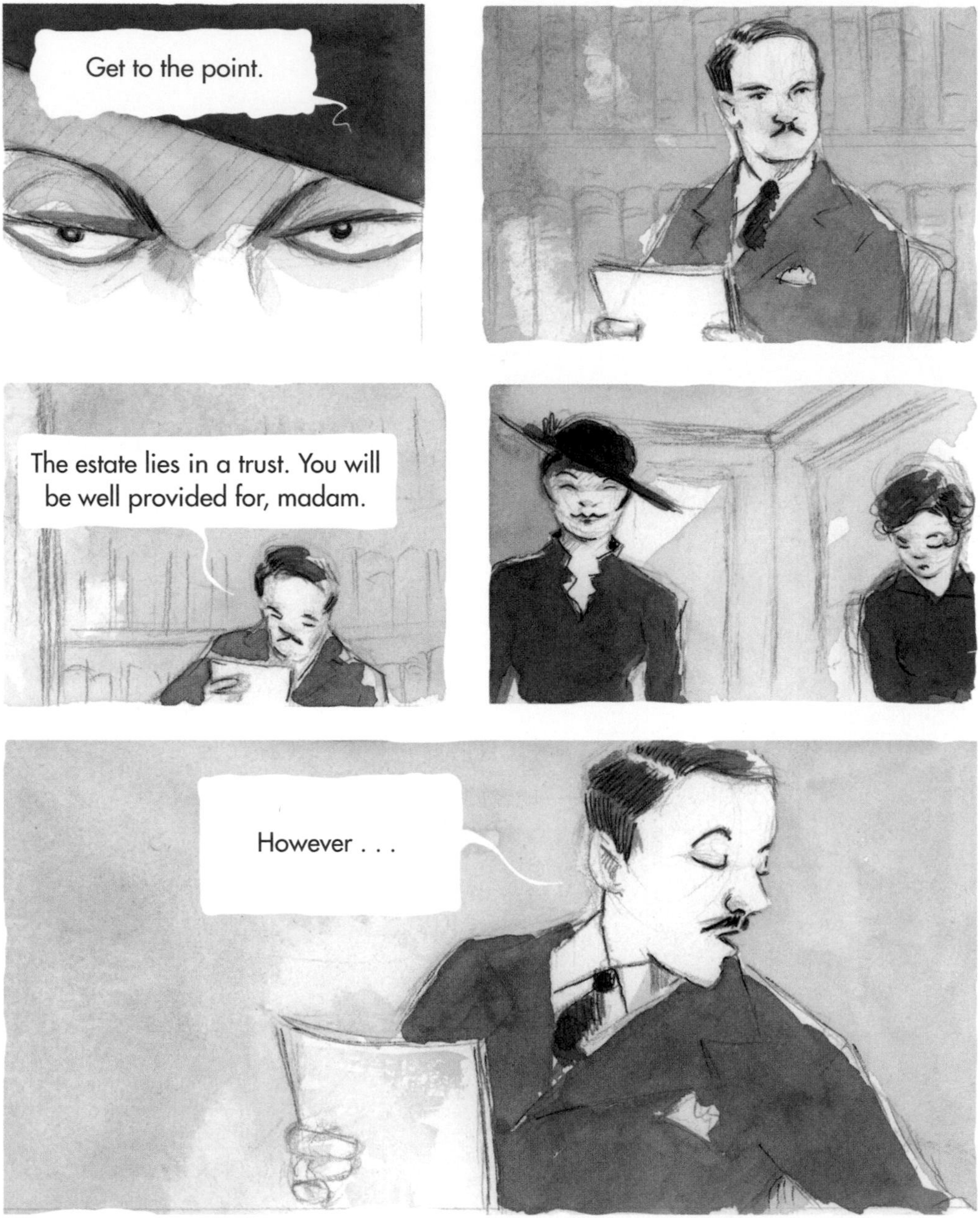
Get to the point.
The estate lies in a trust. You will be well provided for, madam.
However . . .

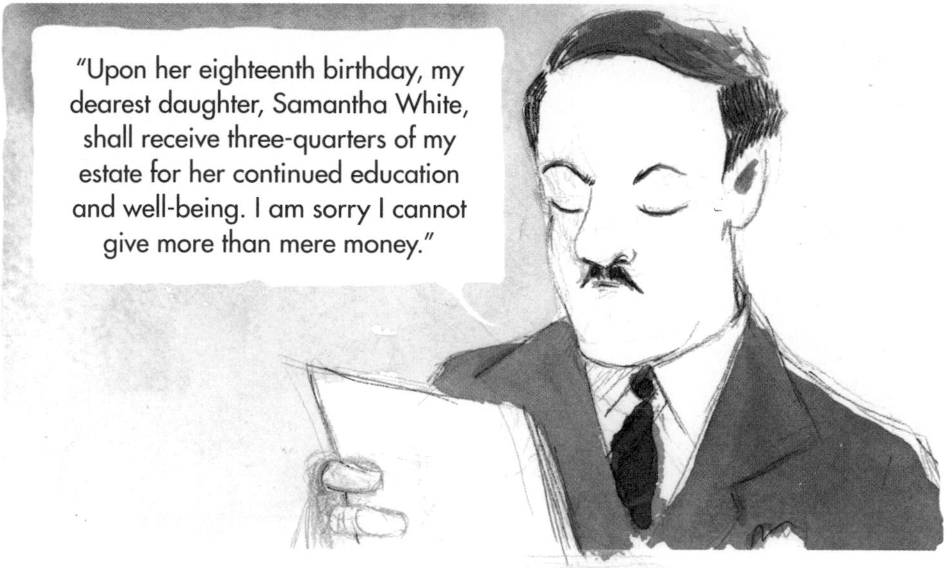
"Upon her eighteenth birthday, my dearest daughter, Samantha White, shall receive three-quarters of my estate for her continued education and well-being. I am sorry I cannot give more than mere money."

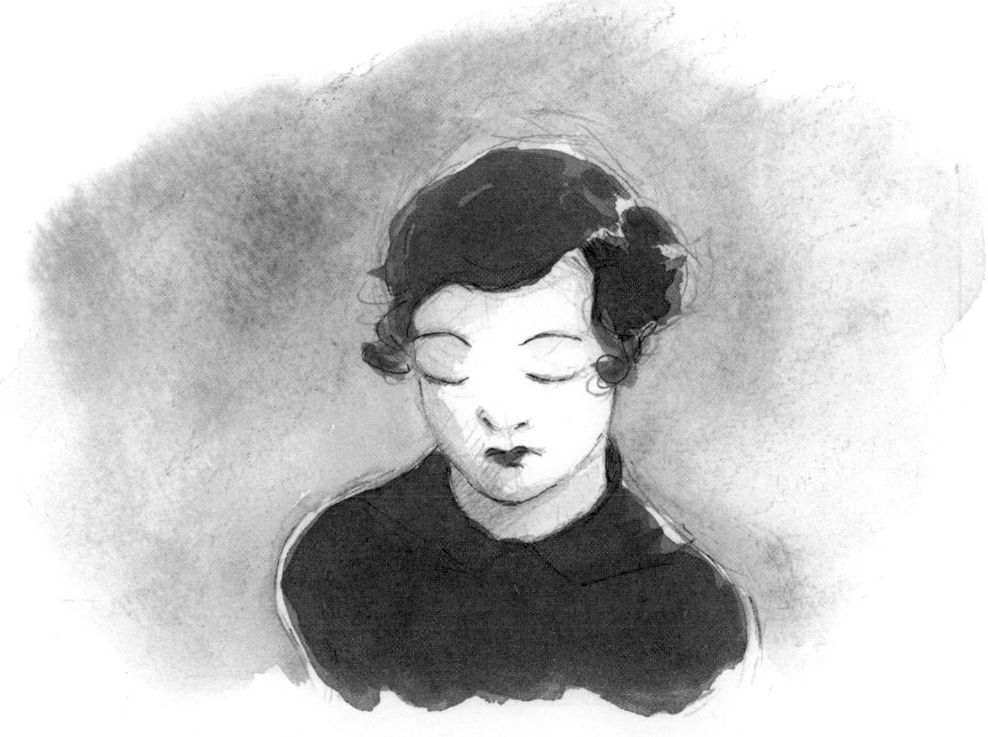

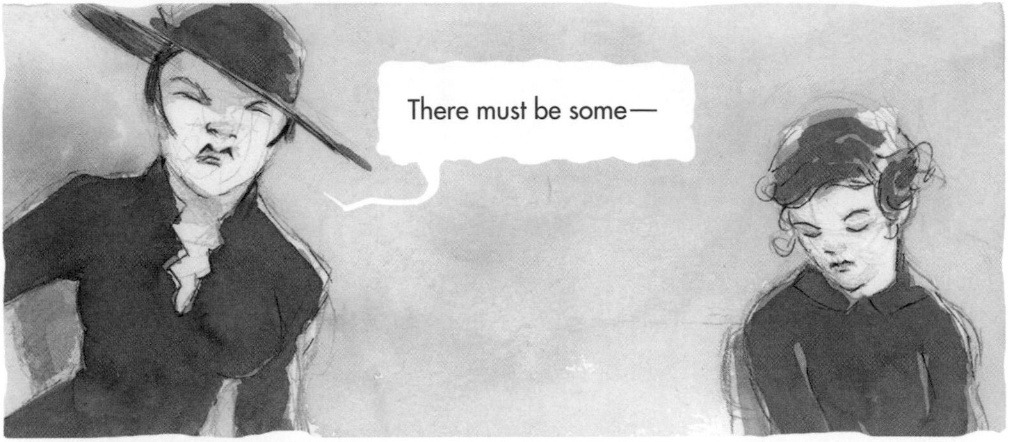
There must be some—

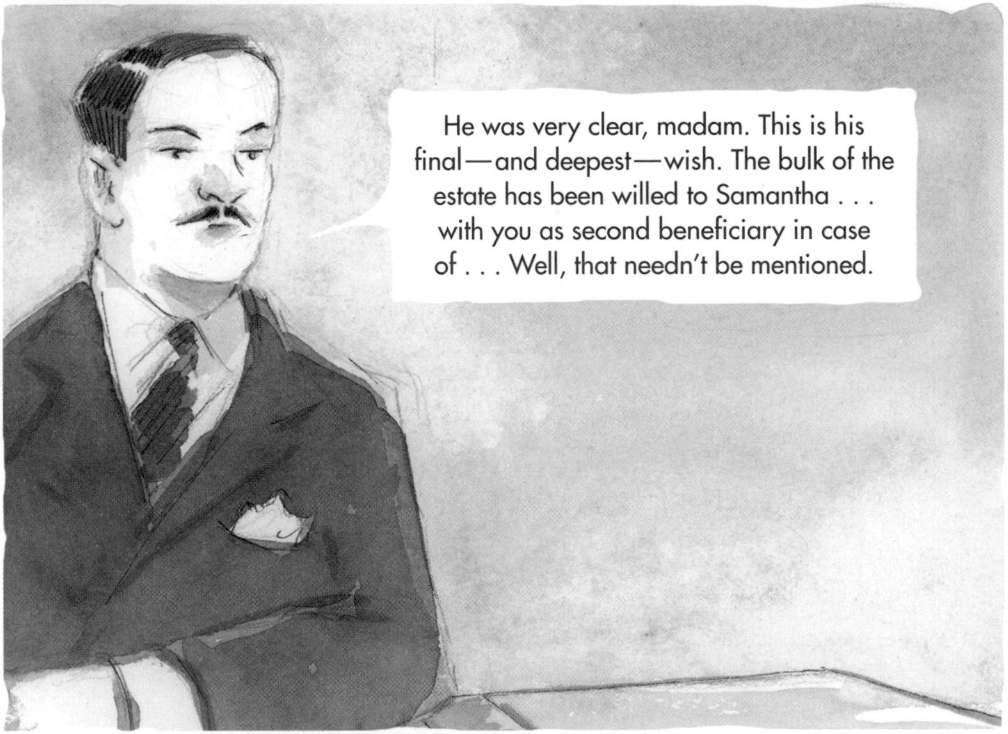
He was very clear, madam. This is his final—and deepest—wish. The bulk of the estate has been willed to Samantha . . . with you as second beneficiary in case of . . . Well, that needn't be mentioned.

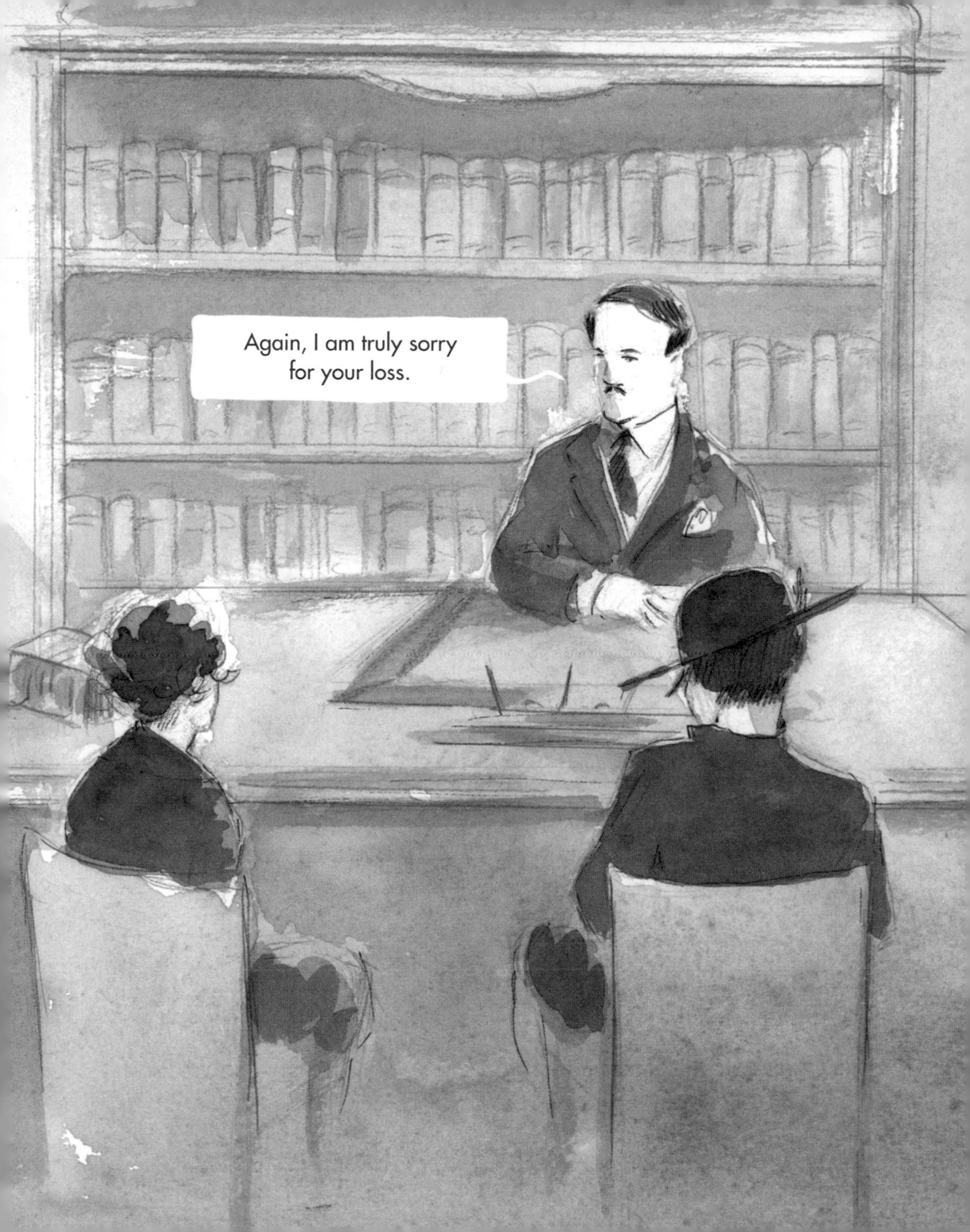
Again, I am truly sorry for your loss.

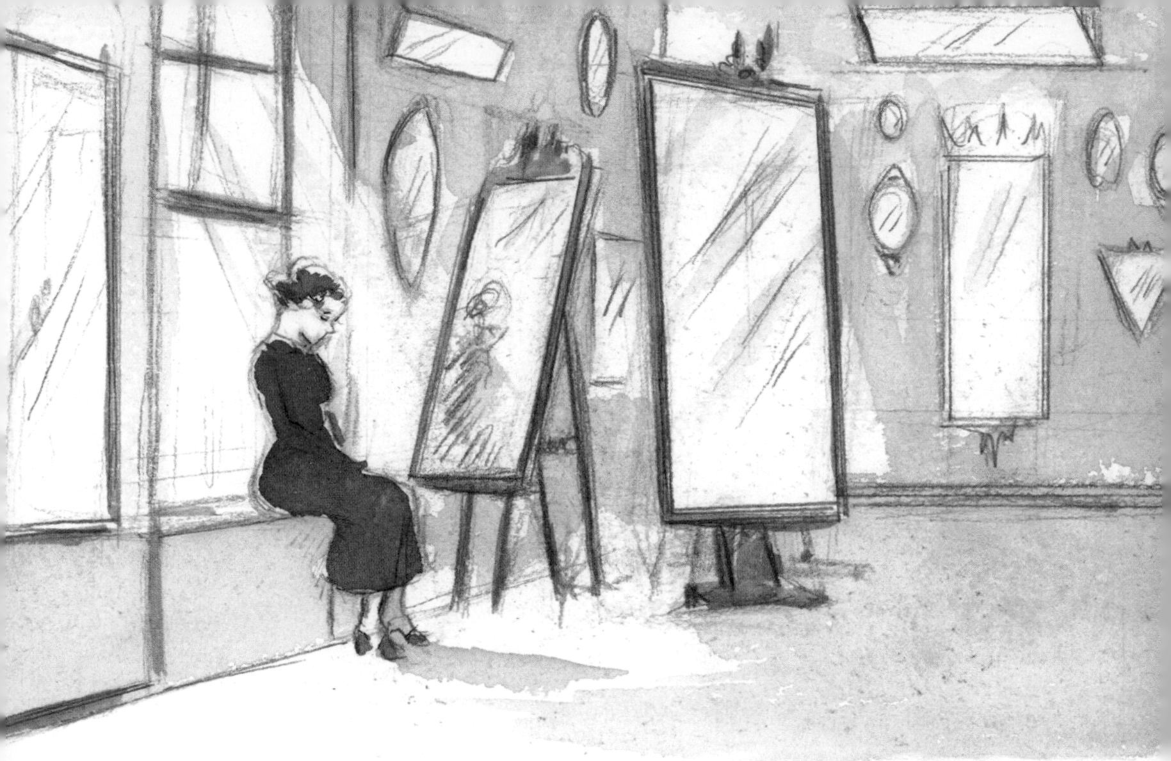

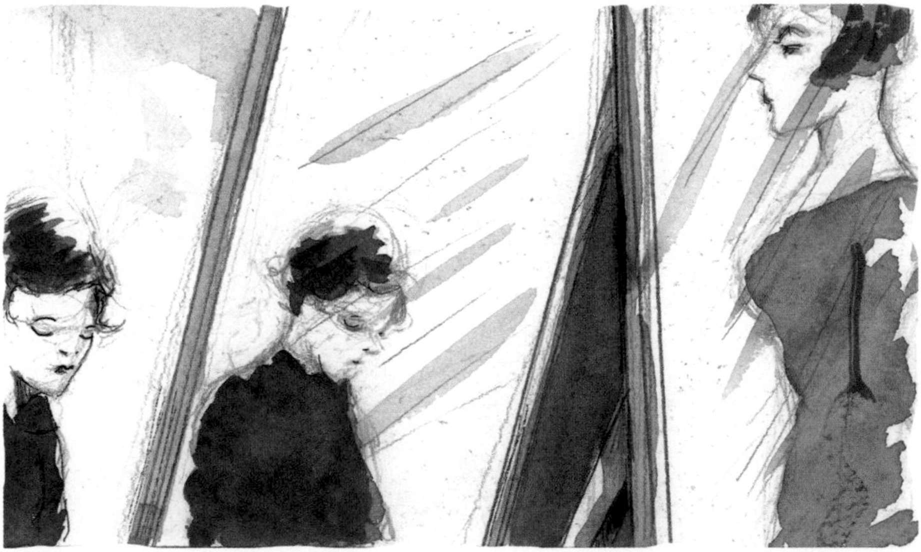

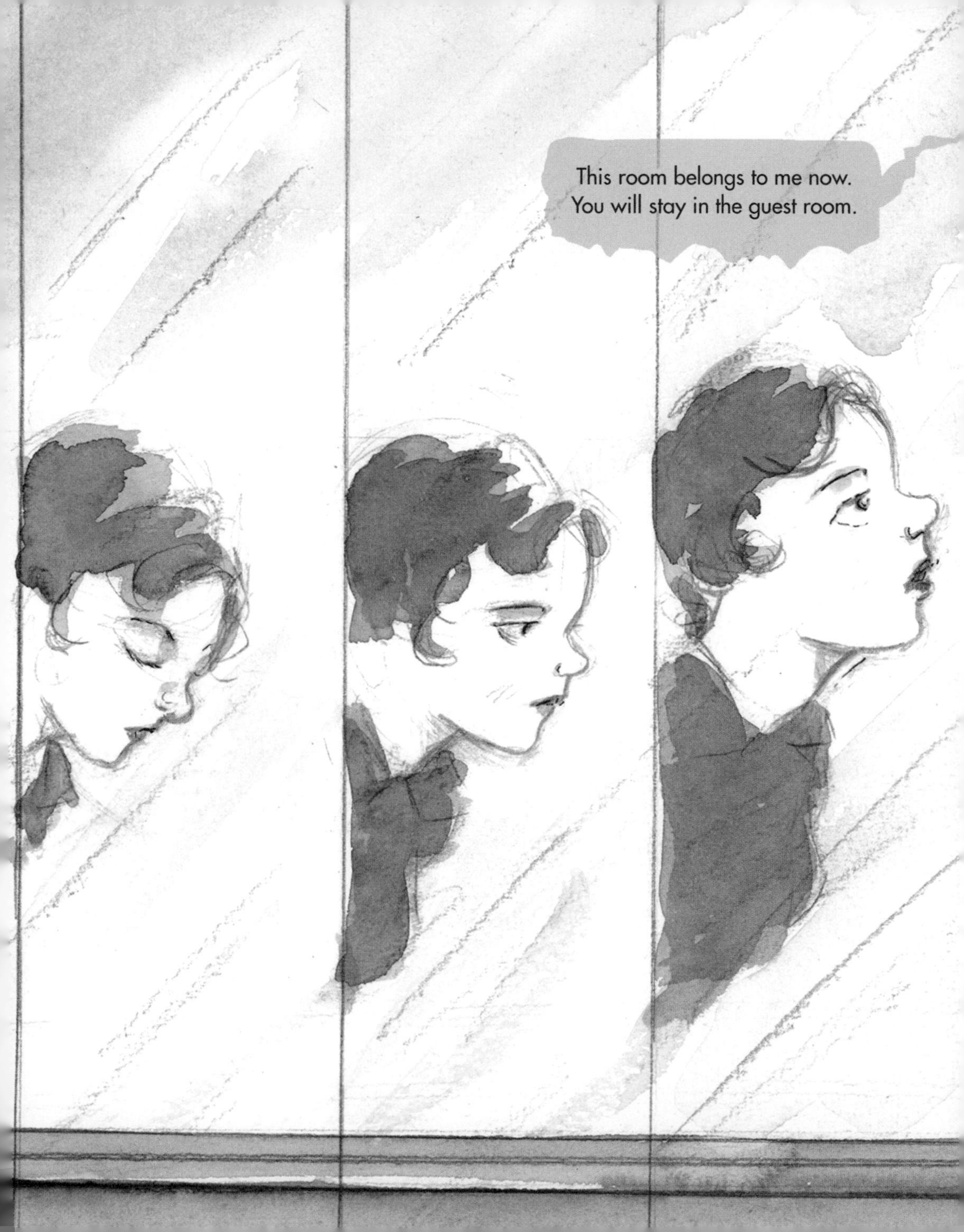
This room belongs to me now.
You will stay in the guest room.

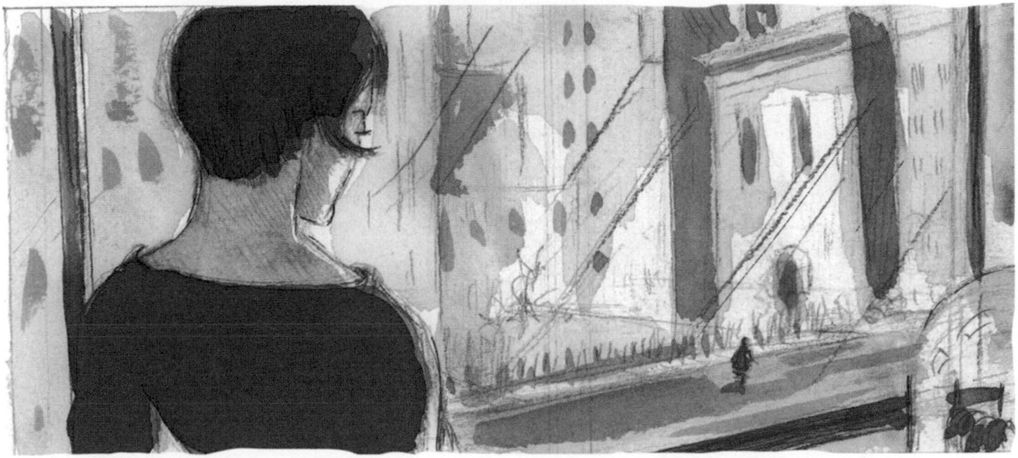

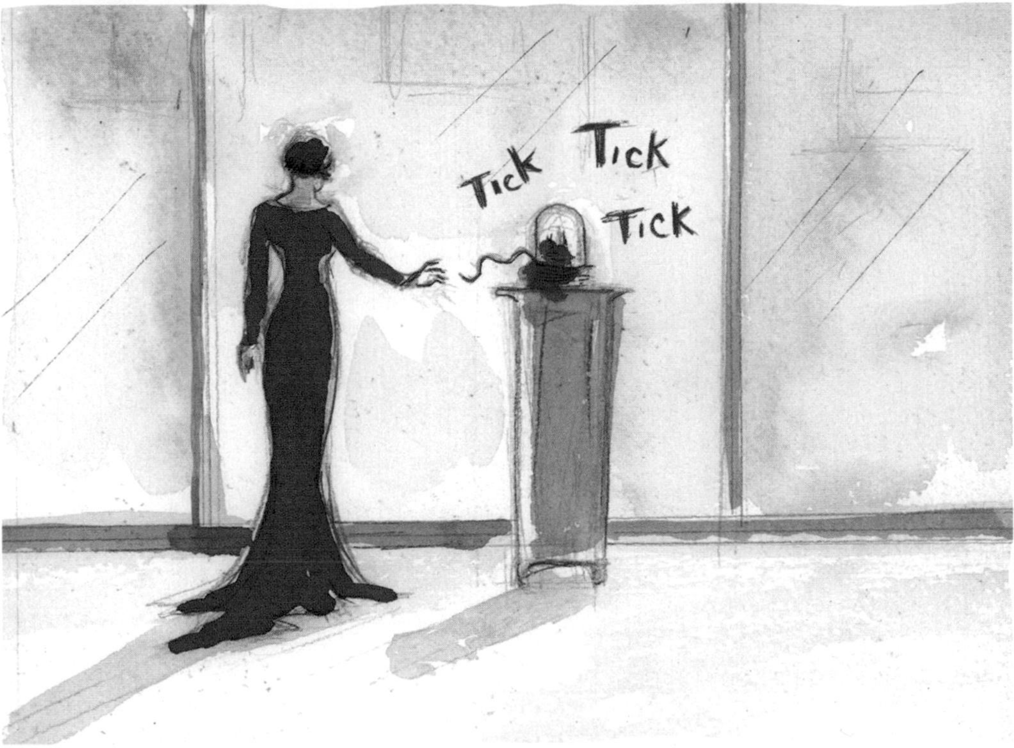
Tick Tick
Tick

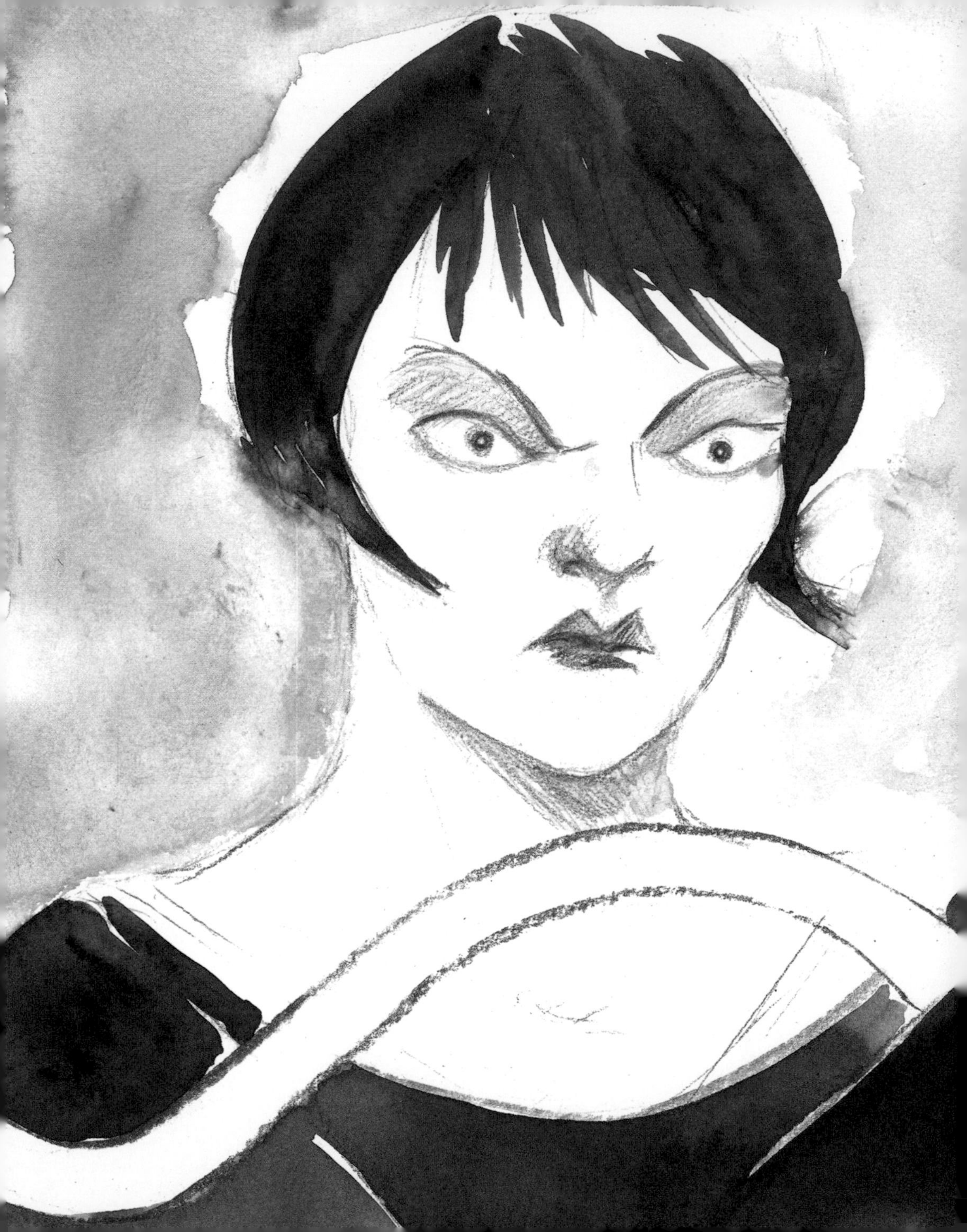

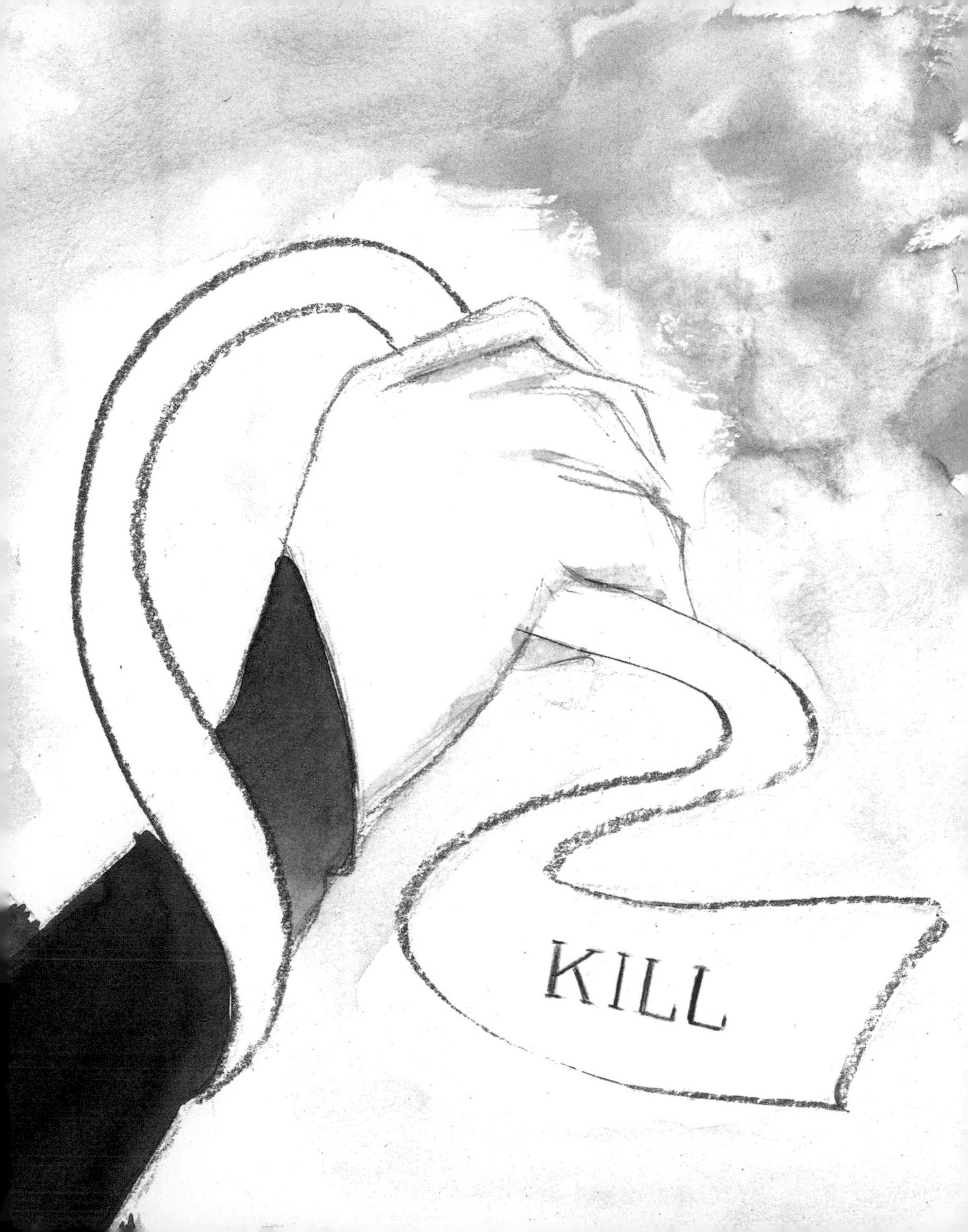
KILL

MR. HUNT

HAS A

DRINK

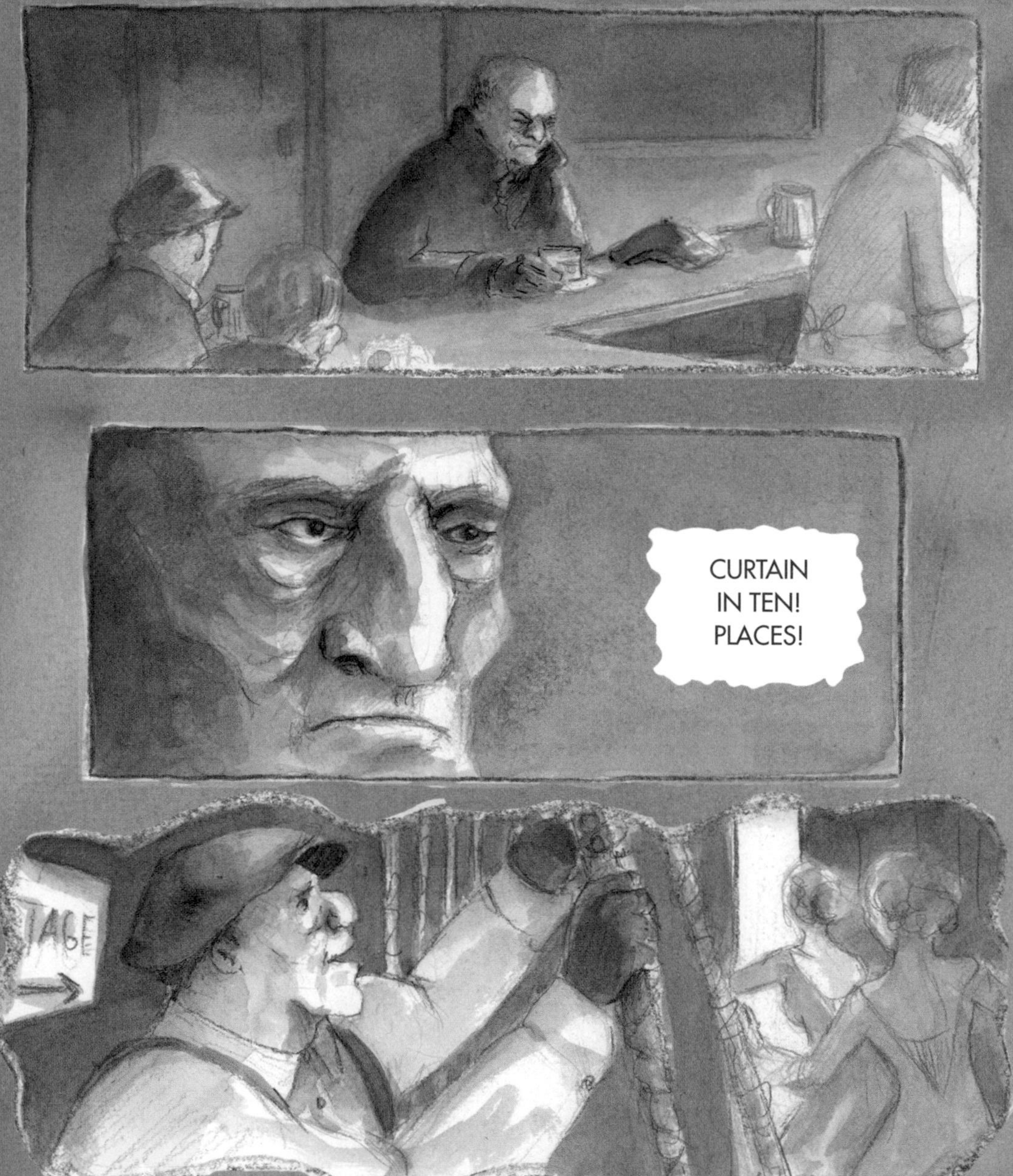
CURTAIN IN TEN! PLACES!

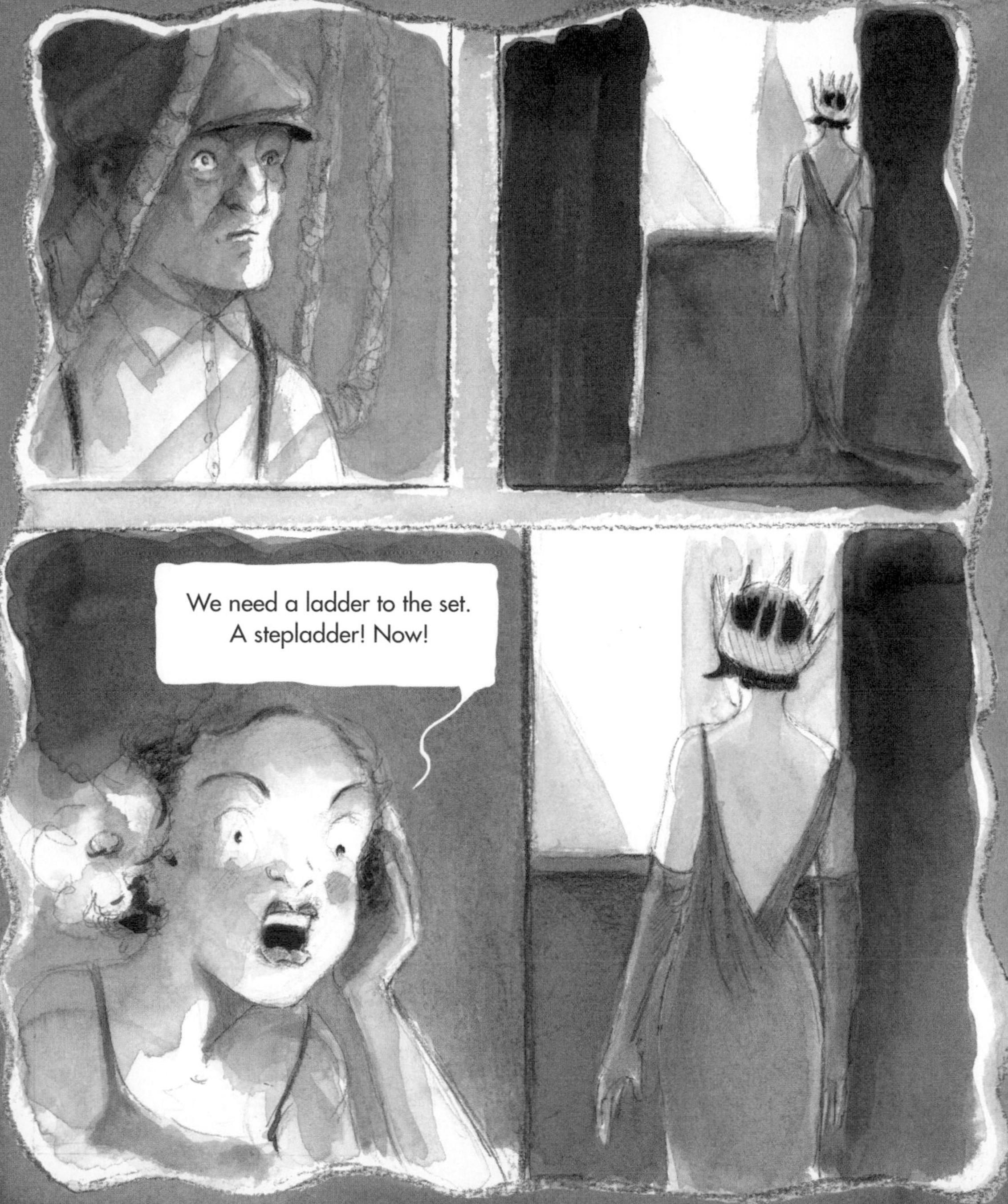
We need a ladder to the set. A stepladder! Now!

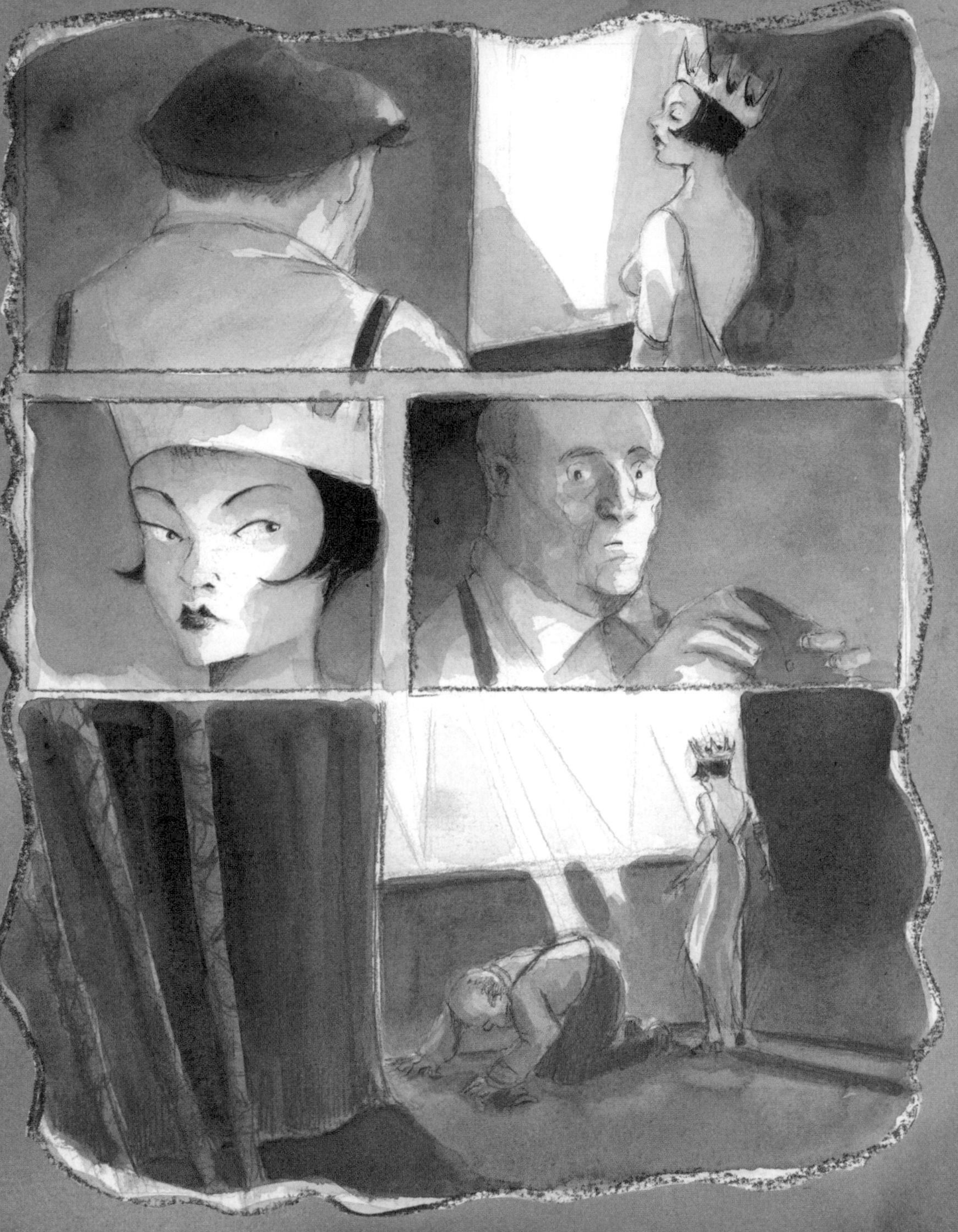

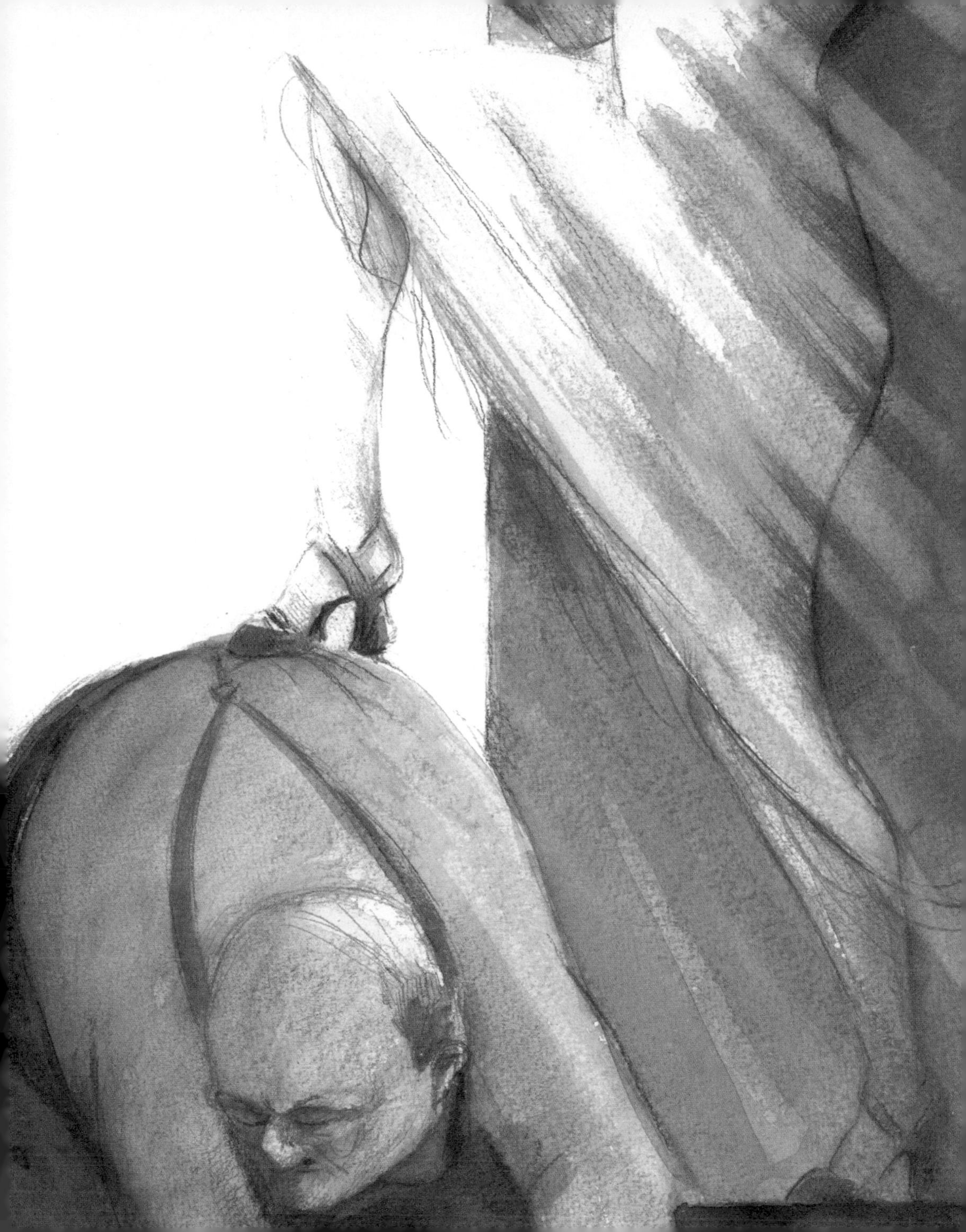

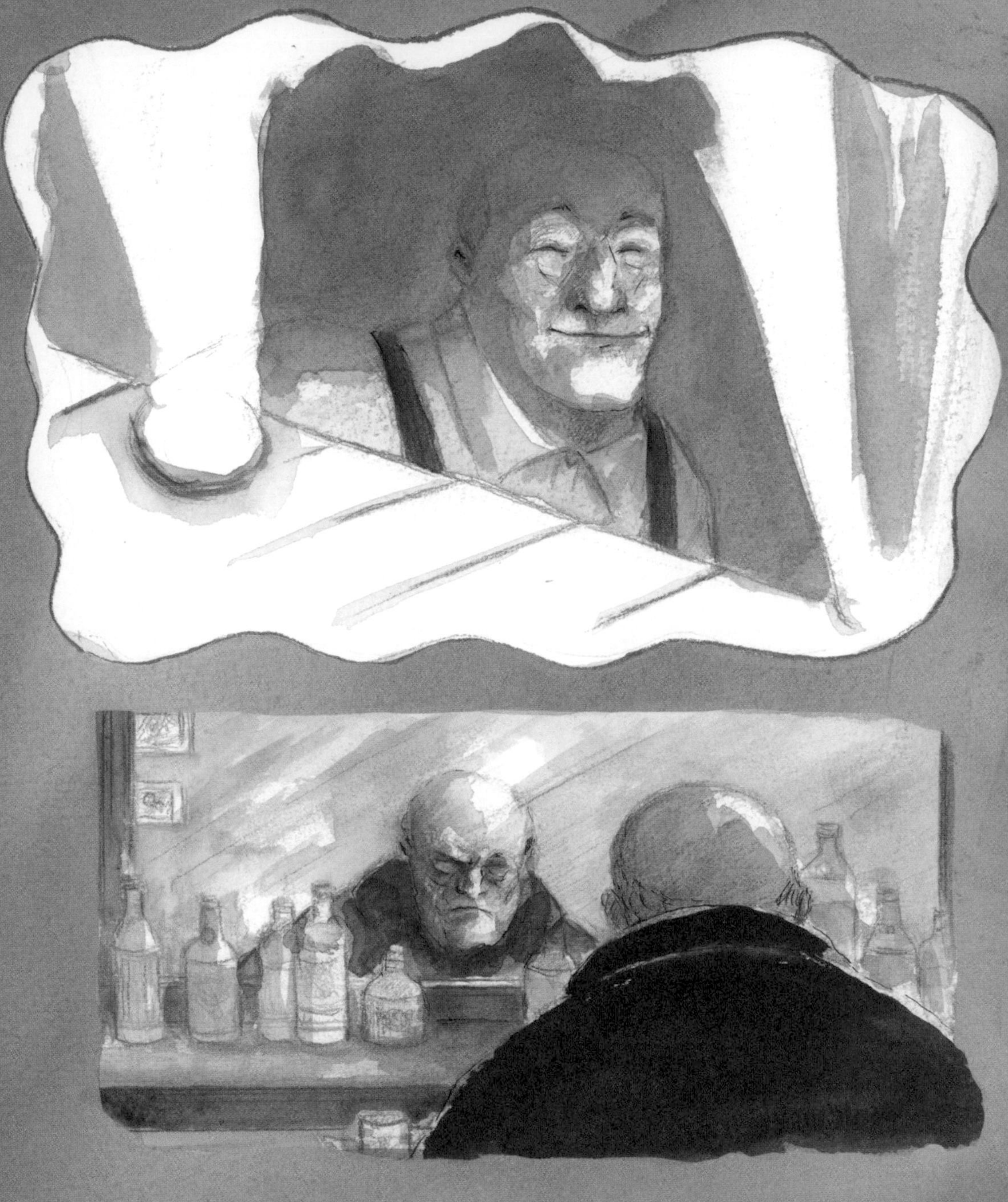

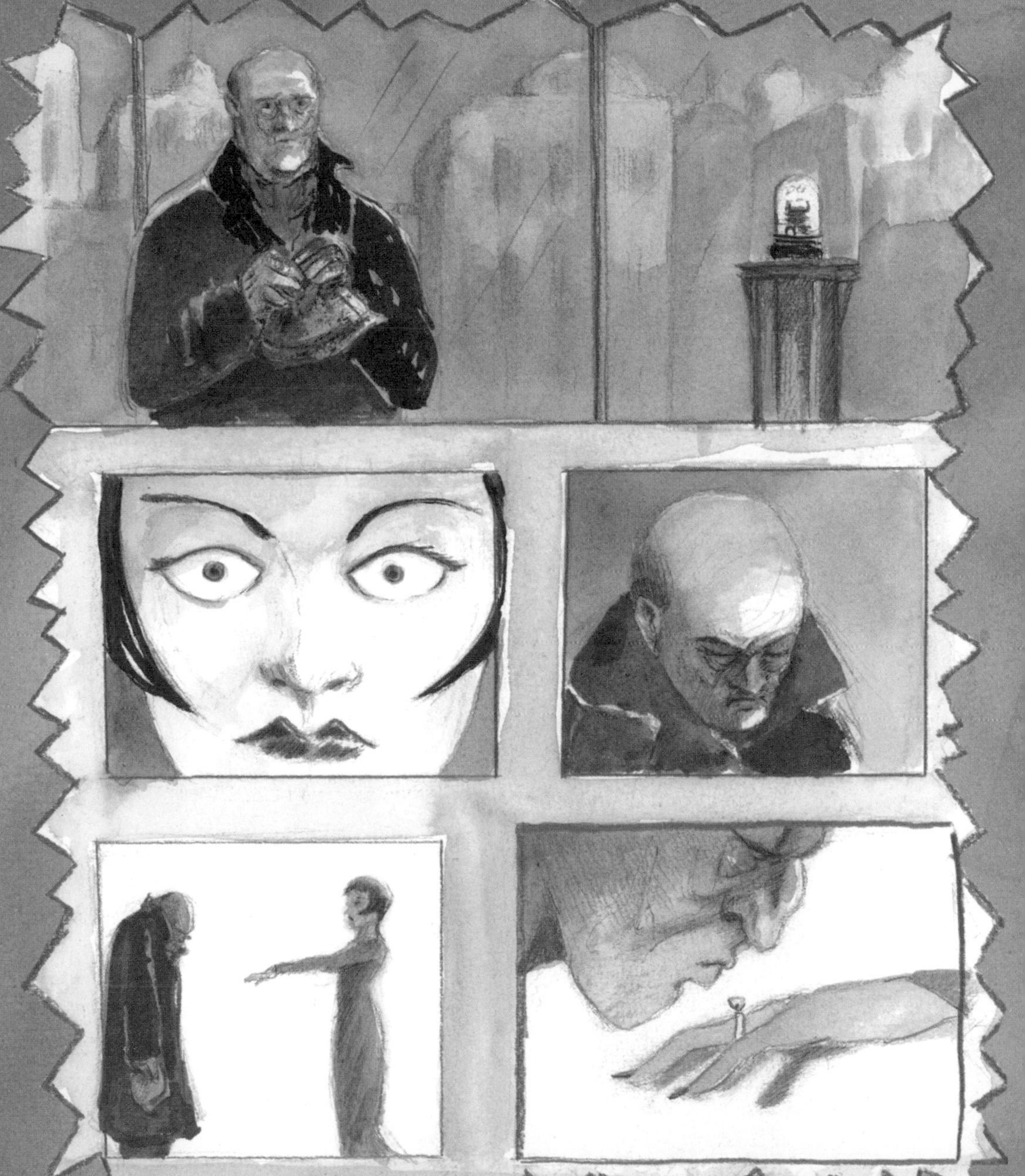

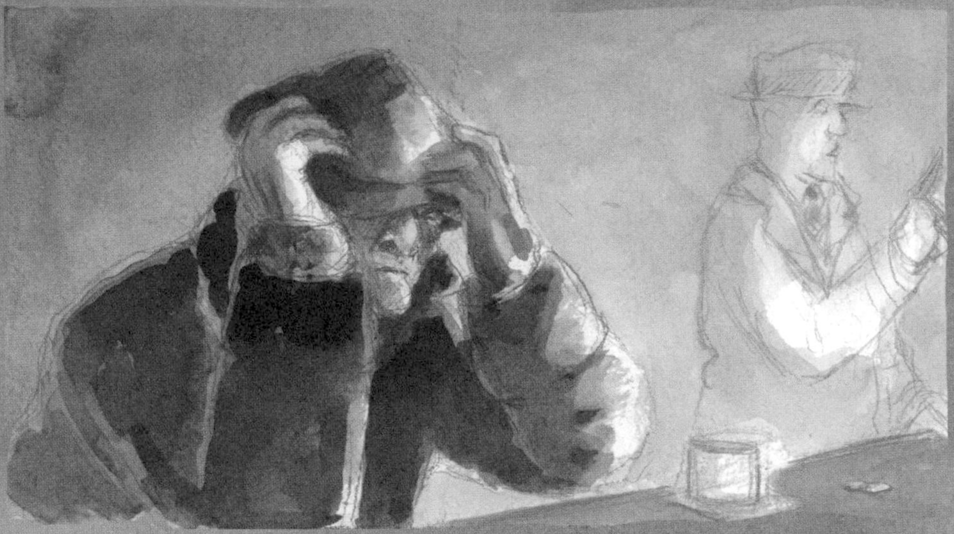

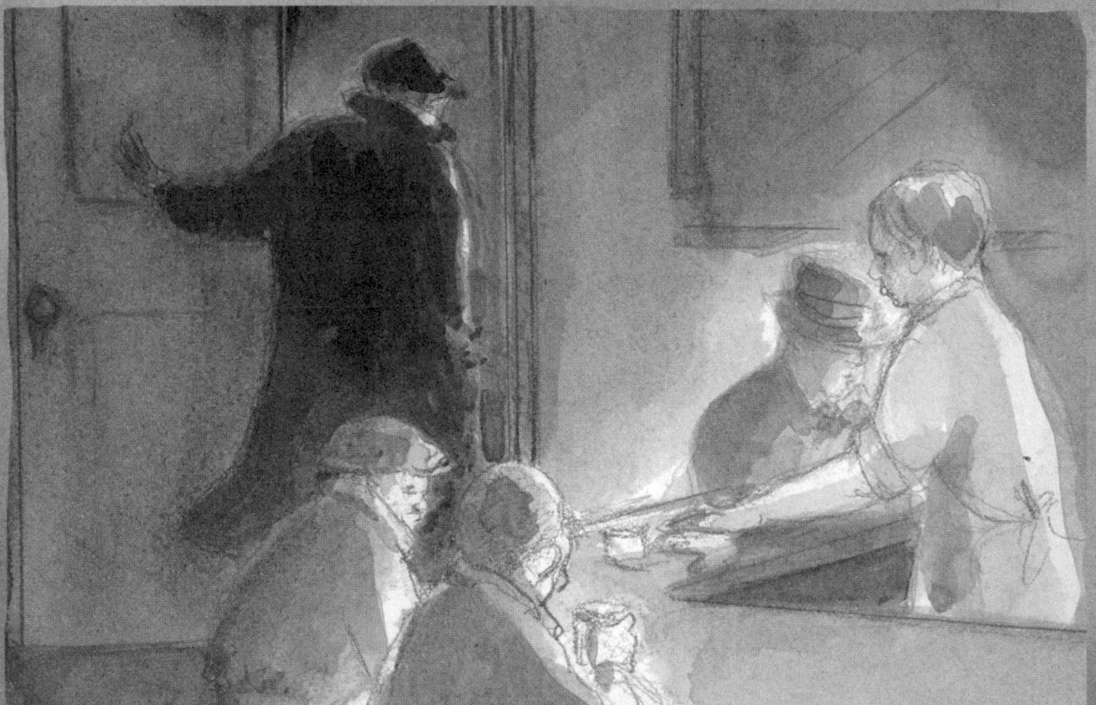

HOOVERVILLE

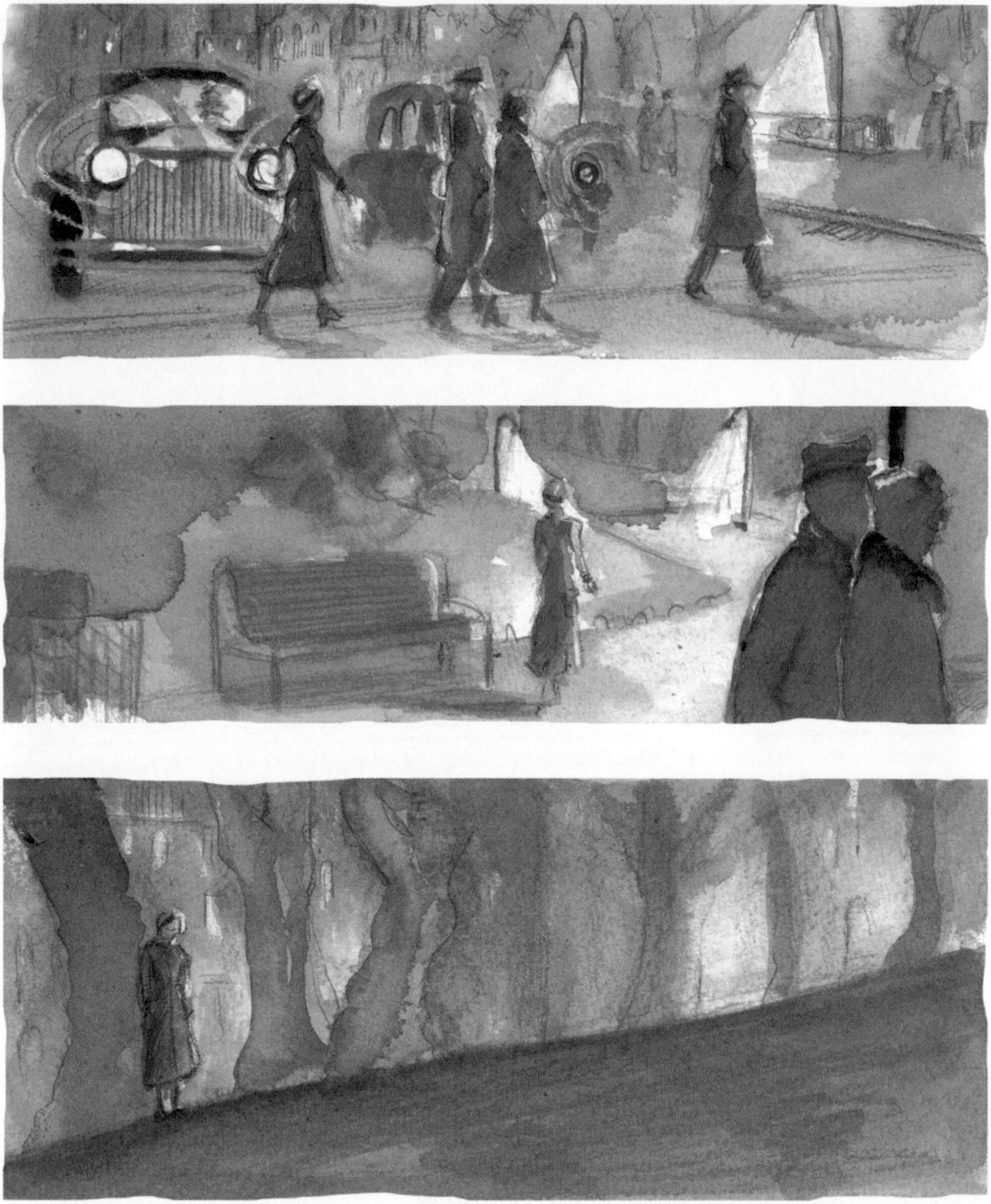

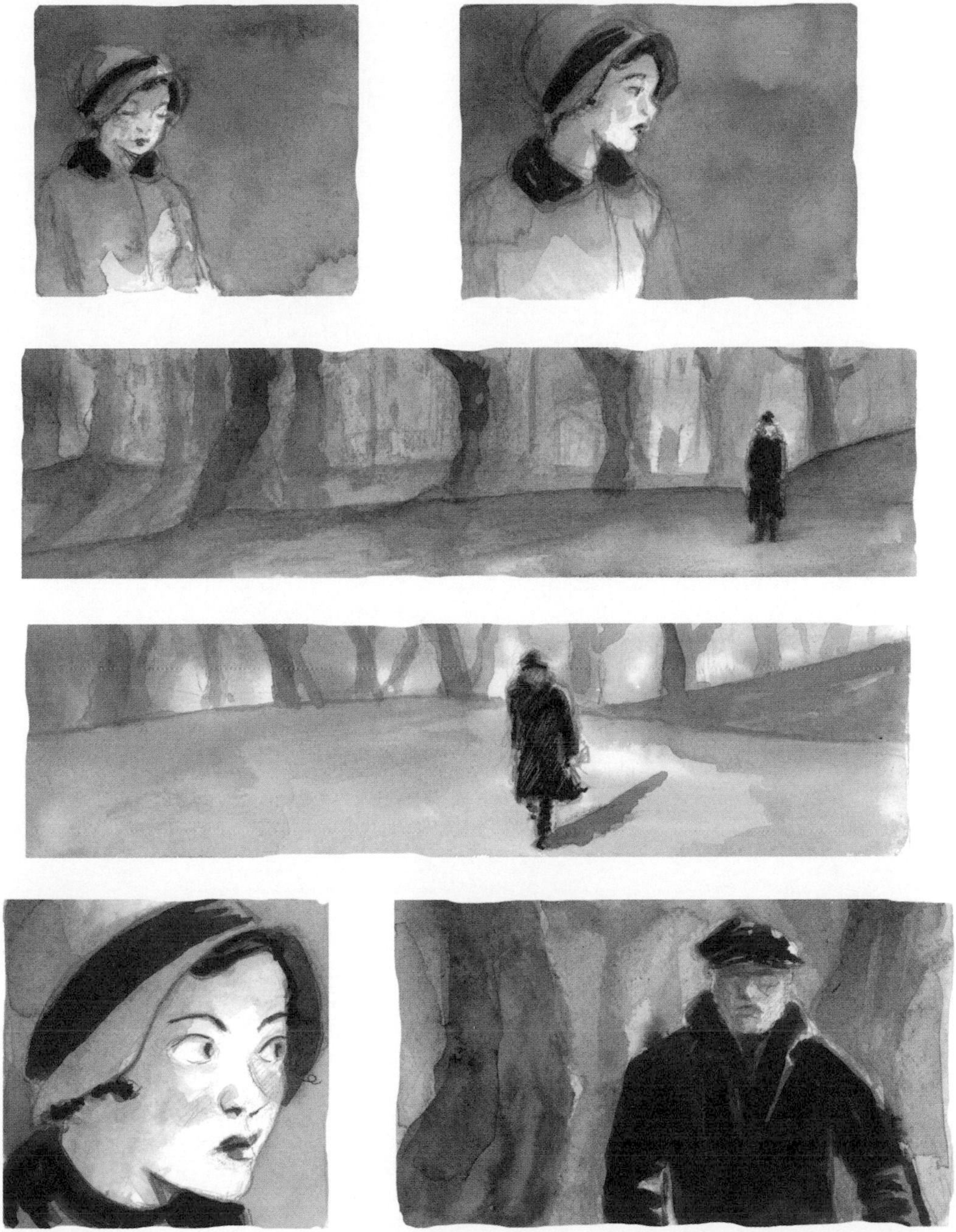

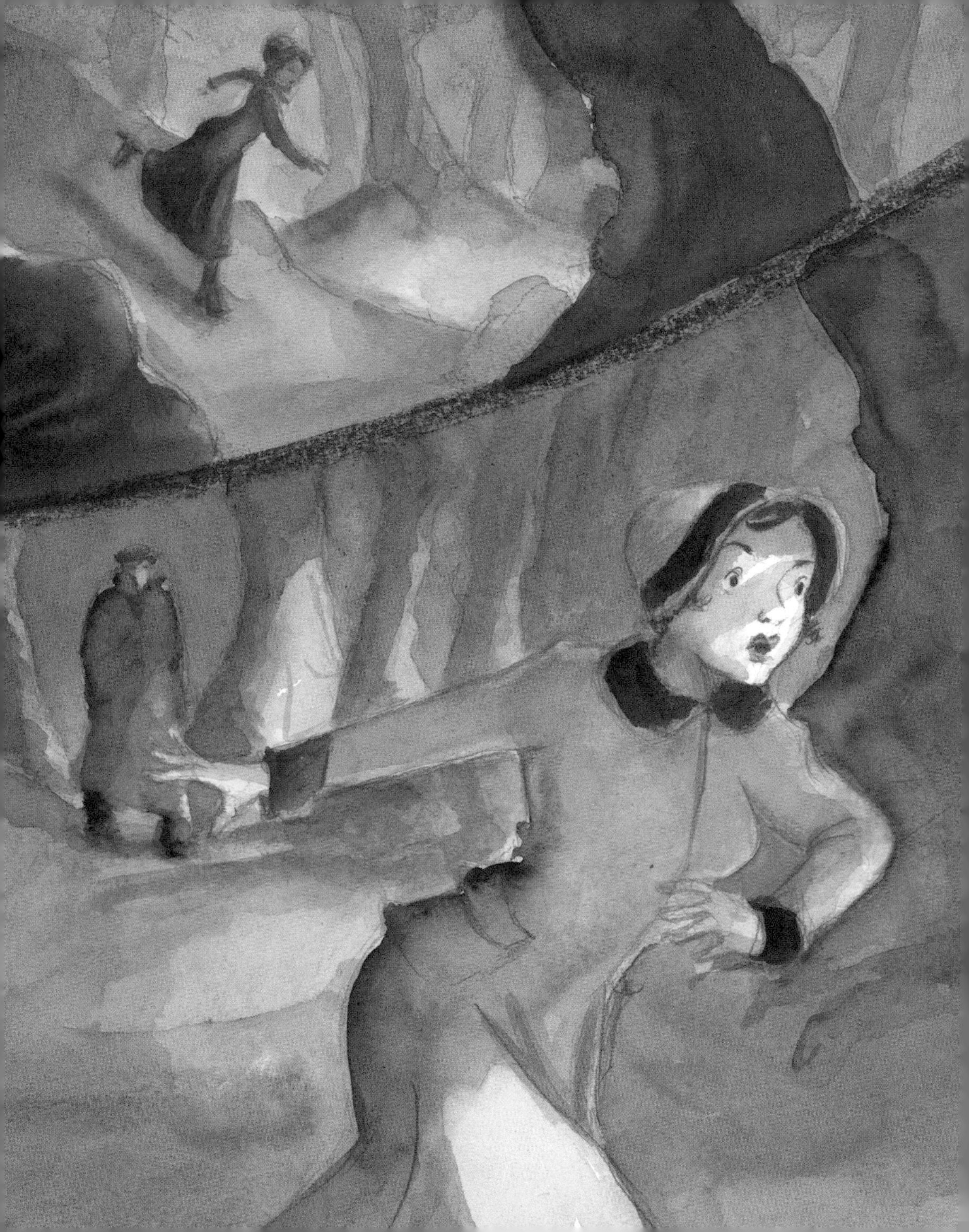

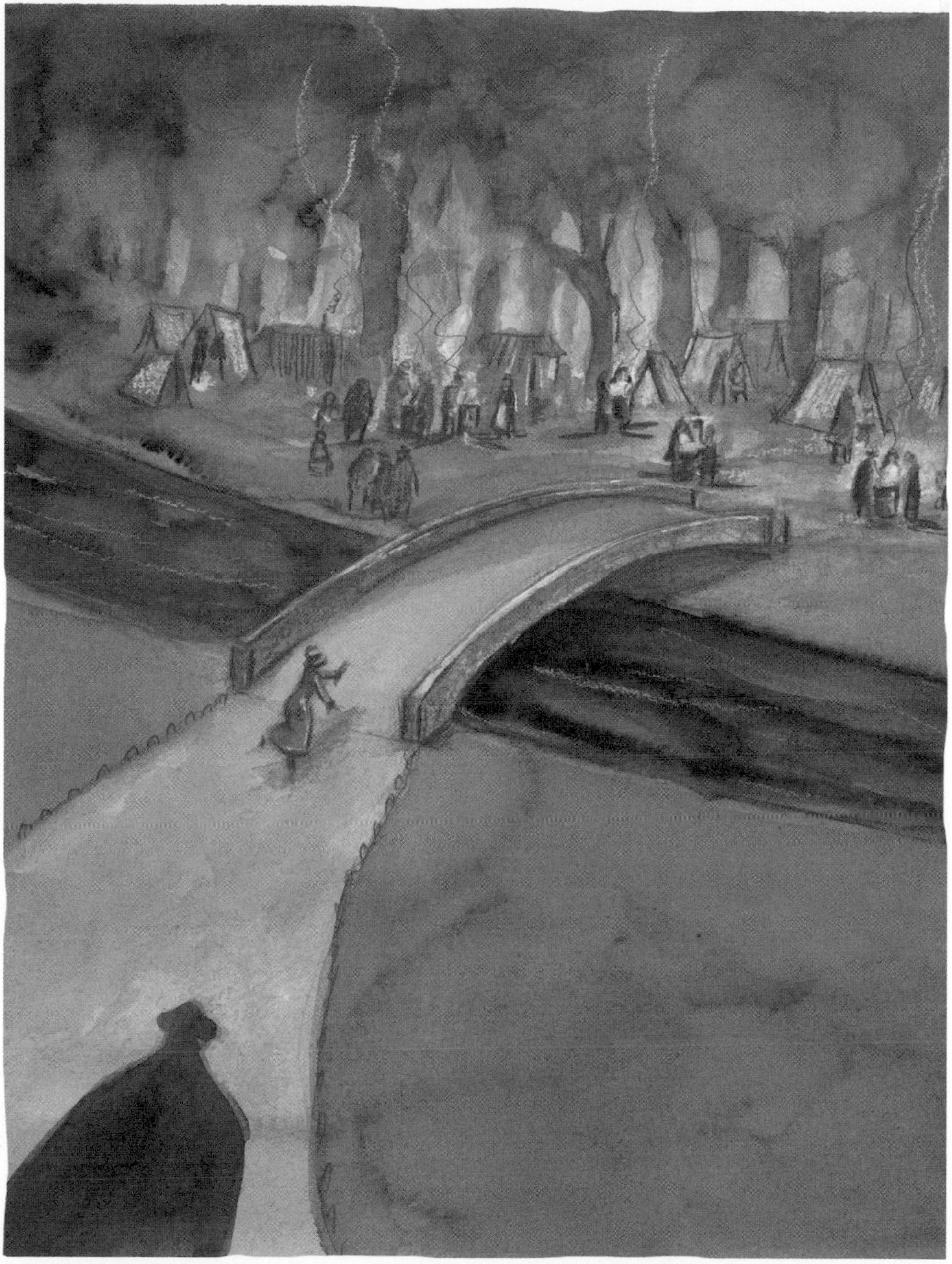

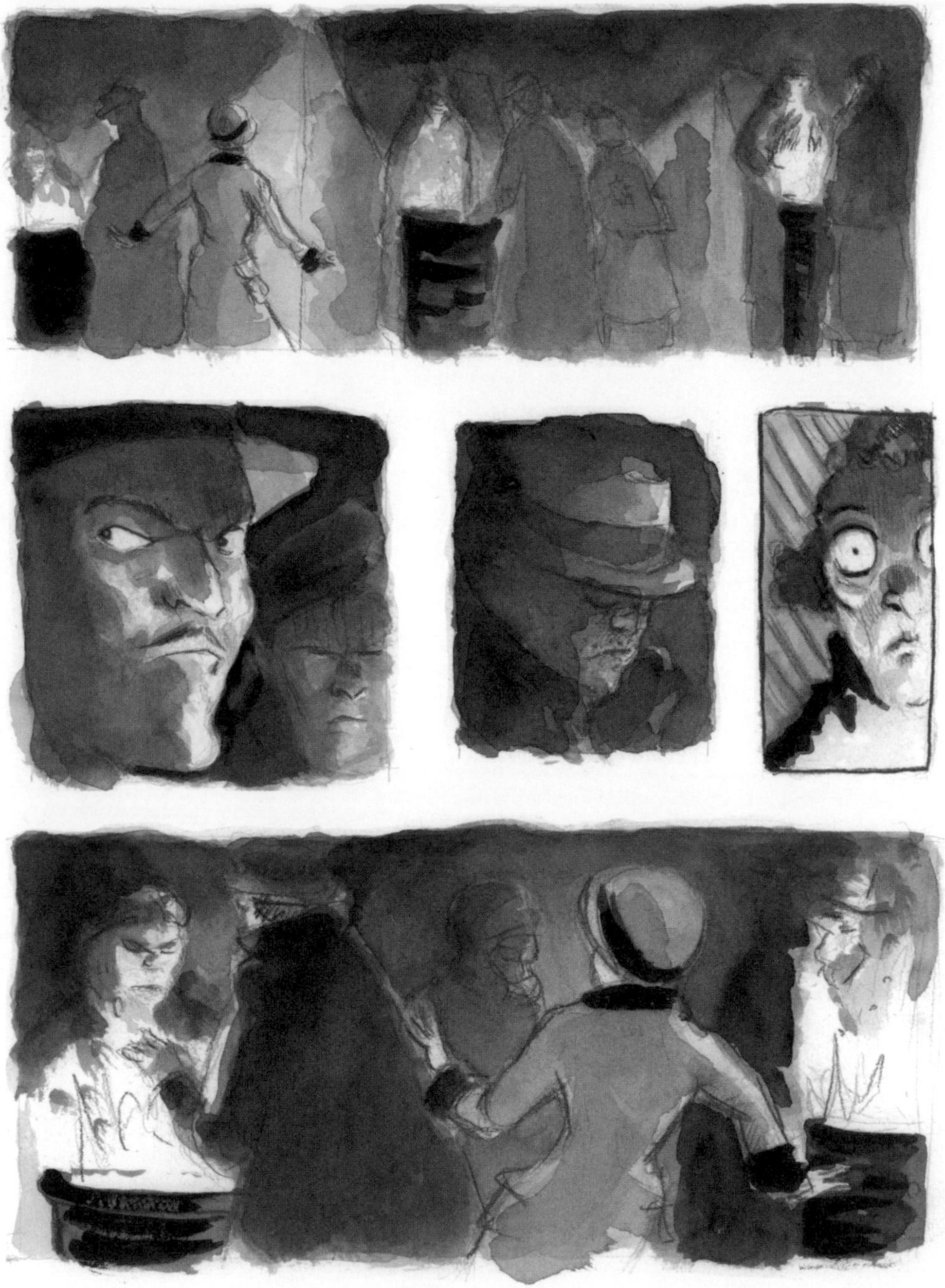

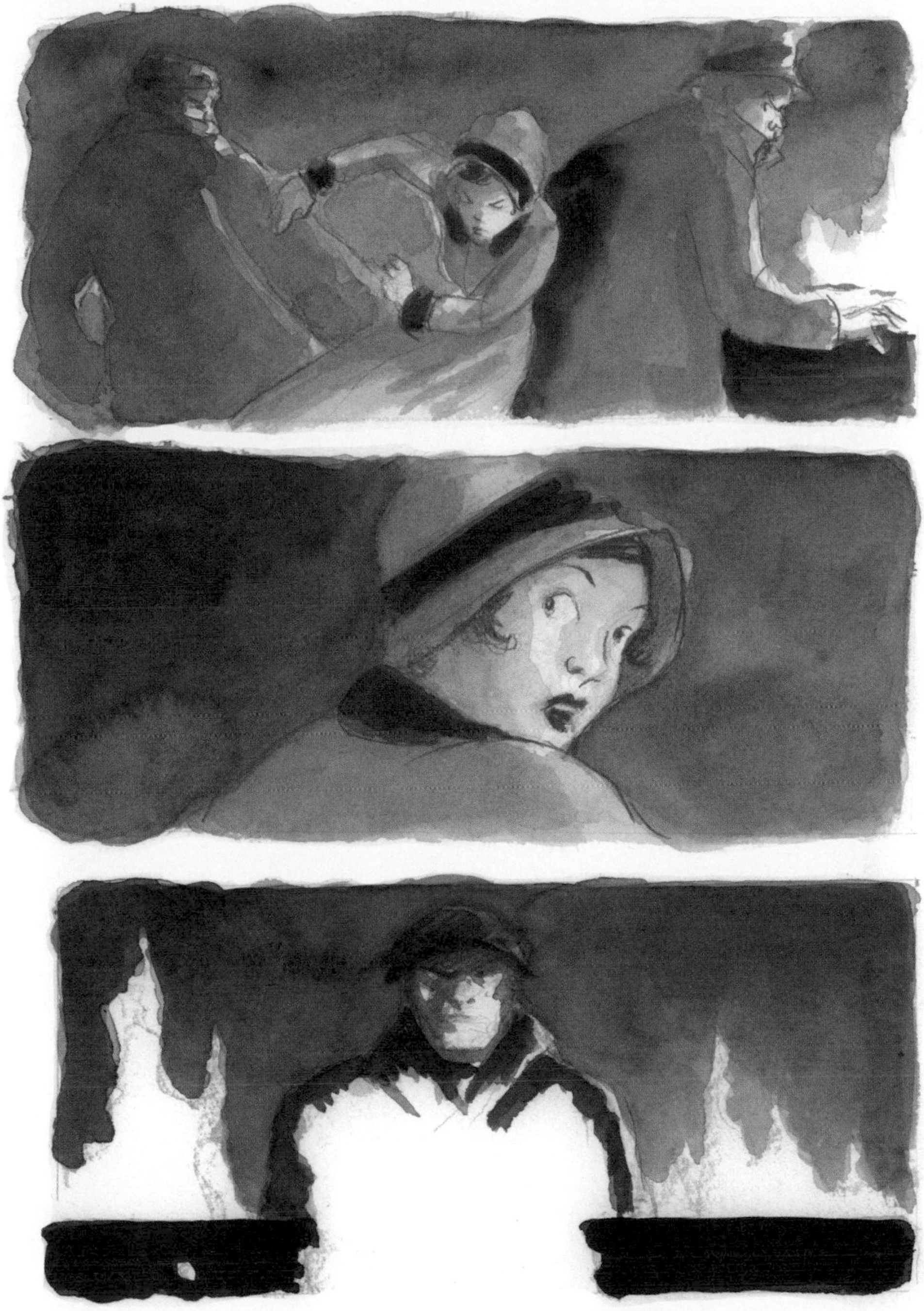

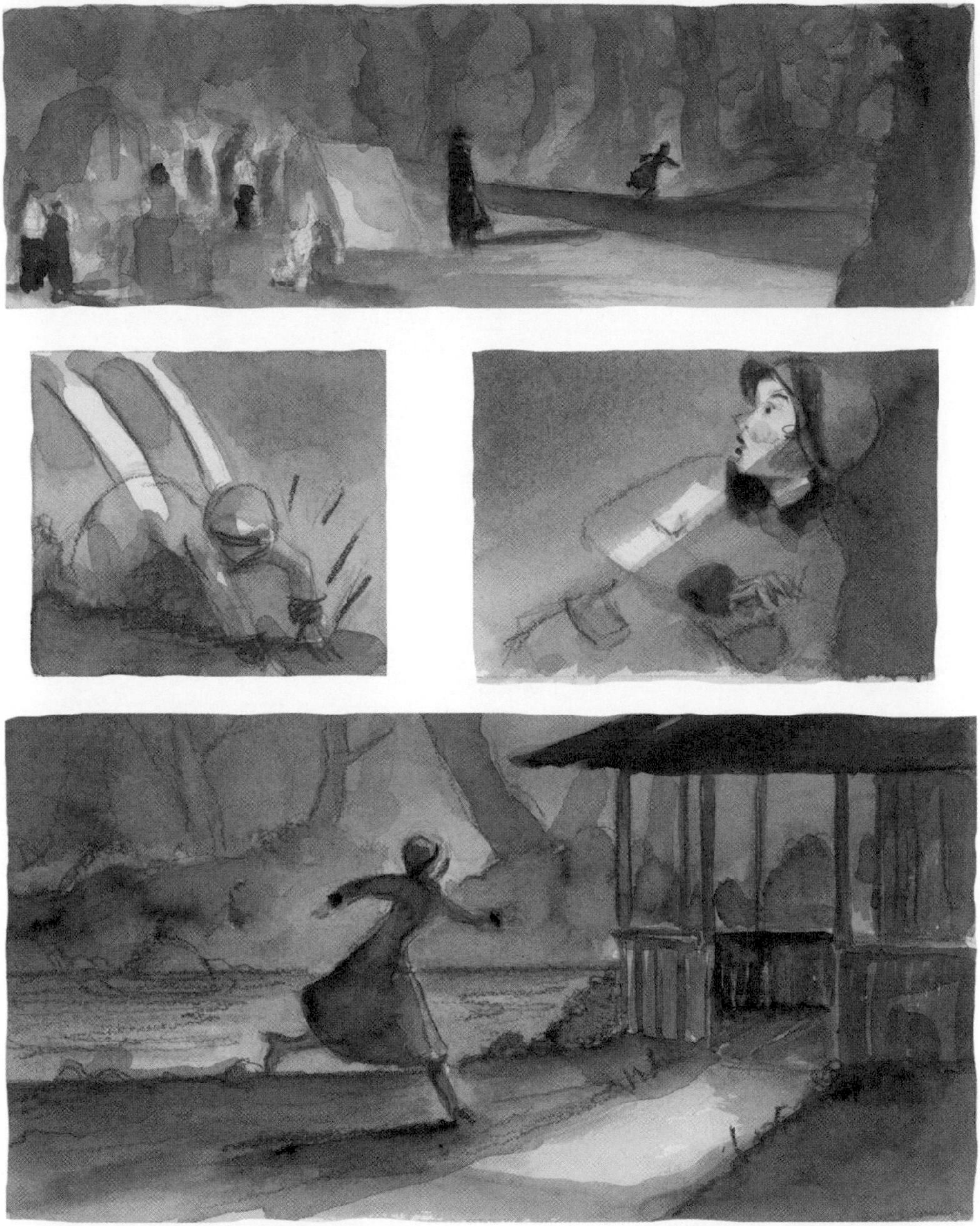

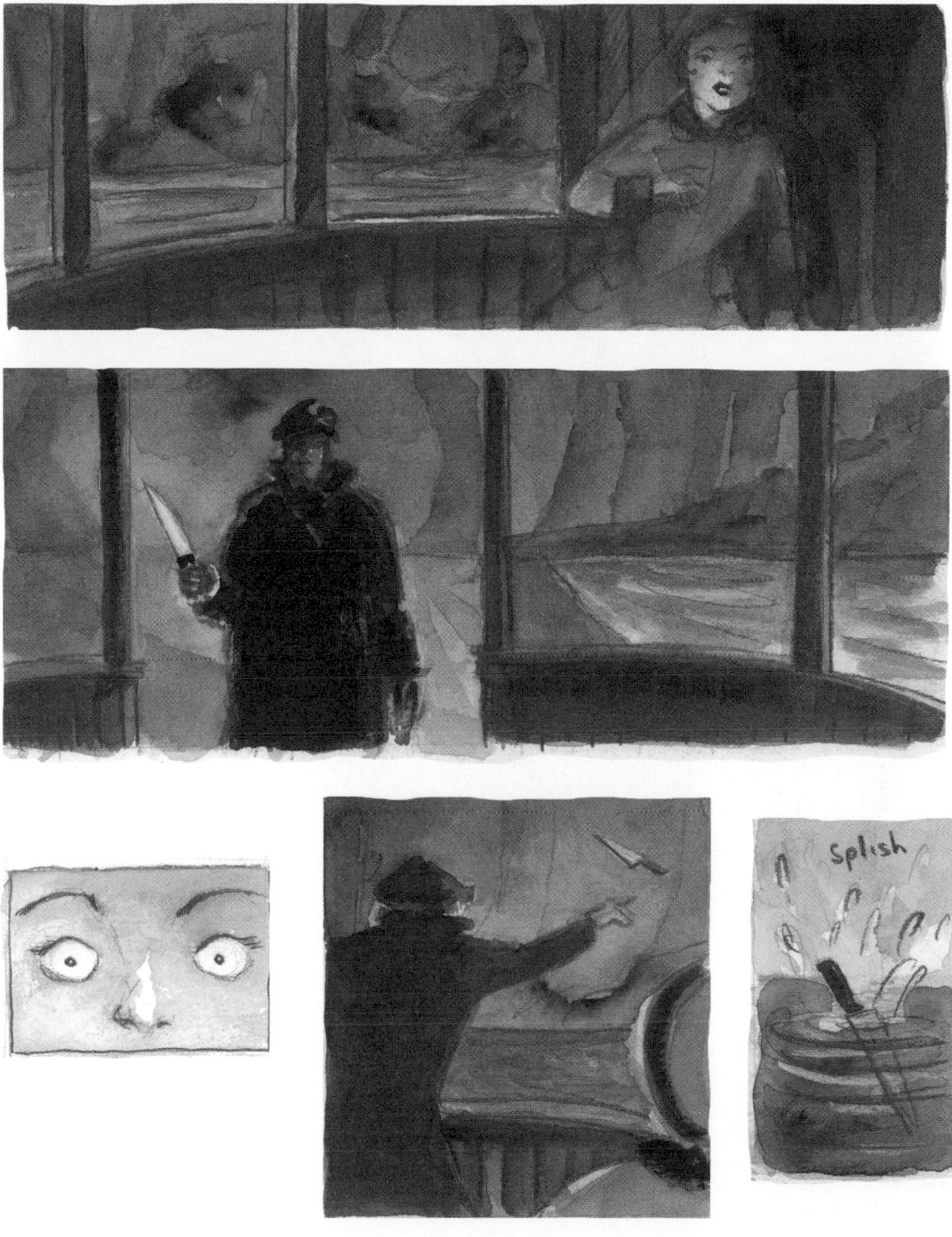
Splish

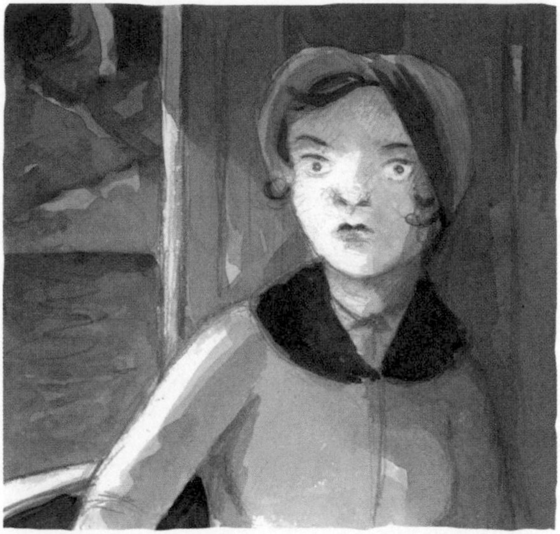

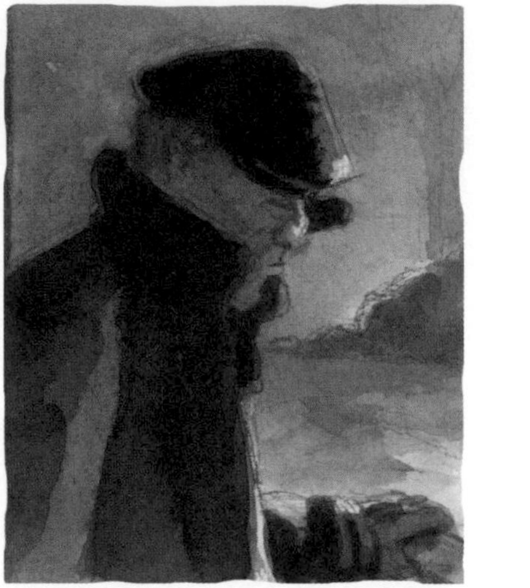

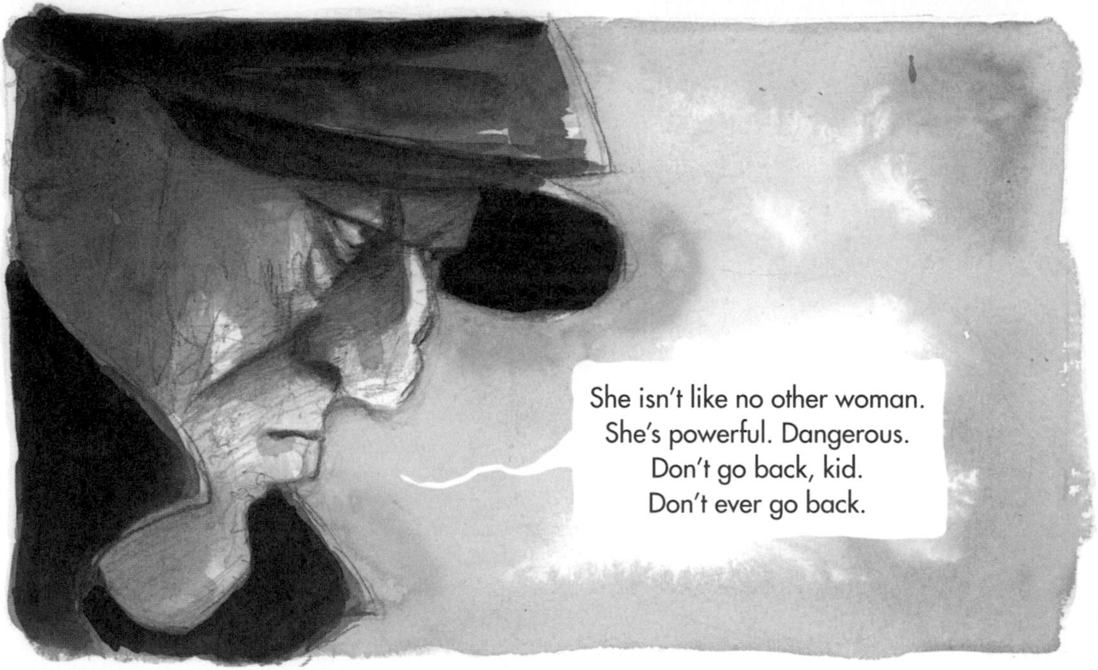
She isn't like no other woman.
She's powerful. Dangerous.
Don't go back, kid.
Don't ever go back.

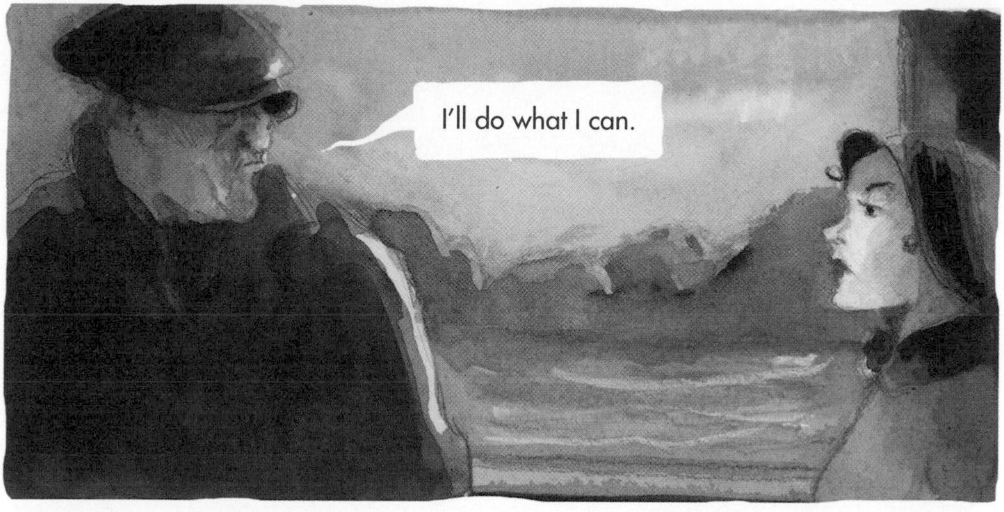
I'll do what I can.

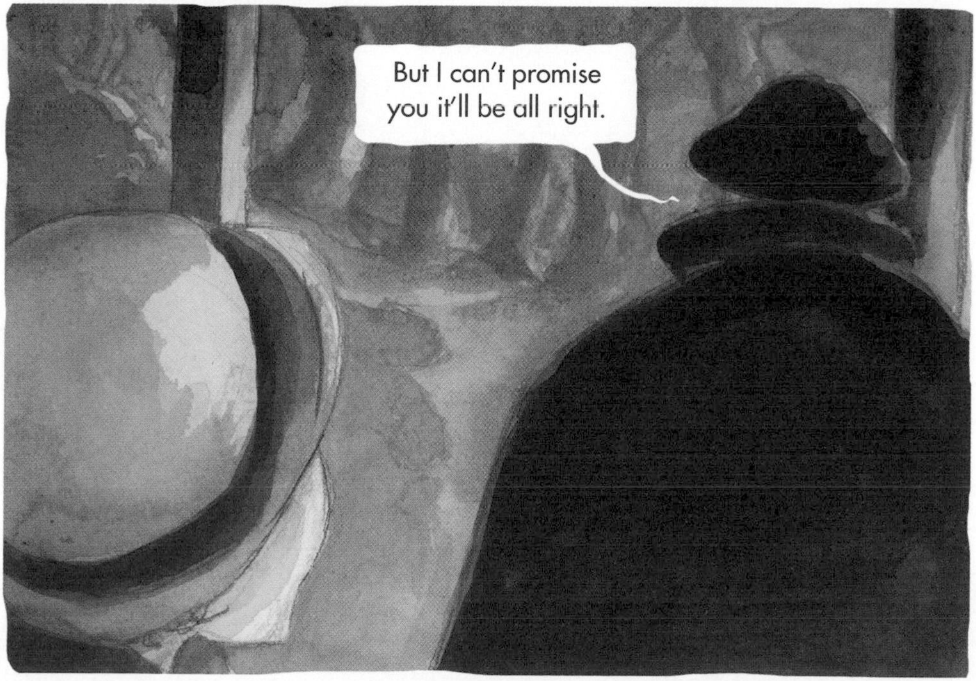
But I can't promise you it'll be all right.

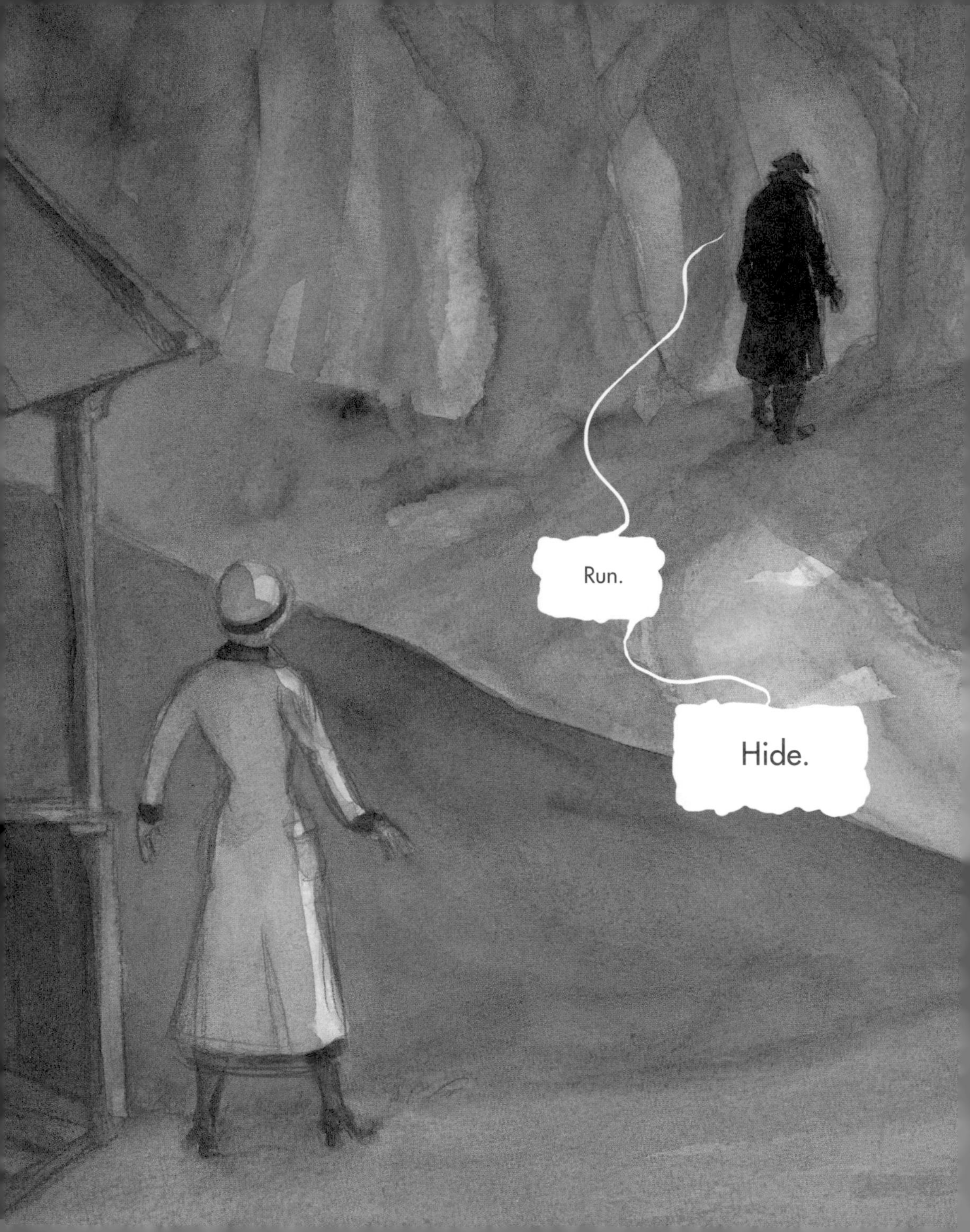
Run.
Hide.

LATE NIGHT
AT THE
BUTCHER'S

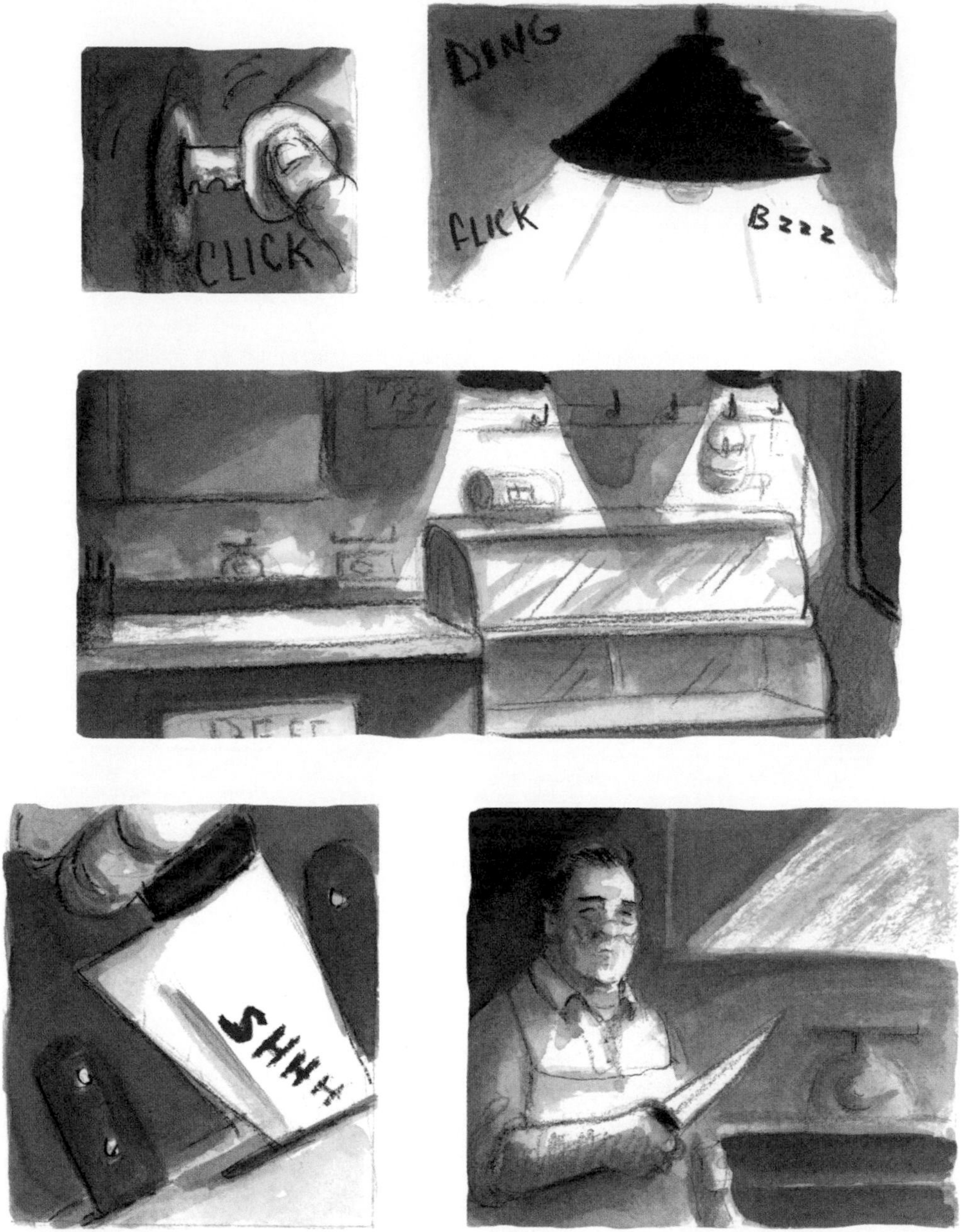
CLICK
DING
FLICK
Bzzz
SHHH

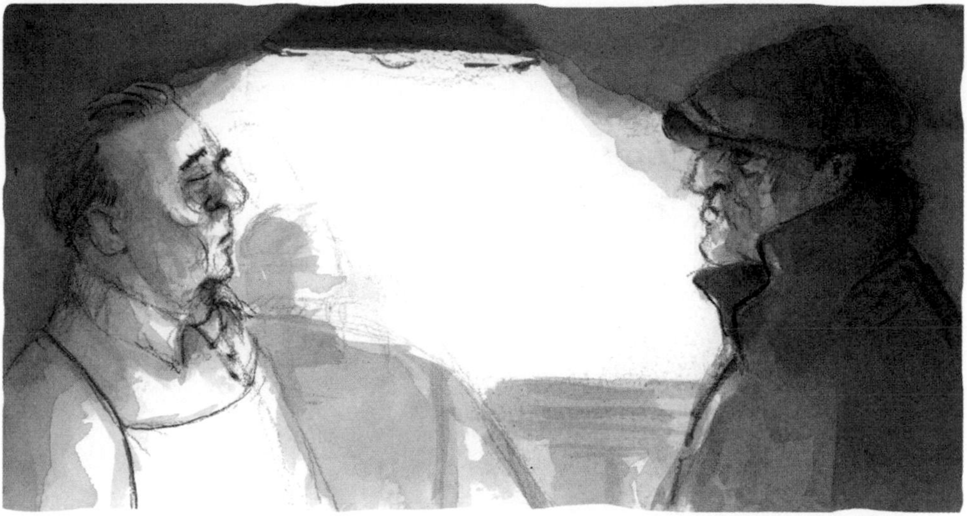

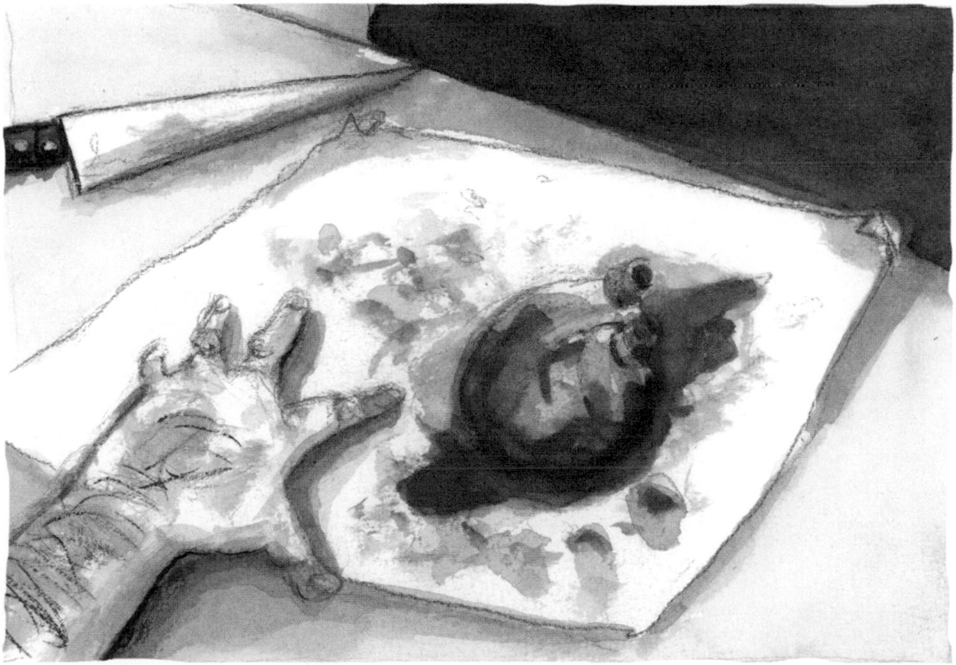

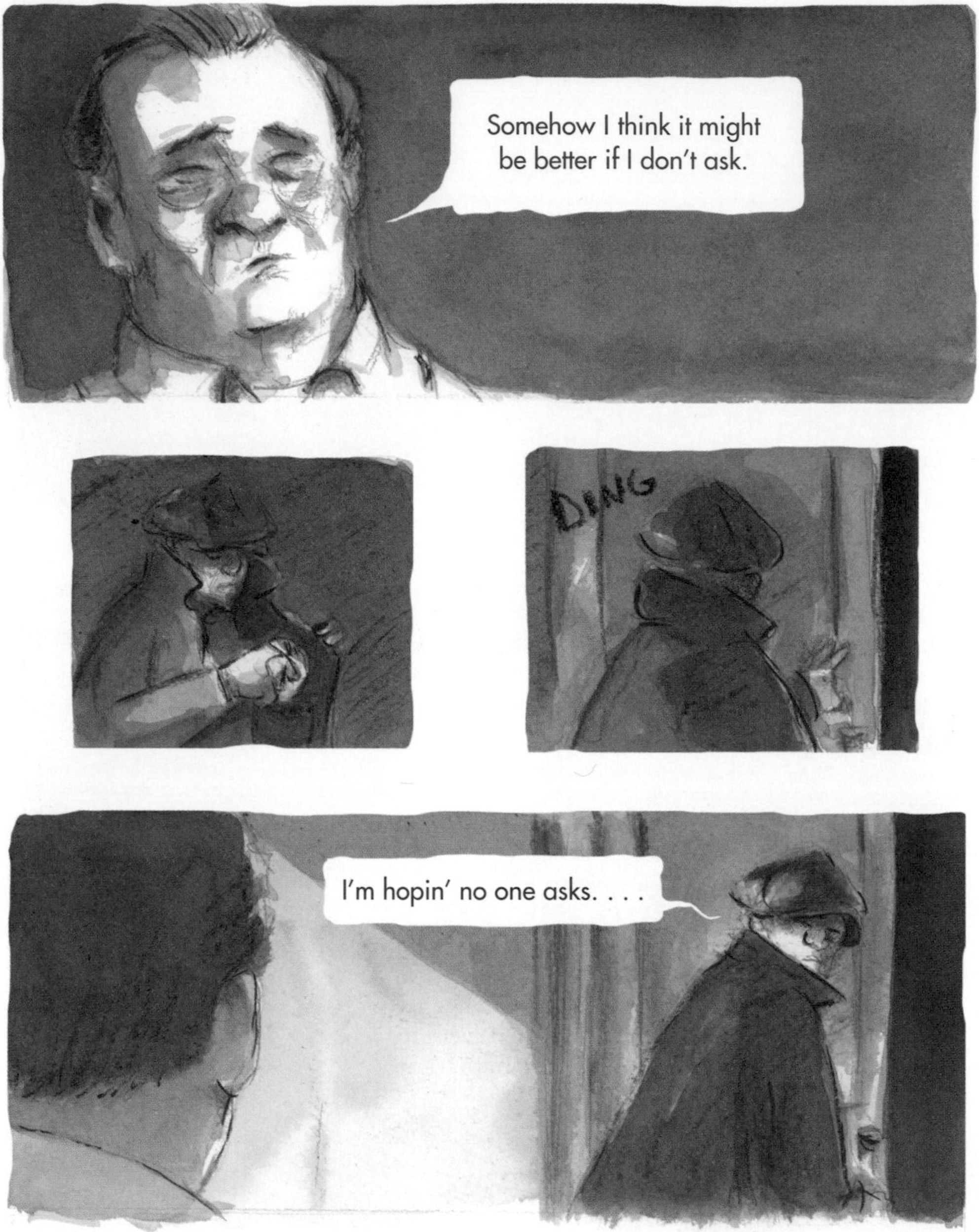
Somehow I think it might be better if I don't ask.
DING
I'm hopin' no one asks. . . .

LOST
IN THE
ALLEYS

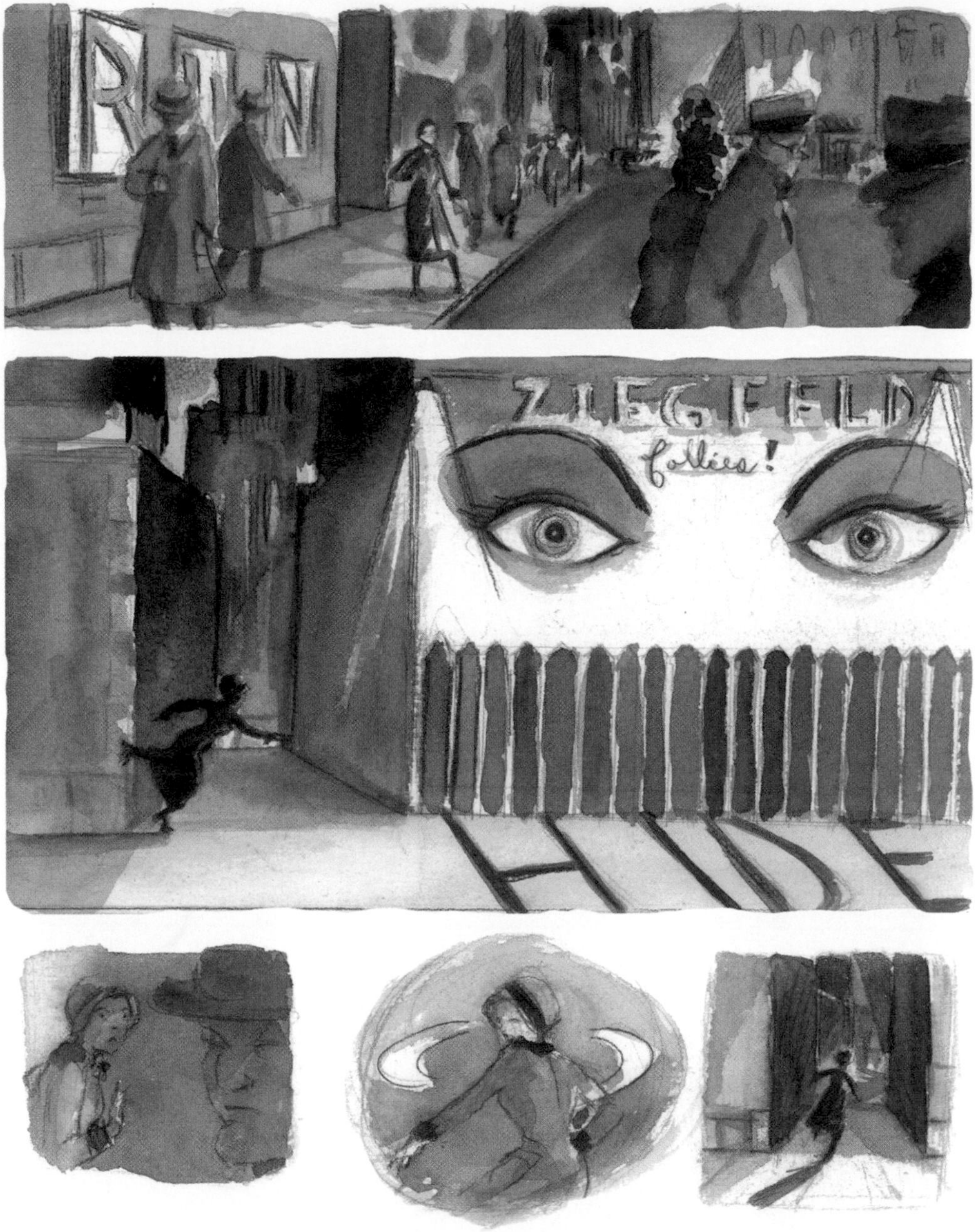
ZIEGFELD
follies!

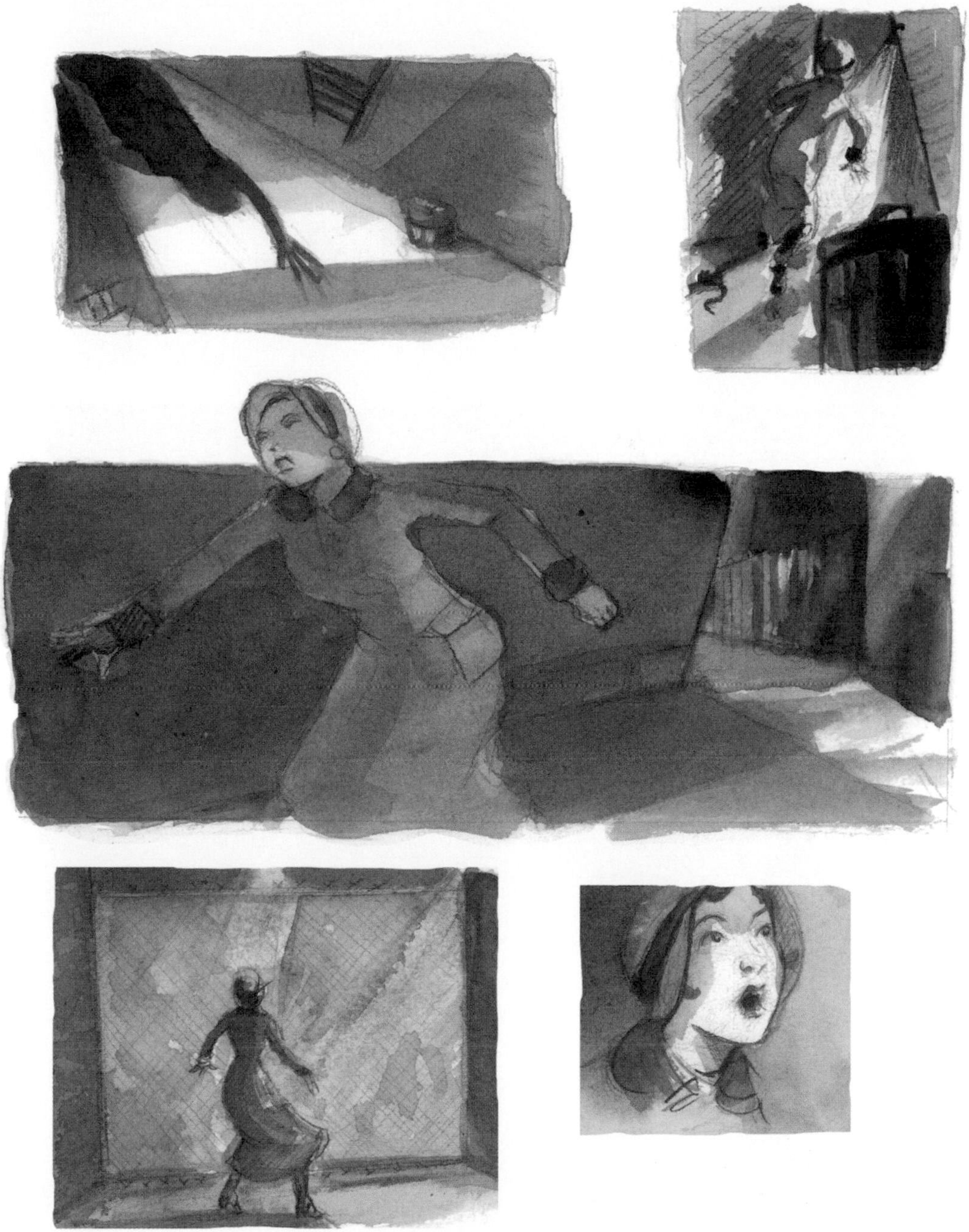

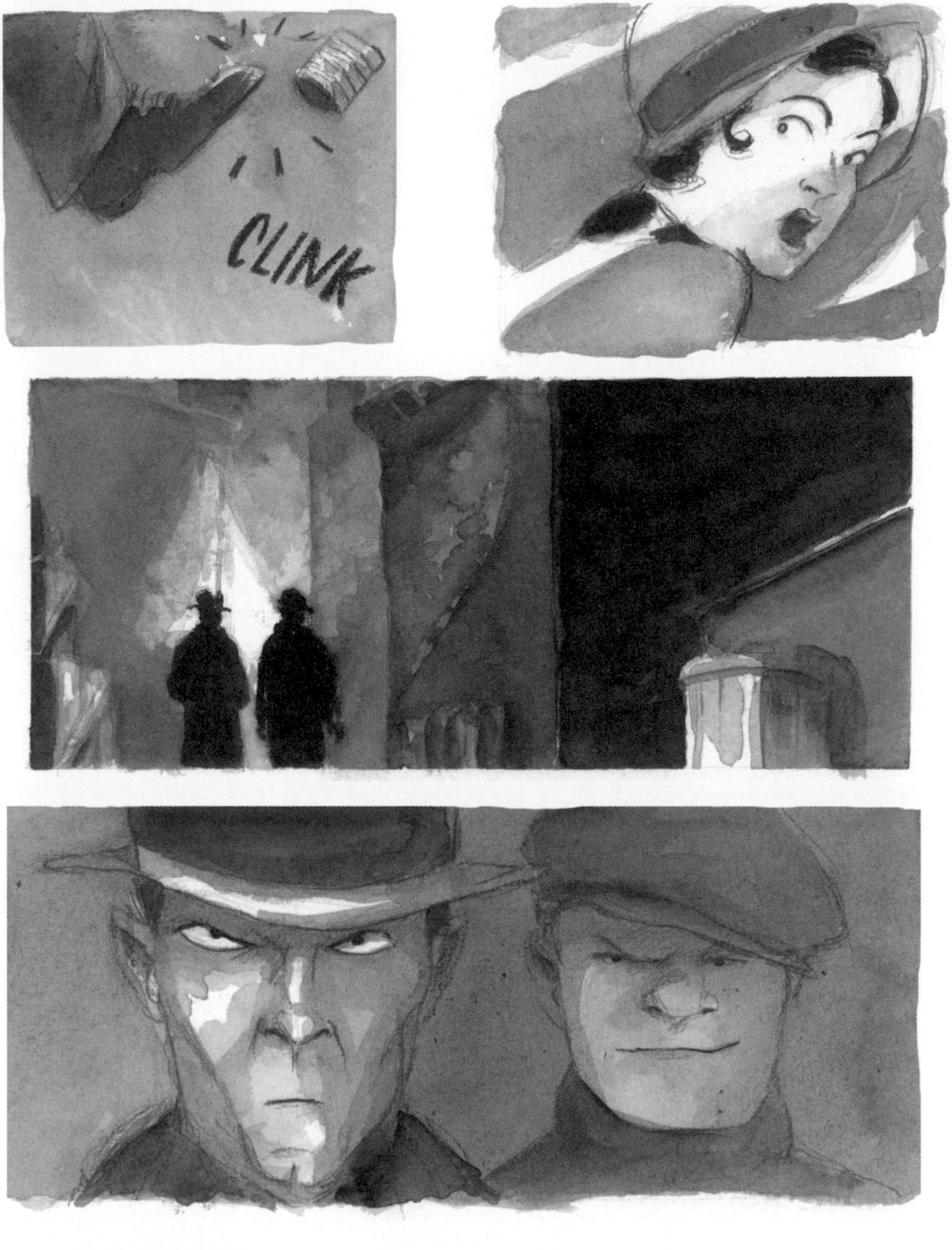
CLINK

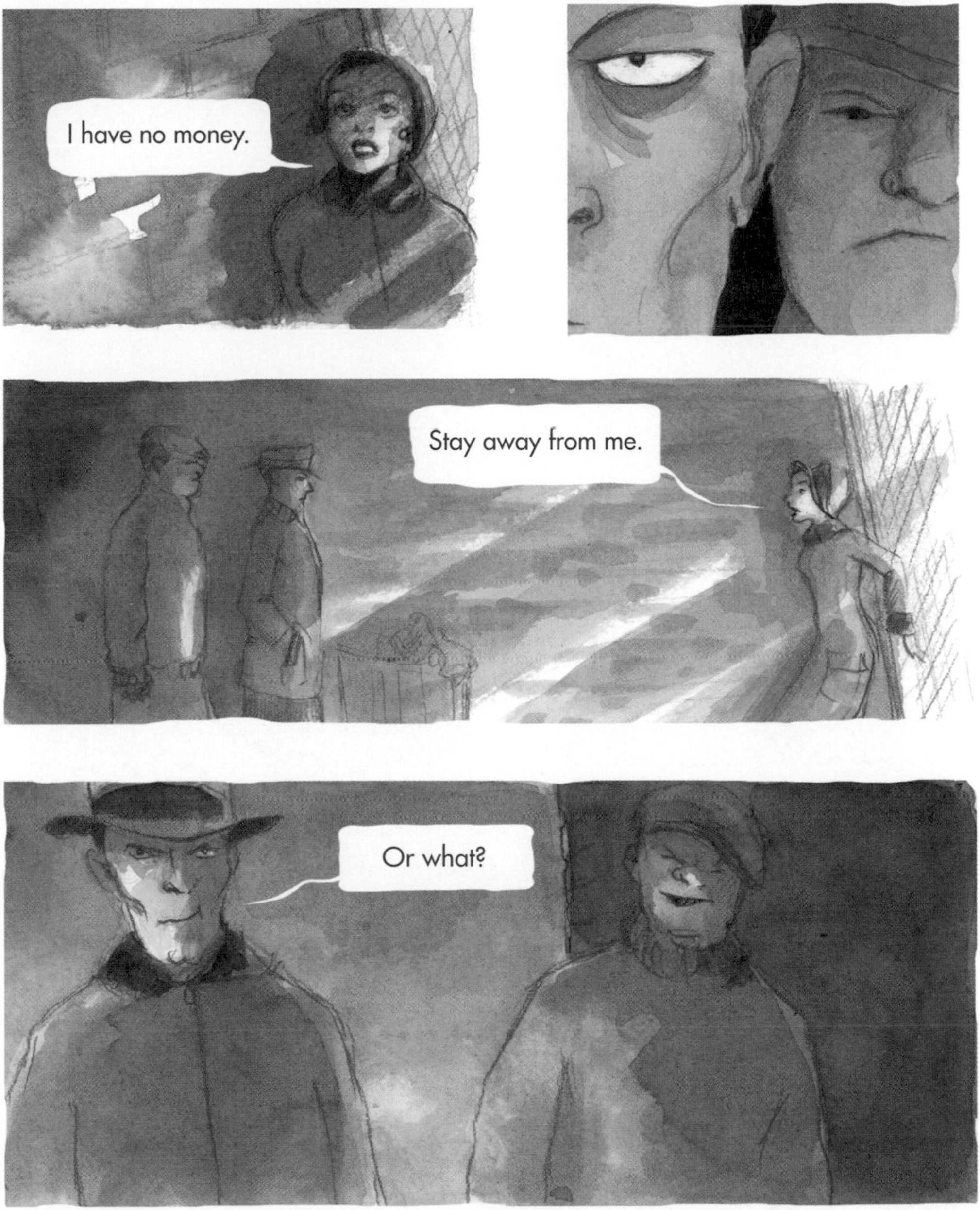
I have no money.
Stay away from me.
Or what?

What the . . . ?
THUD

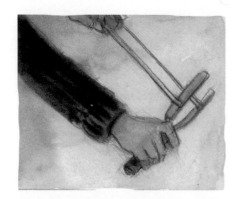

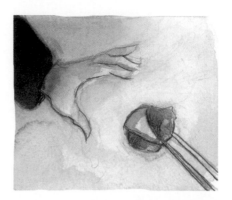

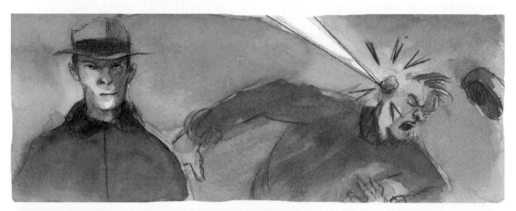

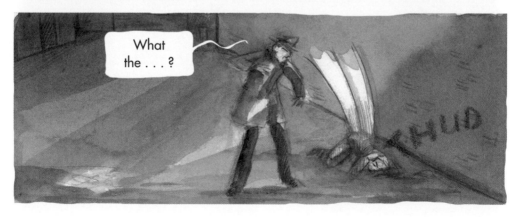

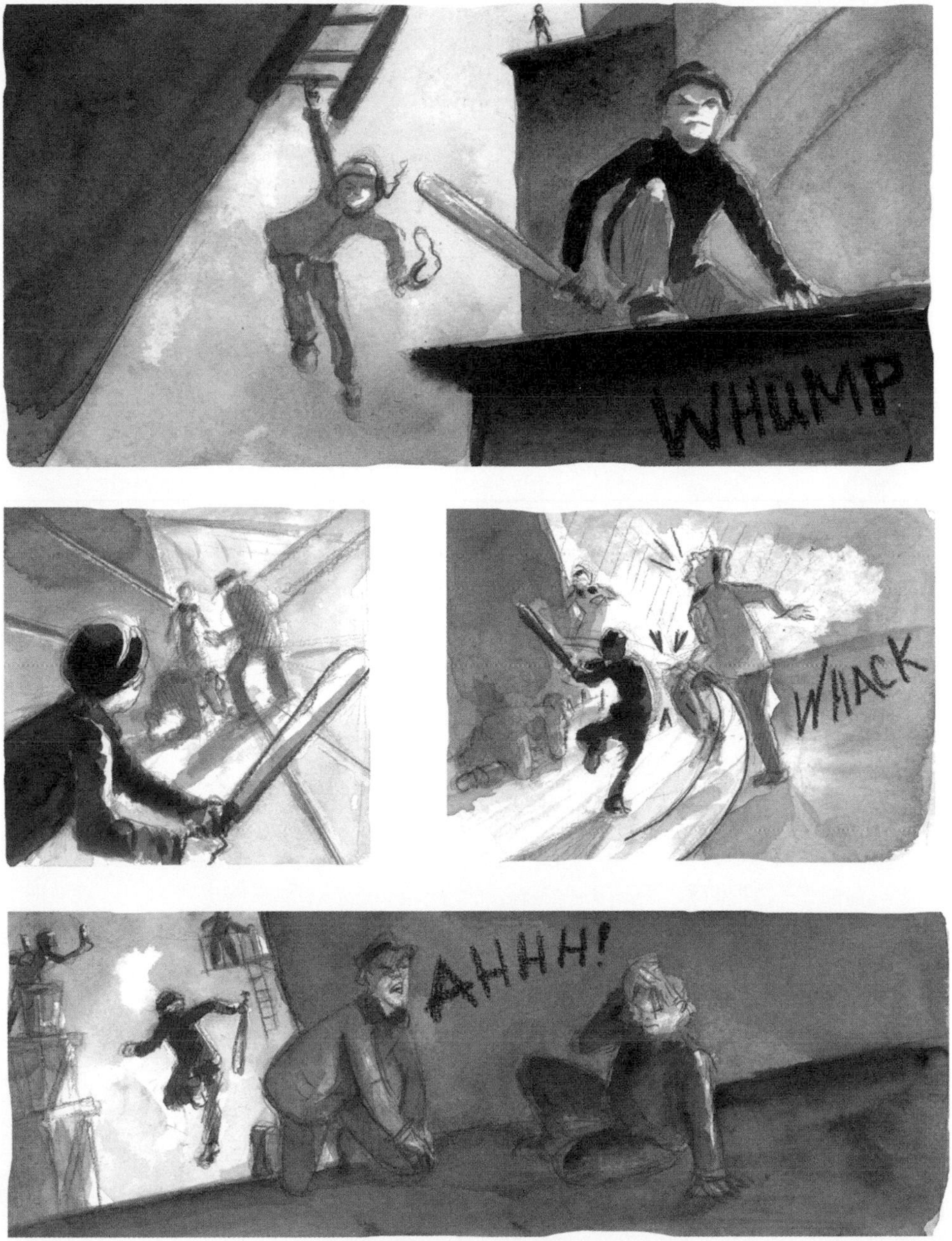
WHUMP
WHACK
AHHH!

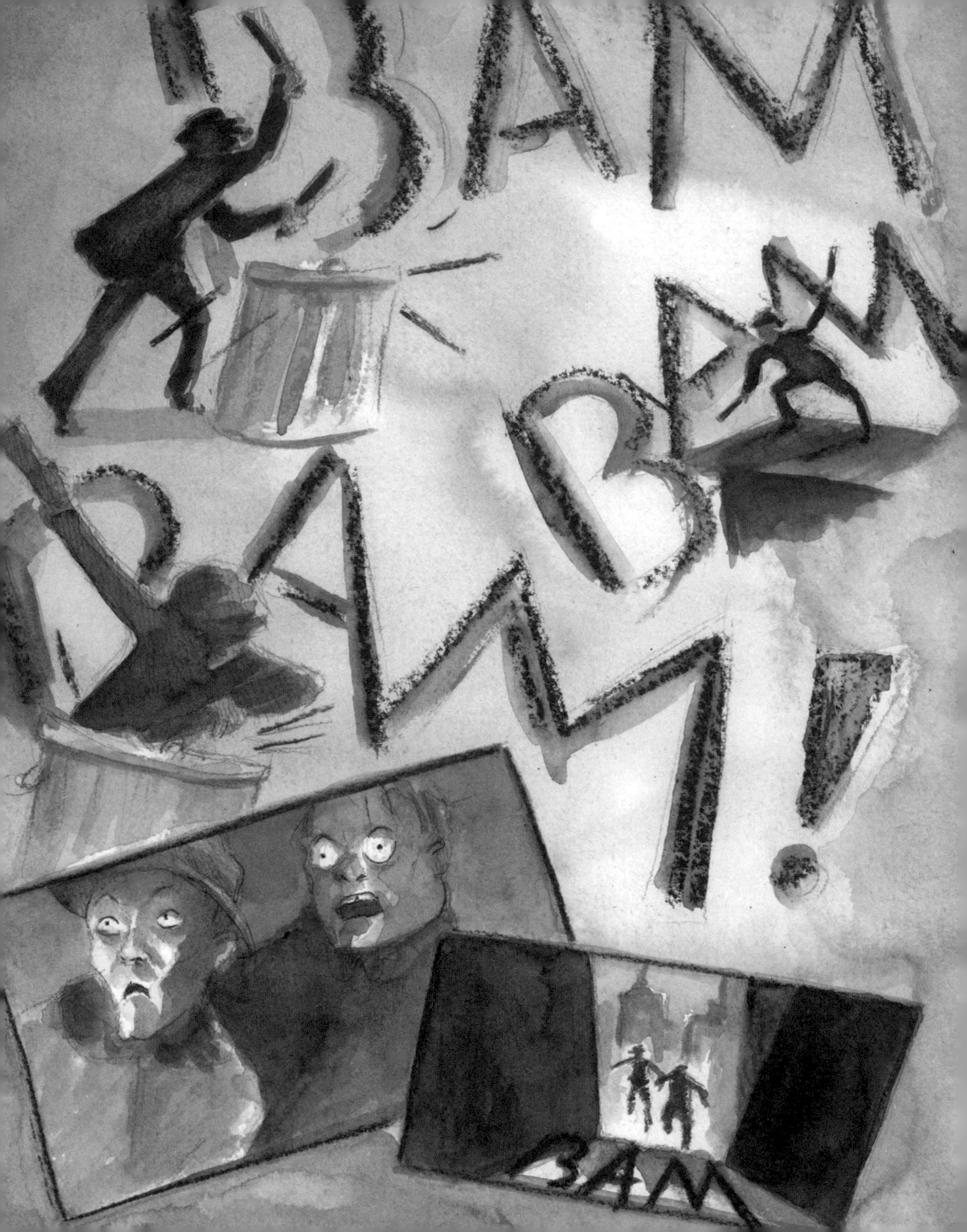
BAM
BAM
BAM!
BAM

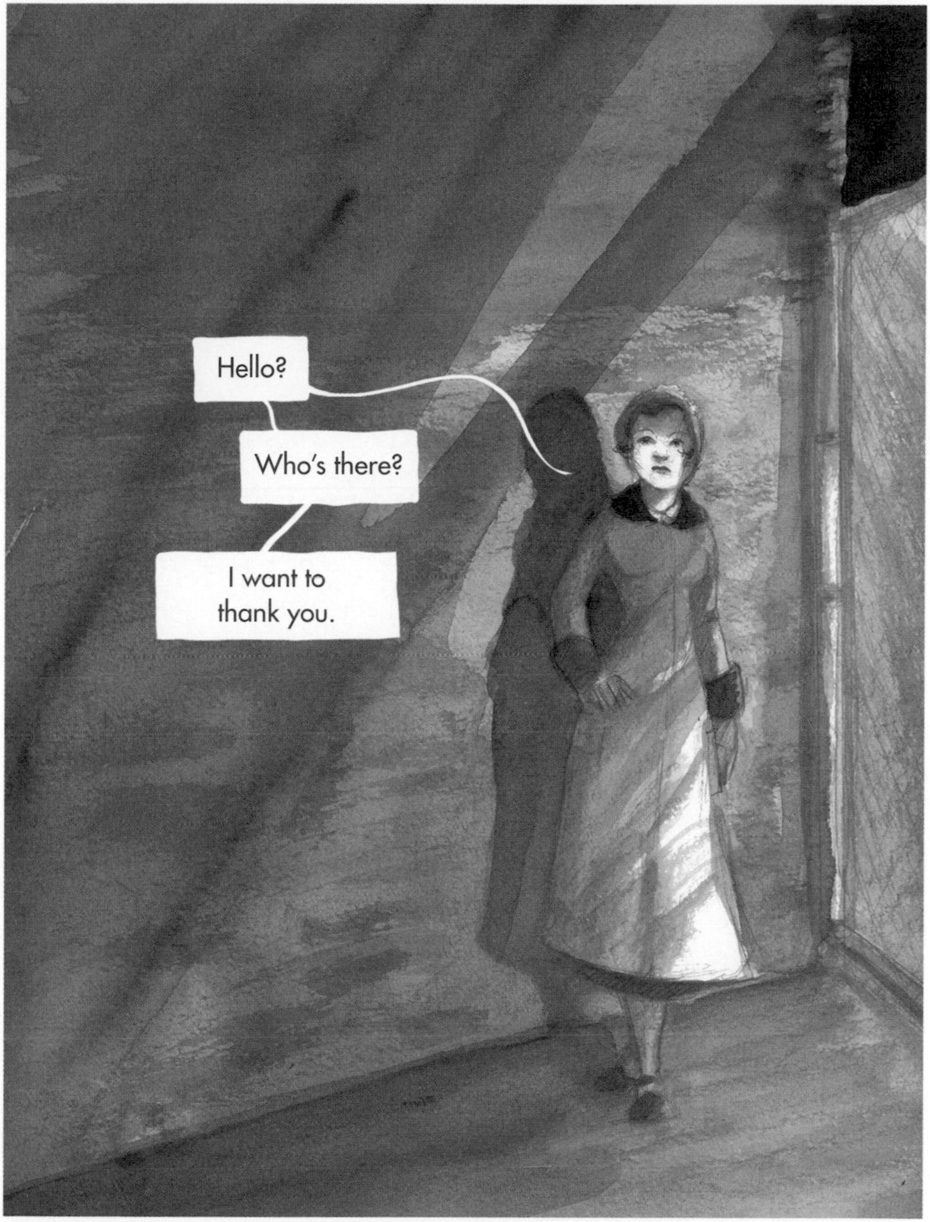
Hello?
Who's there?
I want to thank you.

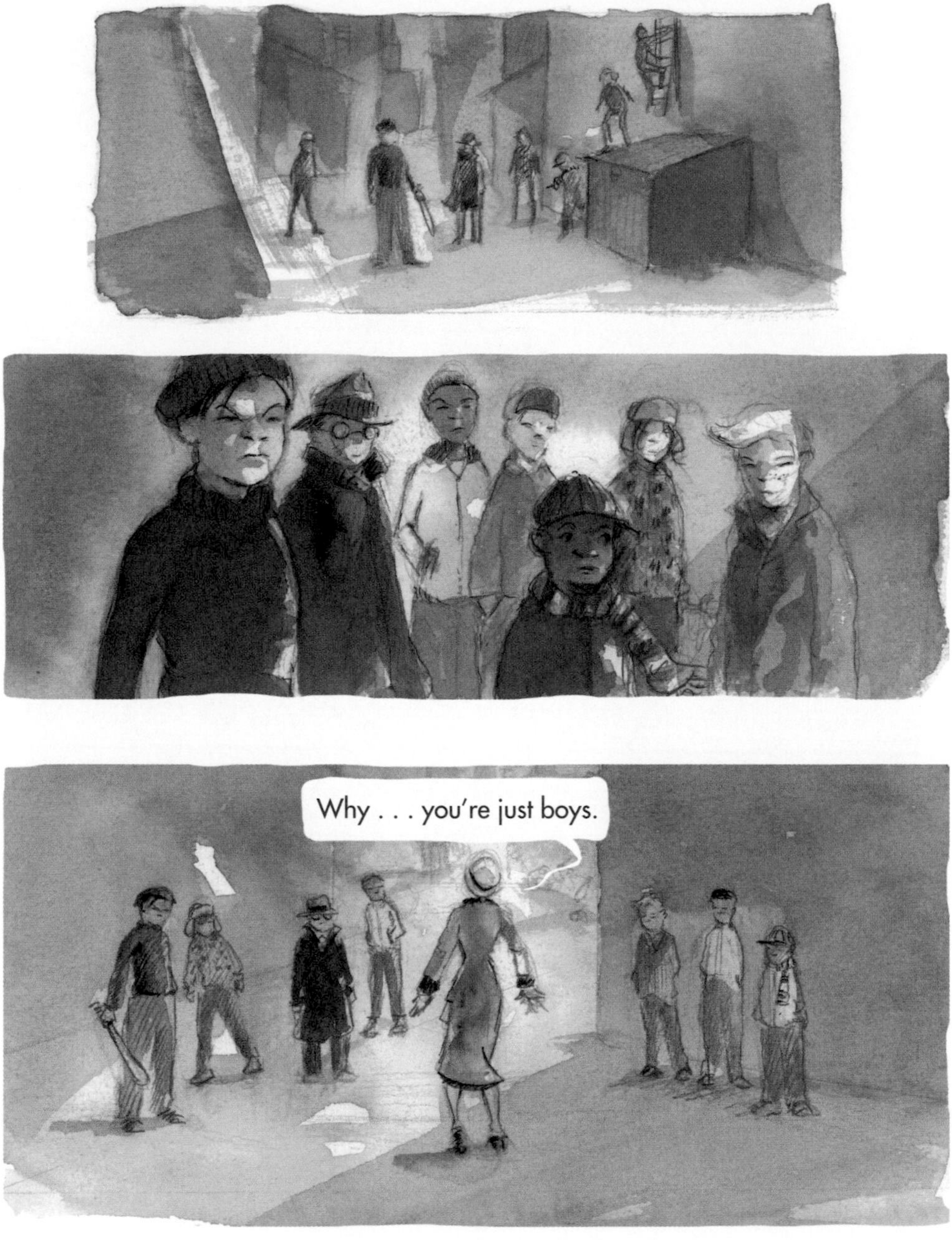
Why . . . you're just boys.

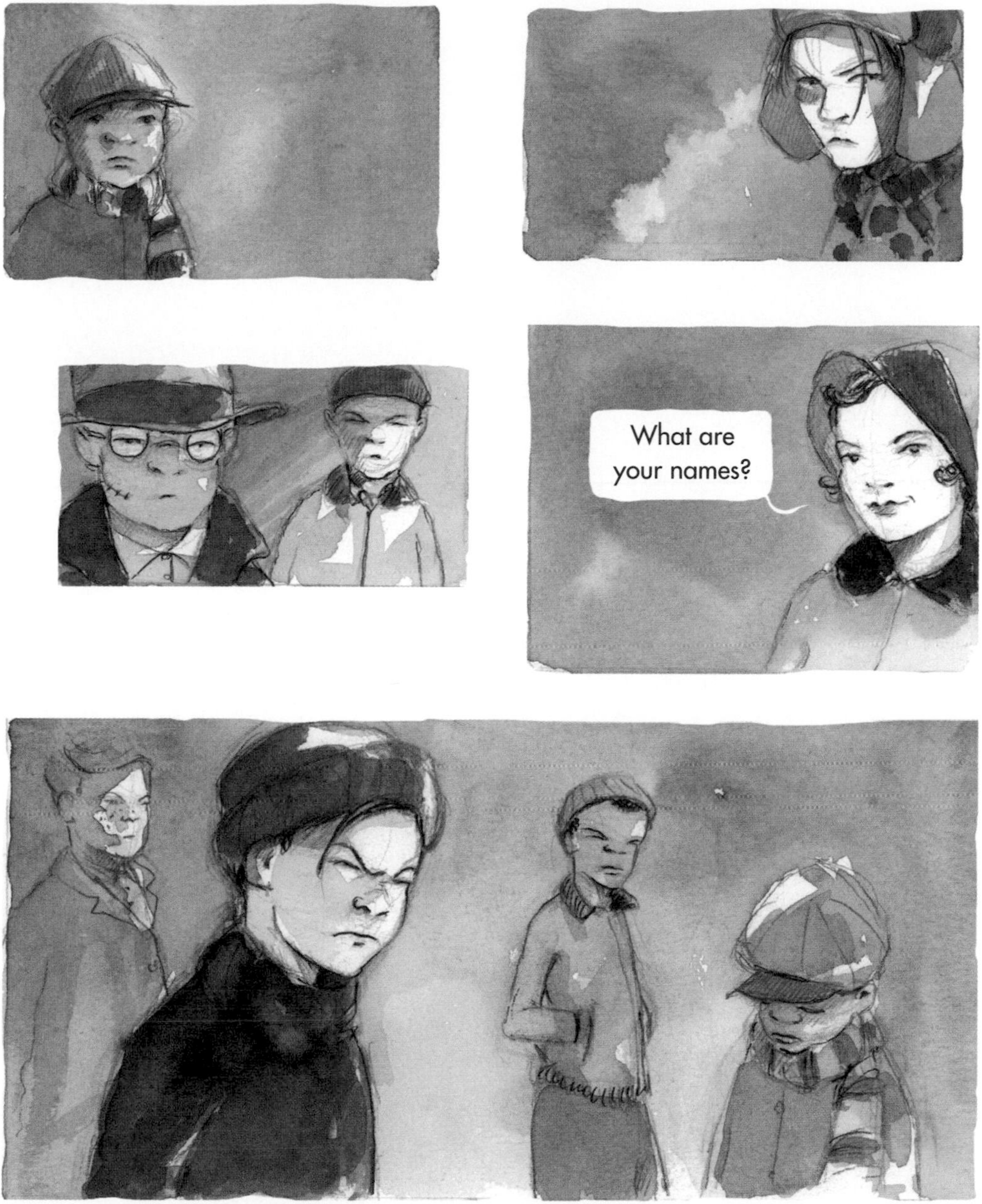
What are your names?

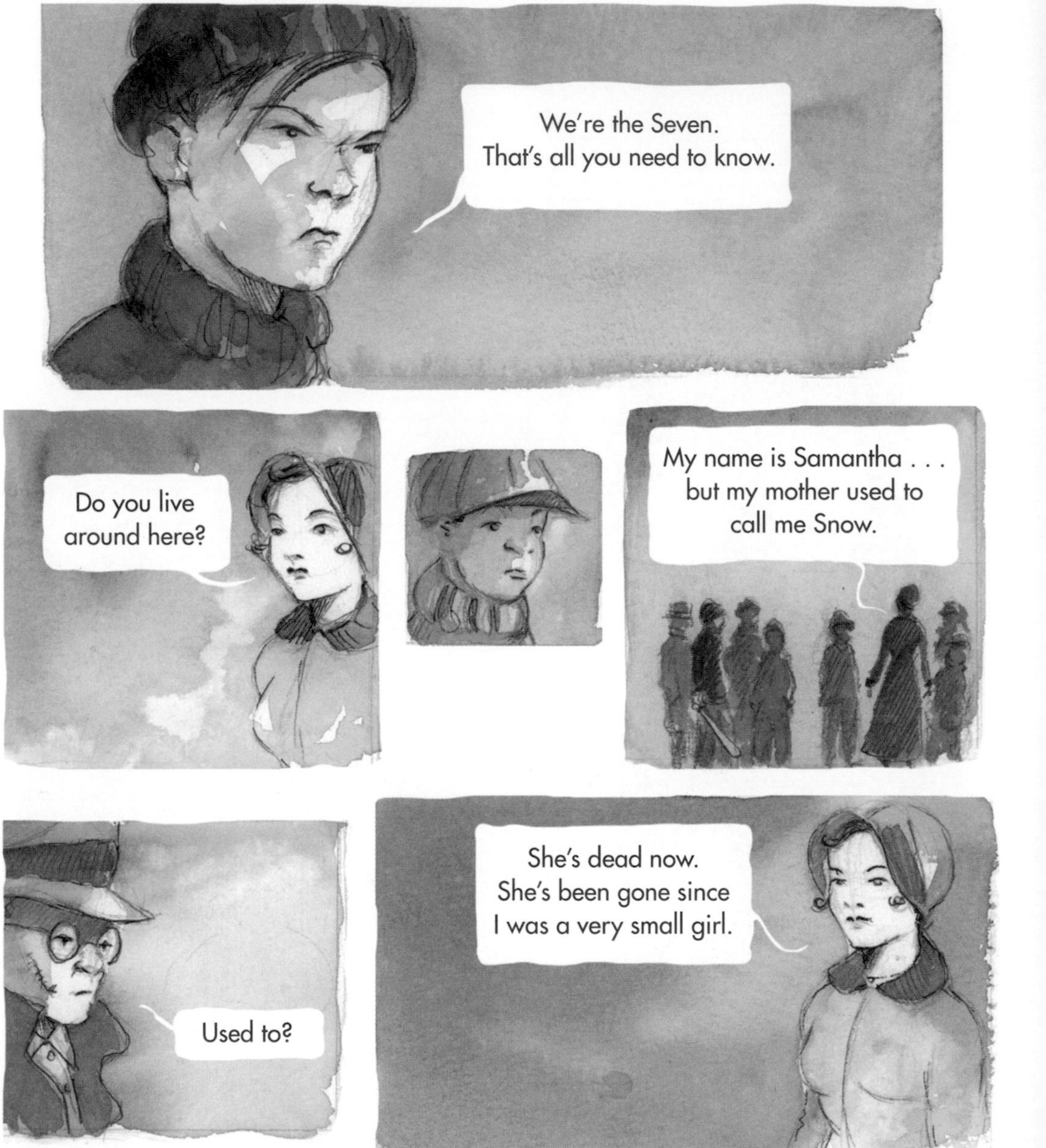
We're the Seven.
That's all you need to know.
Do you live around here?
My name is Samantha . . . but my mother used to call me Snow.
Used to?
She's dead now. She's been gone since I was a very small girl.

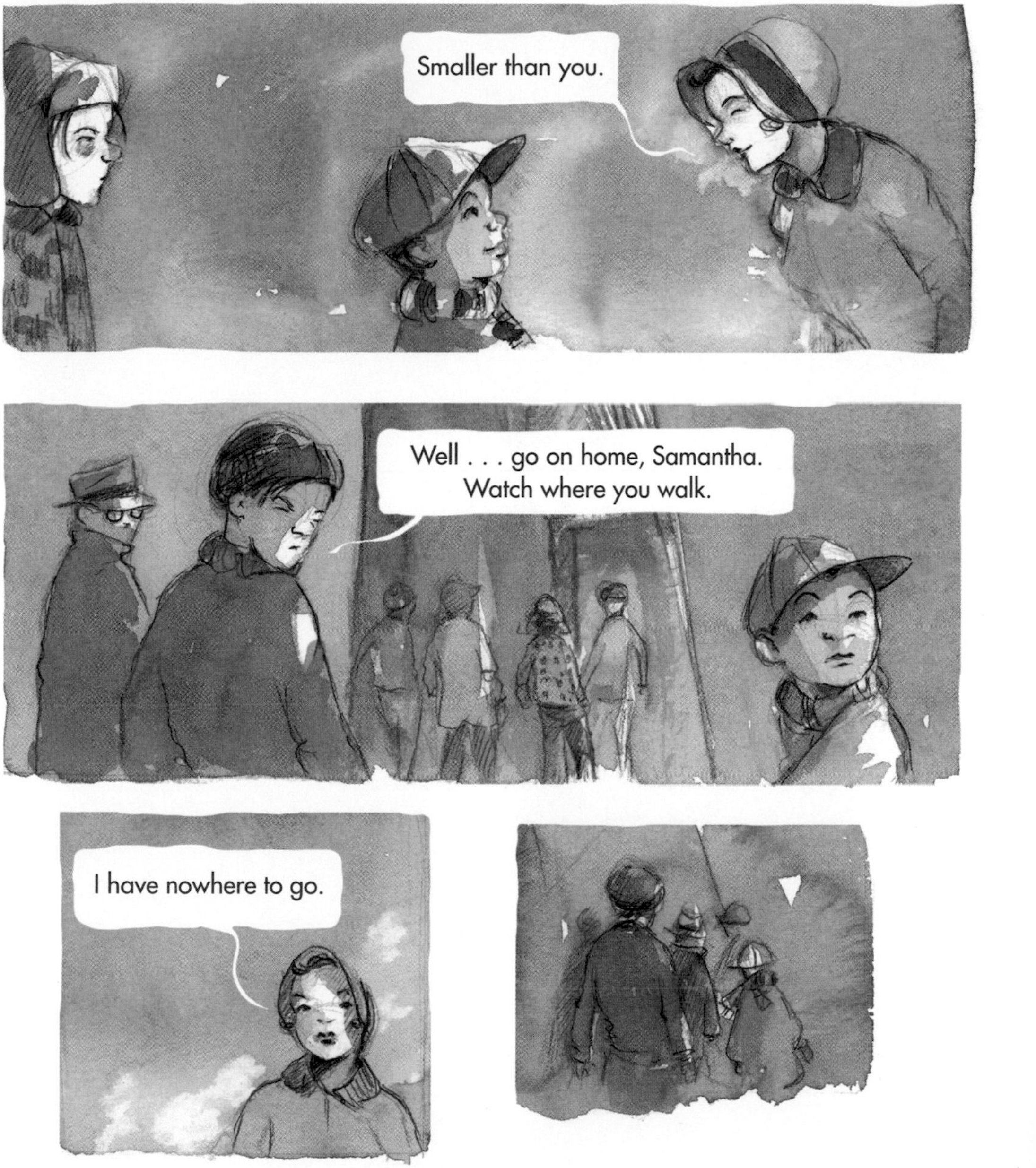
Smaller than you.
Well . . . go on home, Samantha. Watch where you walk.
I have nowhere to go.

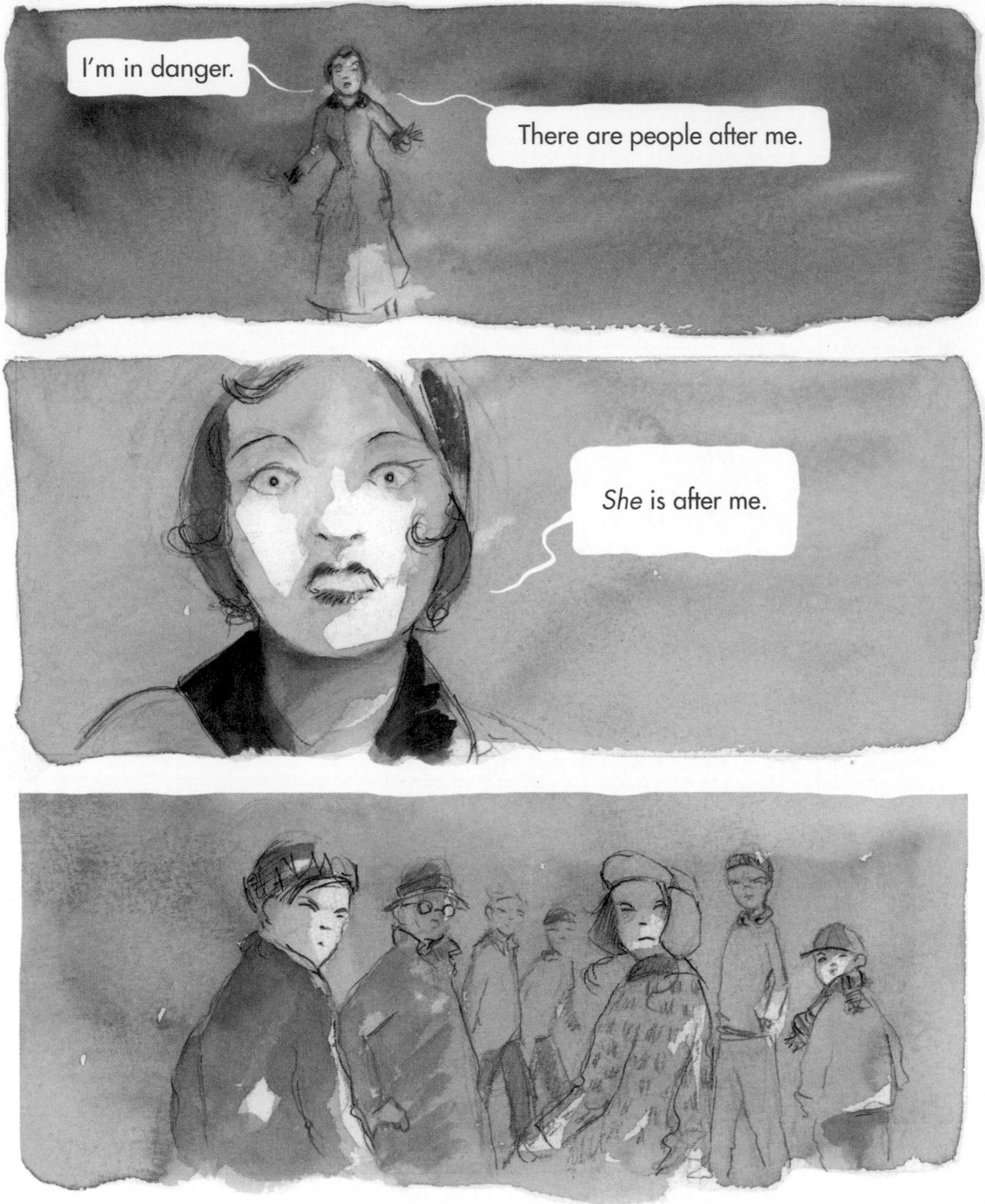
I'm in danger.
There are people after me.
She is after me.

SEVEN SMALL MEN

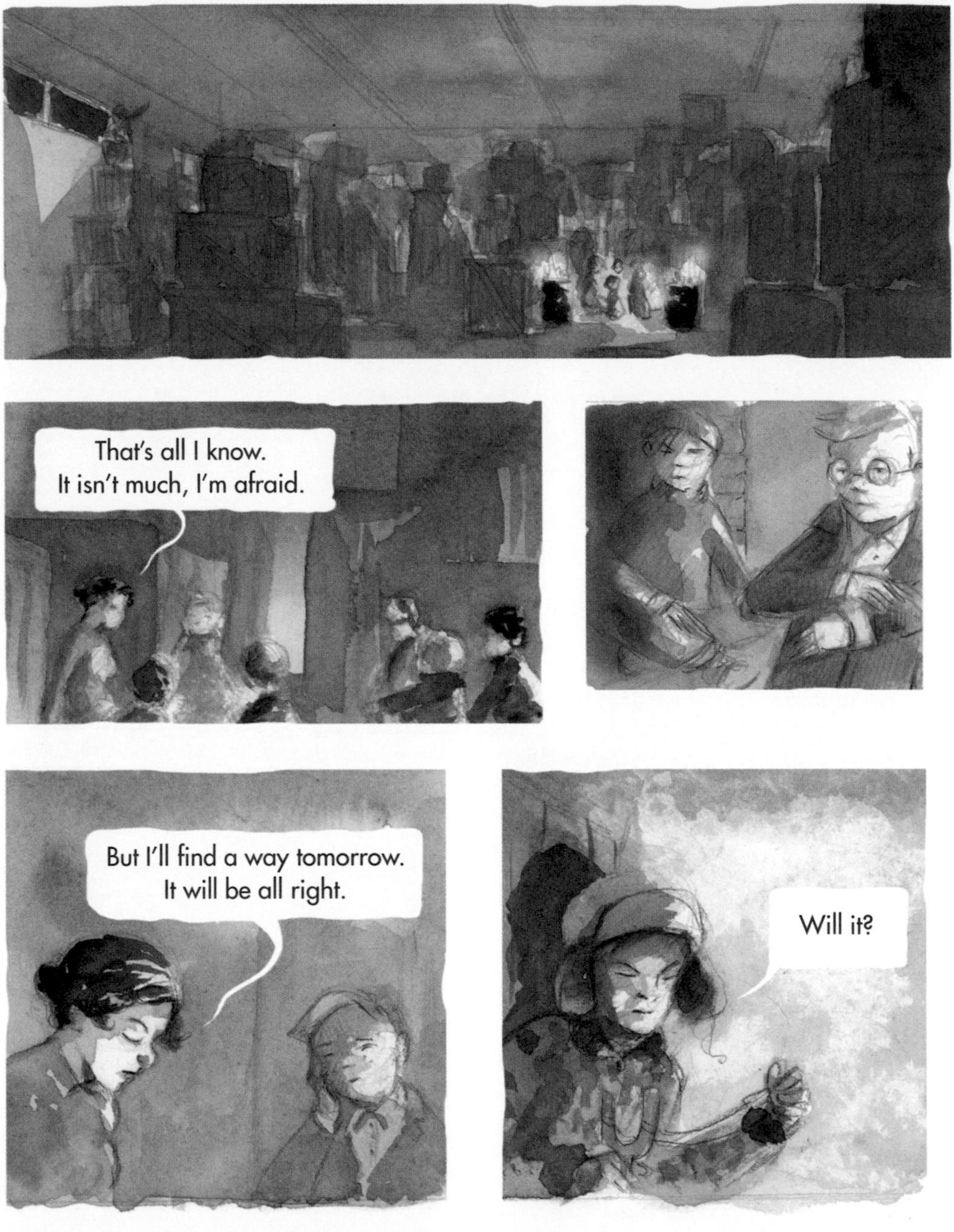
That's all I know.
It isn't much, I'm afraid.
But I'll find a way tomorrow.
It will be all right.
Will it?

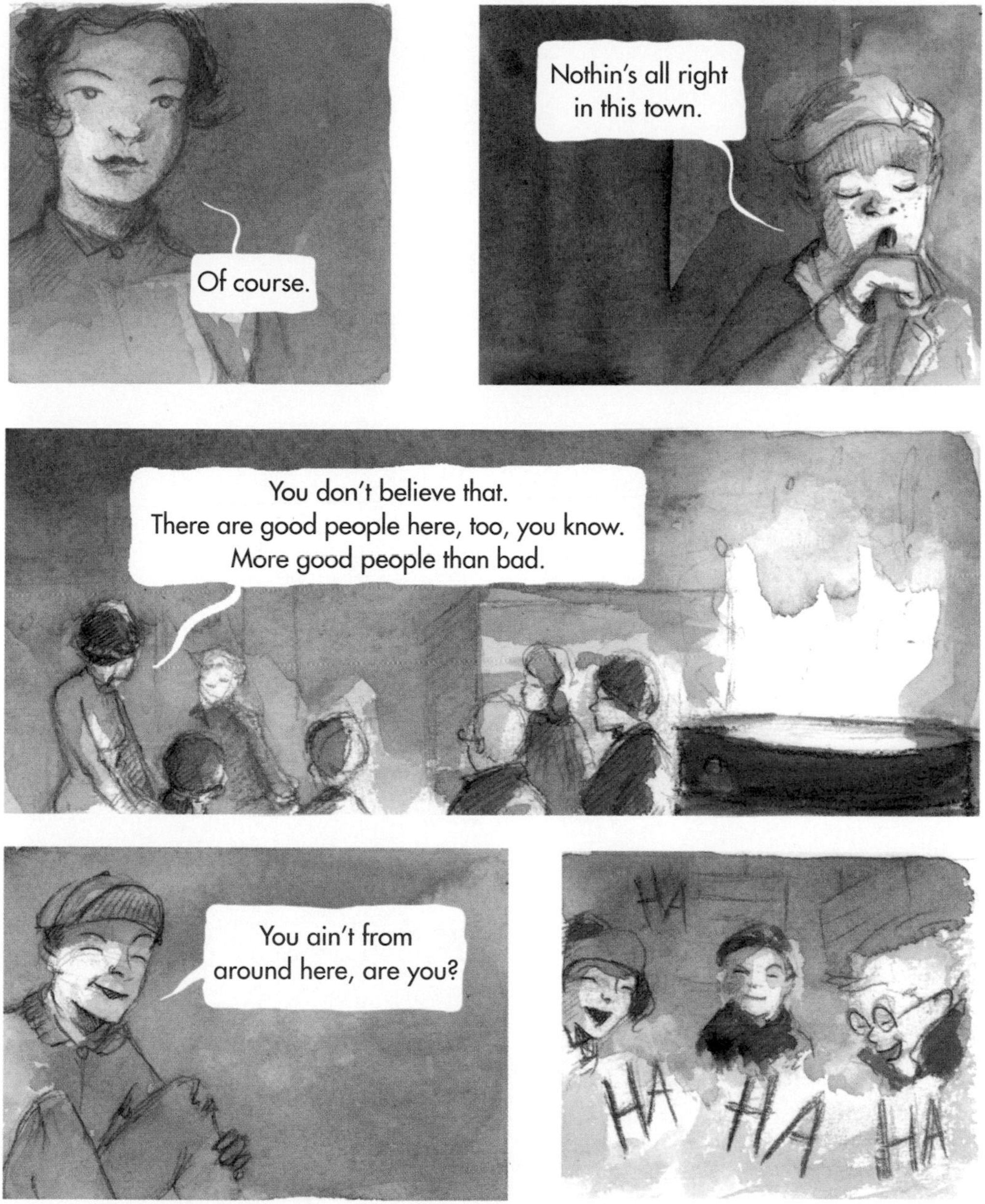
Of course.
Nothin's all right in this town.
You don't believe that. There are good people here, too, you know. More good people than bad.
You ain't from around here, are you?
HA
HA HA HA

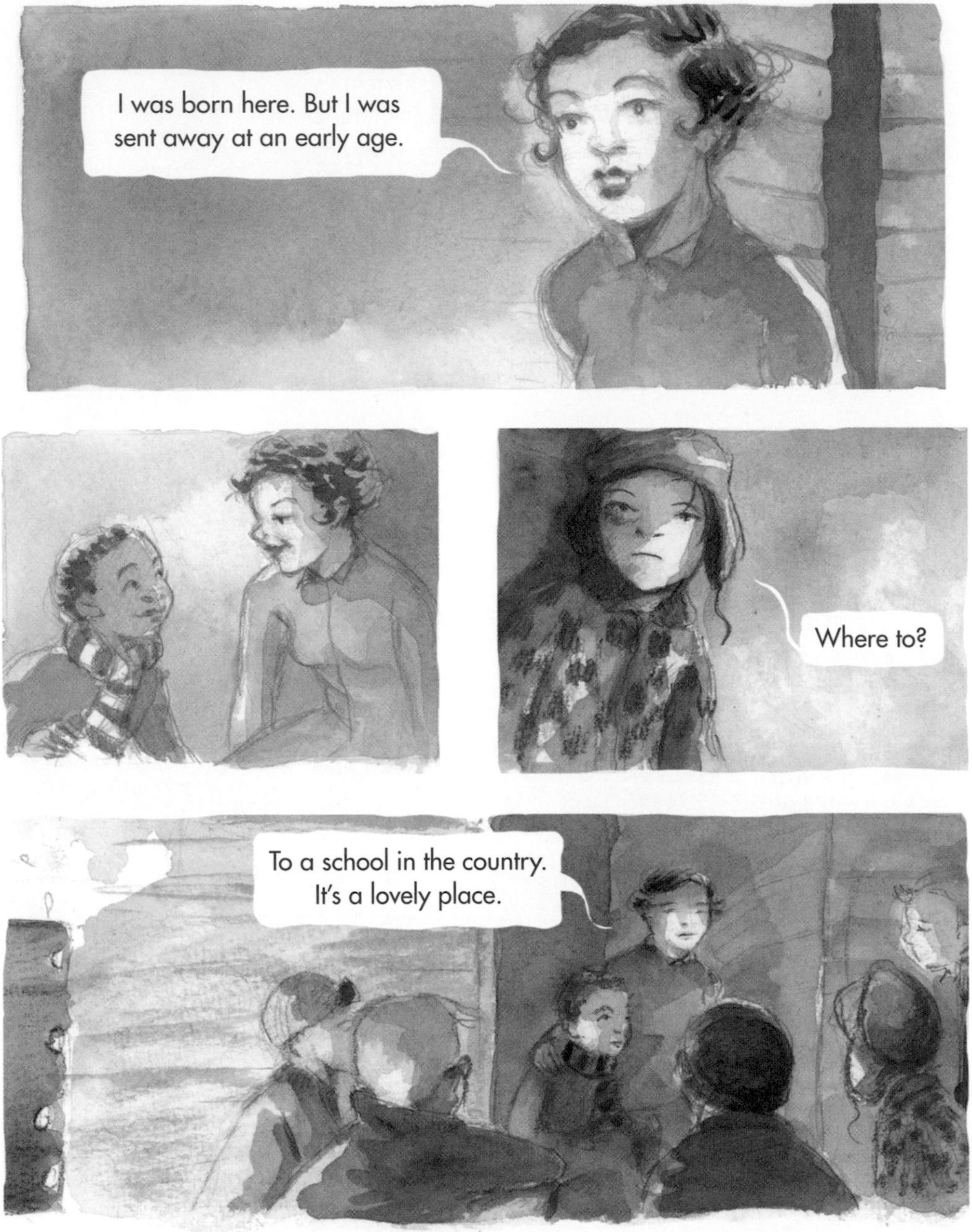
I was born here. But I was sent away at an early age.
Where to?
To a school in the country. It's a lovely place.

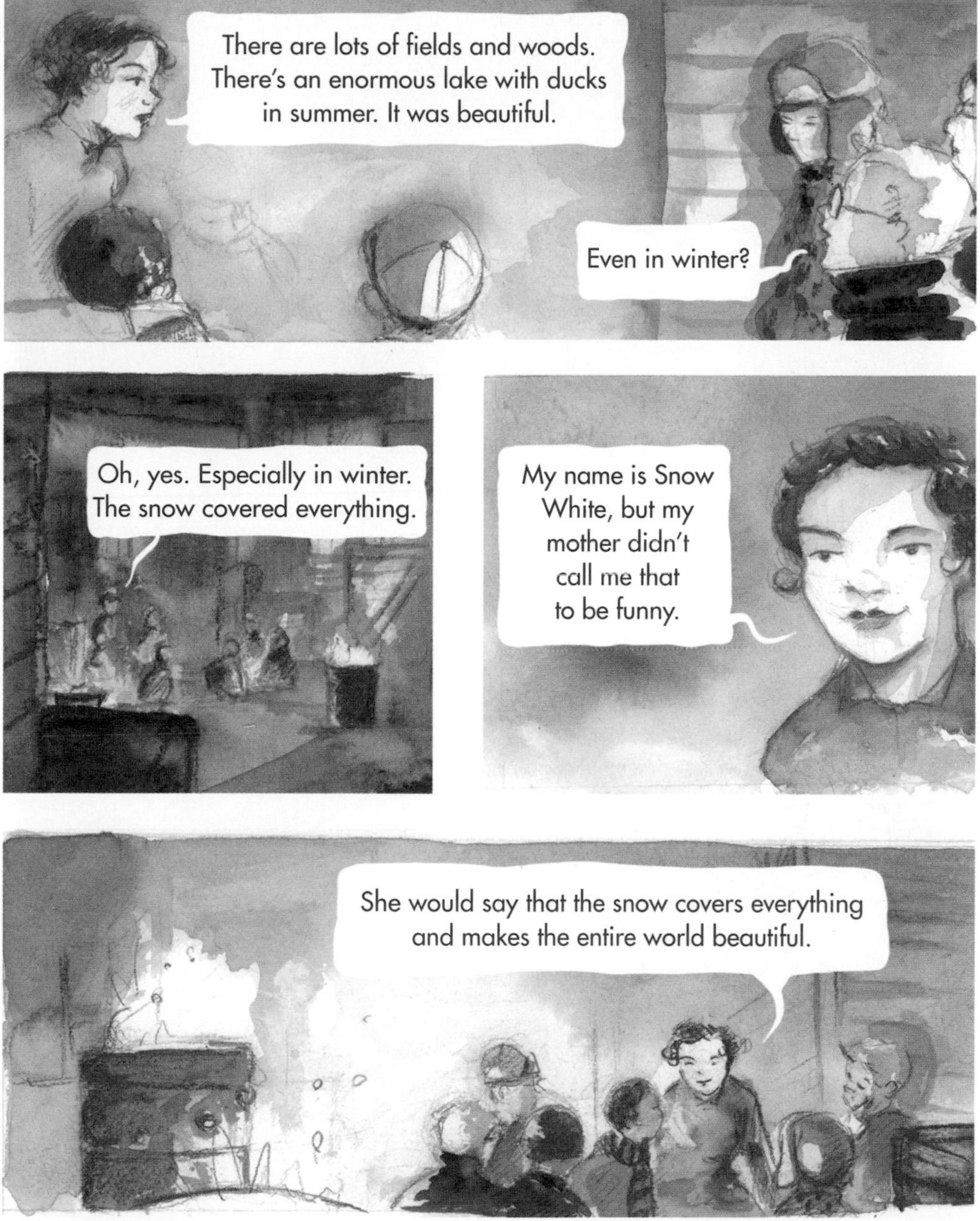
There are lots of fields and woods. There's an enormous lake with ducks in summer. It was beautiful.
Even in winter?
Oh, yes. Especially in winter. The snow covered everything.
My name is Snow White, but my mother didn't call me that to be funny.
She would say that the snow covers everything and makes the entire world beautiful.

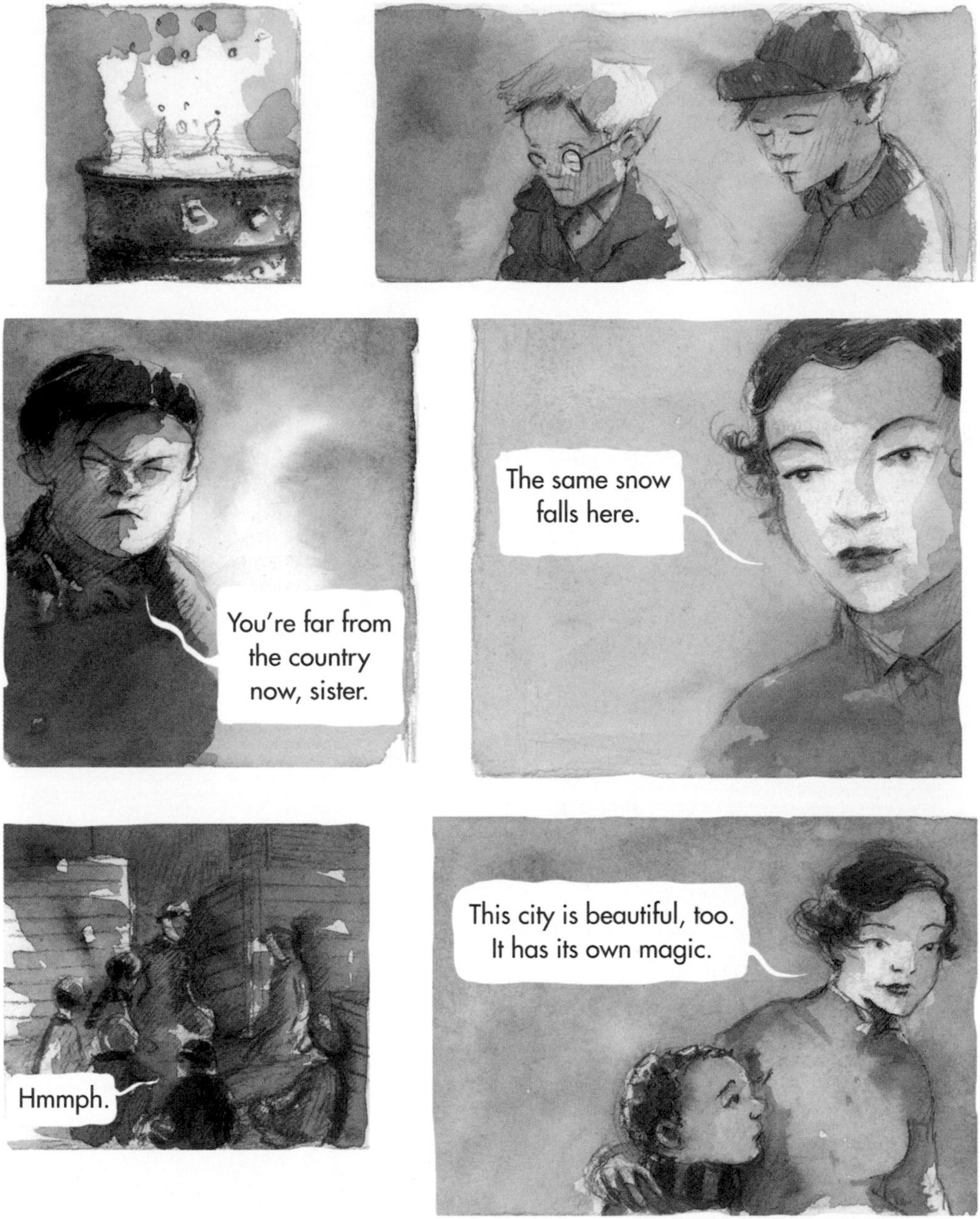
You're far from the country now, sister.
The same snow falls here.
Hmmph.
This city is beautiful, too. It has its own magic.

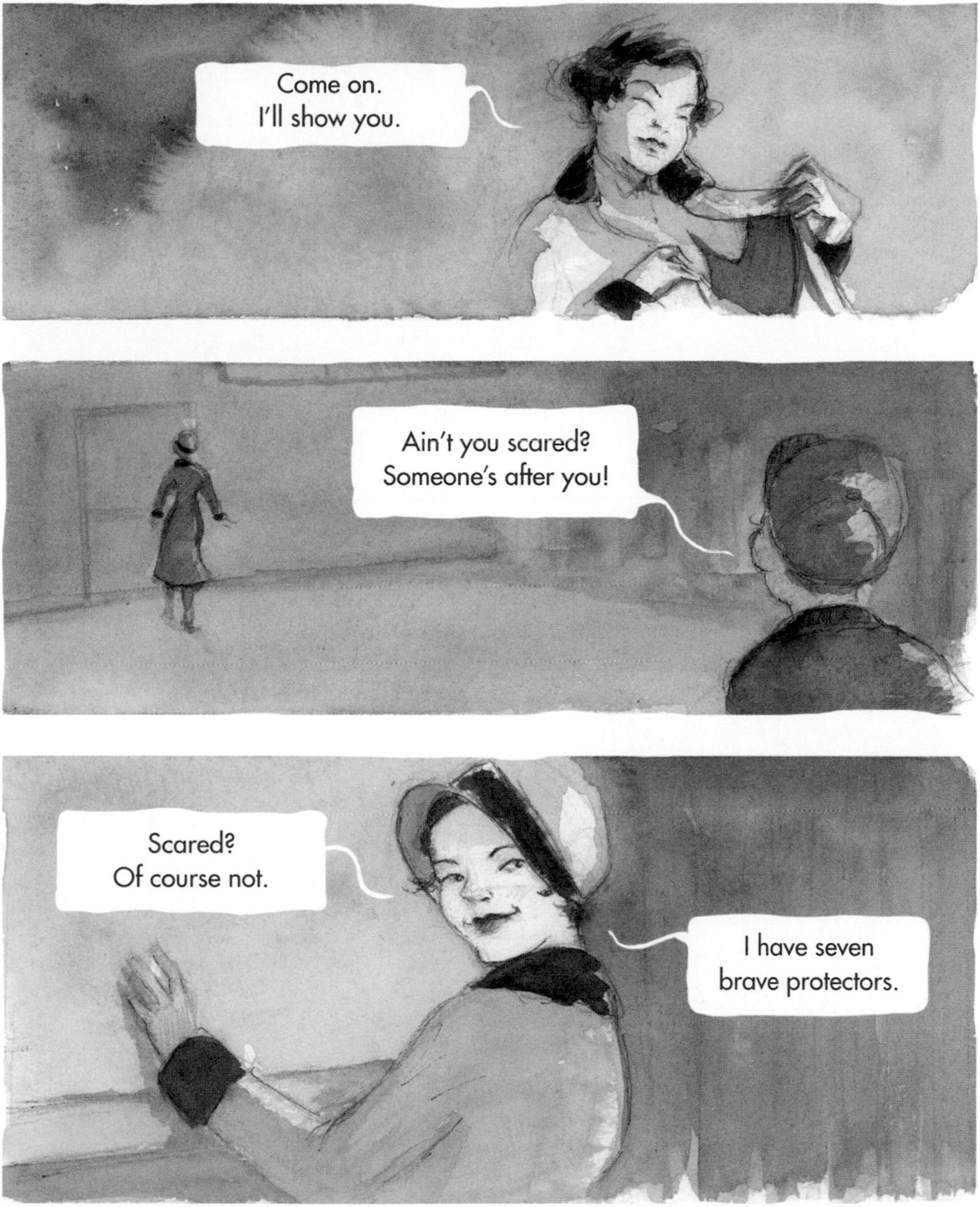
Come on. I'll show you.
Ain't you scared? Someone's after you!
Scared? Of course not.
I have seven brave protectors.

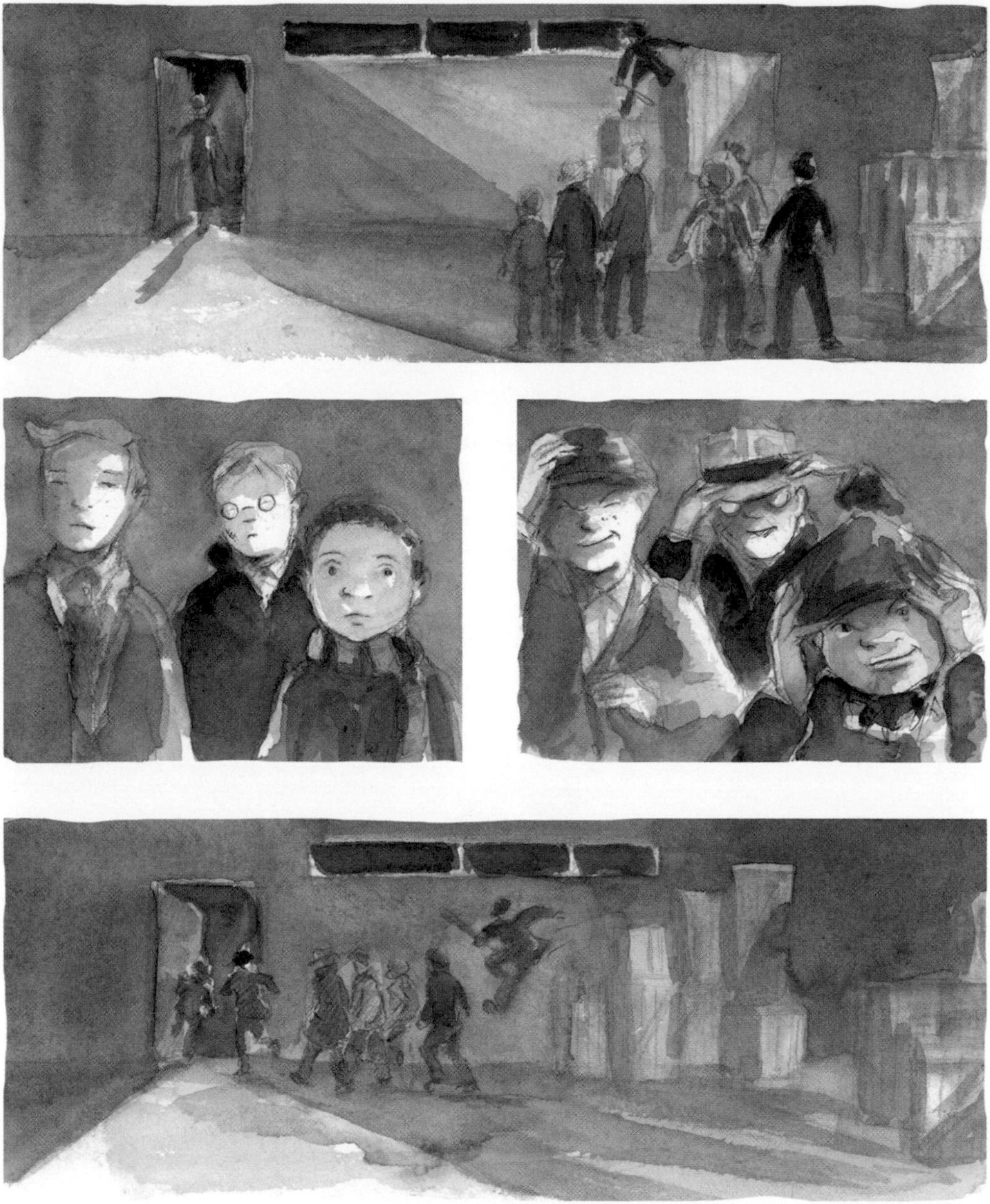

THE
WINDOW
AT
MACY'S

Here it is.

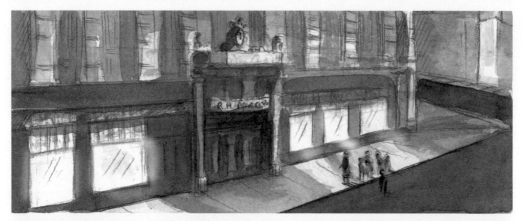

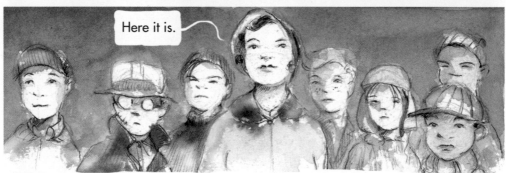

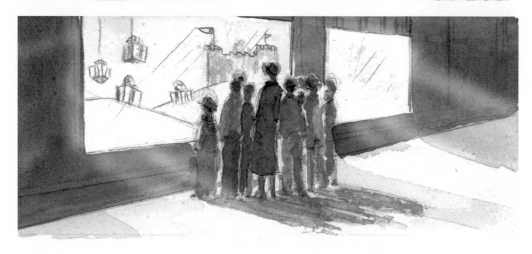

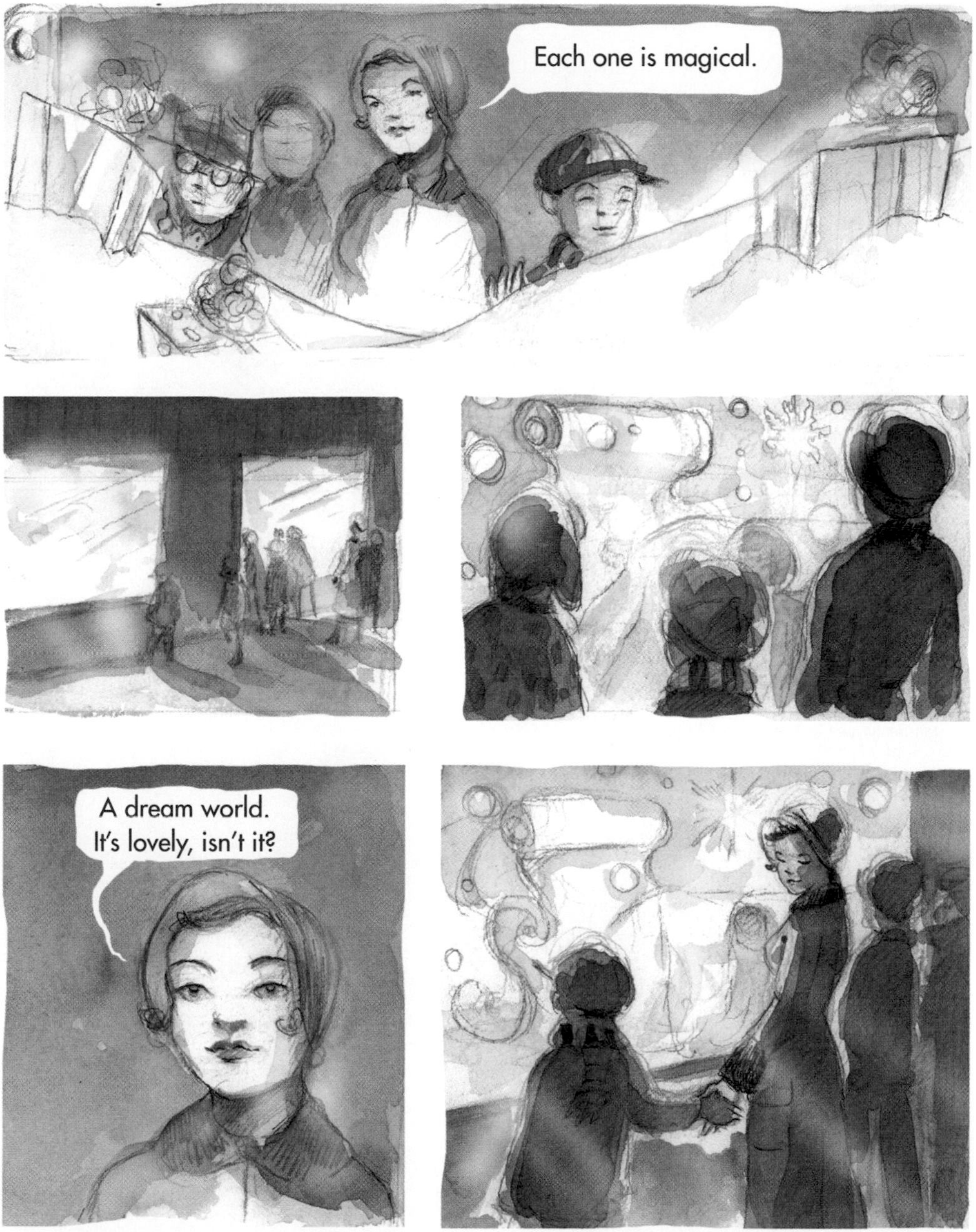
Each one is magical.
A dream world. It's lovely, isn't it?

INSANE
WITH
JEALOUSY

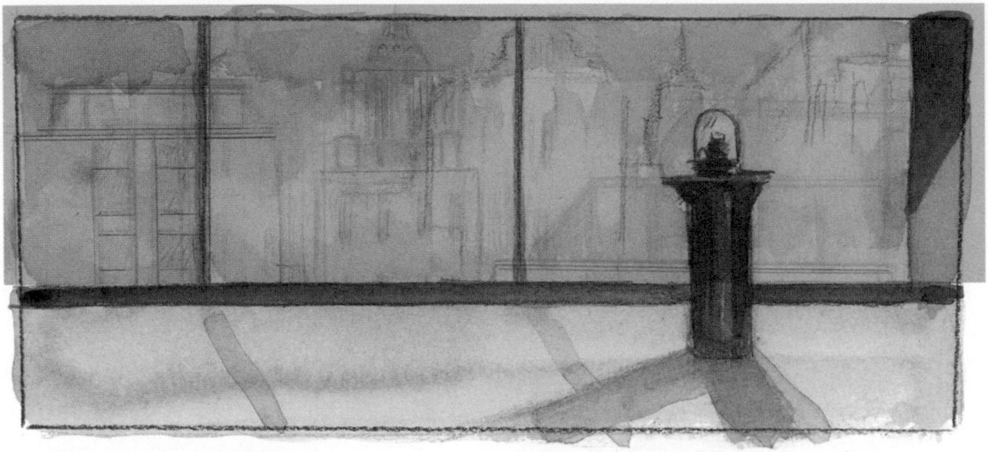
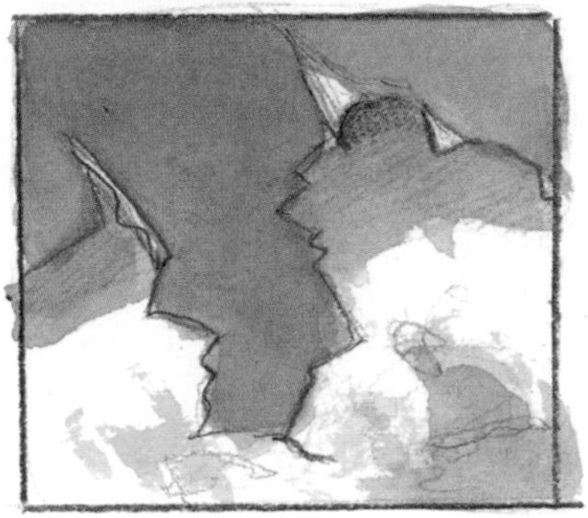
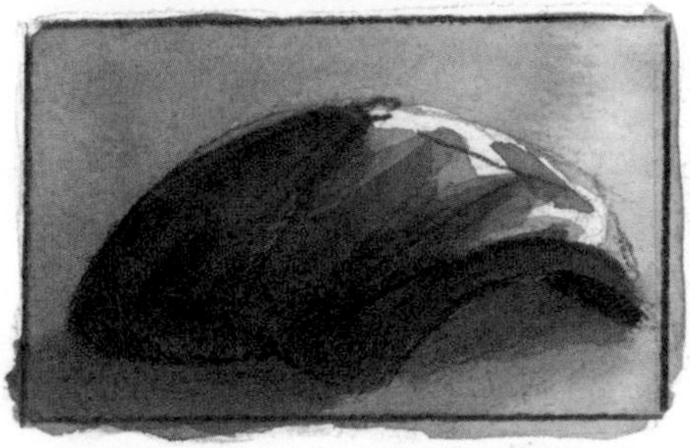
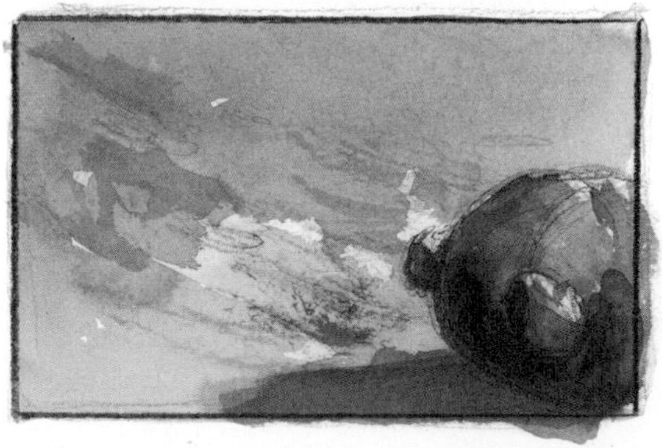

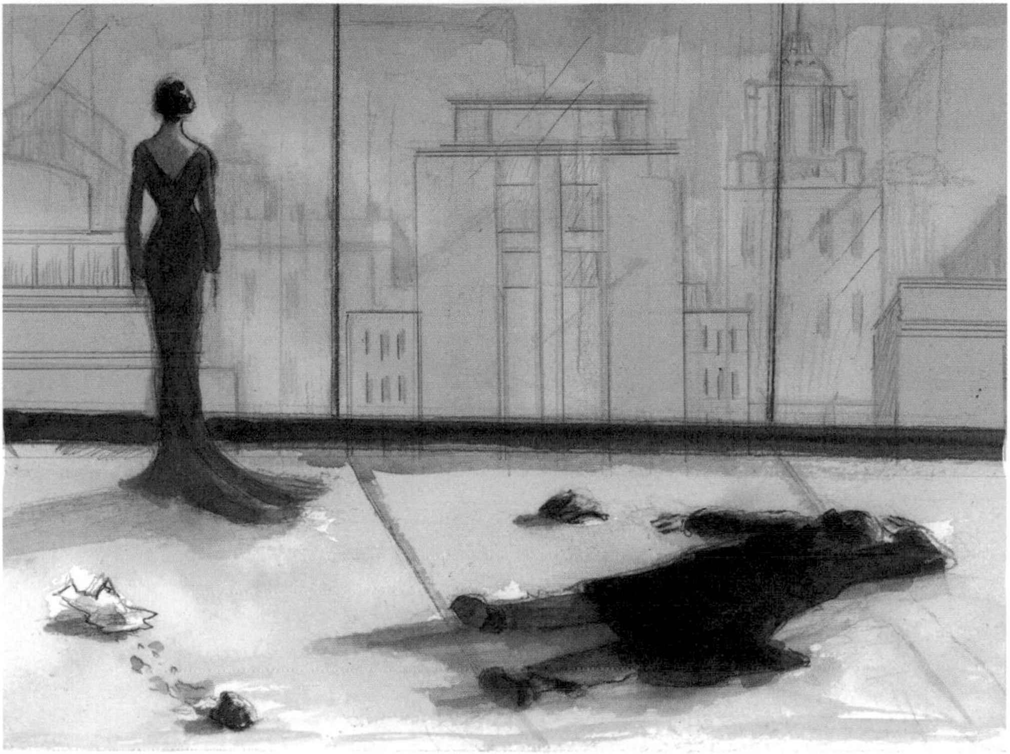

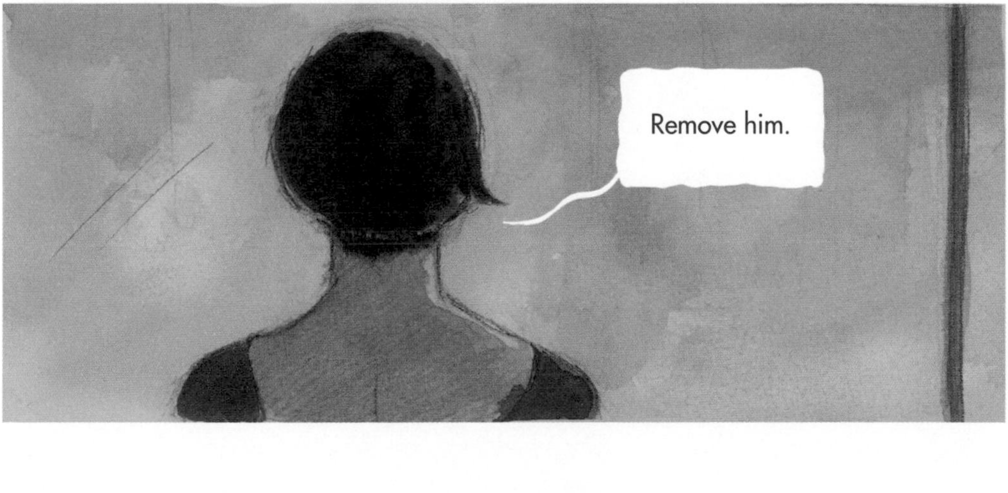
Remove him.

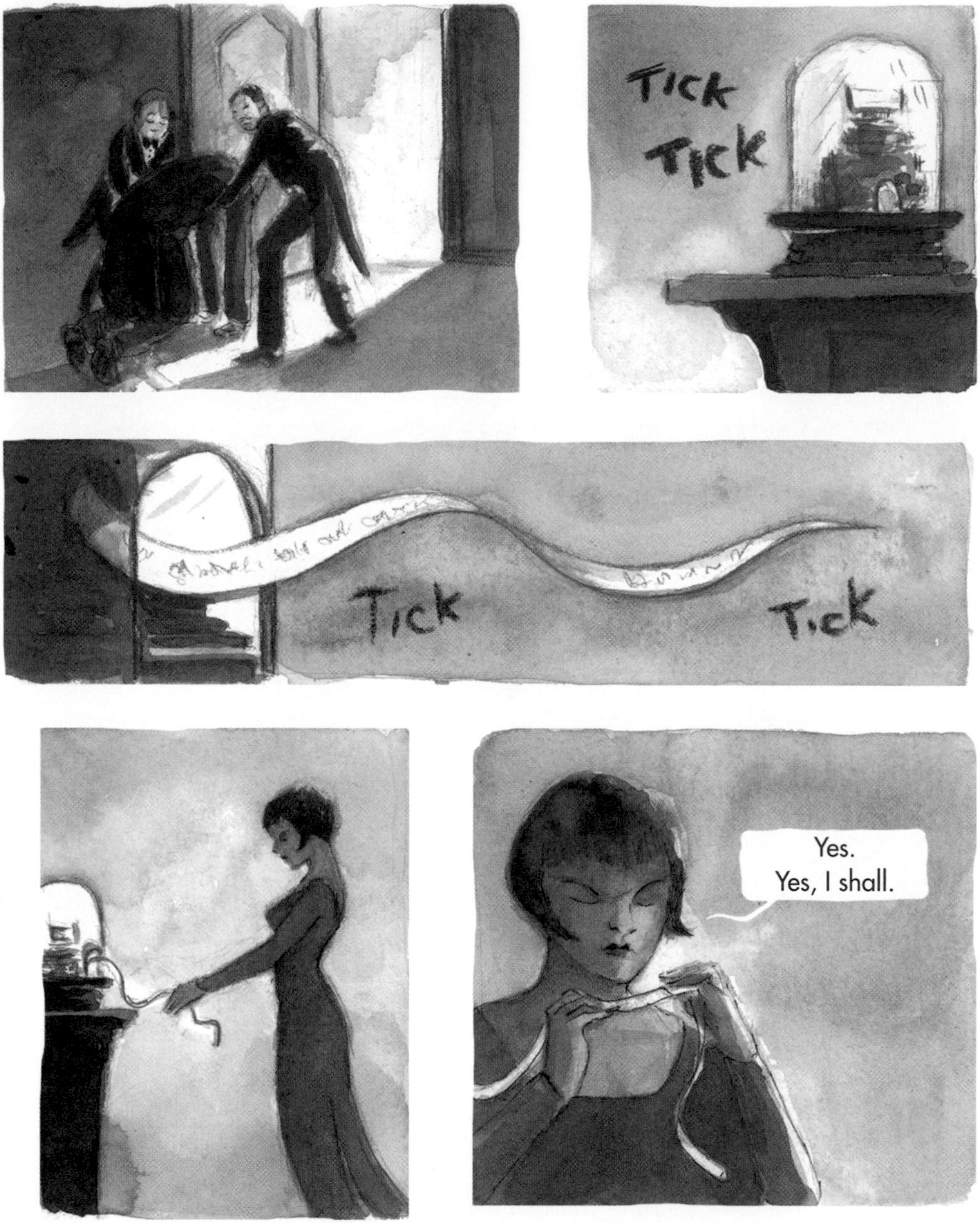
TICK
TICK
TICK
TICK
Yes.
Yes, I shall.

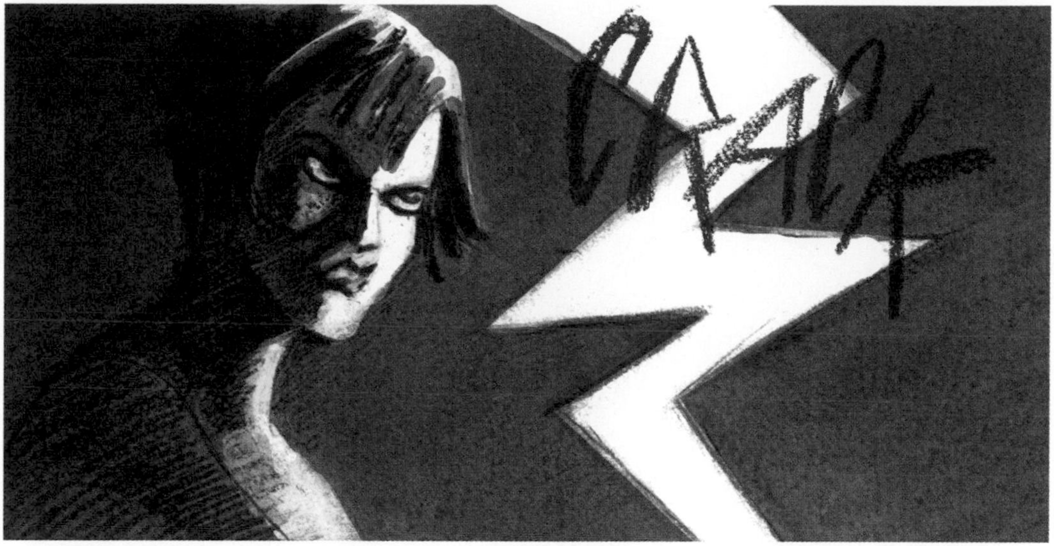
CRACK

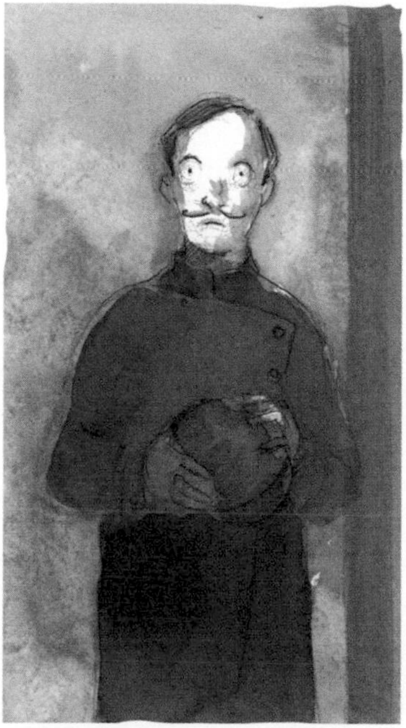

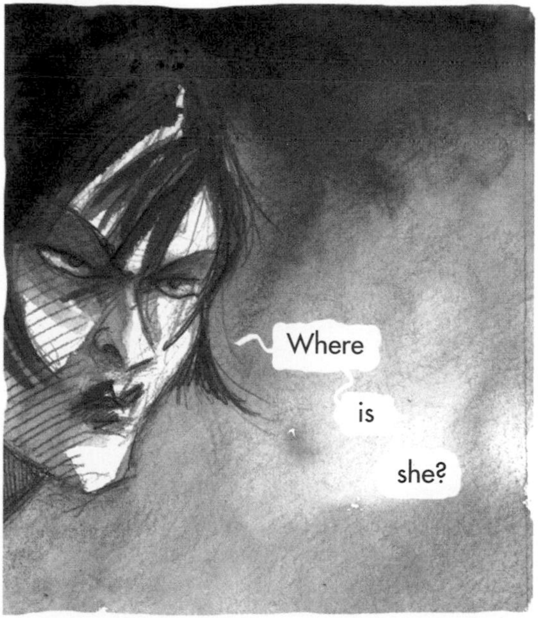
Where is she?

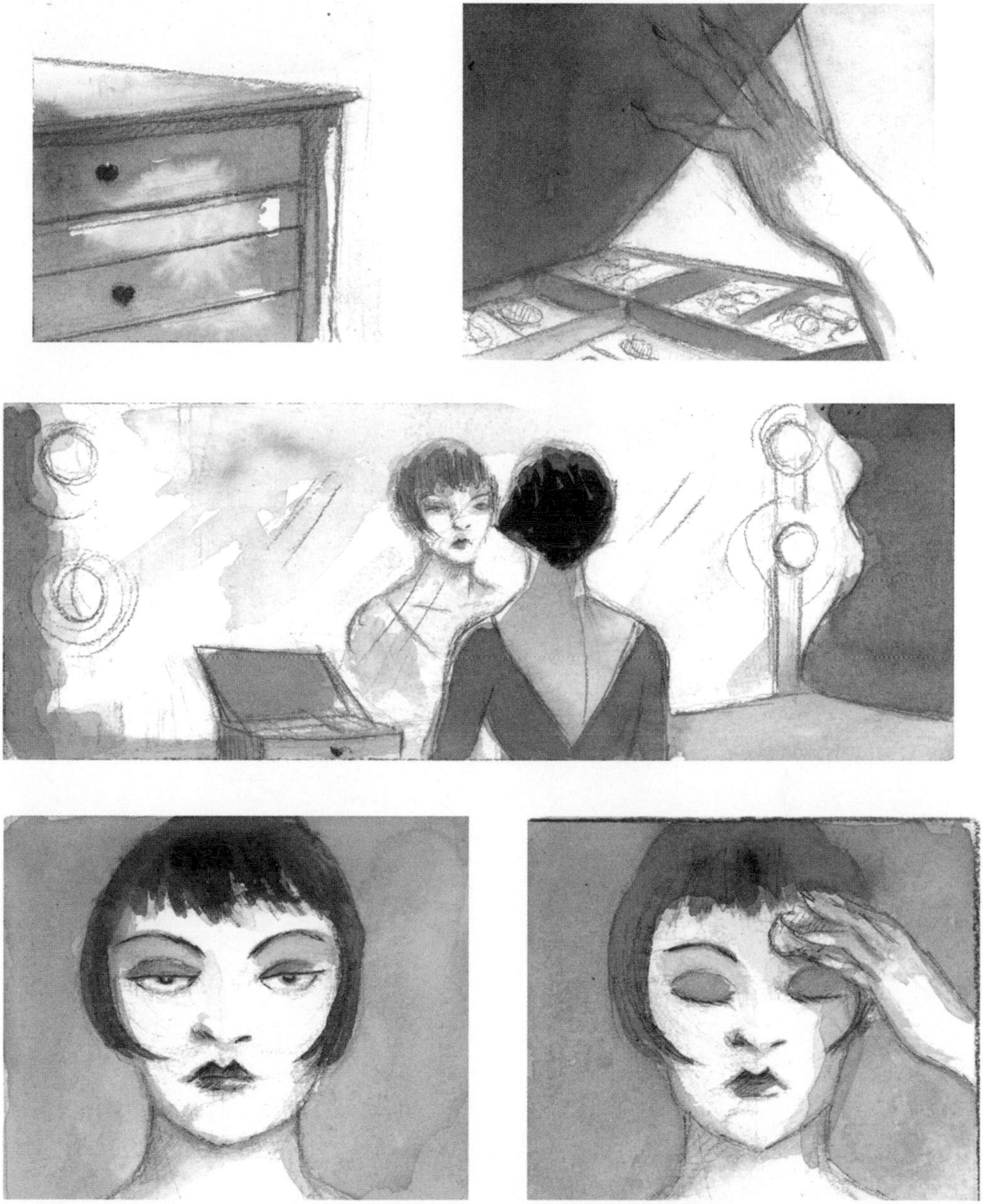

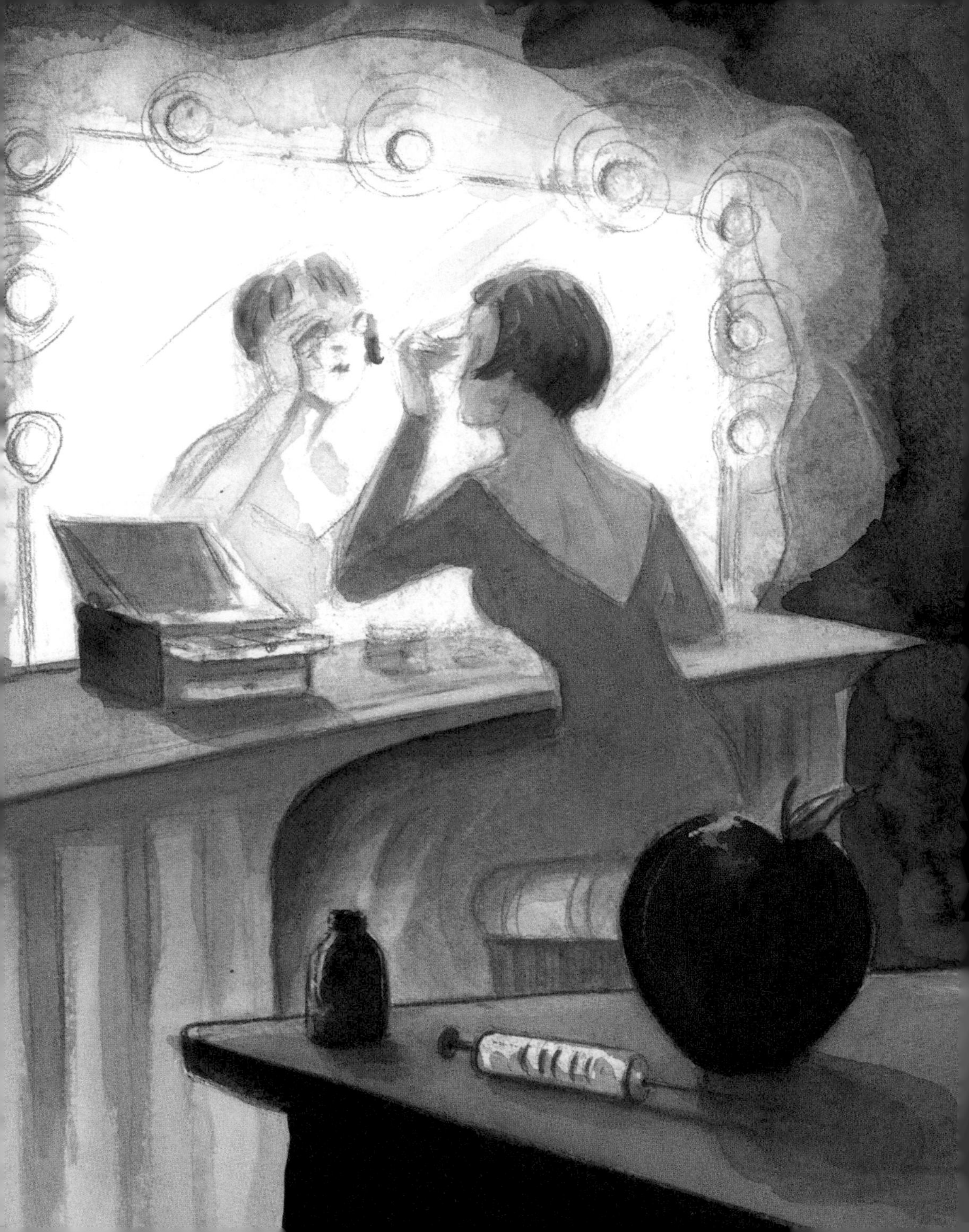

AN
APPLE
FOR A
PRETTY
THING

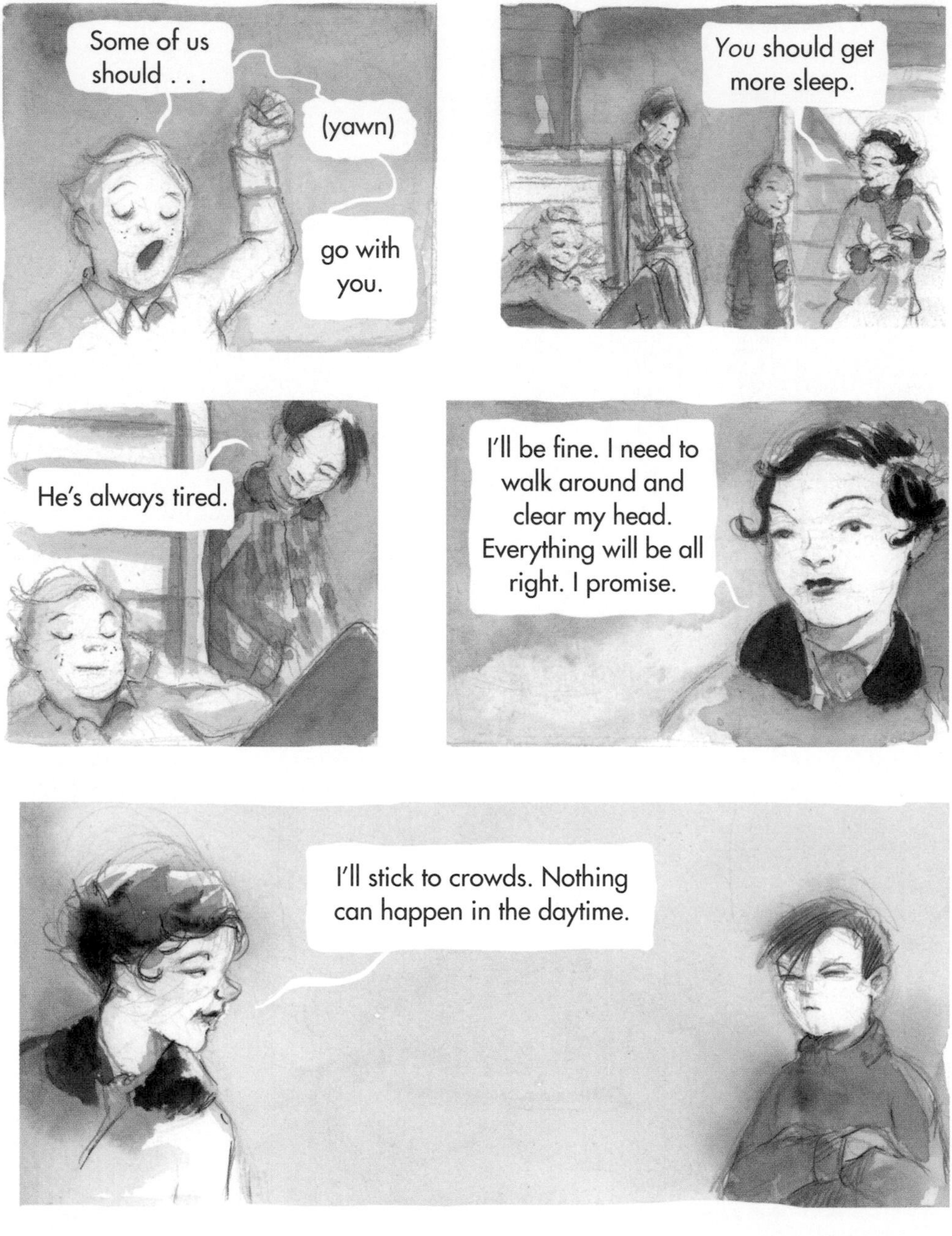
Some of us should . . .
(yawn)
go with you.
You should get more sleep.
He's always tired.
I'll be fine. I need to walk around and clear my head. Everything will be all right. I promise.
I'll stick to crowds. Nothing can happen in the daytime.

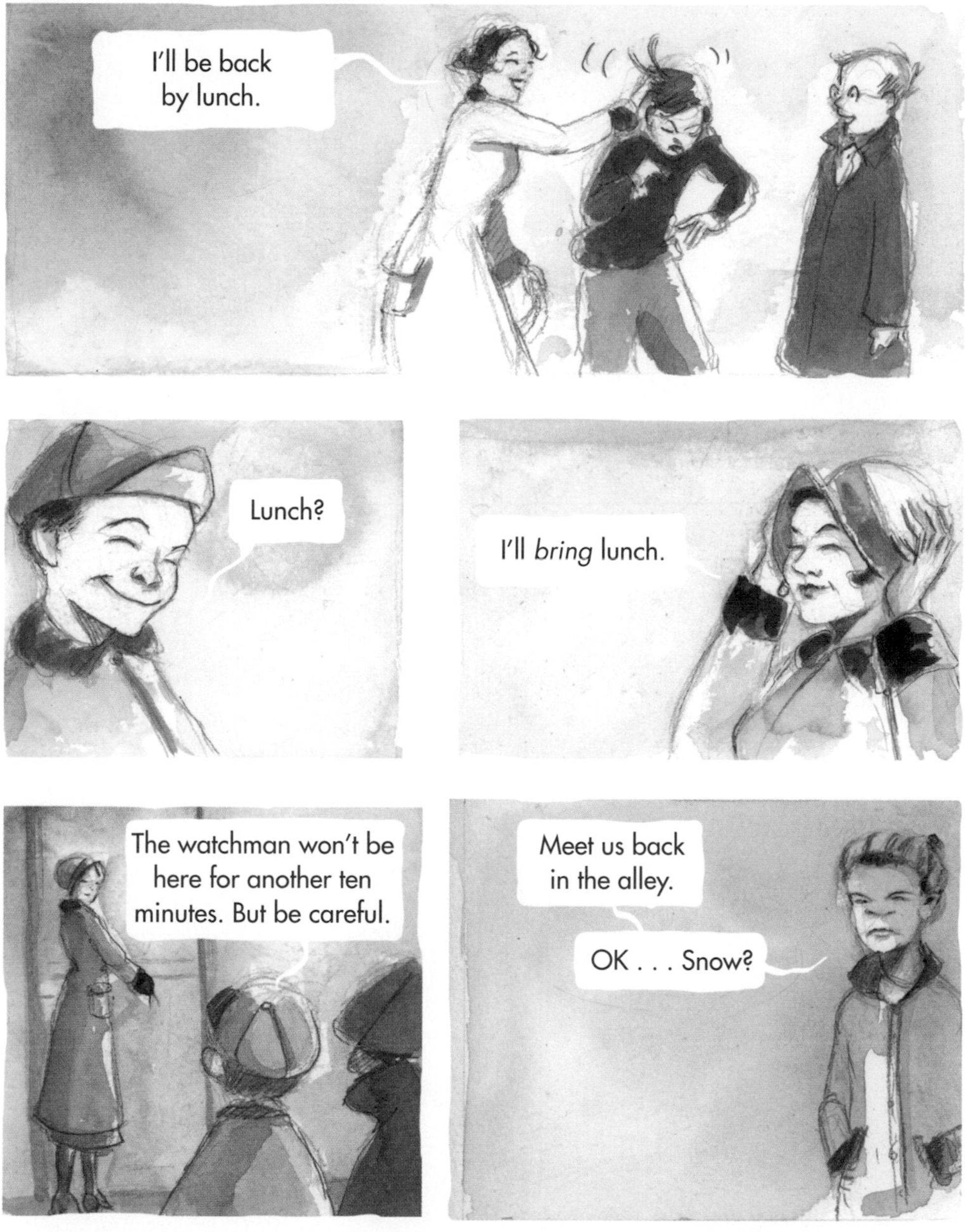
I'll be back by lunch.
Lunch?
I'll *bring* lunch.
The watchman won't be here for another ten minutes. But be careful.
Meet us back in the alley.
OK . . . Snow?

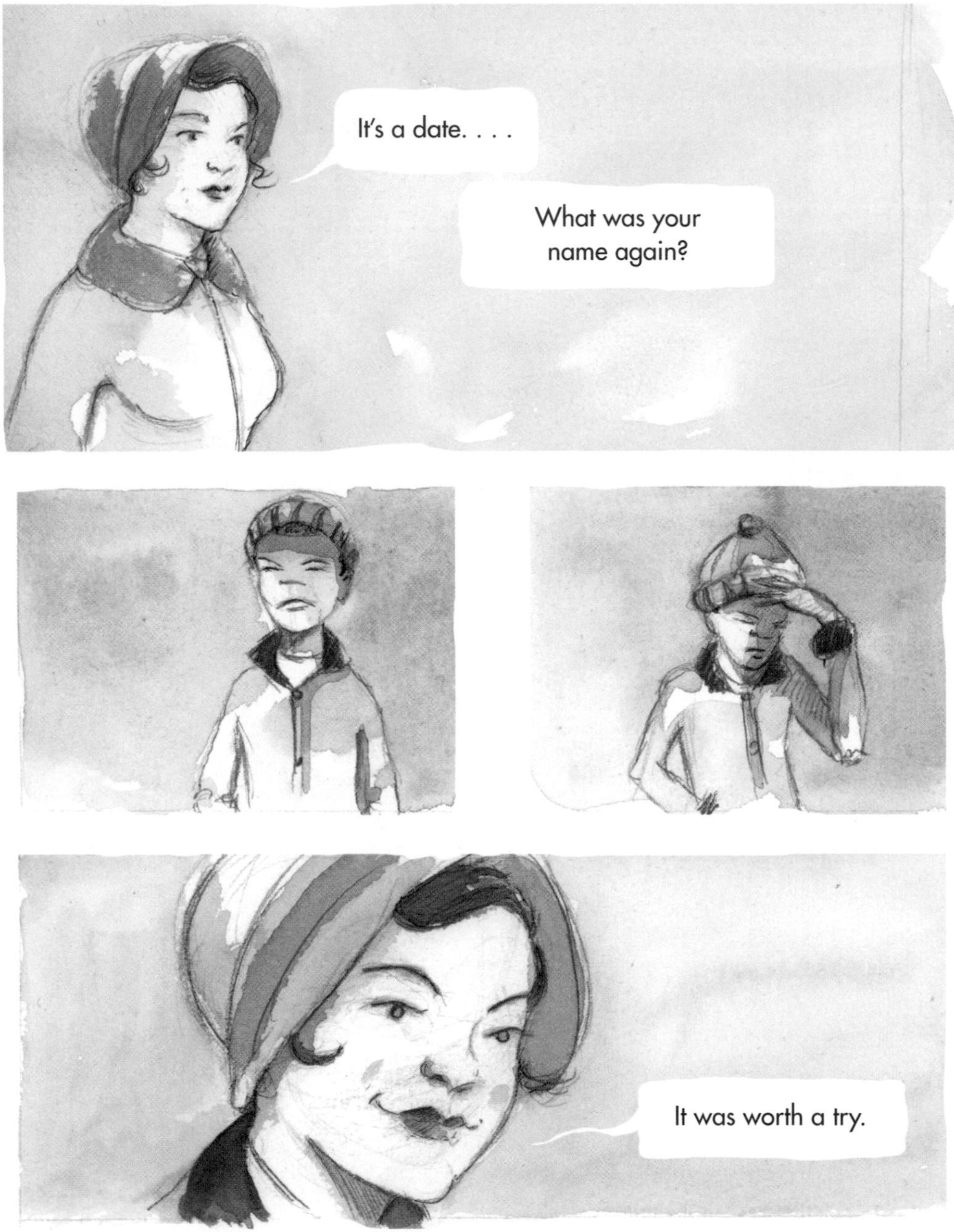
It's a date. . . .
What was your name again?
It was worth a try.

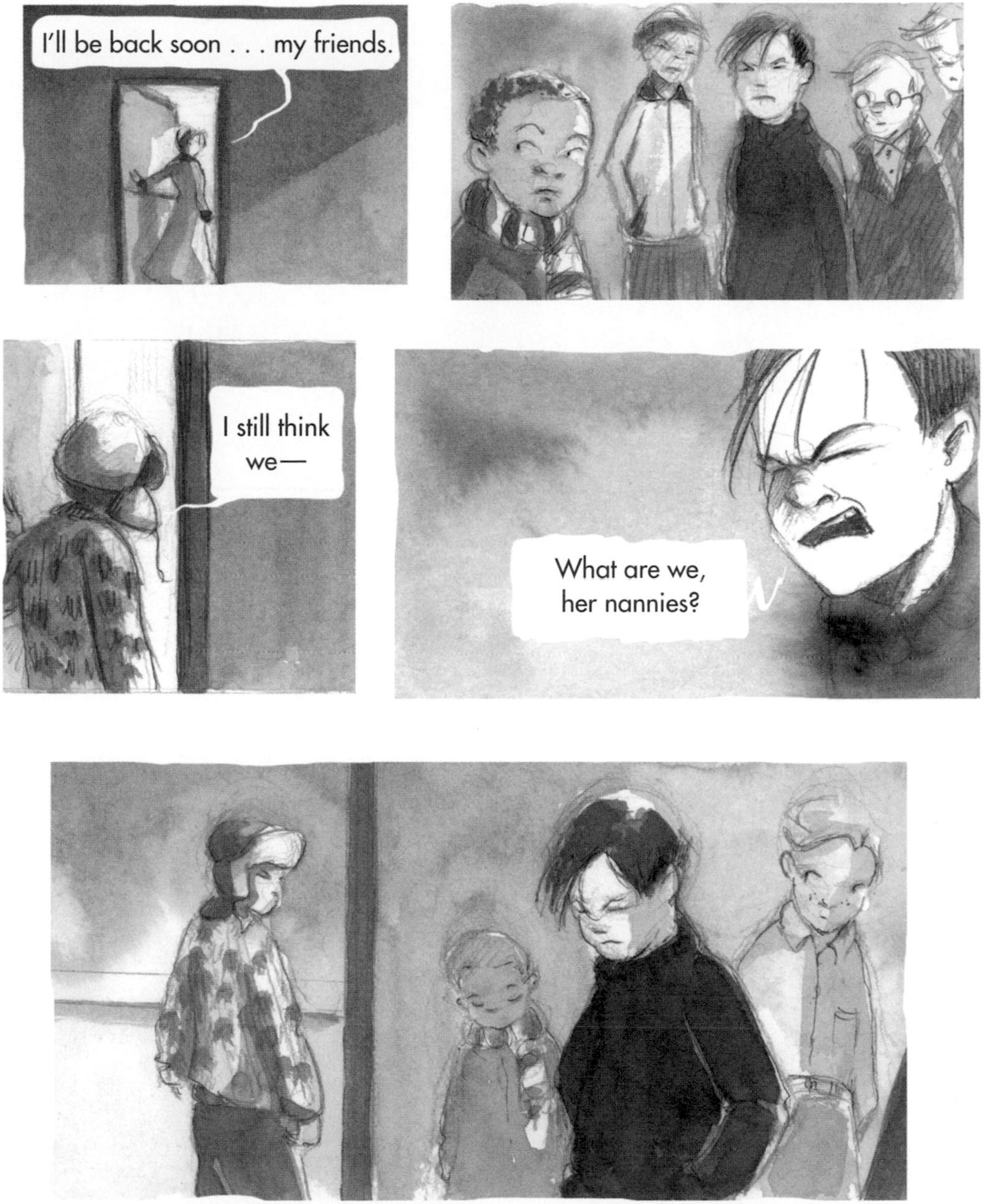
I'll be back soon . . . my friends.
I still think we—
What are we, her nannies?

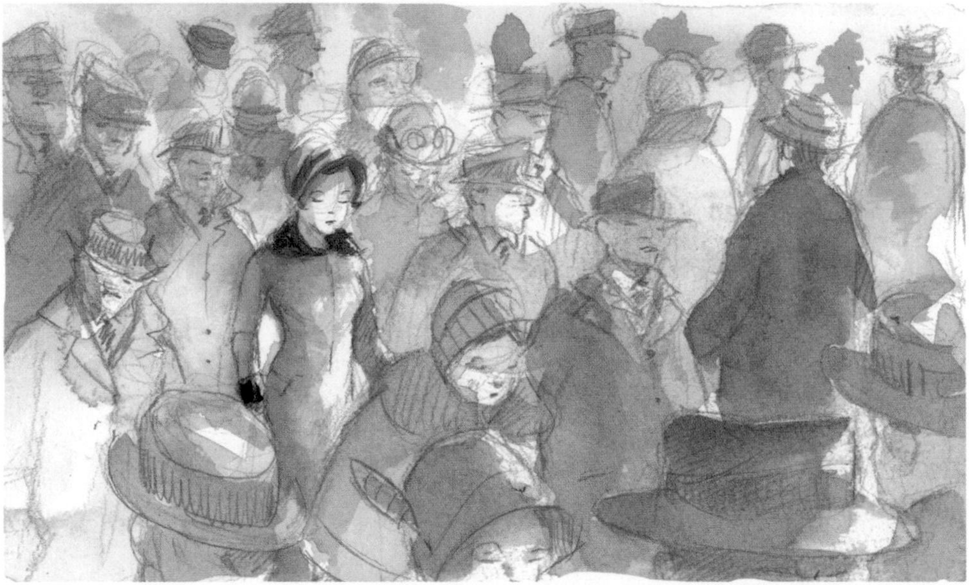

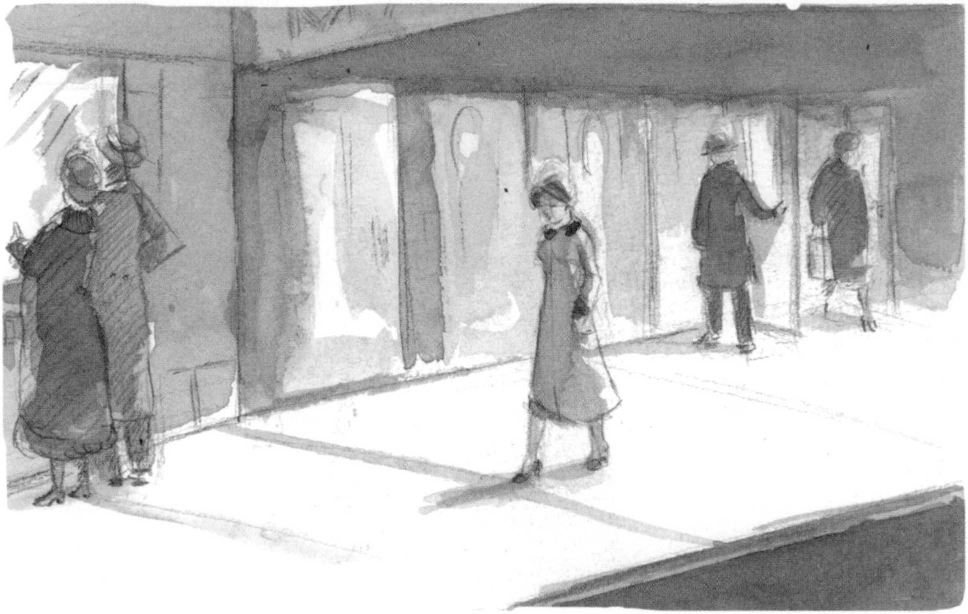

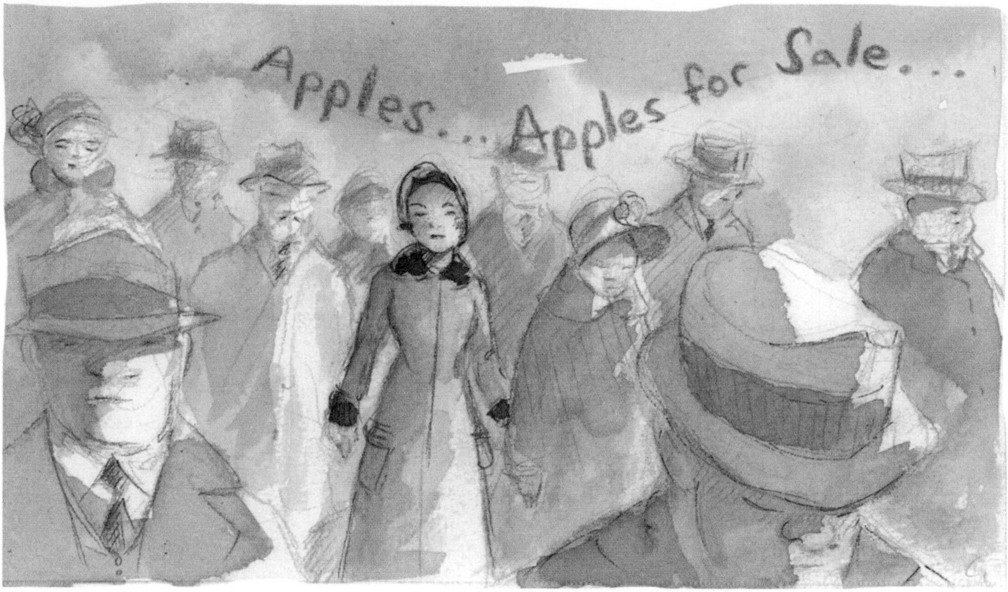
Apples... Apples for Sale...

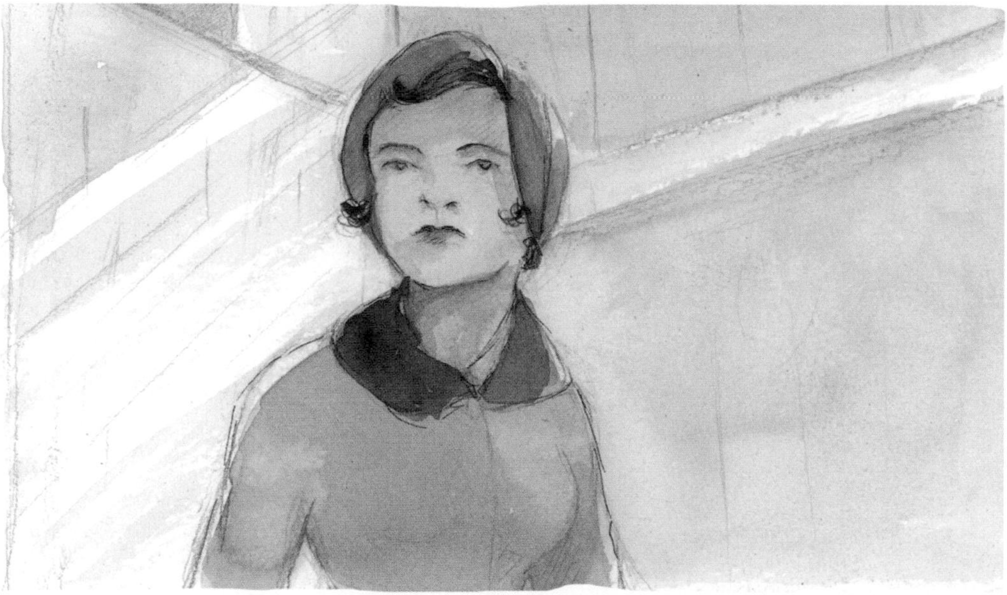

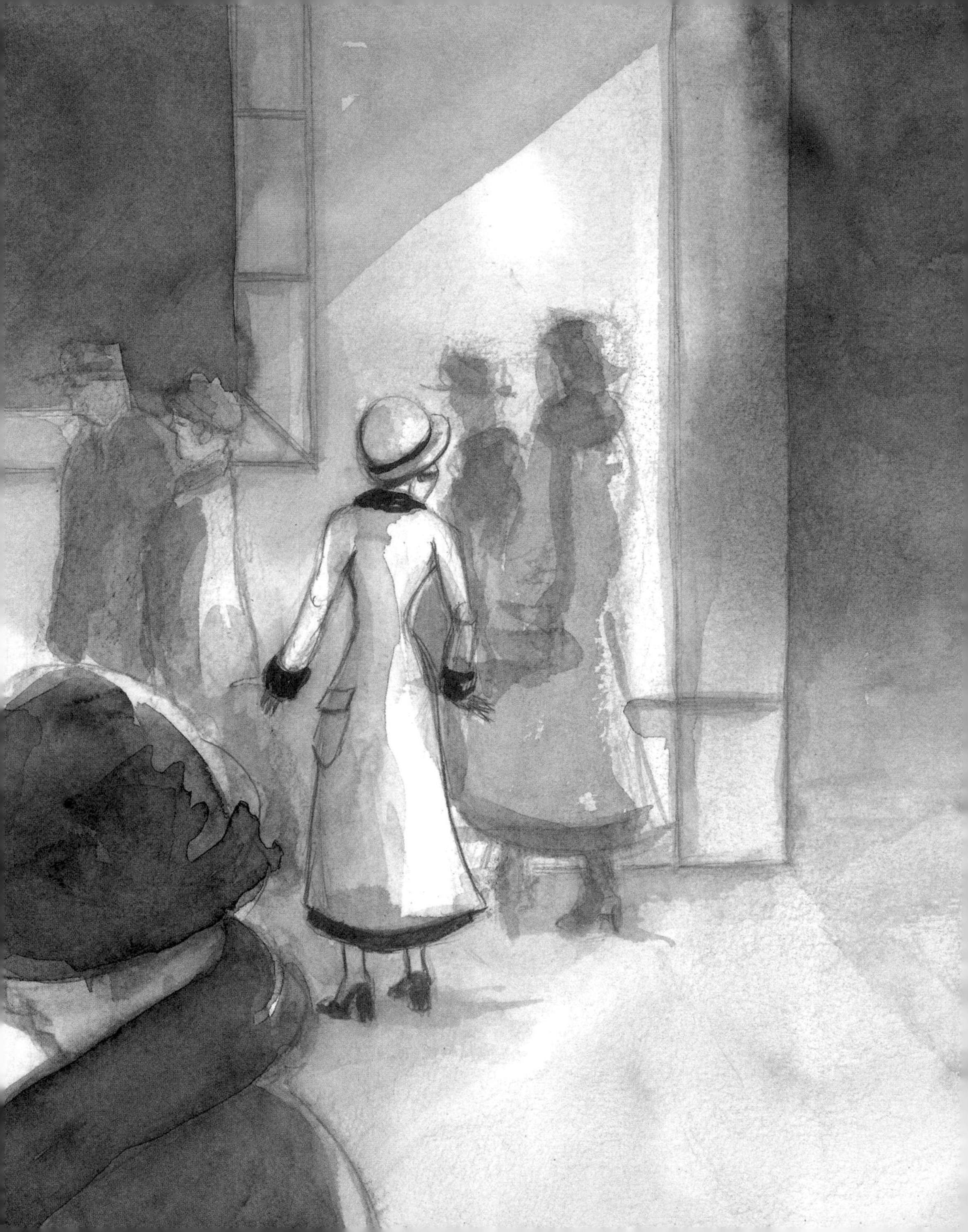

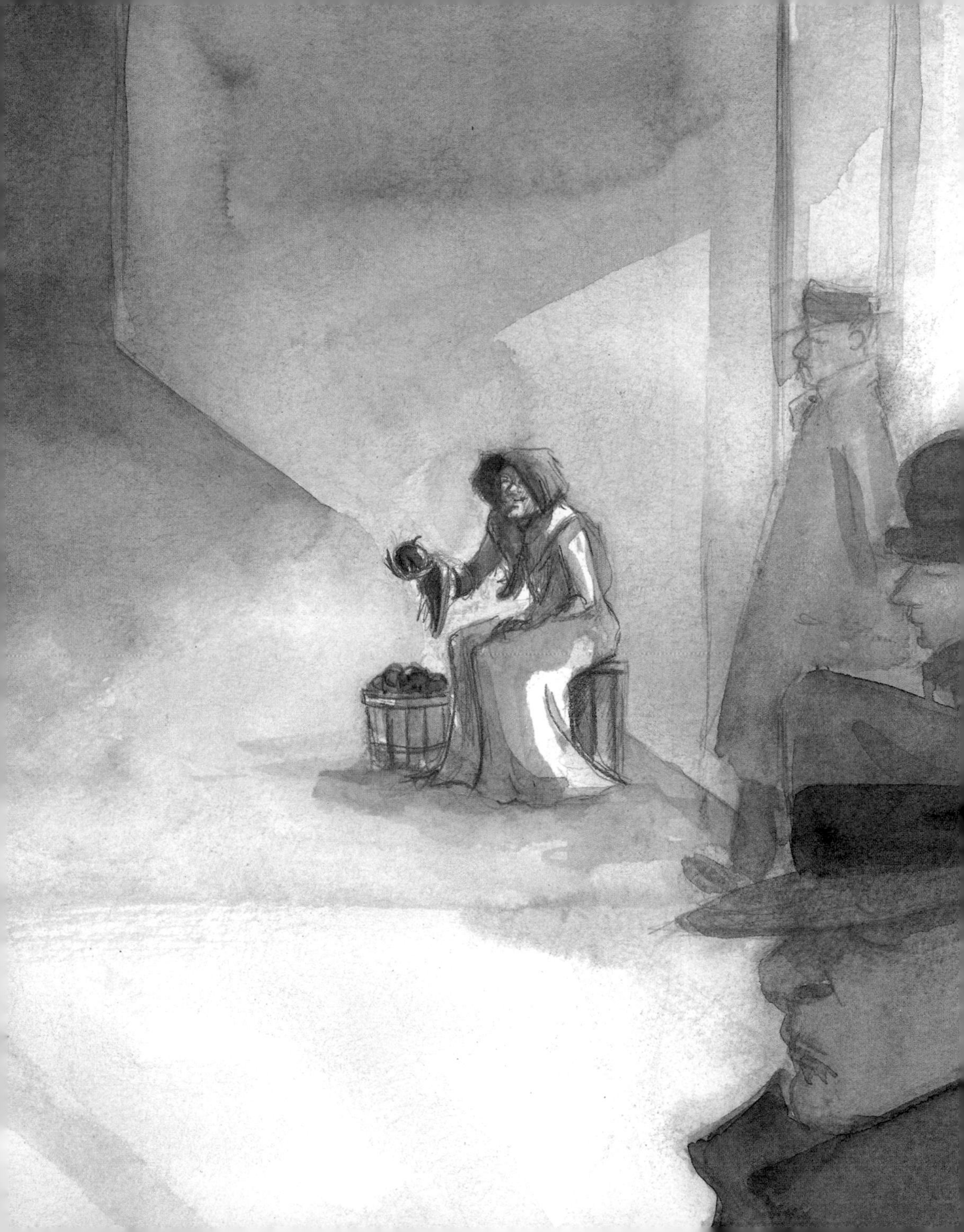

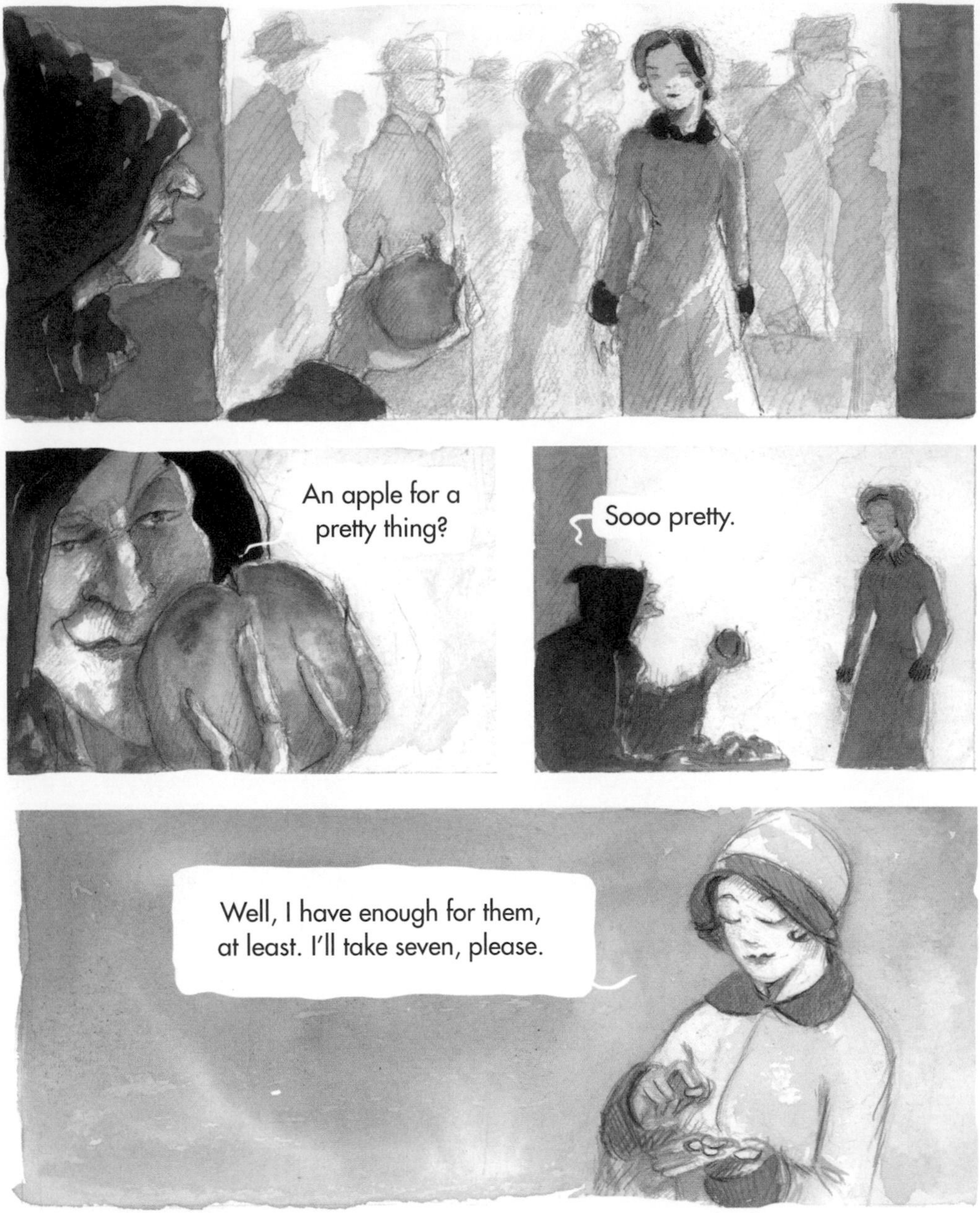
An apple for a pretty thing?
Sooo pretty.
Well, I have enough for them, at least. I'll take seven, please.

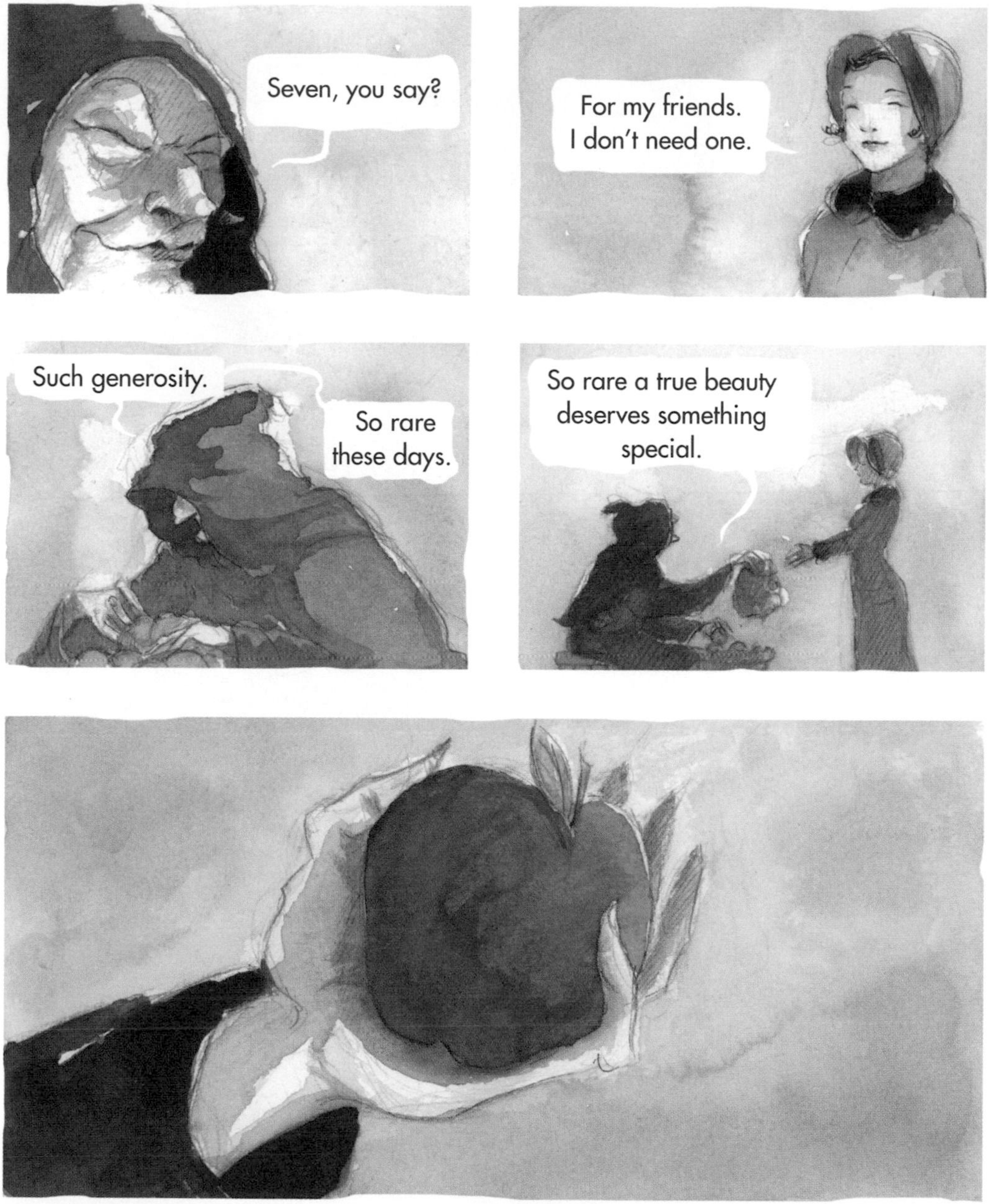
Seven, you say?
For my friends.
I don't need one.
Such generosity.
So rare
these days.
So rare a true beauty
deserves something
special.

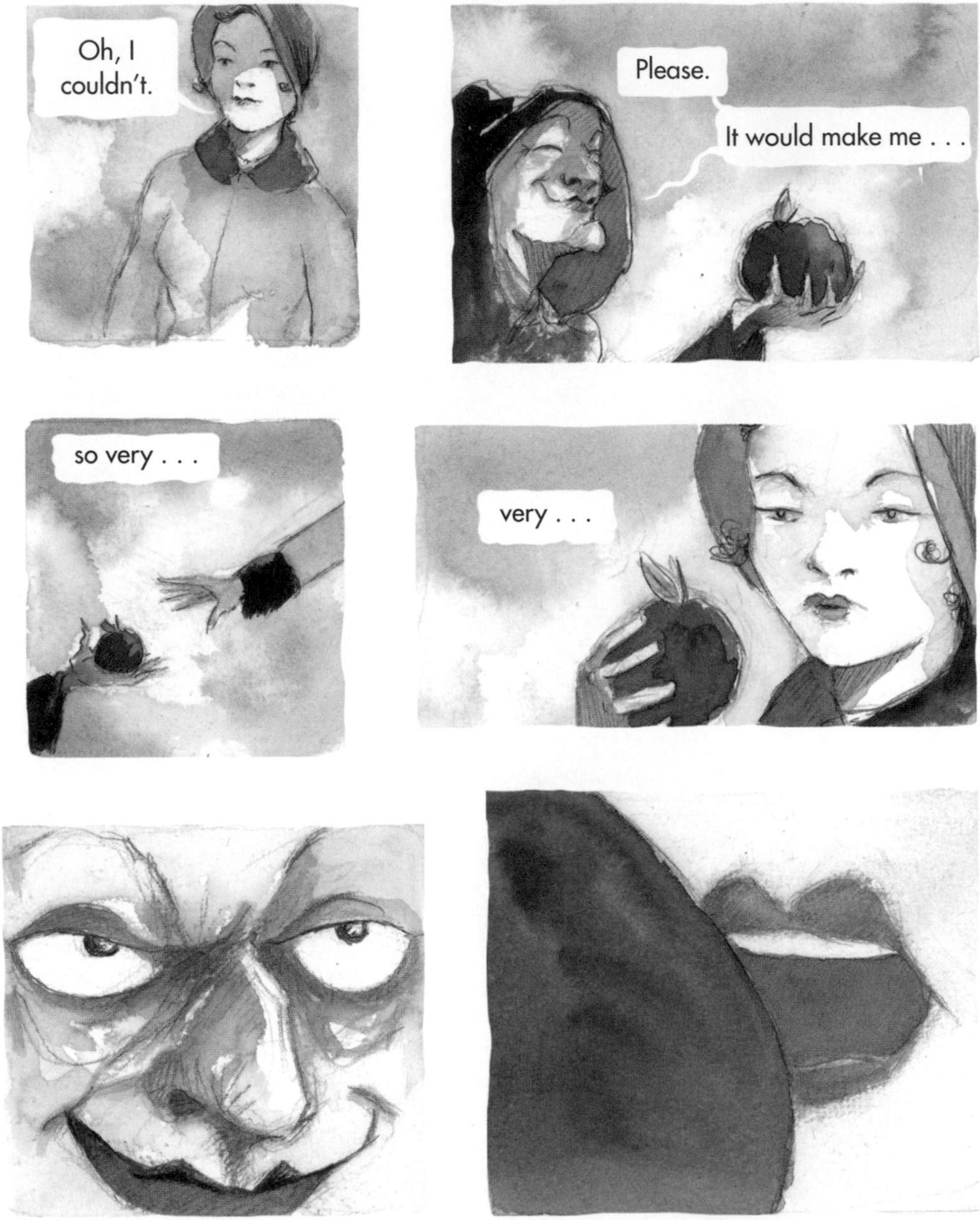
Oh, I couldn't.
Please.
It would make me . . .
so very . . .
very . . .

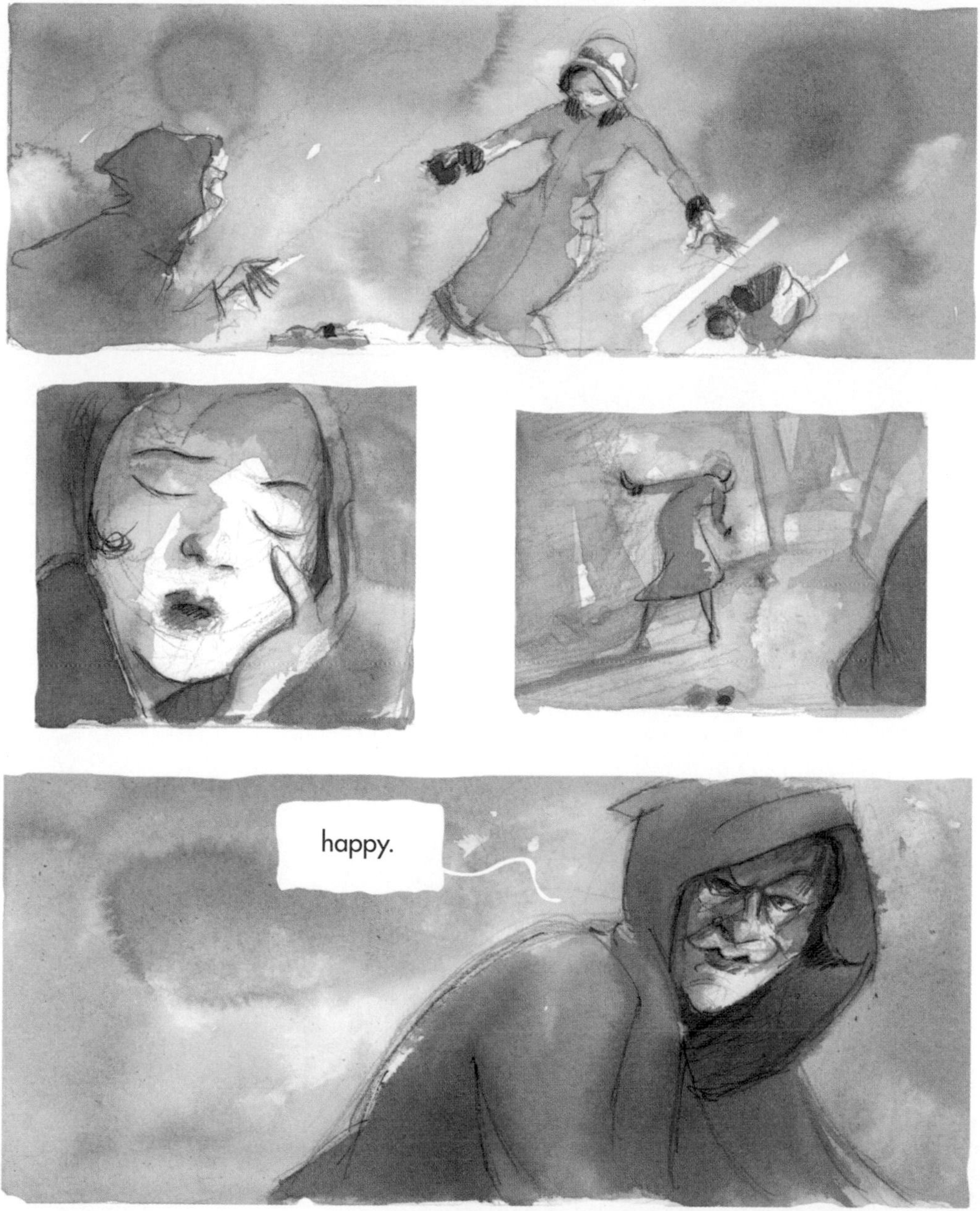
happy.

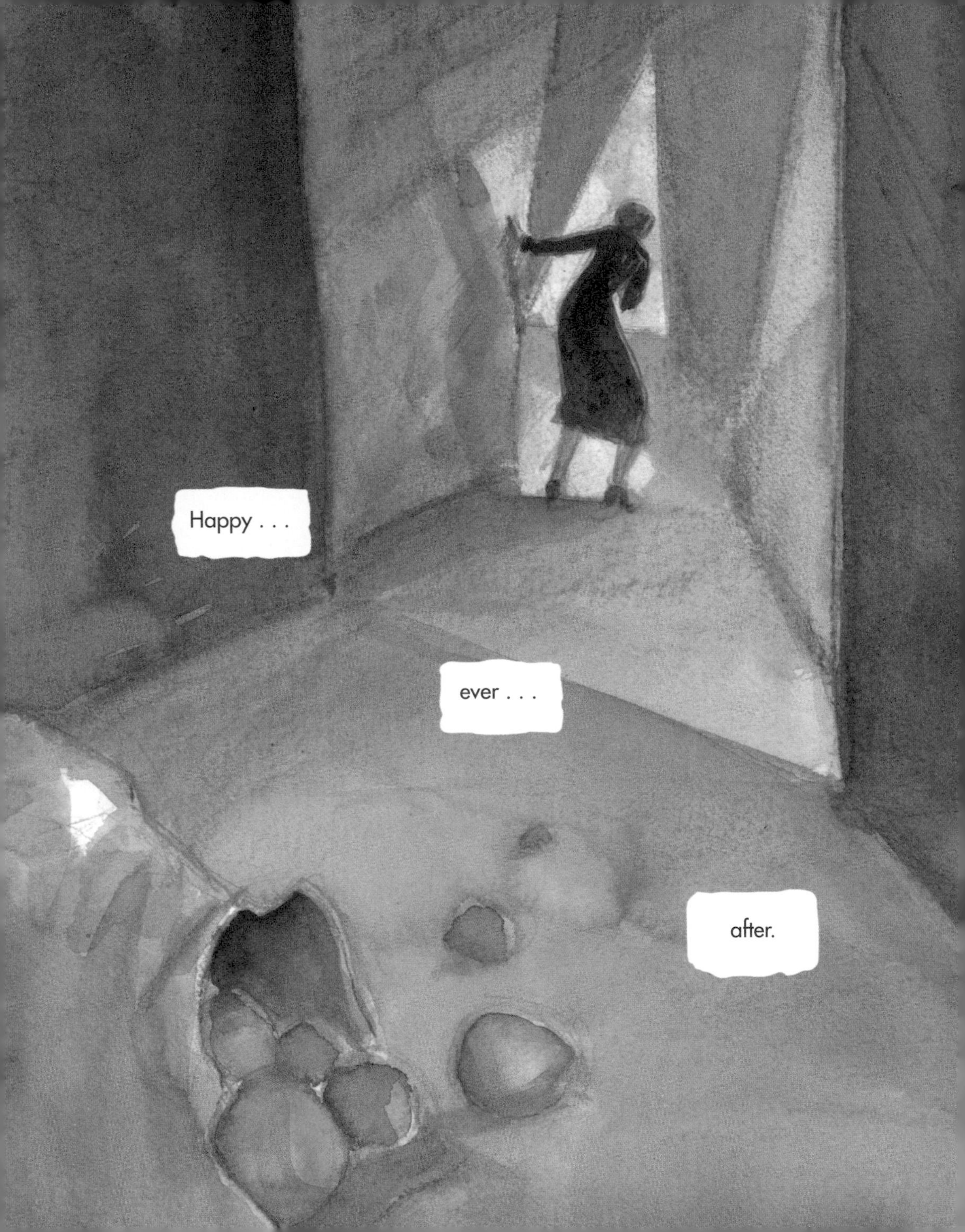
Happy . . .
ever . . .
after.

NAMES

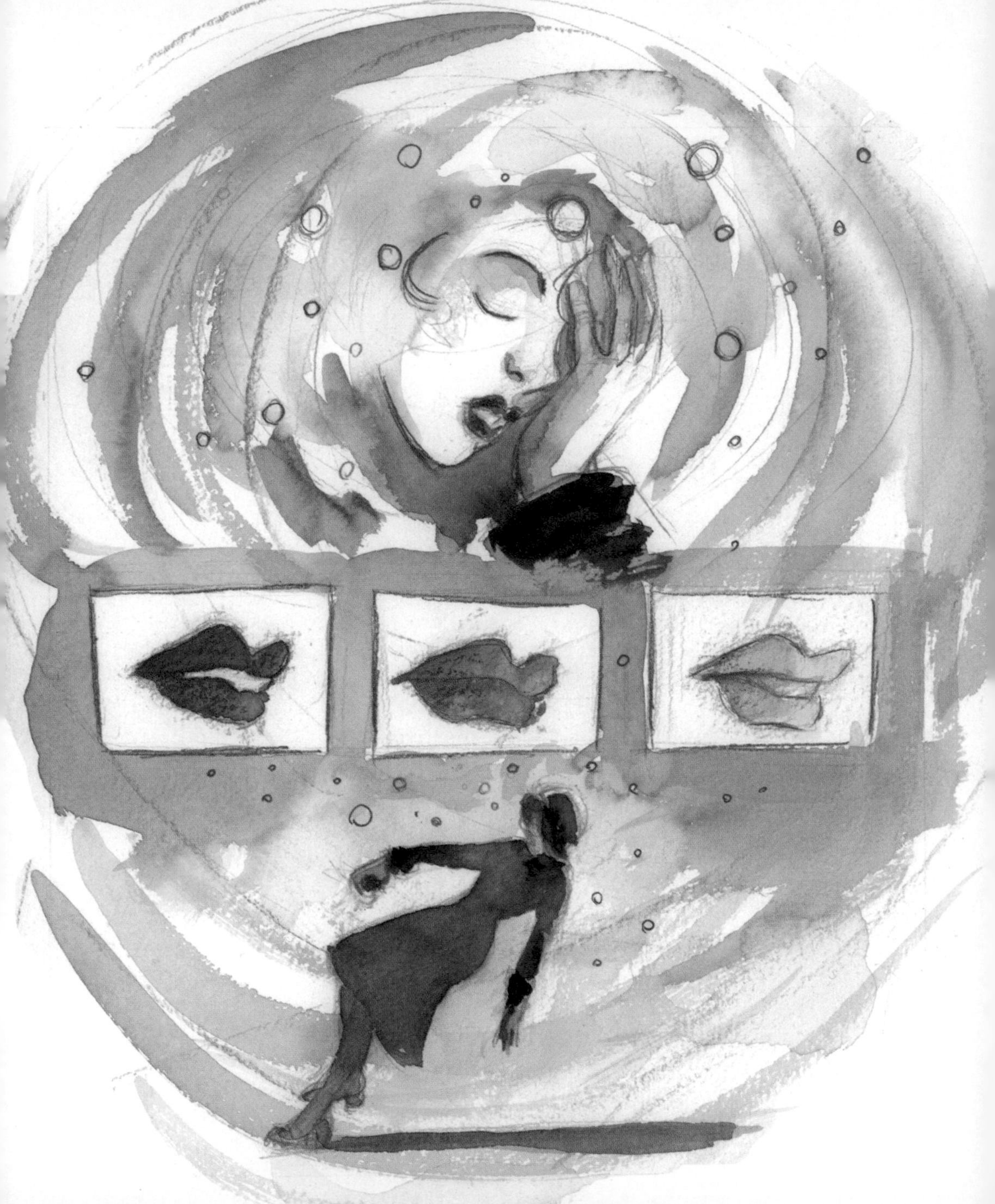

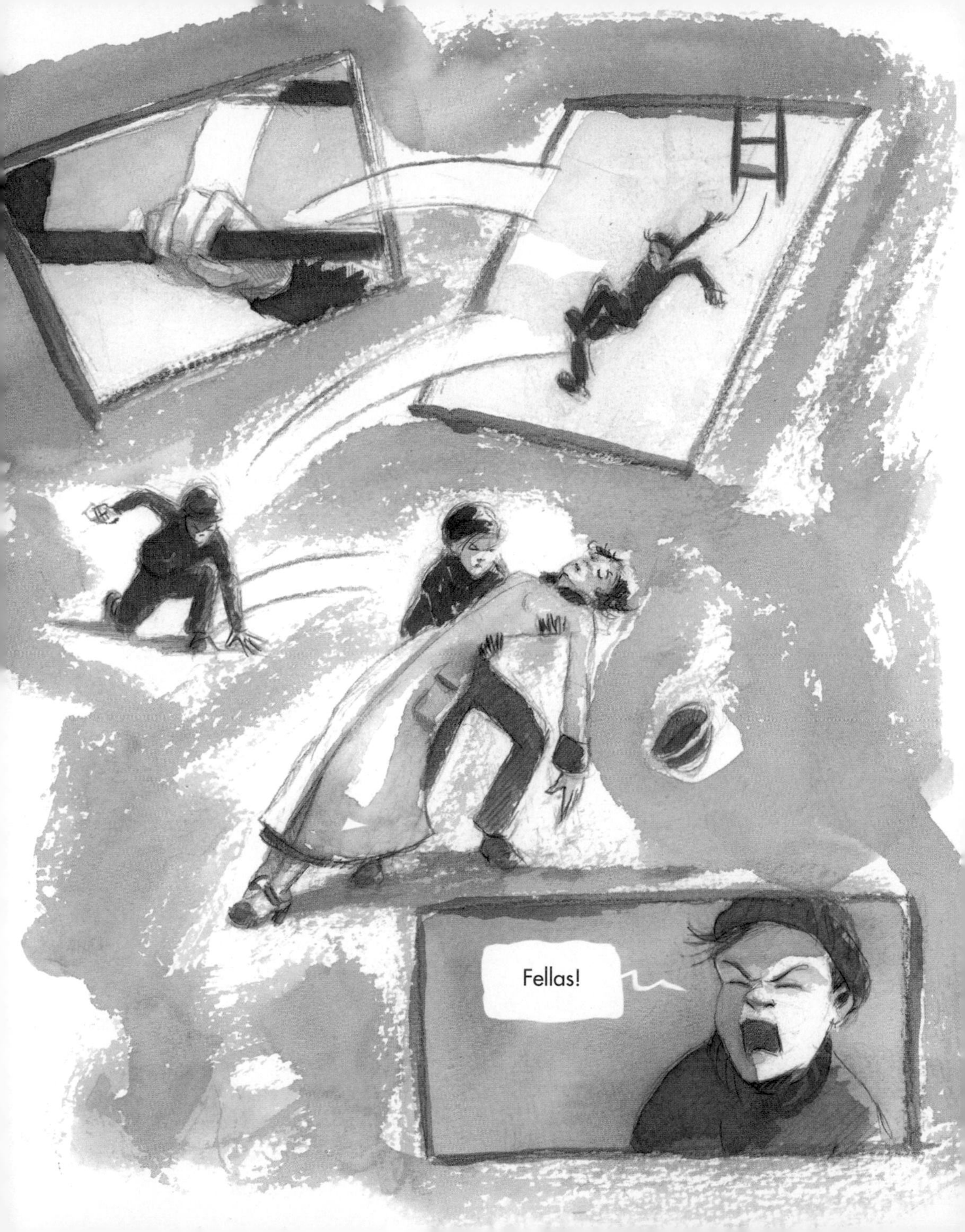
Fellas!

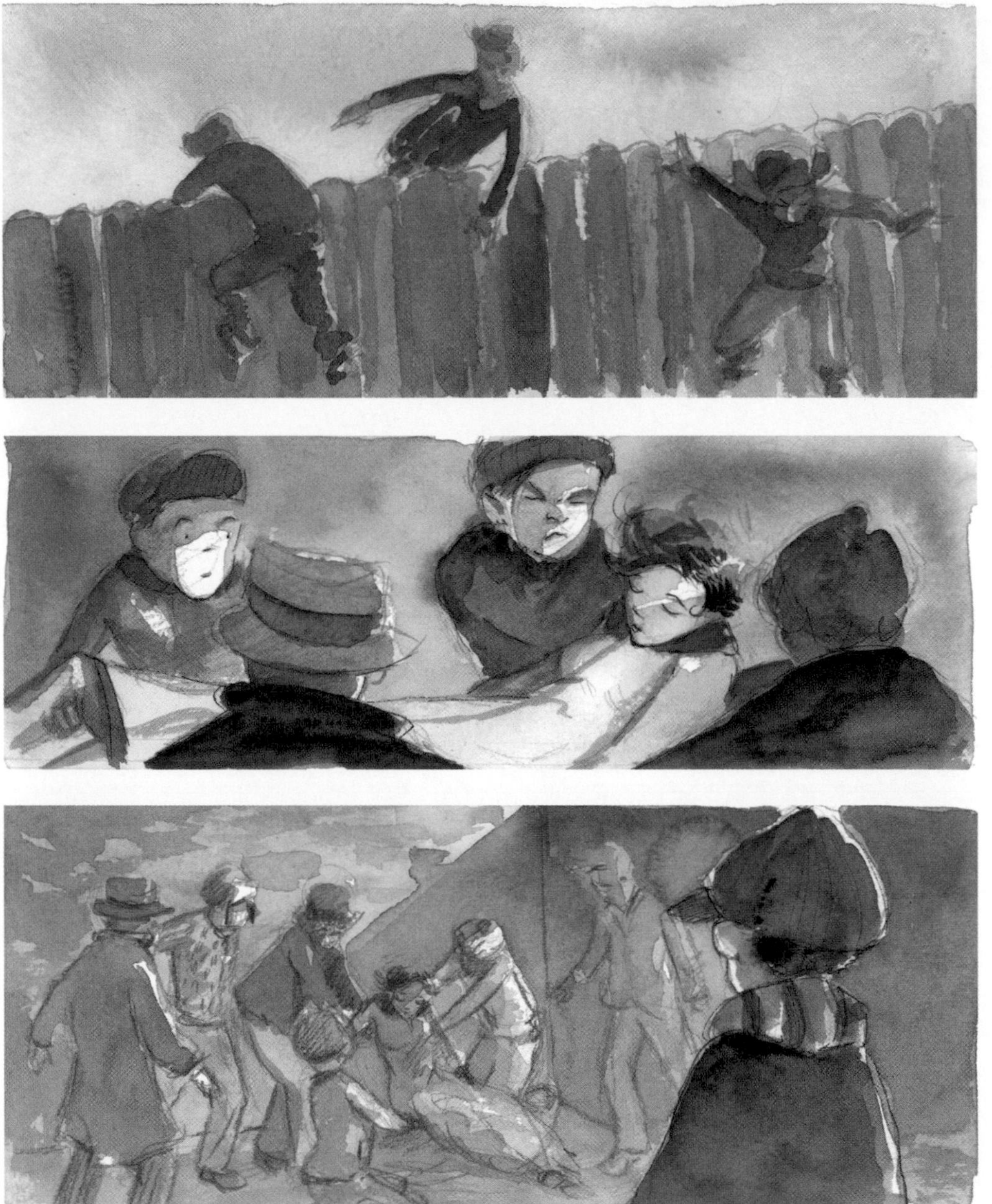

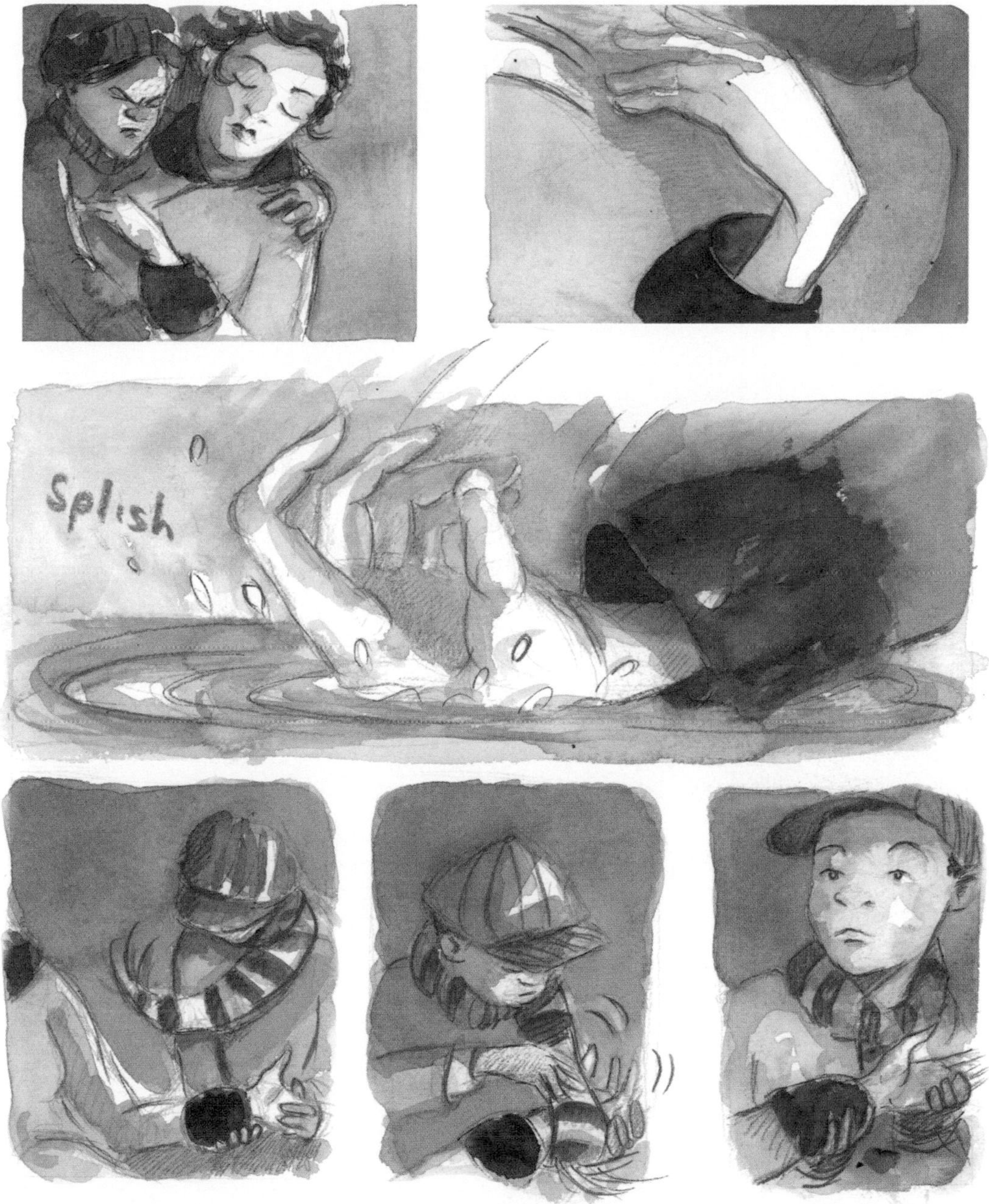
Splish

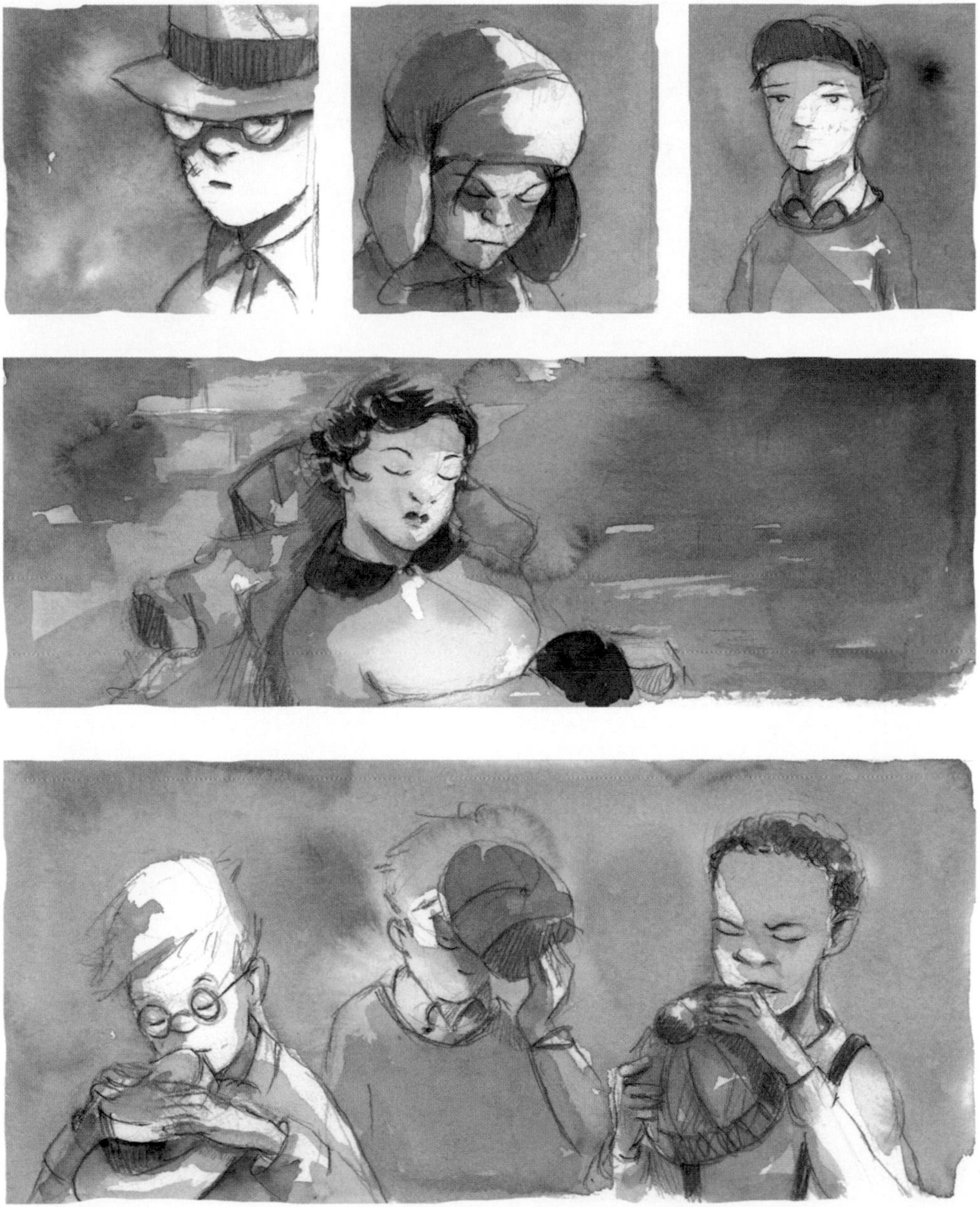

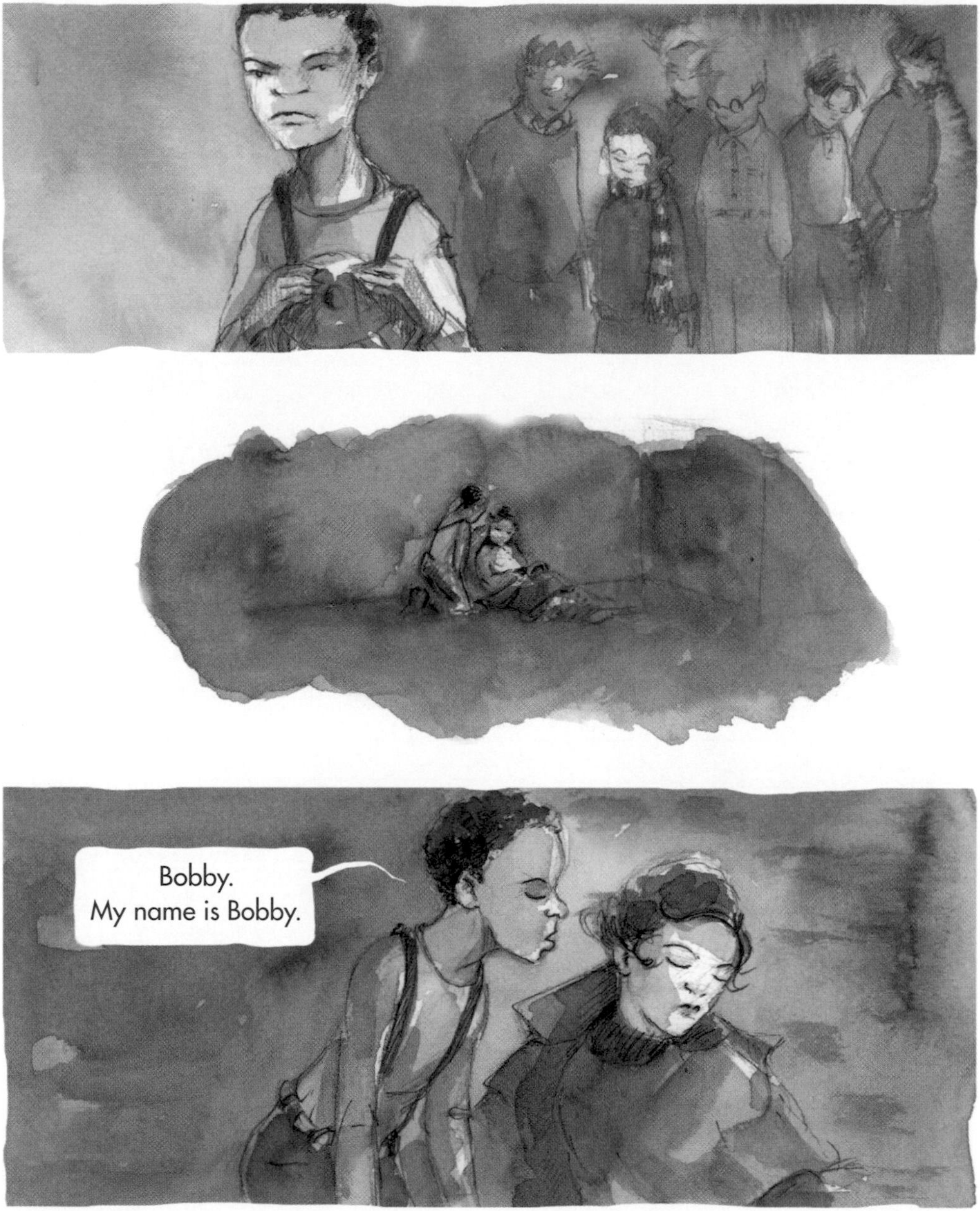
Bobby. My name is Bobby.

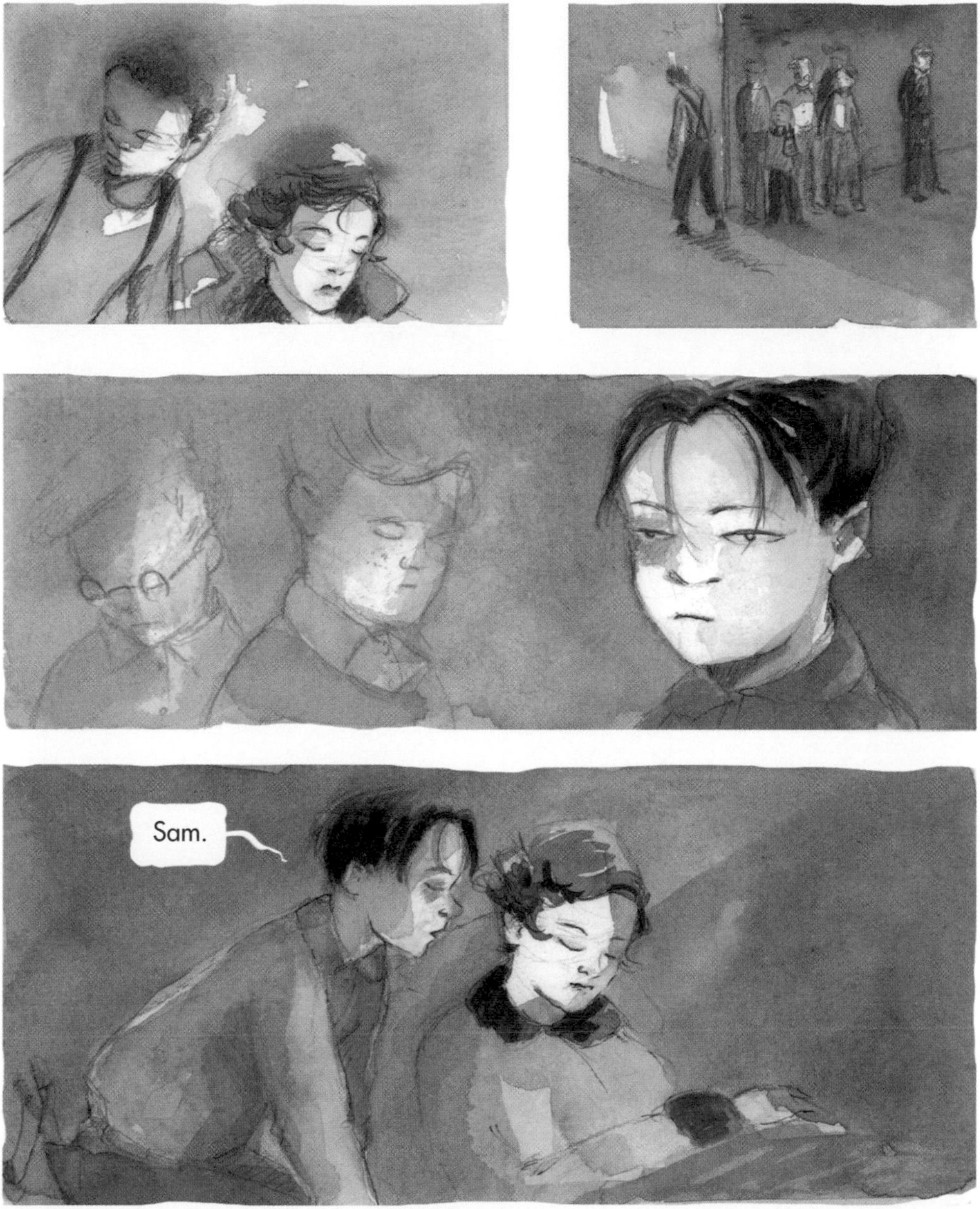
Sam.

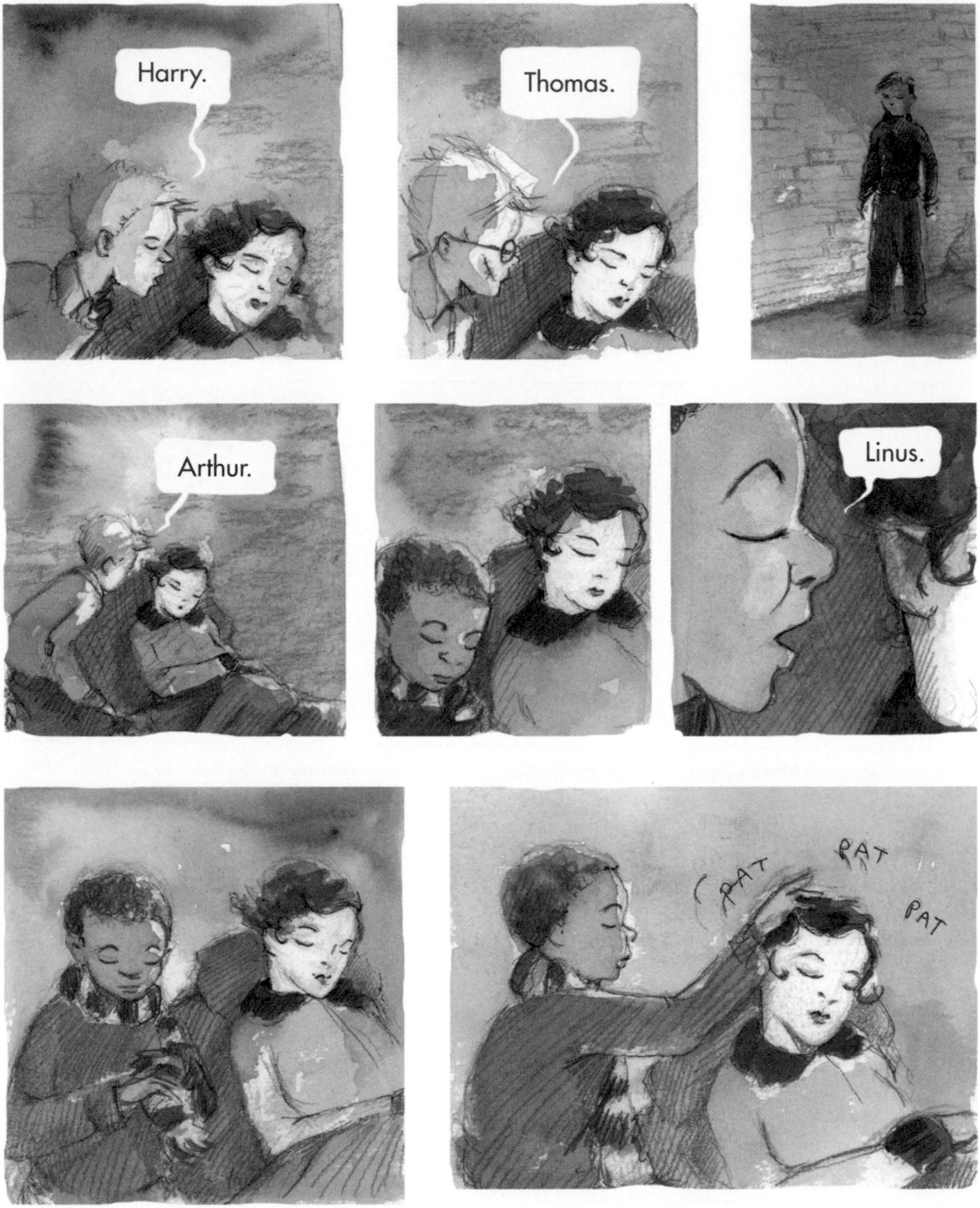
Harry.
Thomas.
Arthur.
Linus.
PAT
PAT
PAT

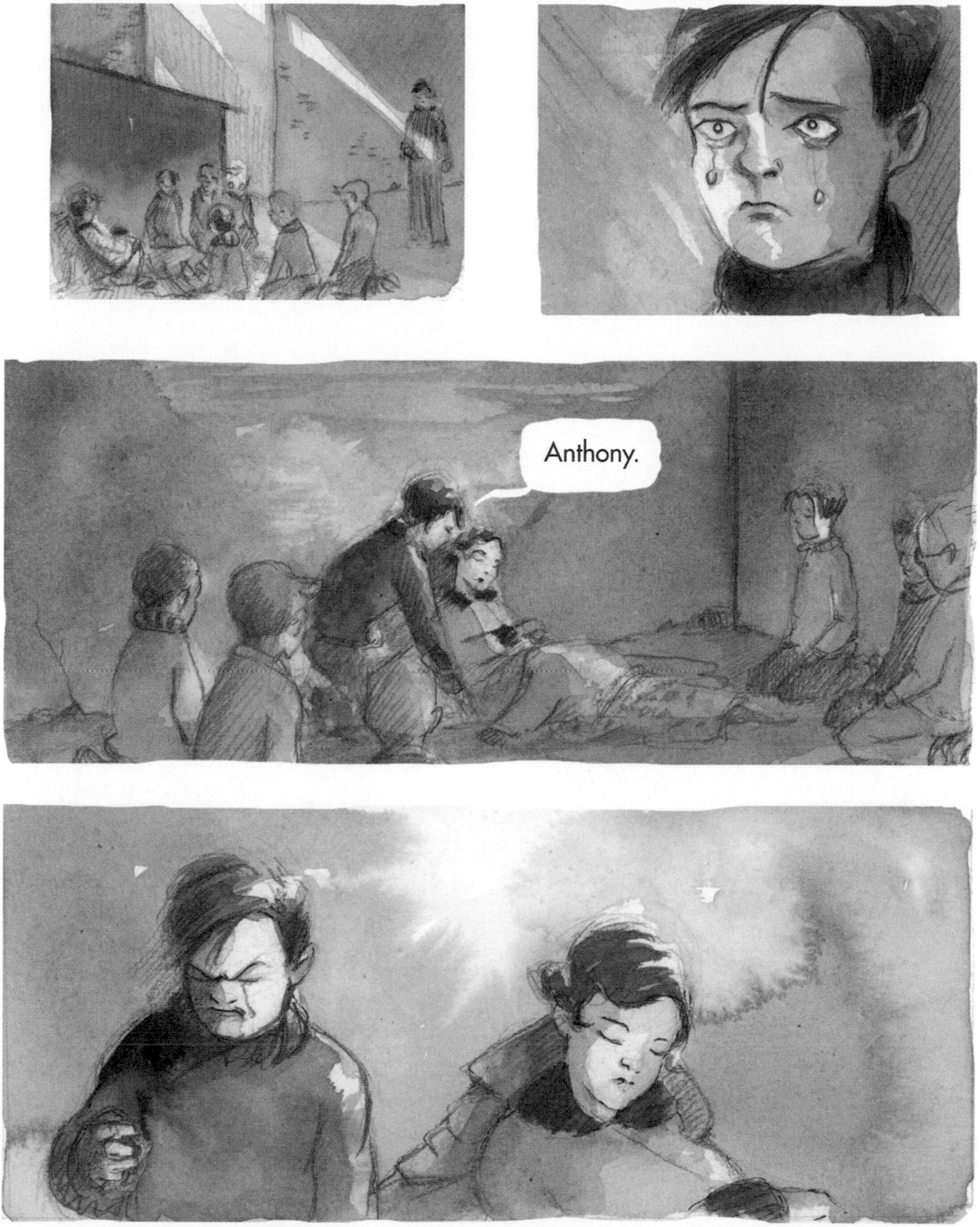
Anthony.

UP IN
LIGHTS

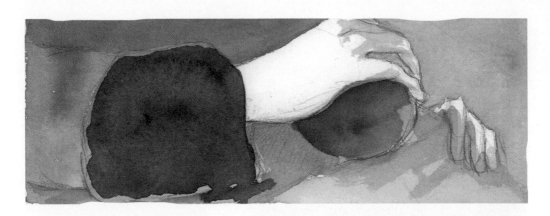

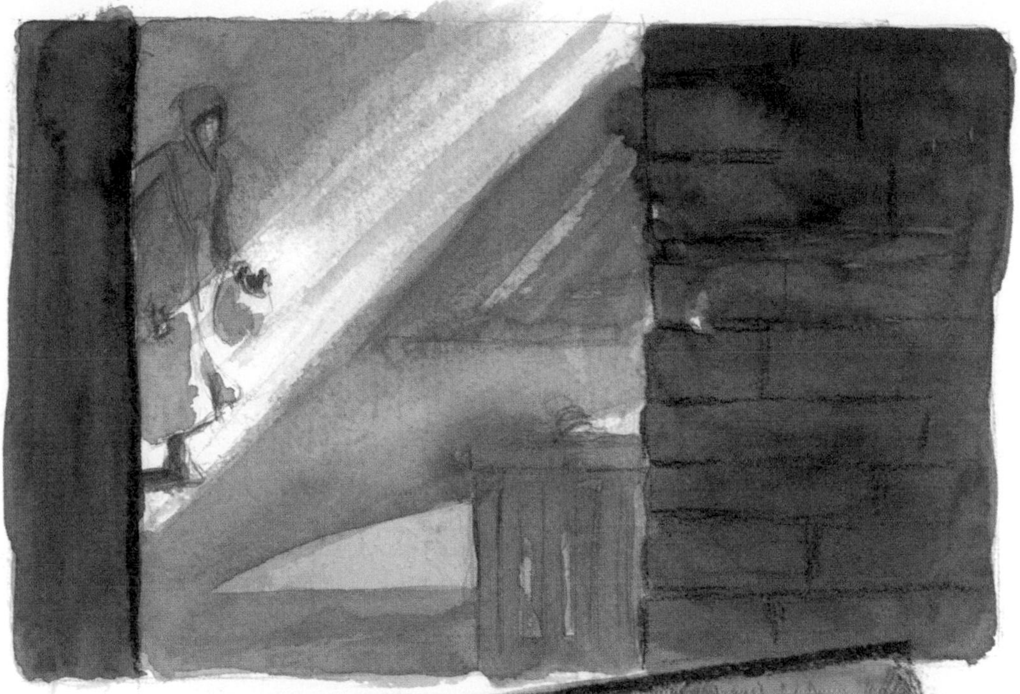

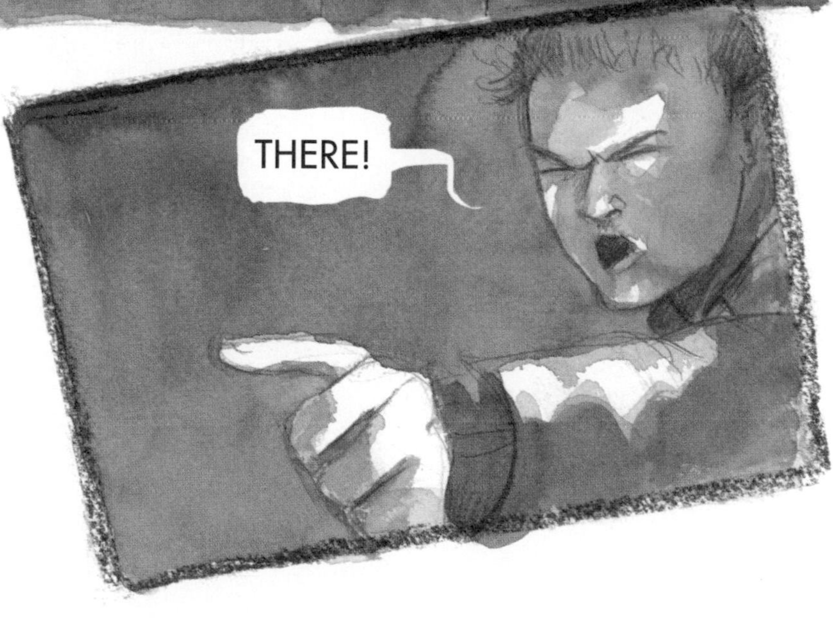
THERE!

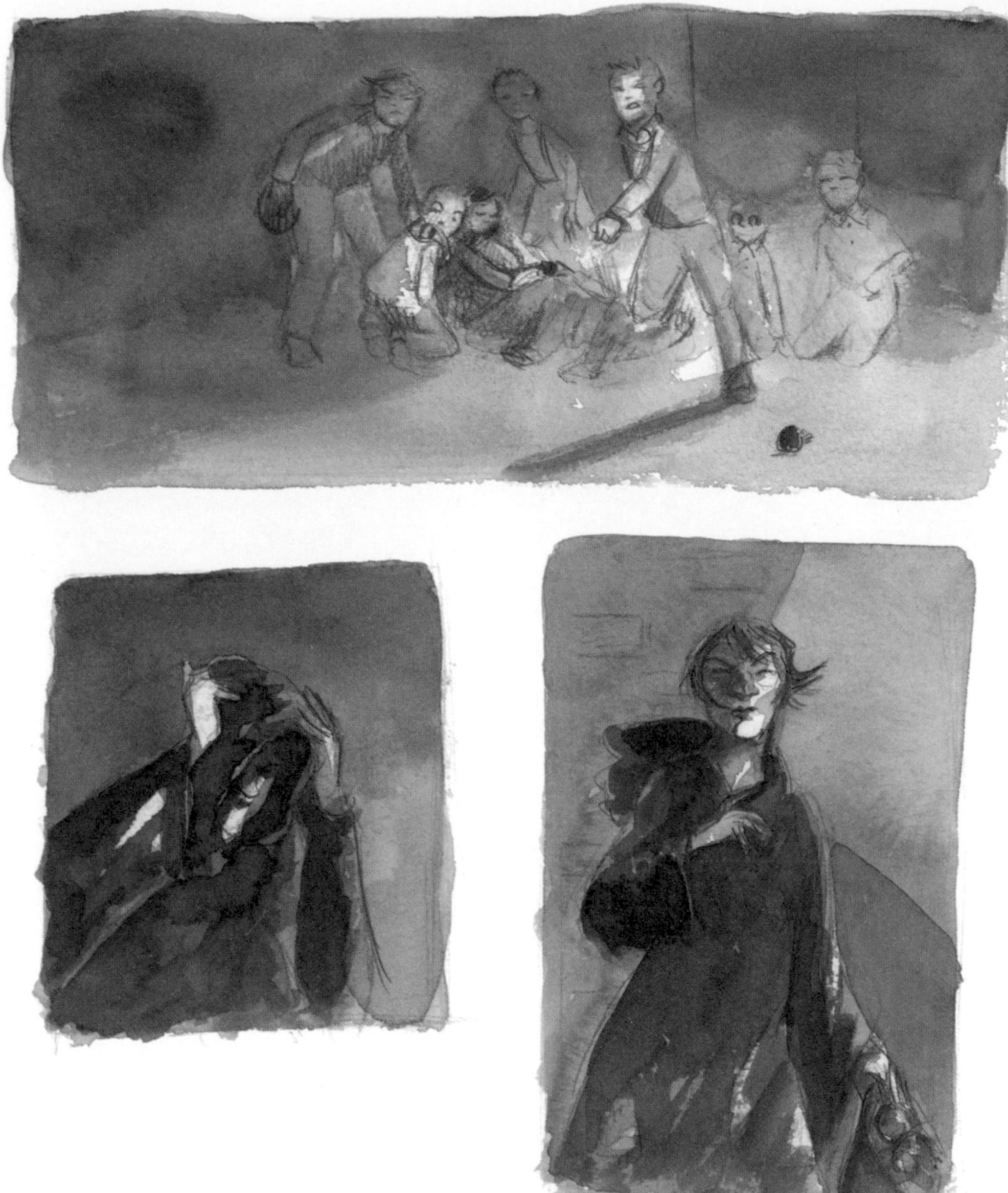

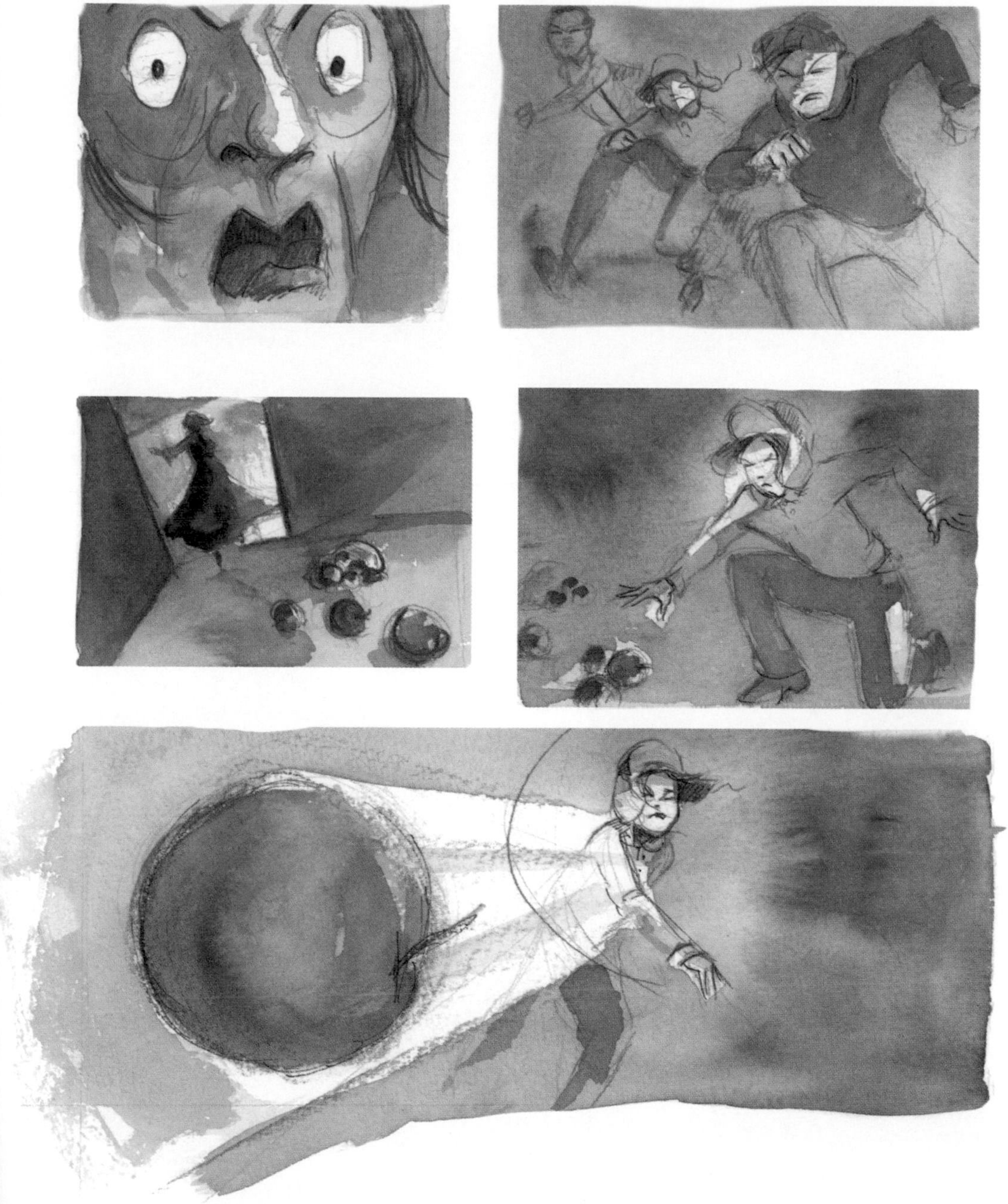

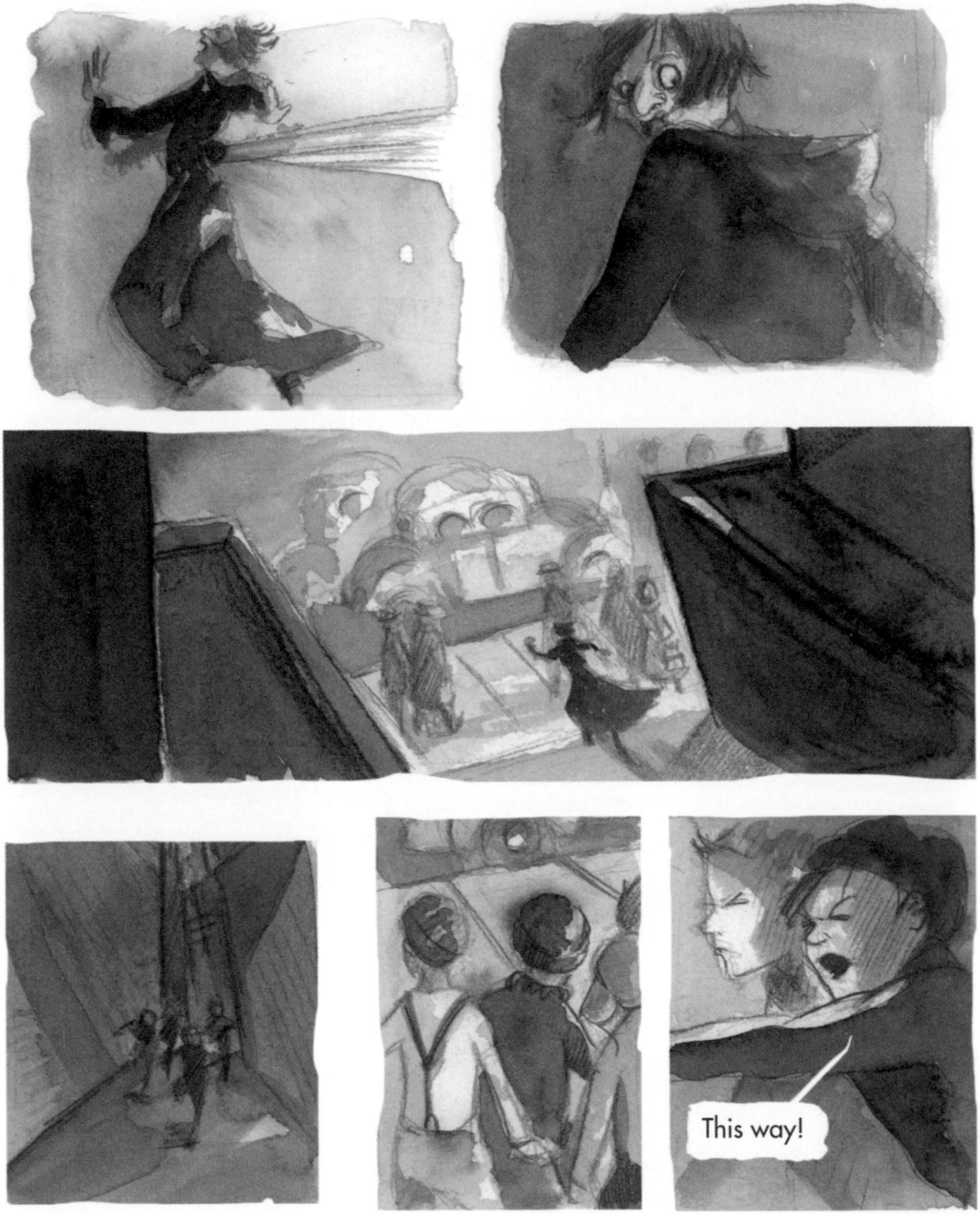
This way!

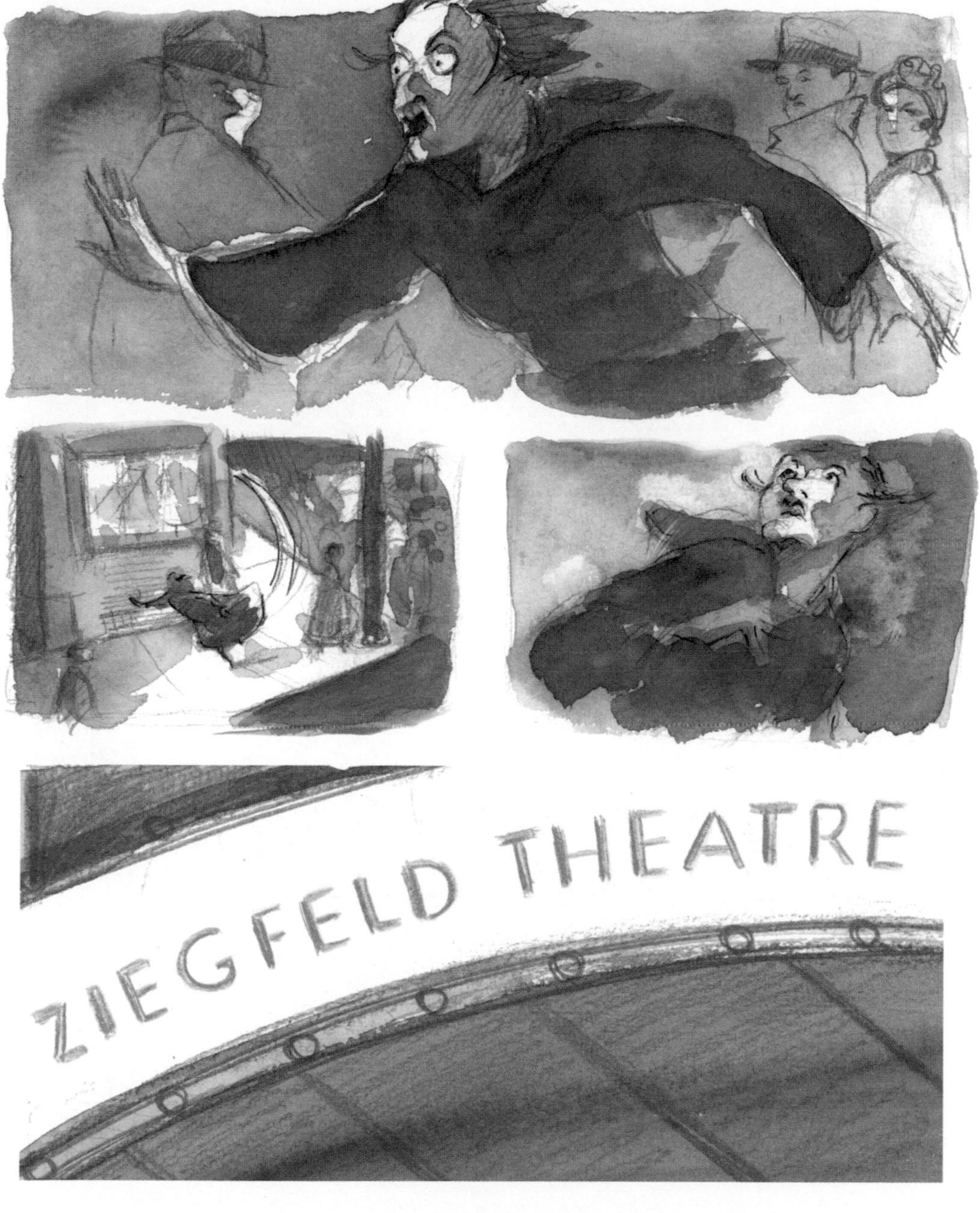
ZIEGFELD THEATRE

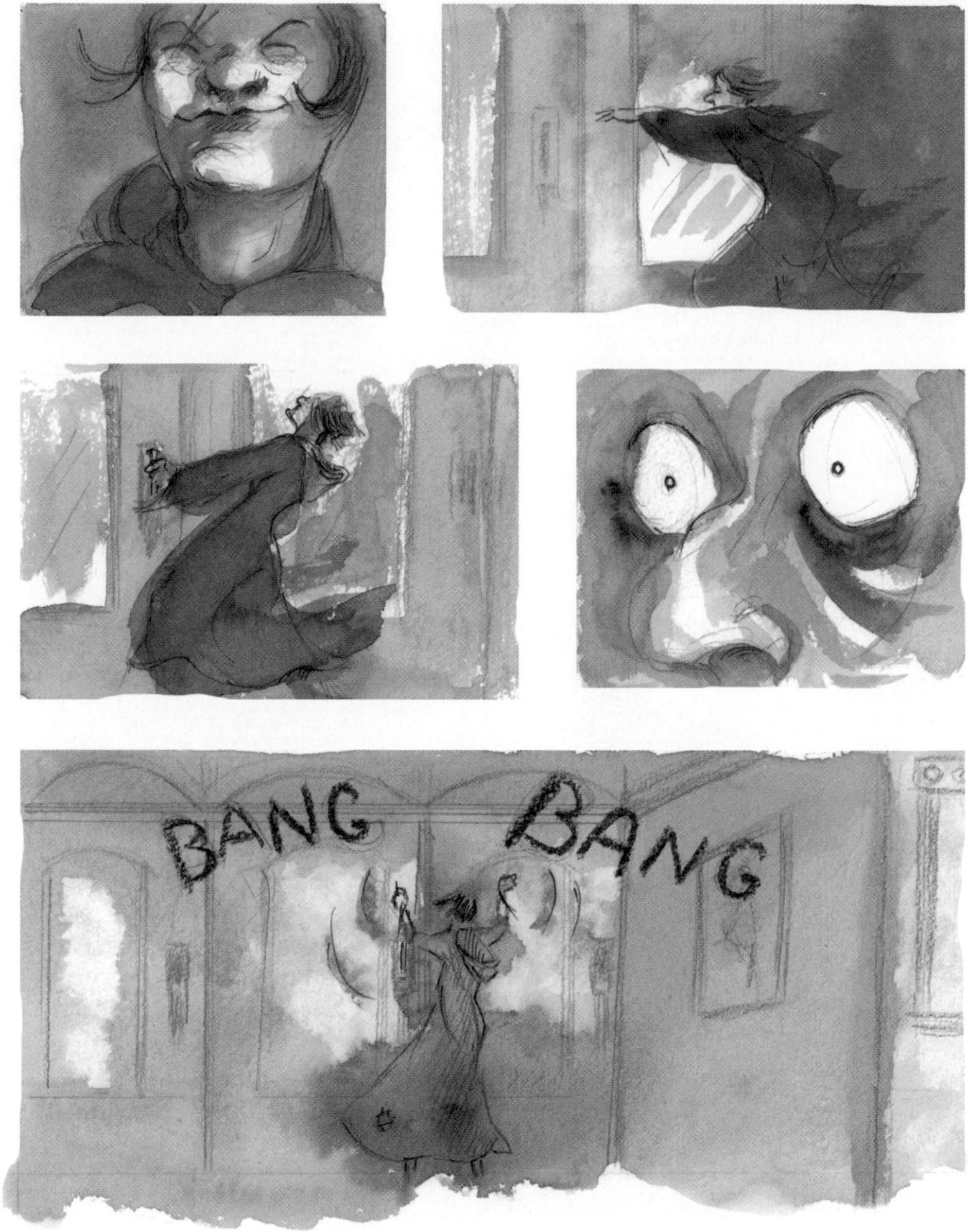
BANG
BANG

BANG
BANG
BANG
BANG
STAGE

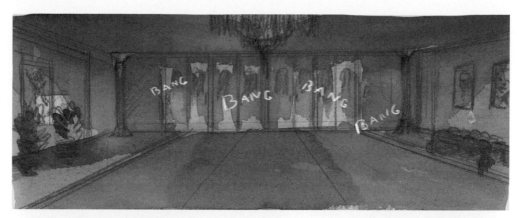

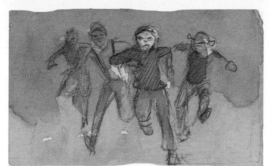

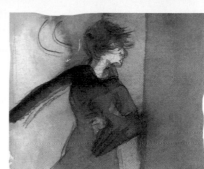

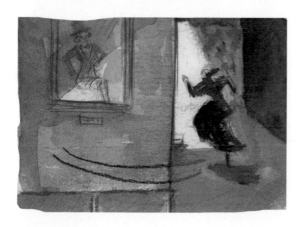

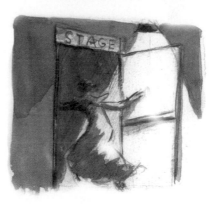

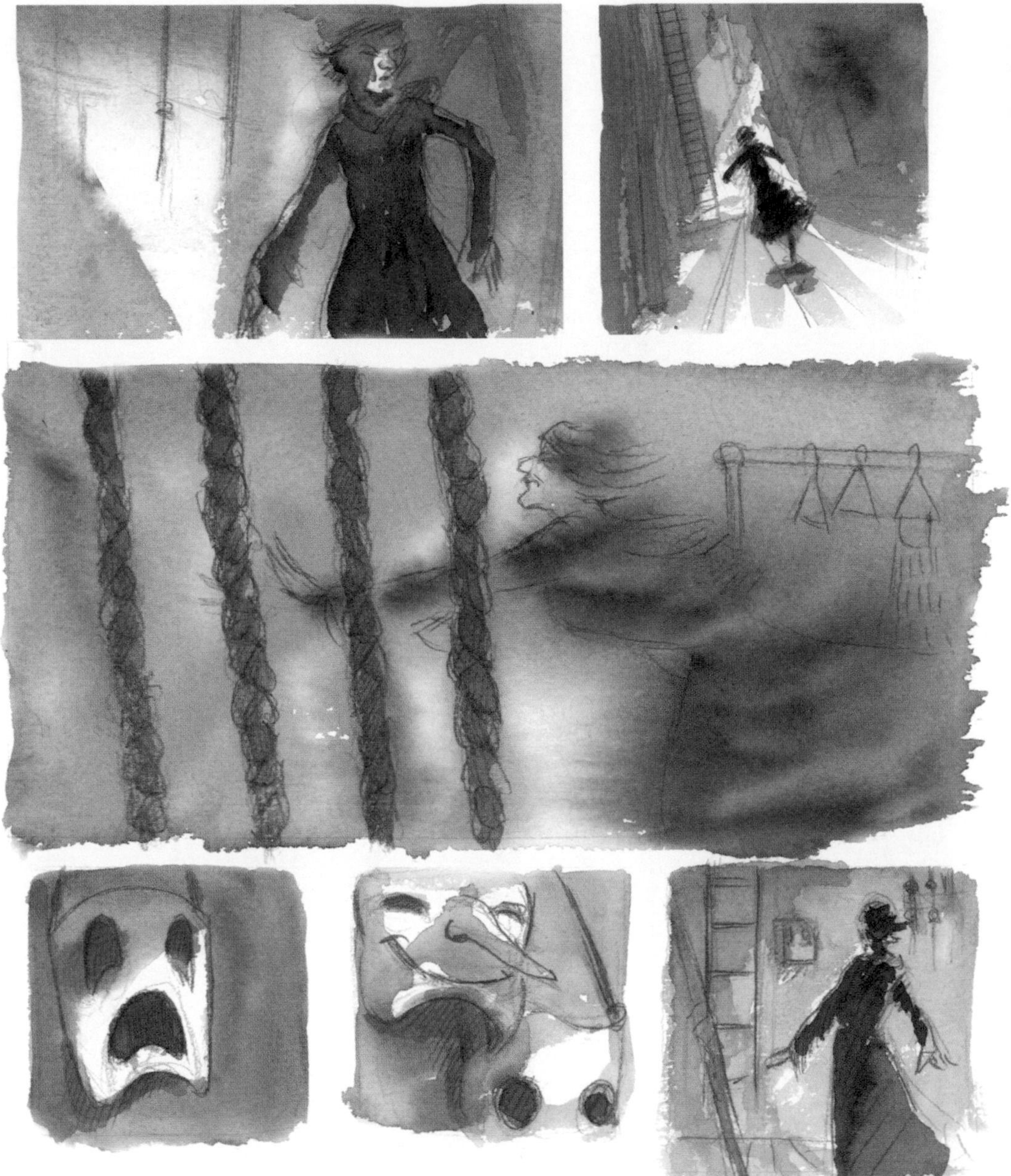

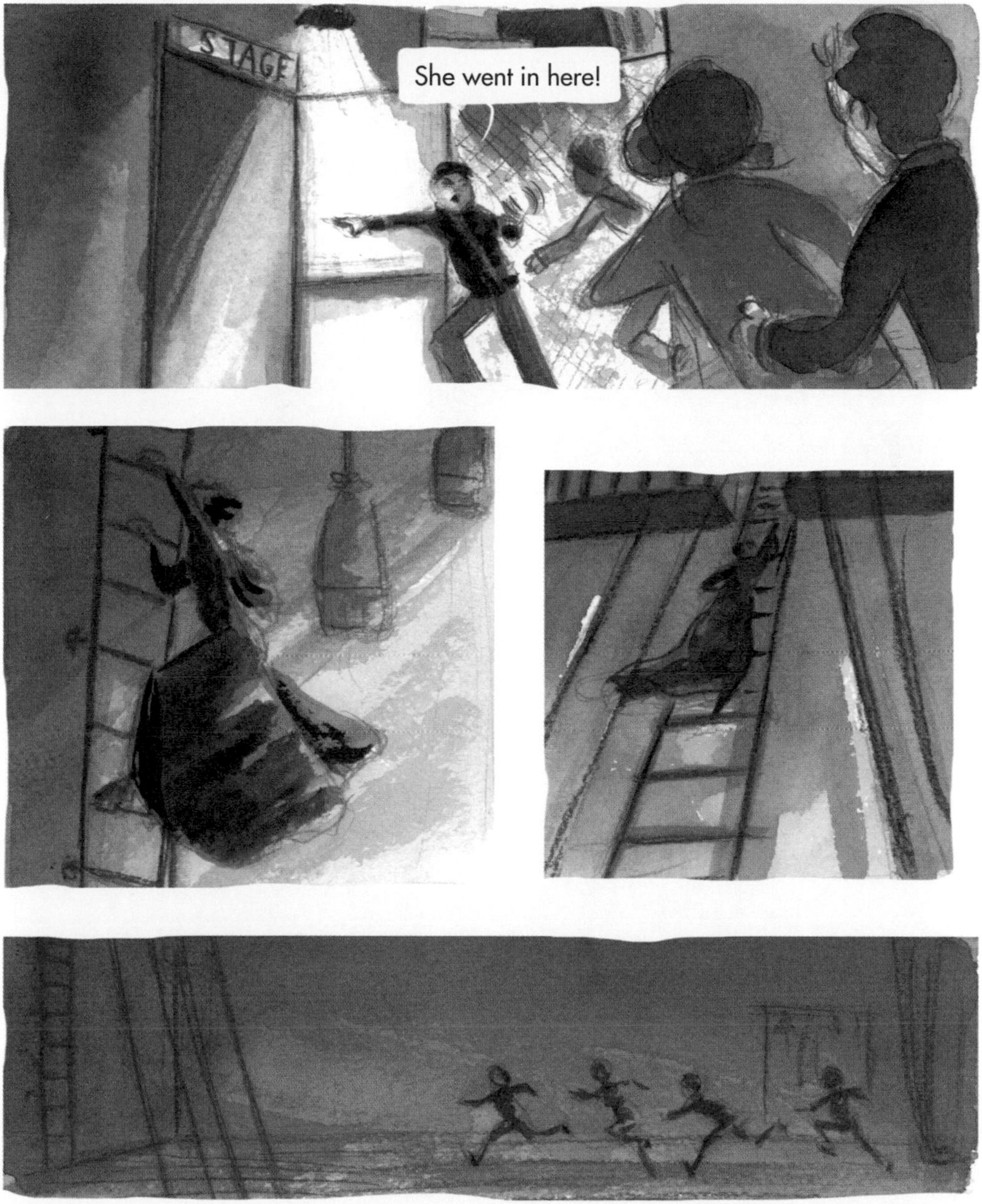
She went in here!
STAGE

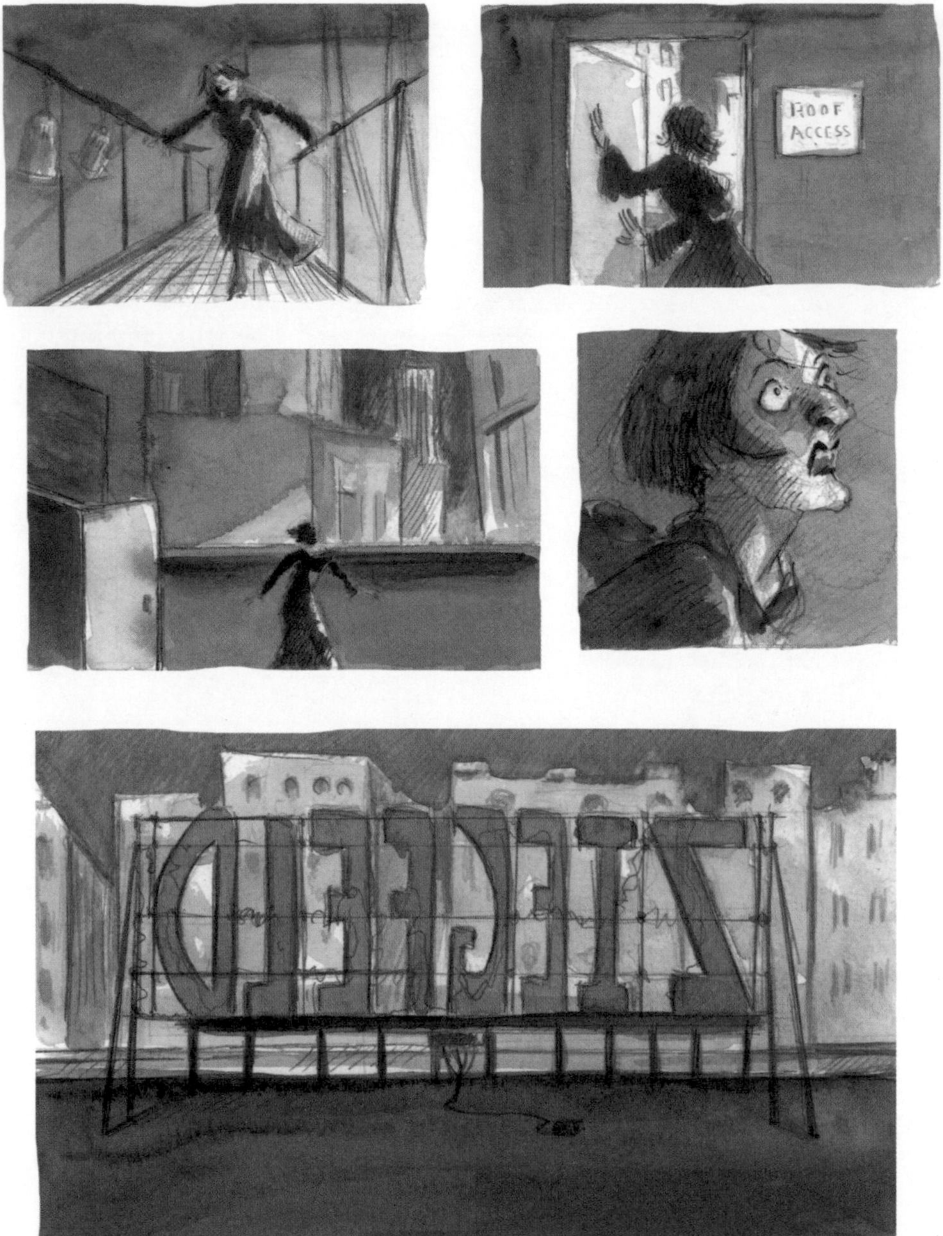
ROOF ACCESS

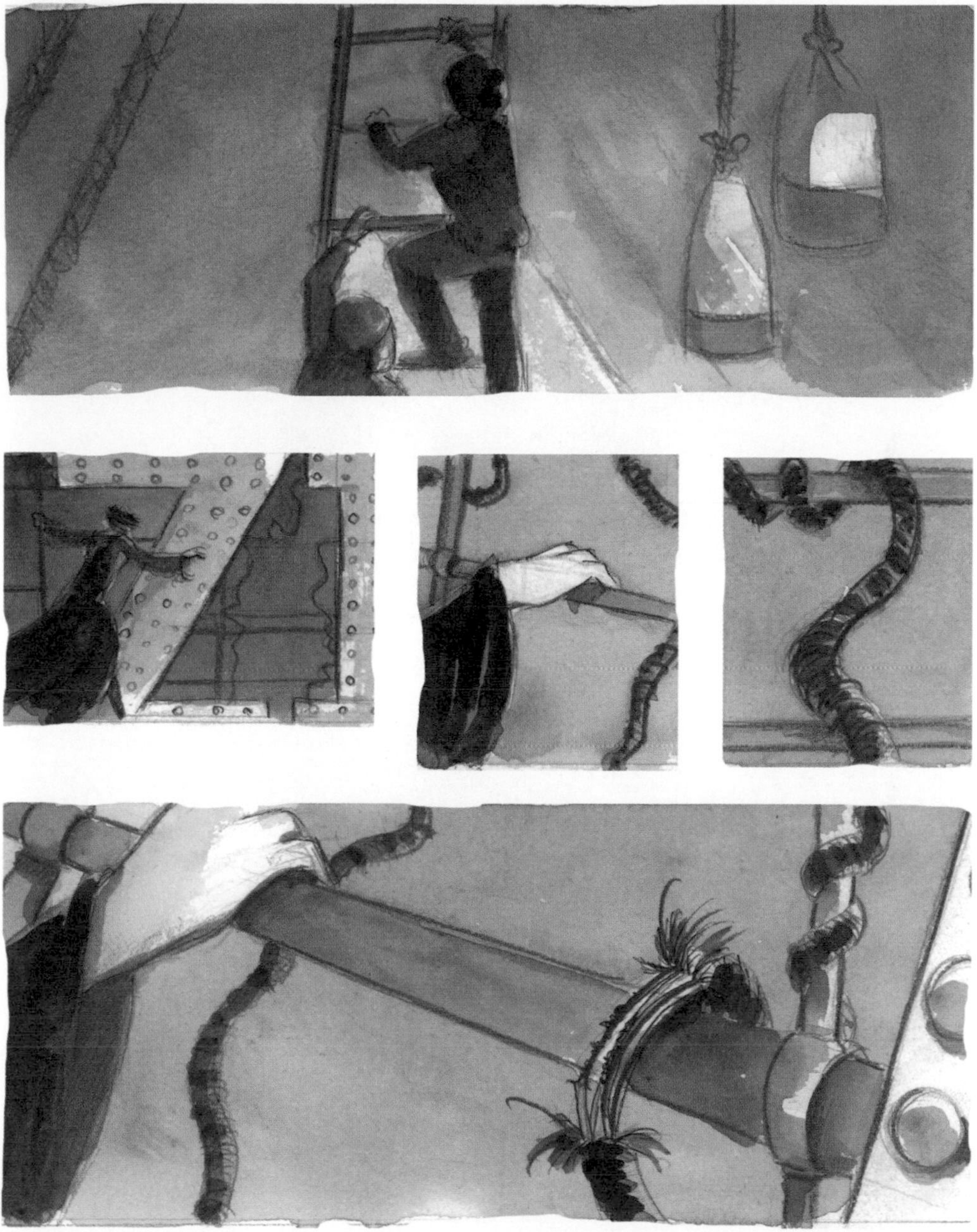

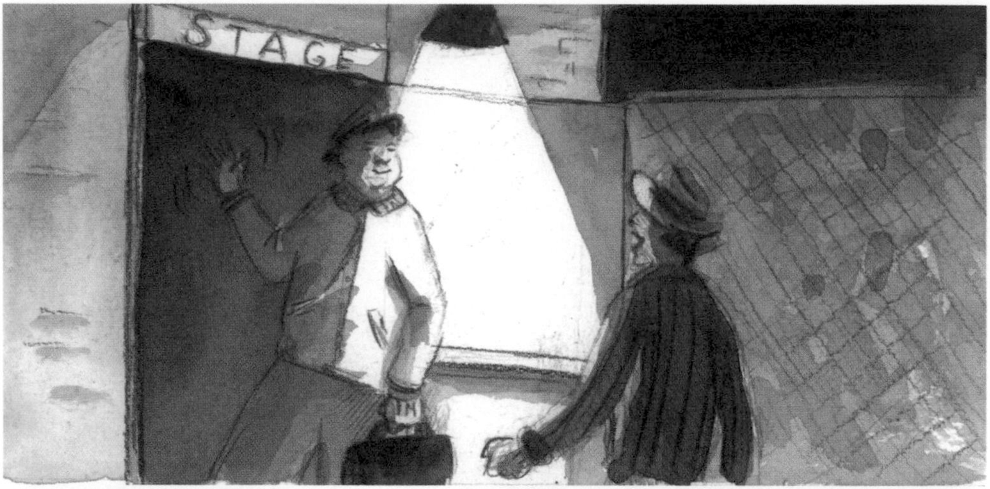
STAGE

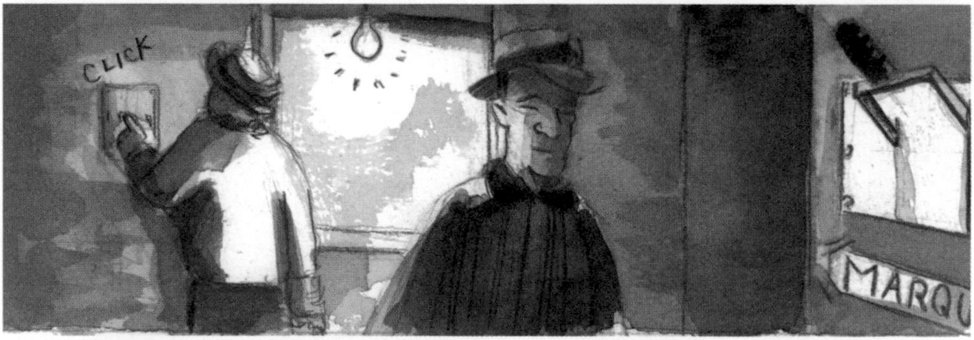
CLICK
MARQU

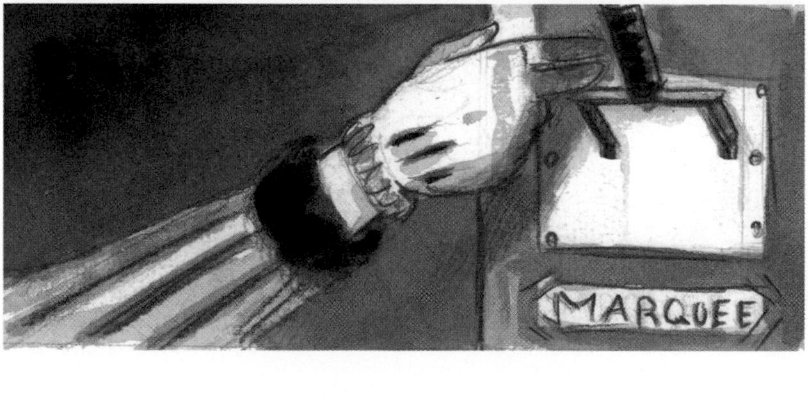
MARQUEE

THUNK
ARQUEE

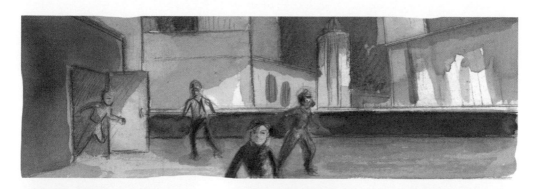

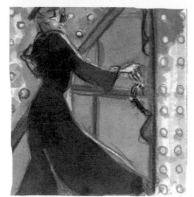

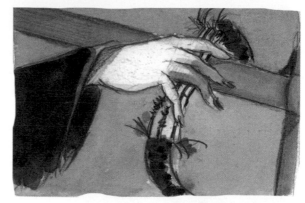

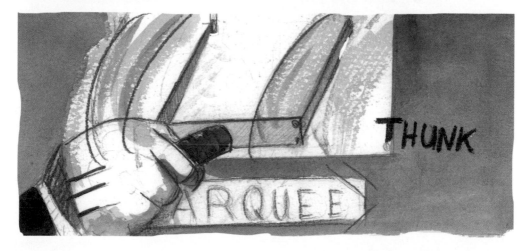

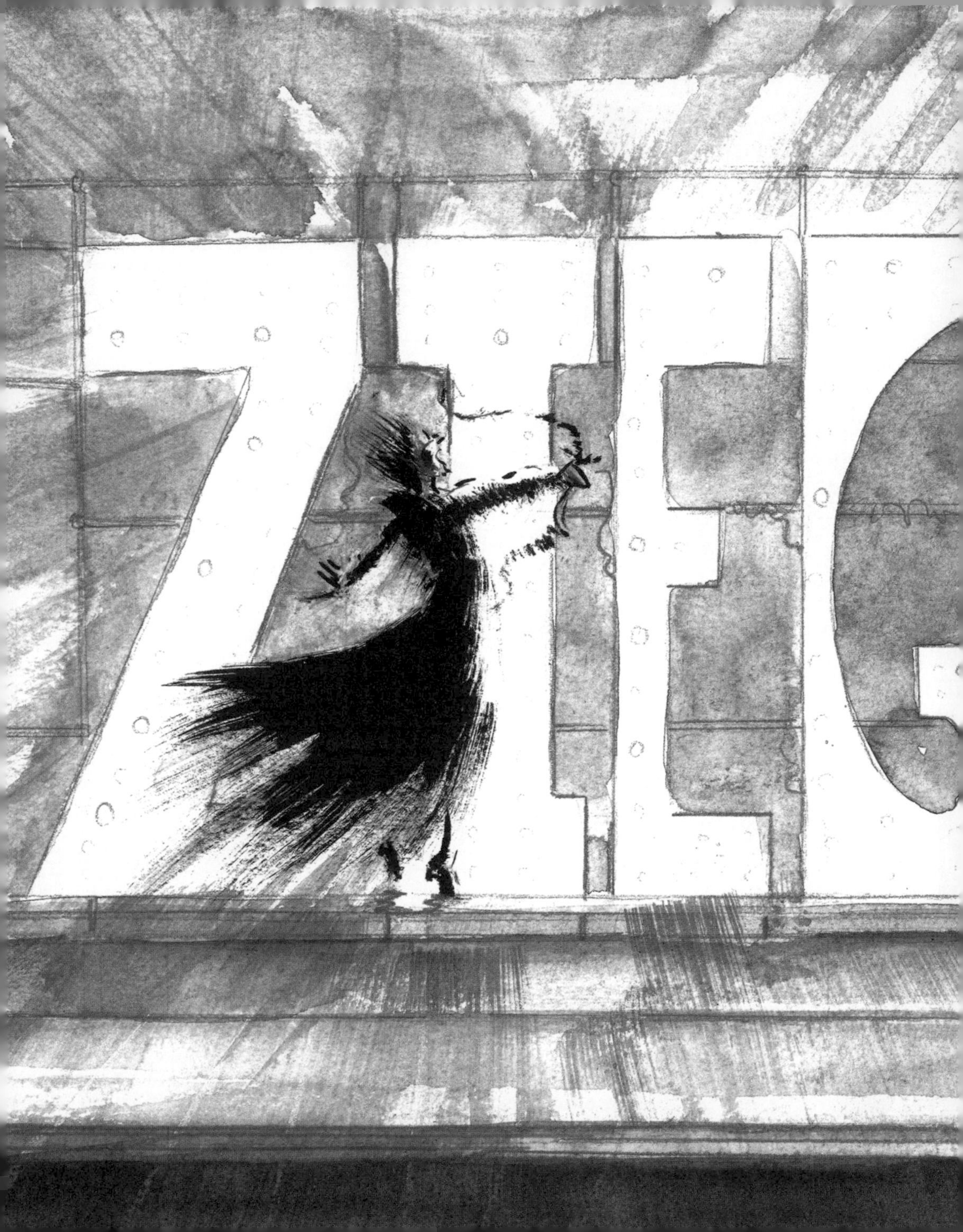

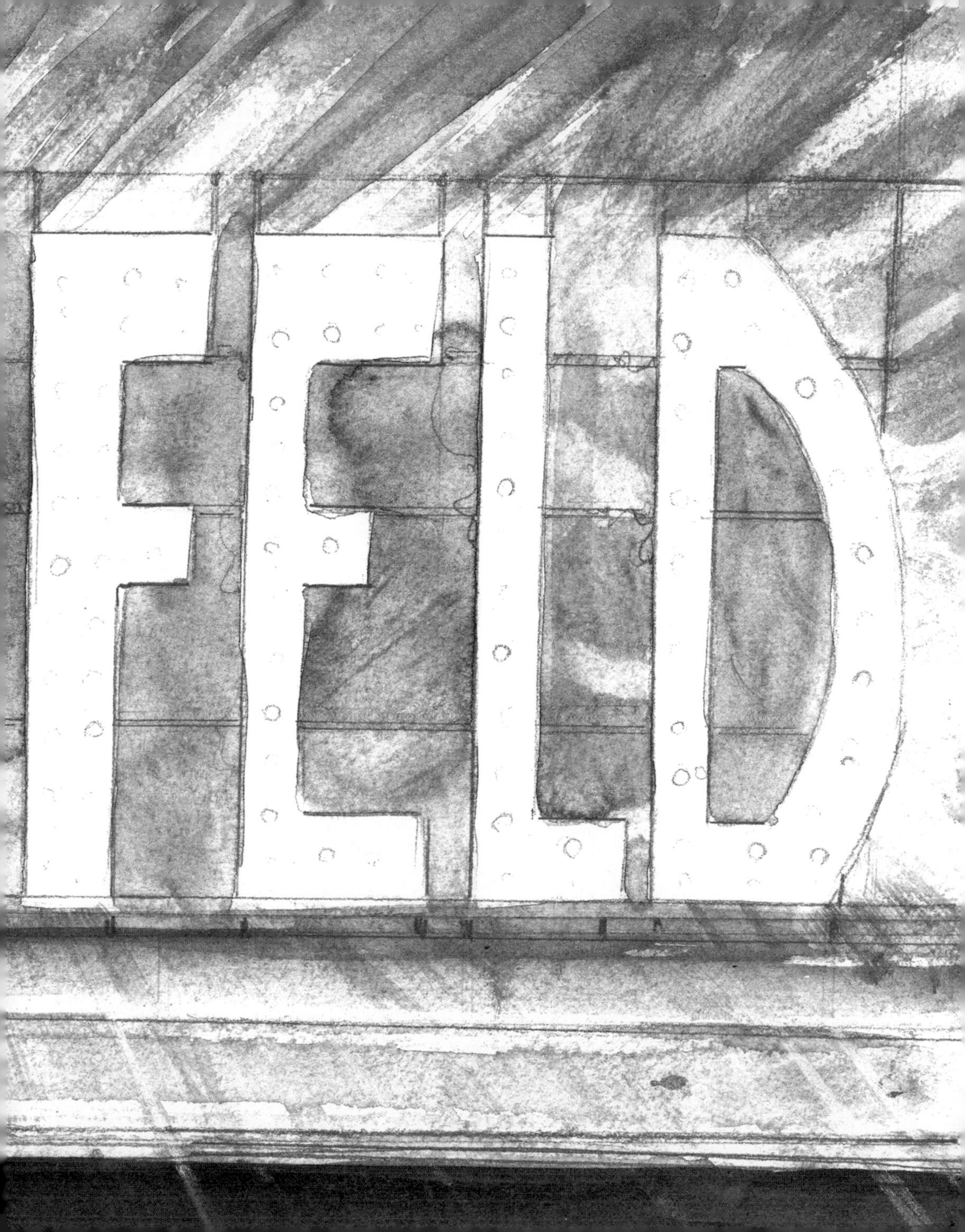
FELD

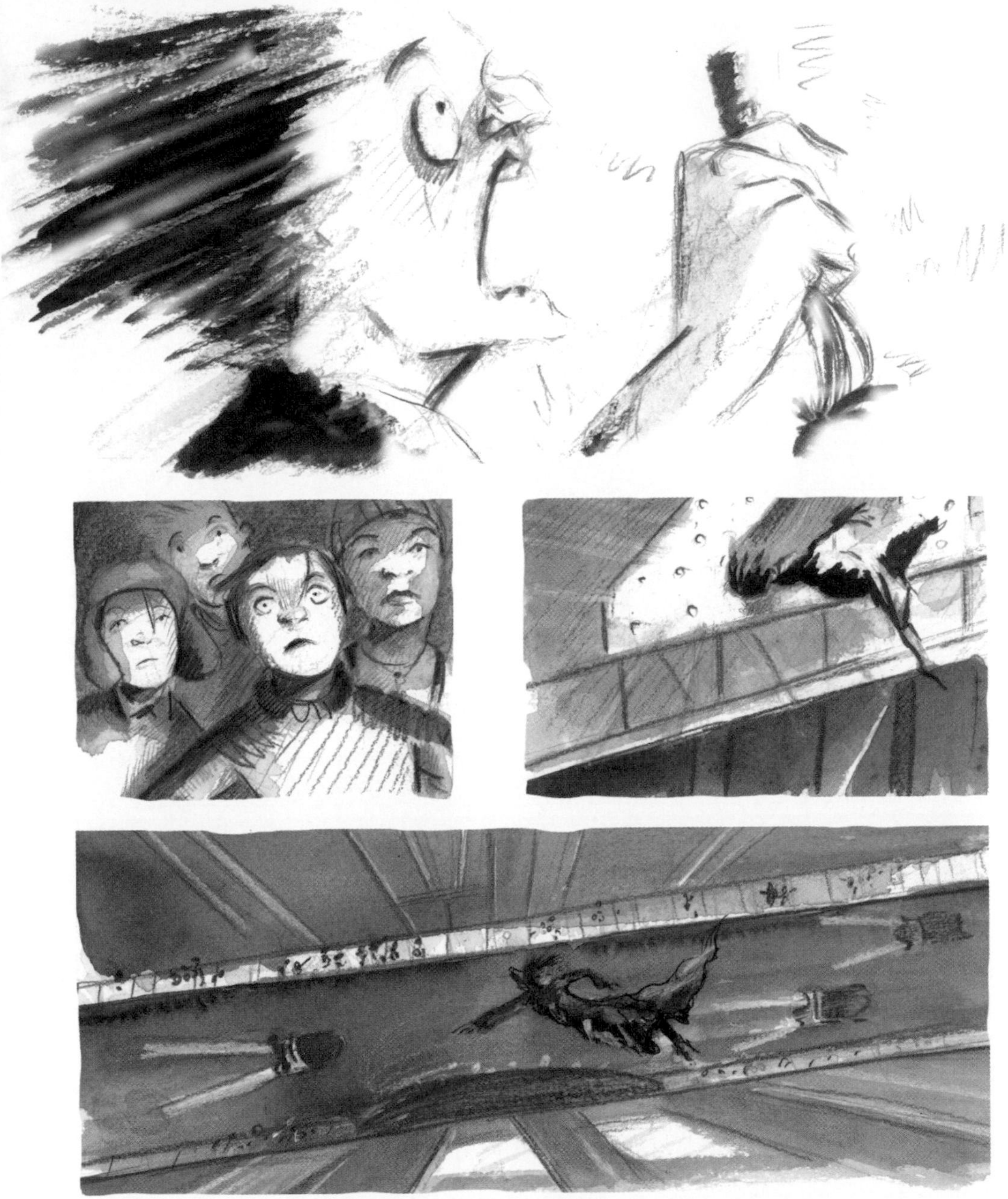

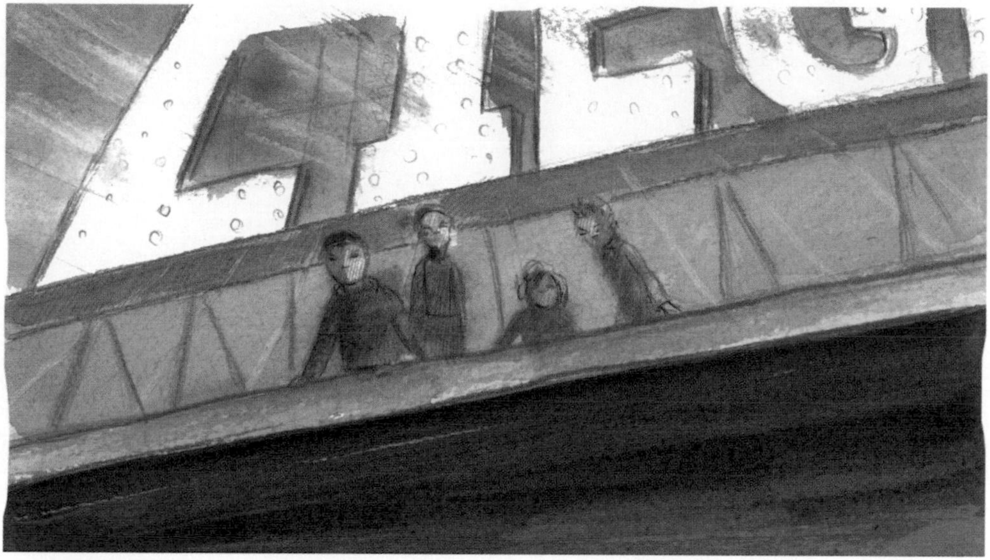

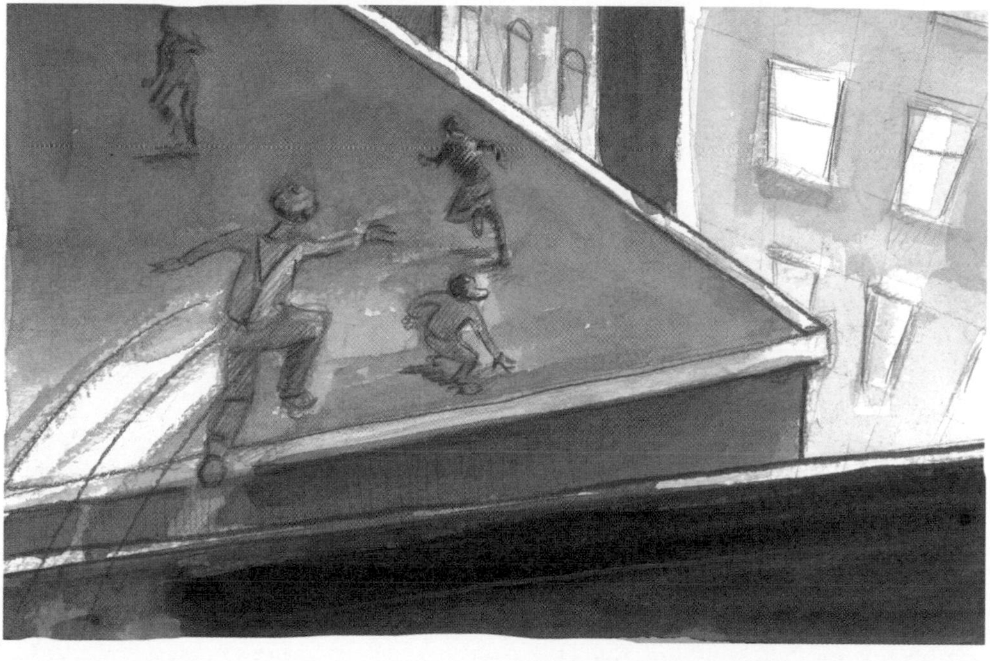

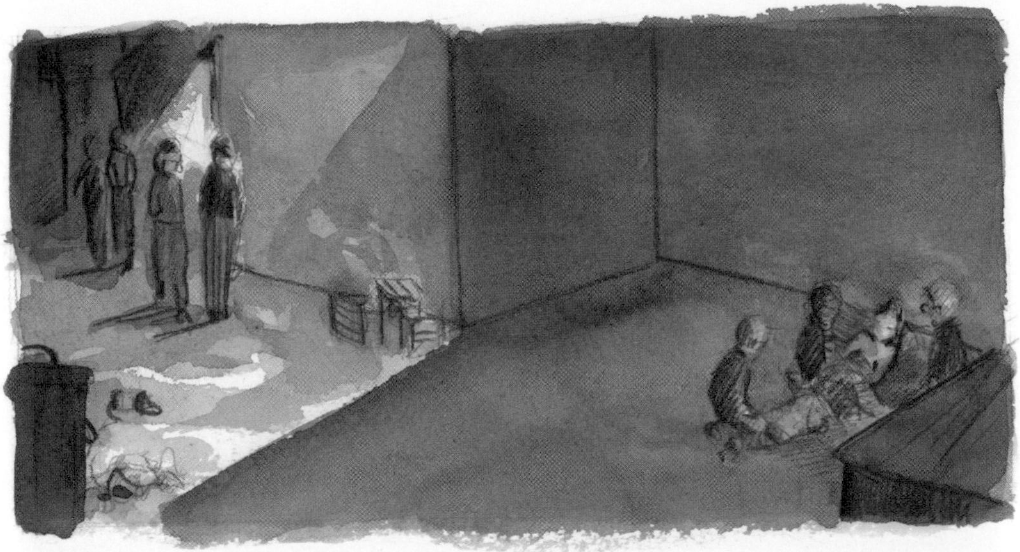

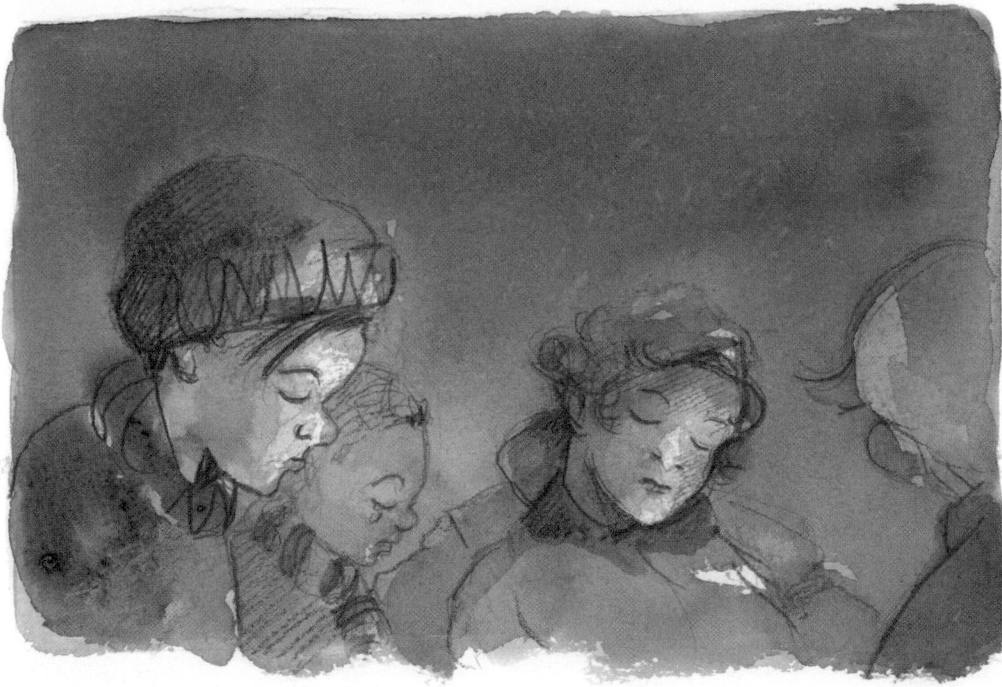

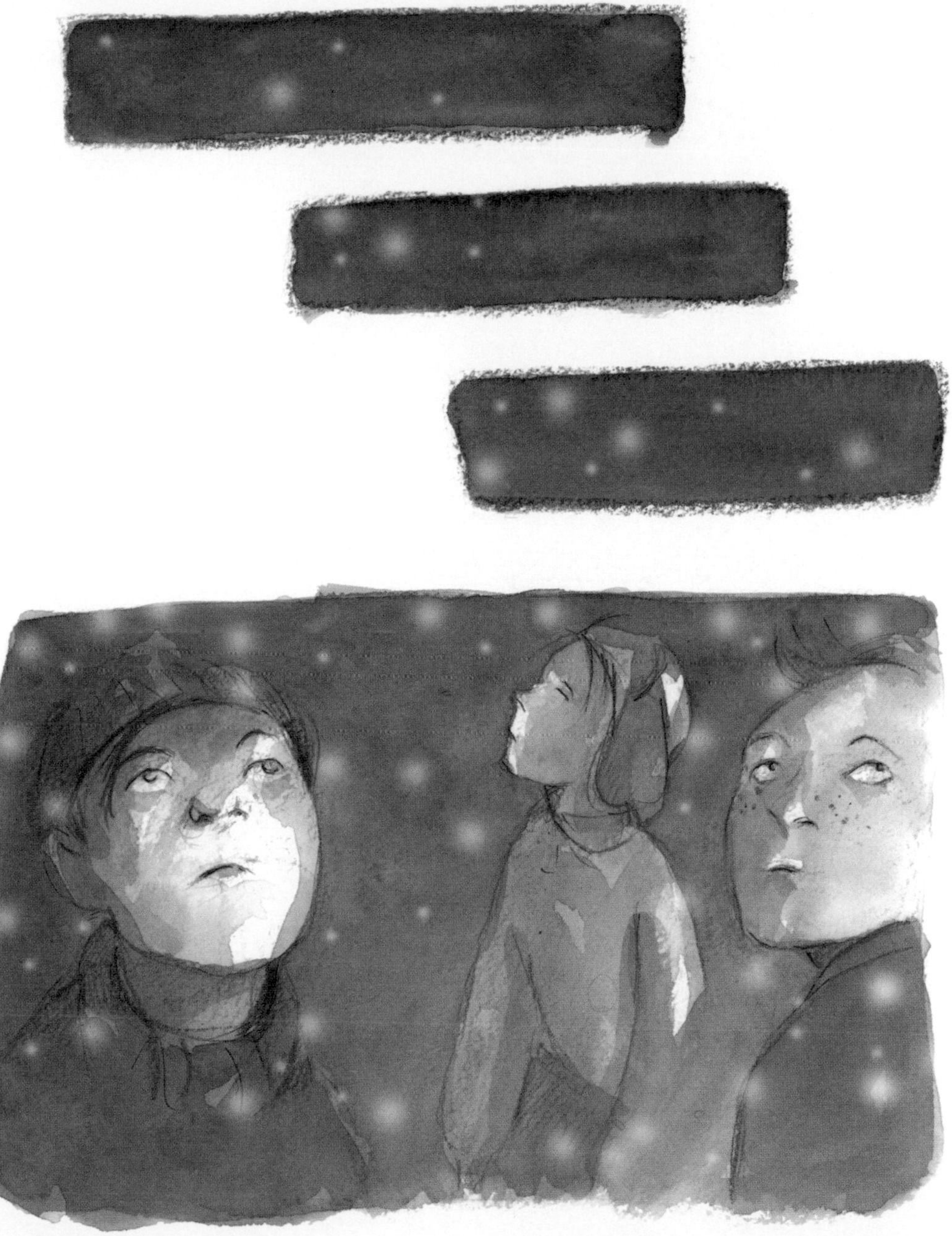

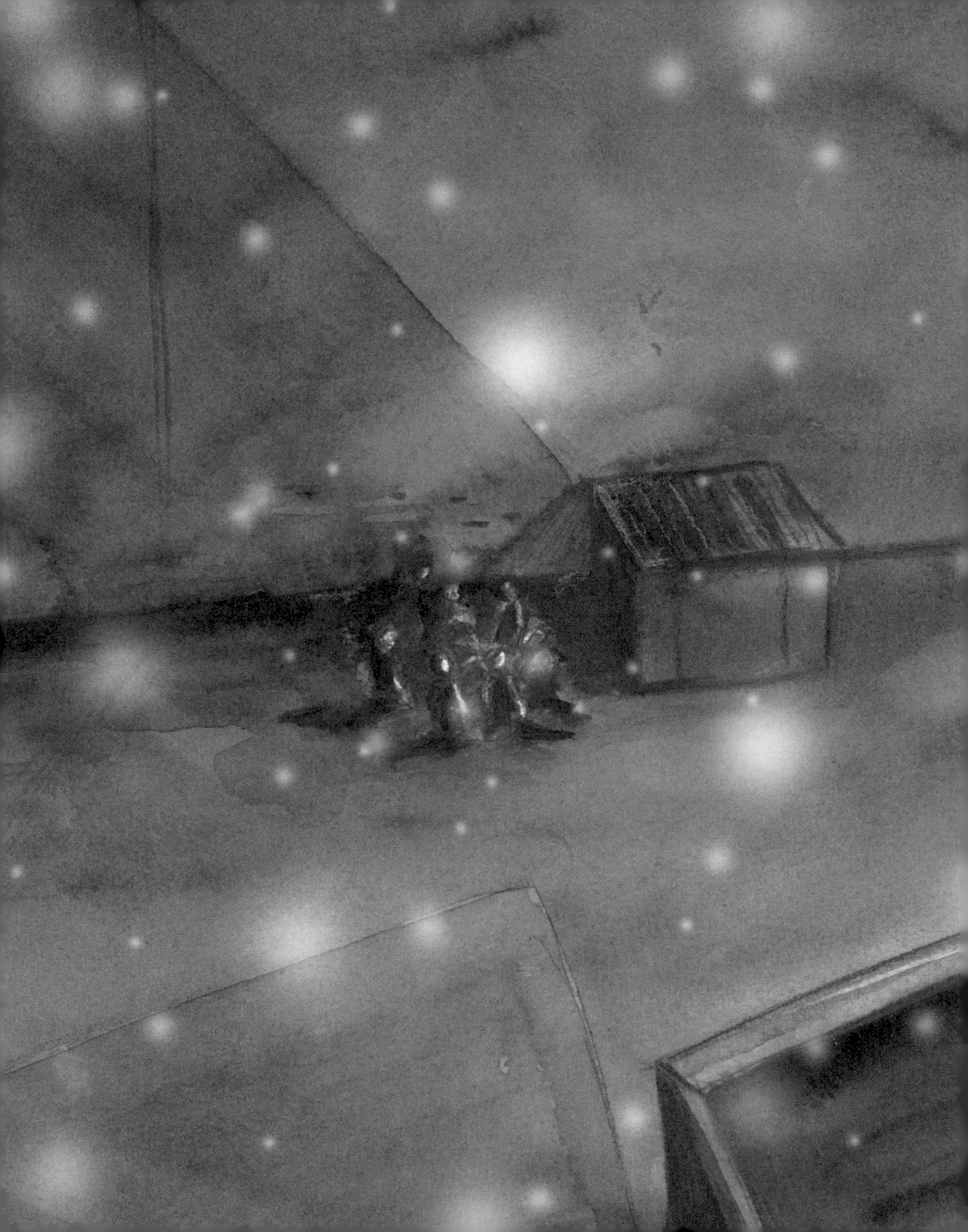

THE
GLASS
COFFIN

Closing in five minutes.
Evening, ladies.
R. H. MACY
SPLOT!
Hey!

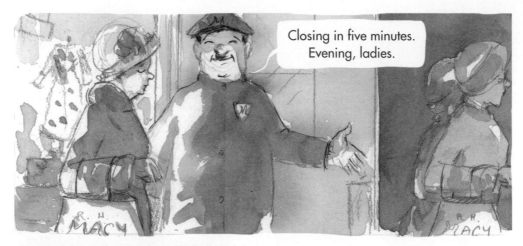

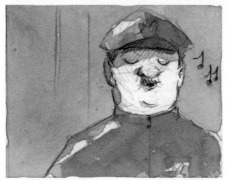

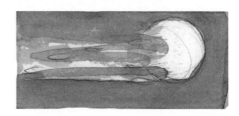

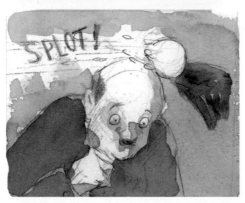

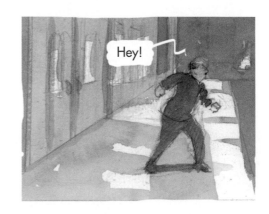

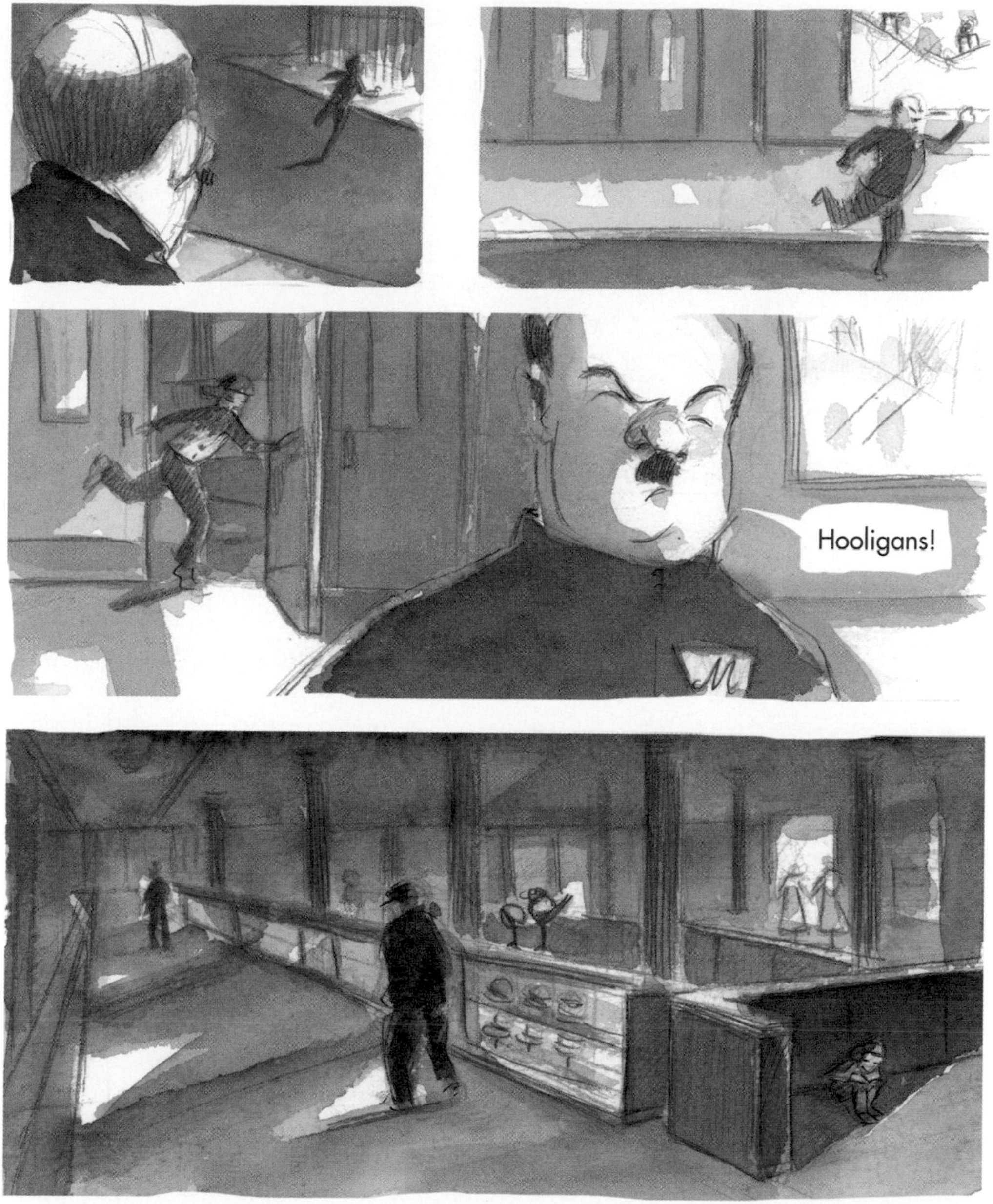
Hooligans!

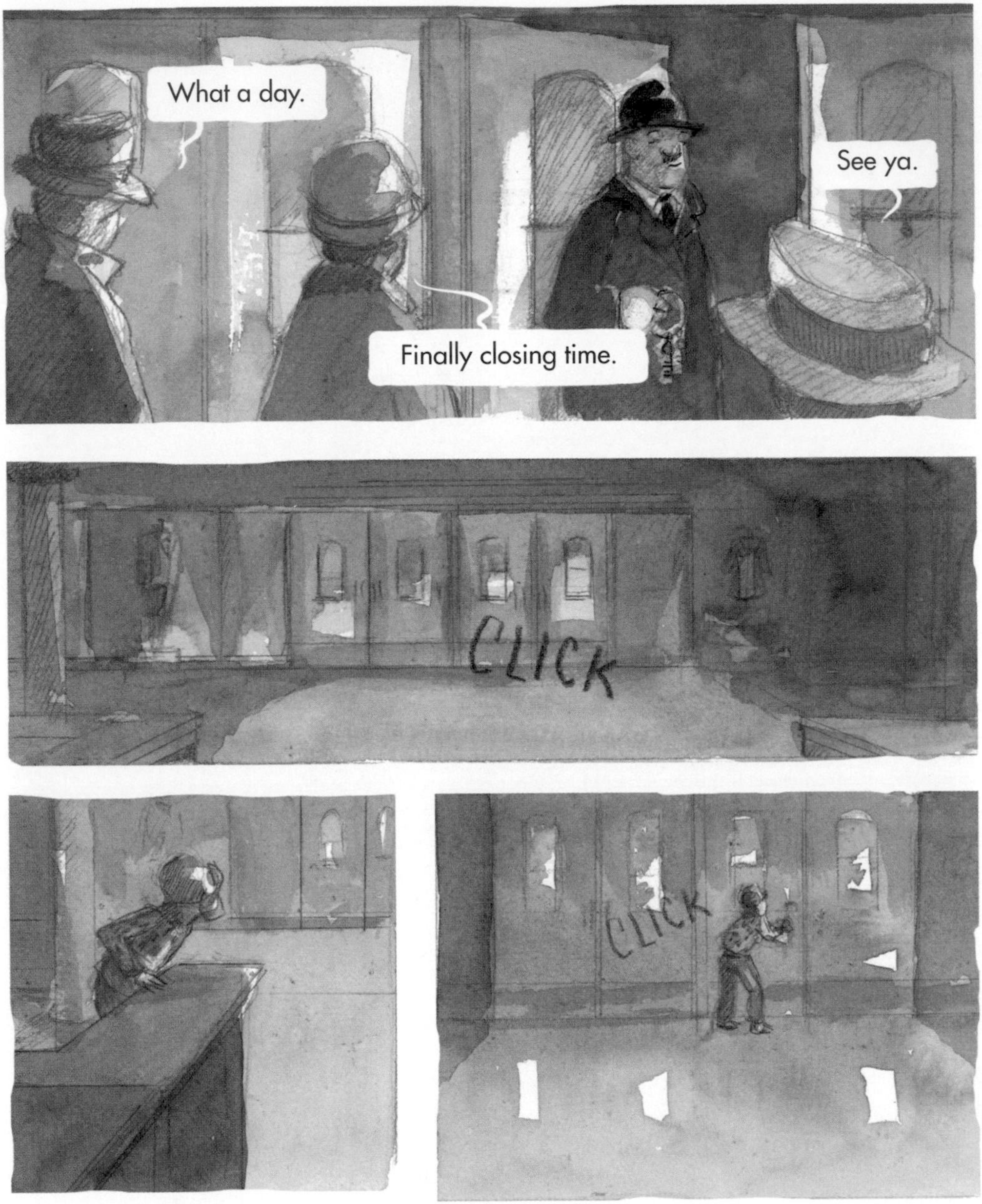
What a day.
Finally closing time.
See ya.
CLICK
CLICK

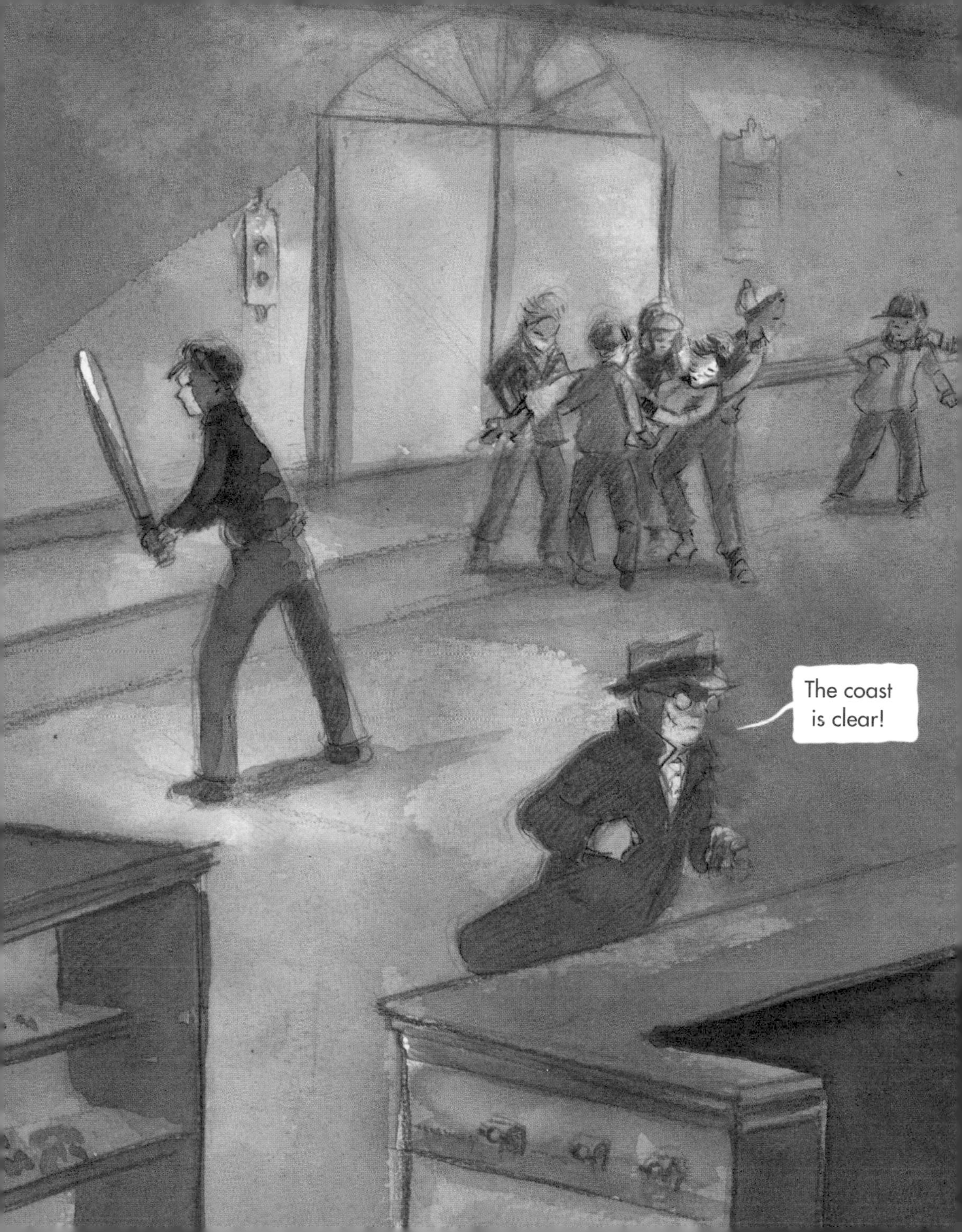
The coast is clear!

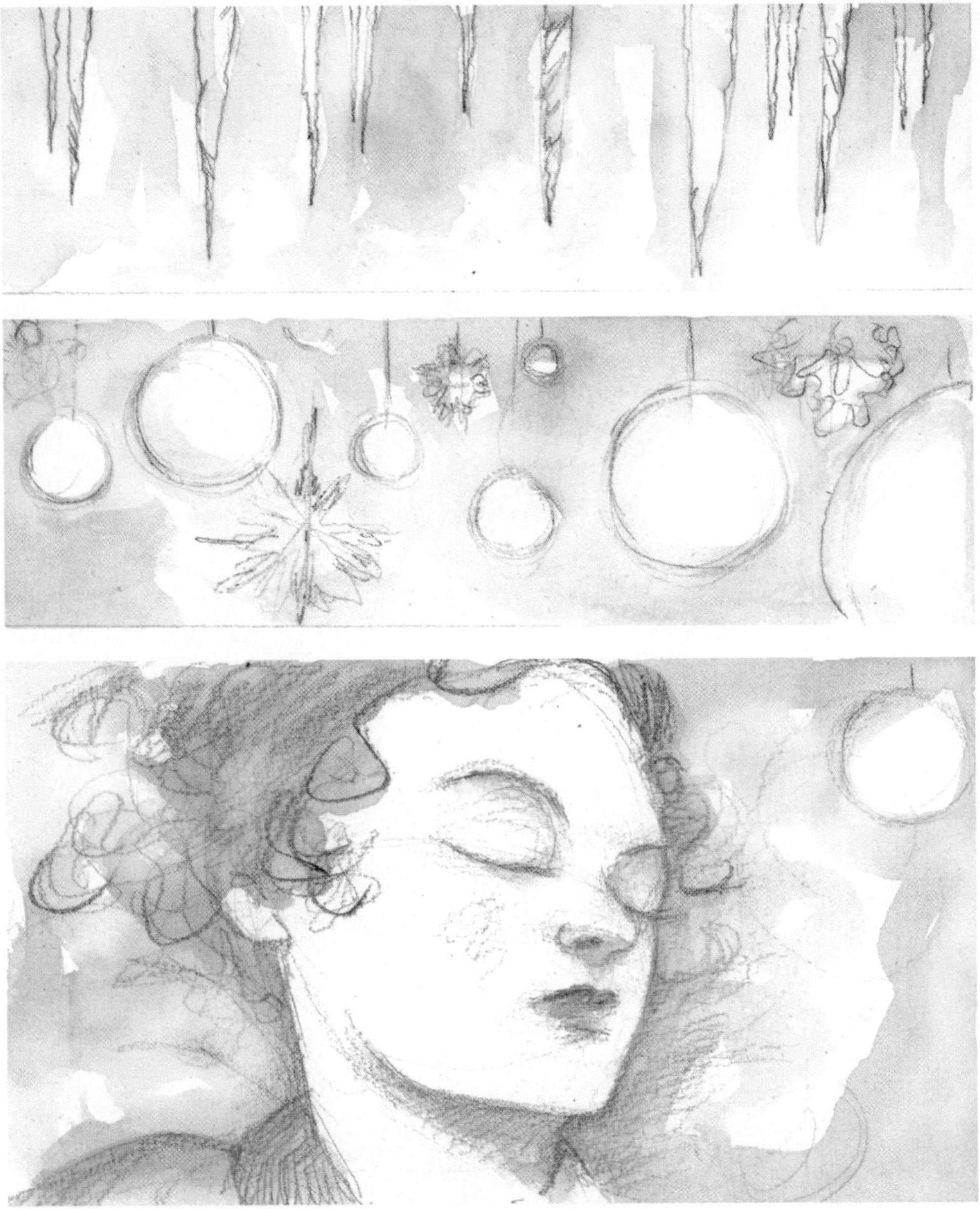

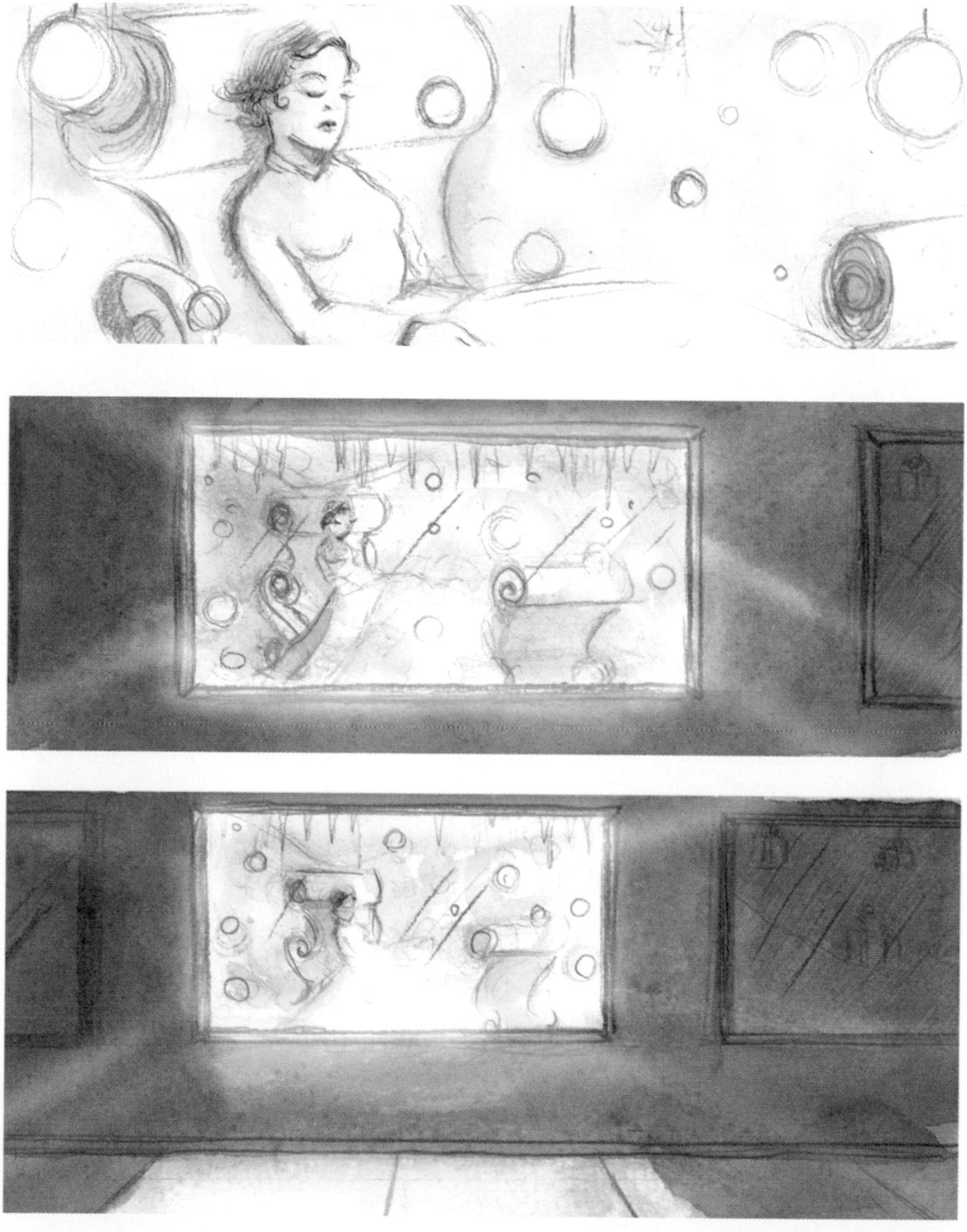

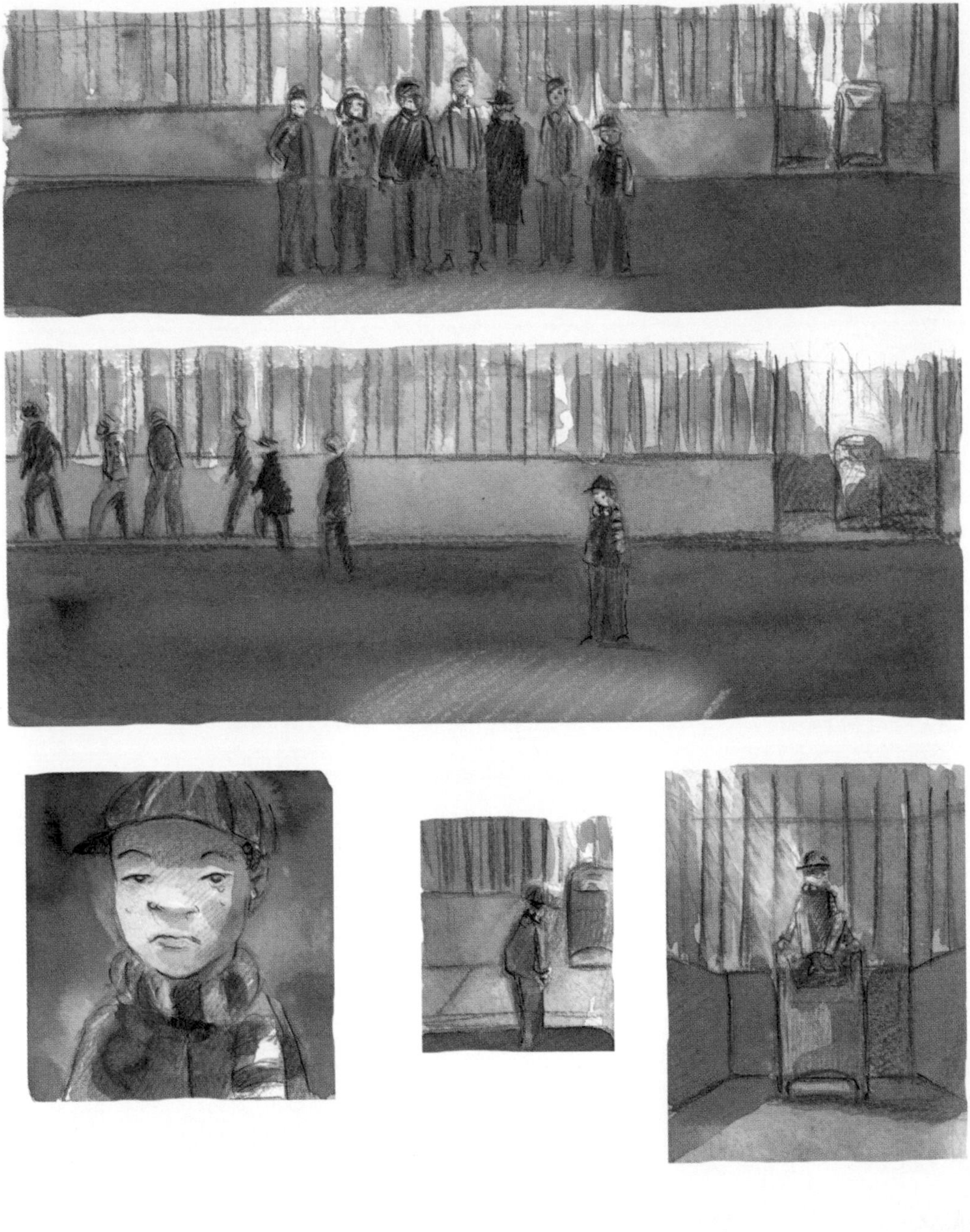

DETECTIVE PRINCE
OVERSTEPS HIS
BOUNDS

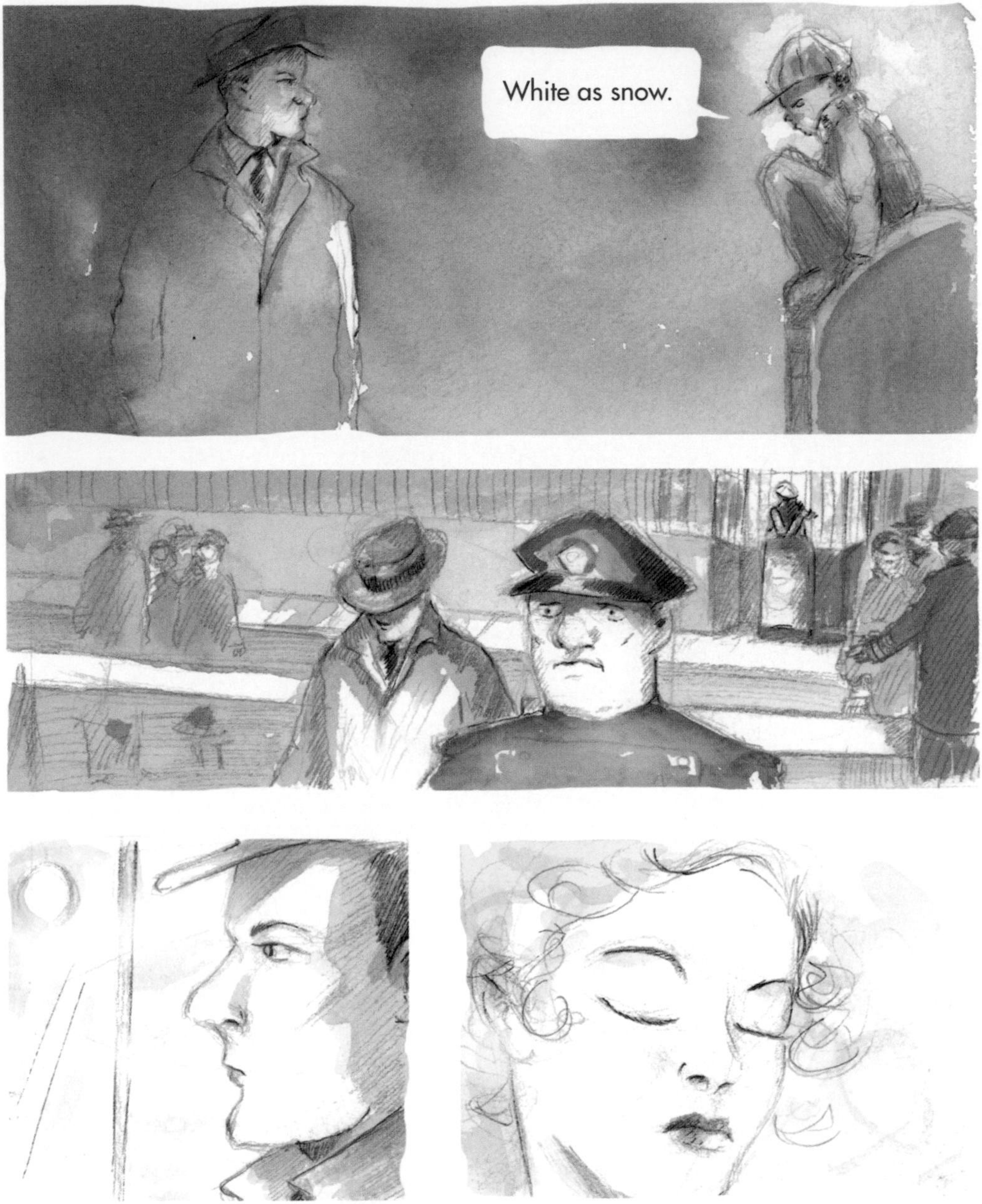
White as snow.

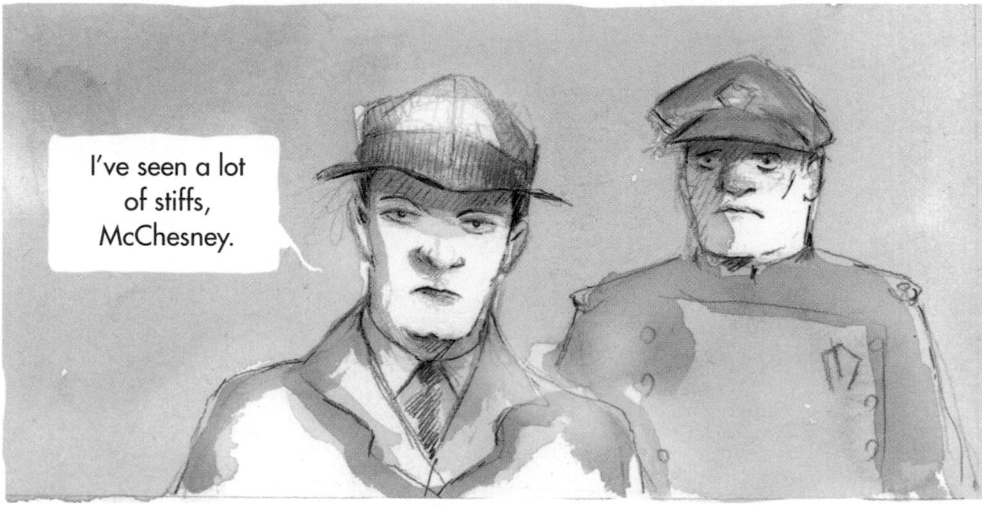
I've seen a lot of stiffs, McChesney.

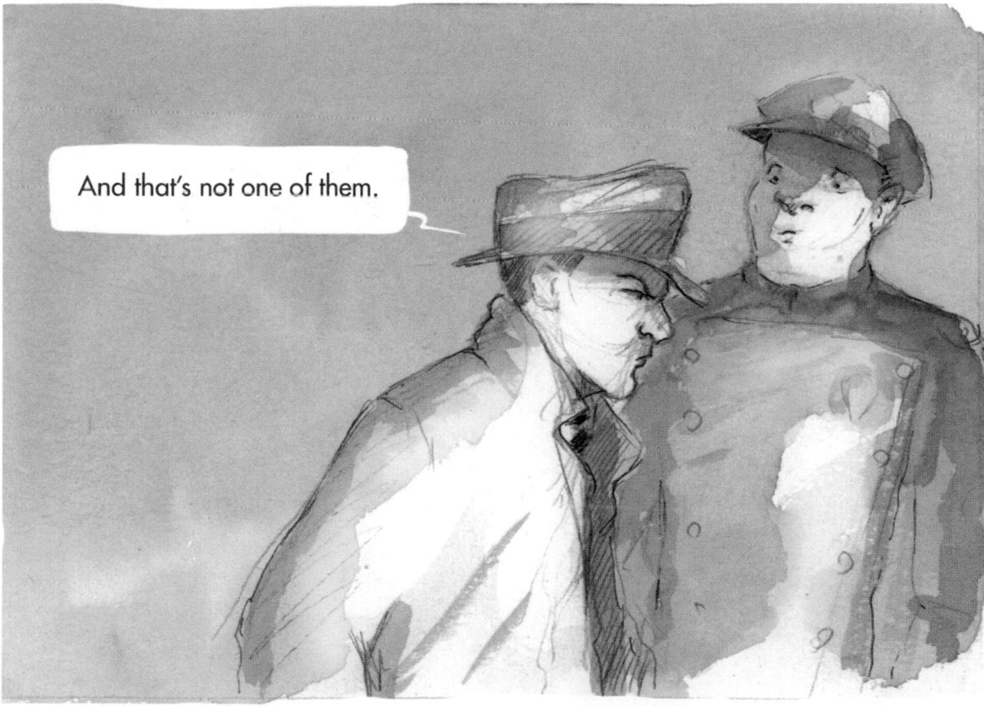
And that's not one of them.

Hold it.

Gimme a minute, Phil.

Sure thing, Detective.

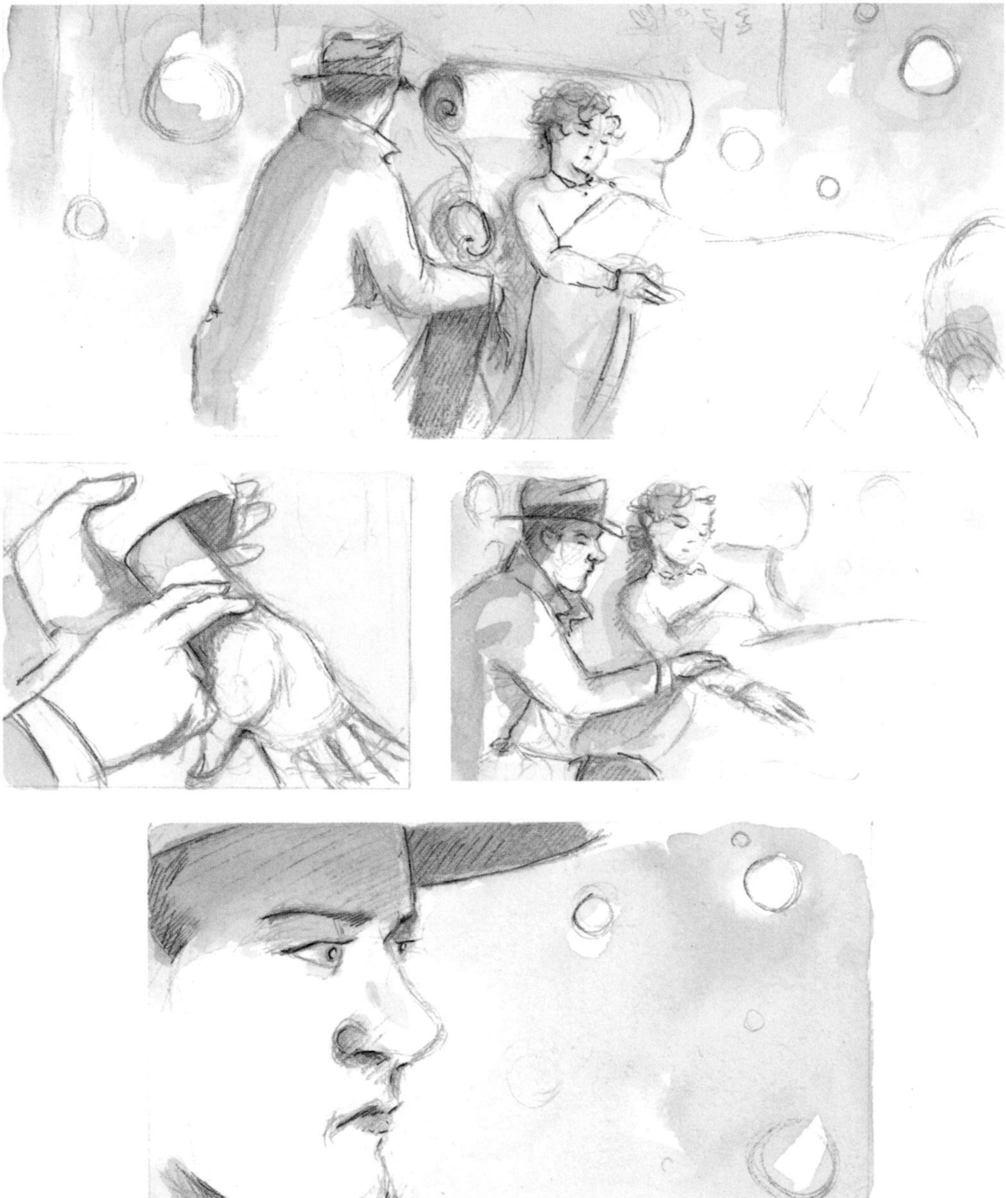

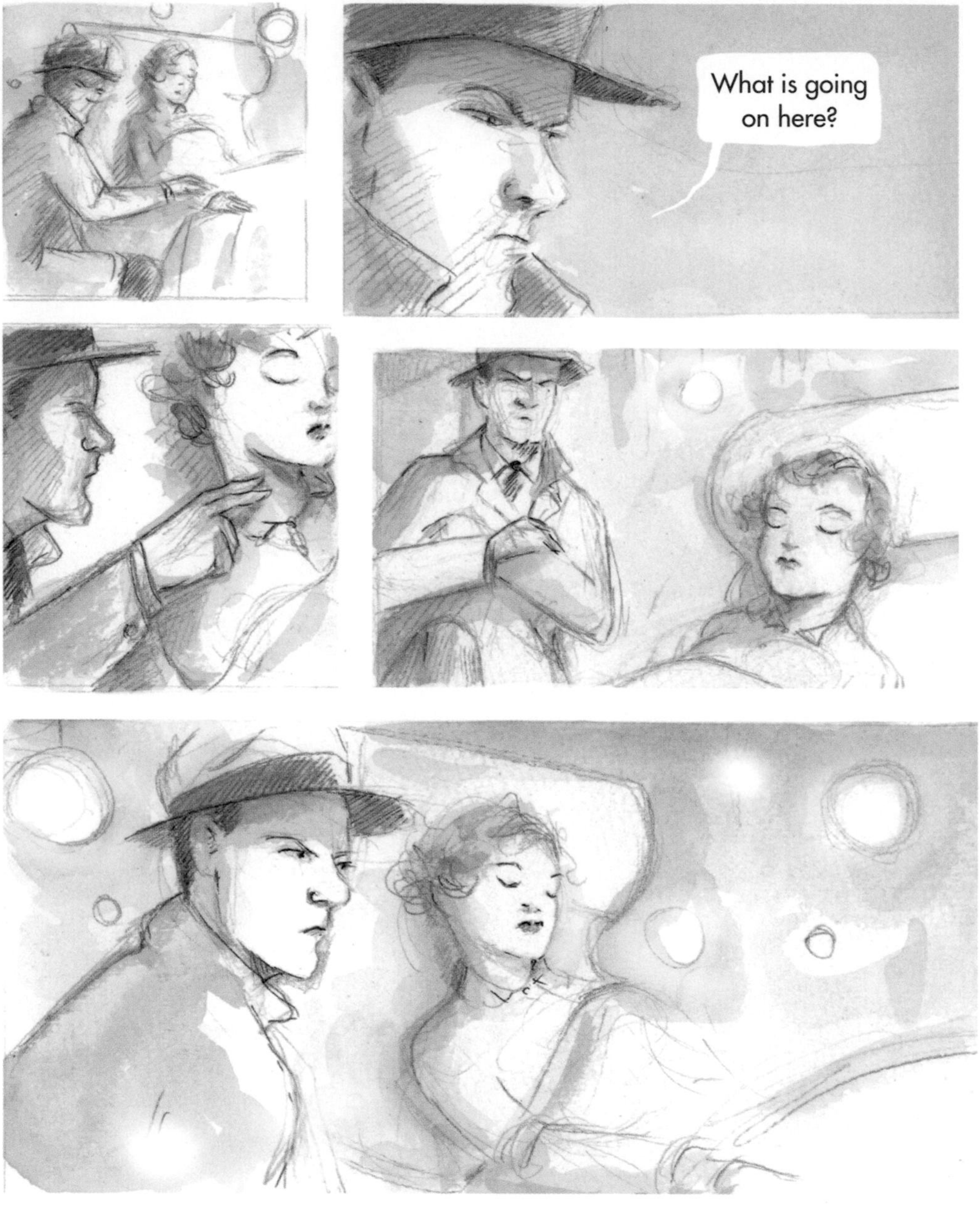
What is going on here?

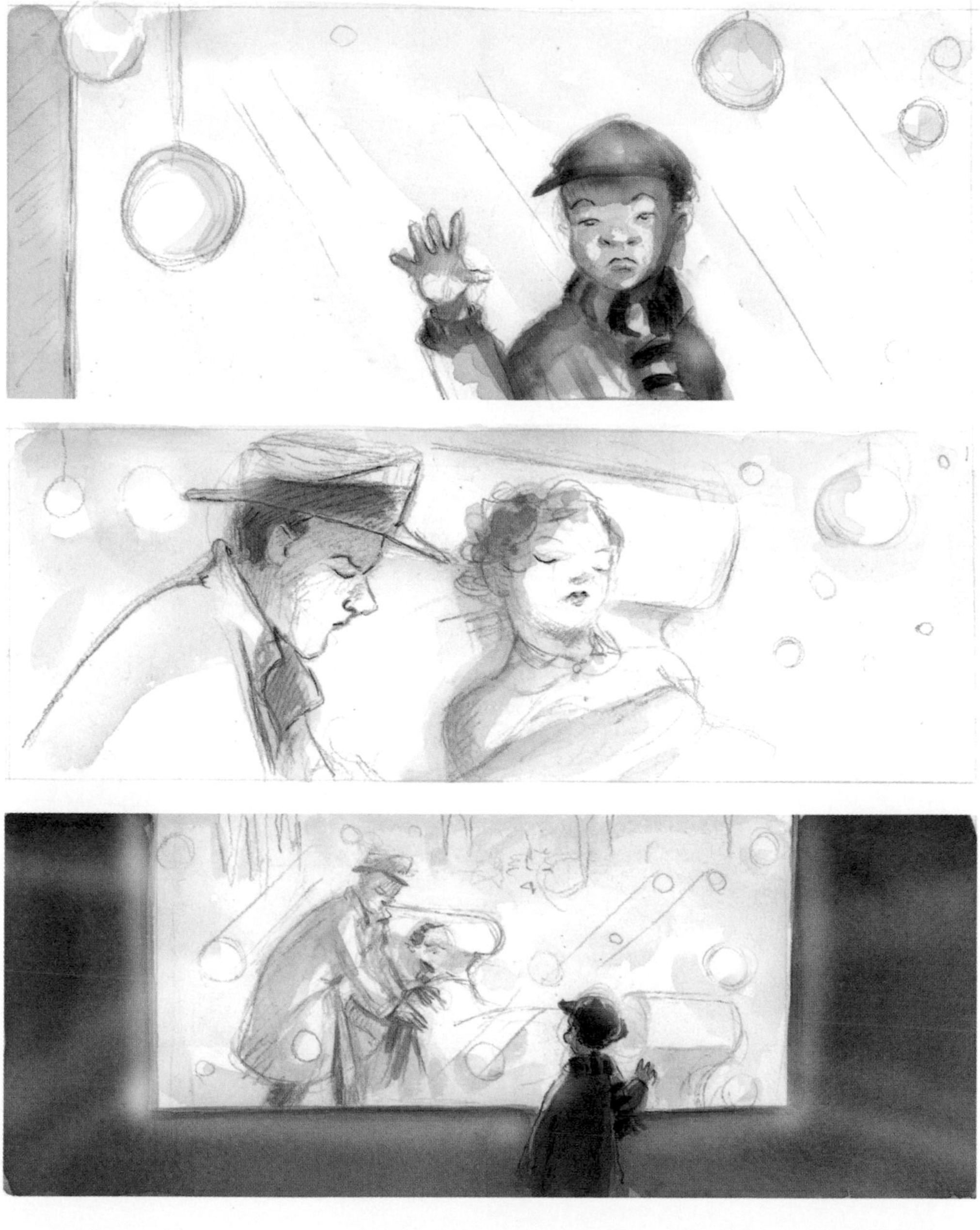

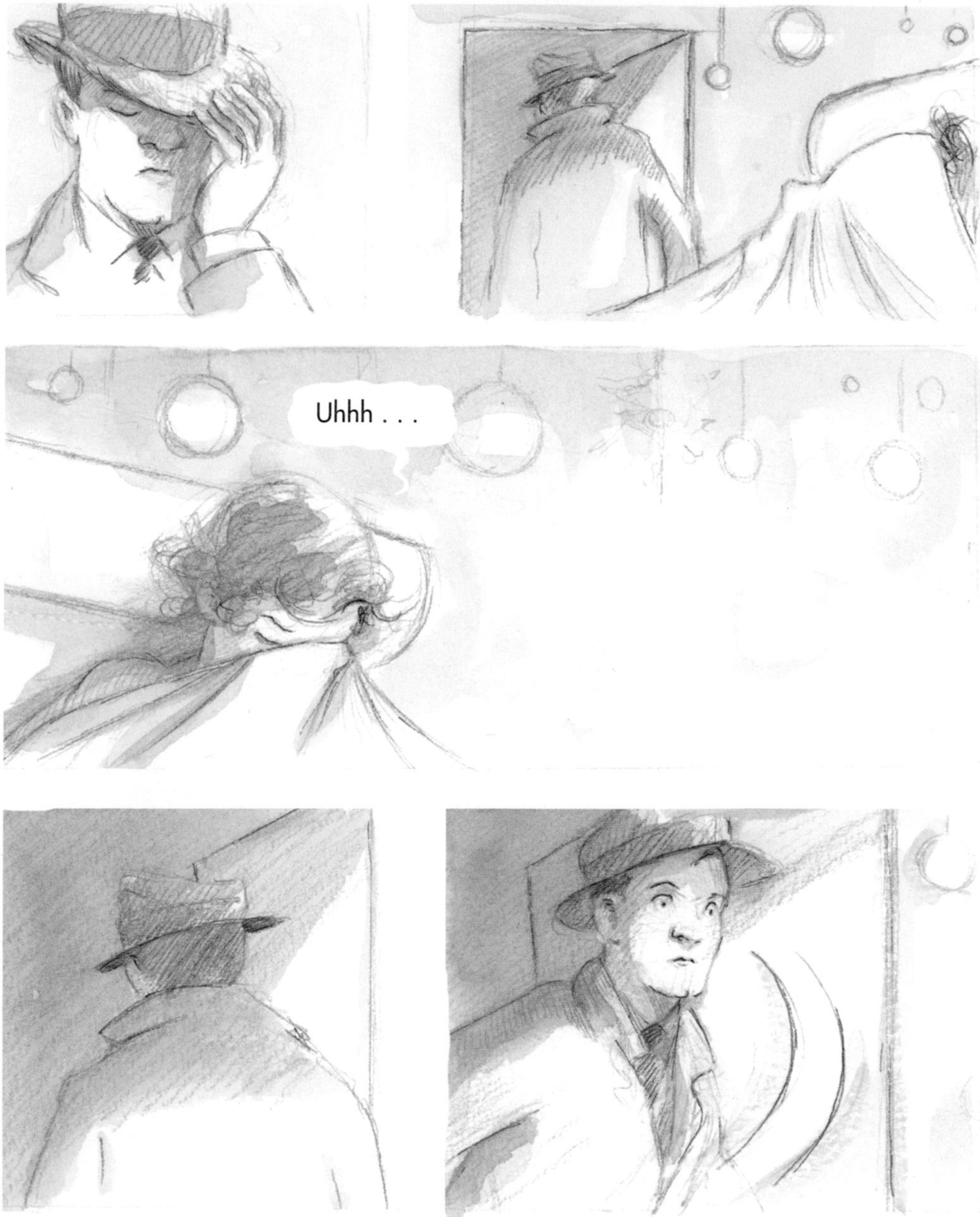
Uhhh . . .

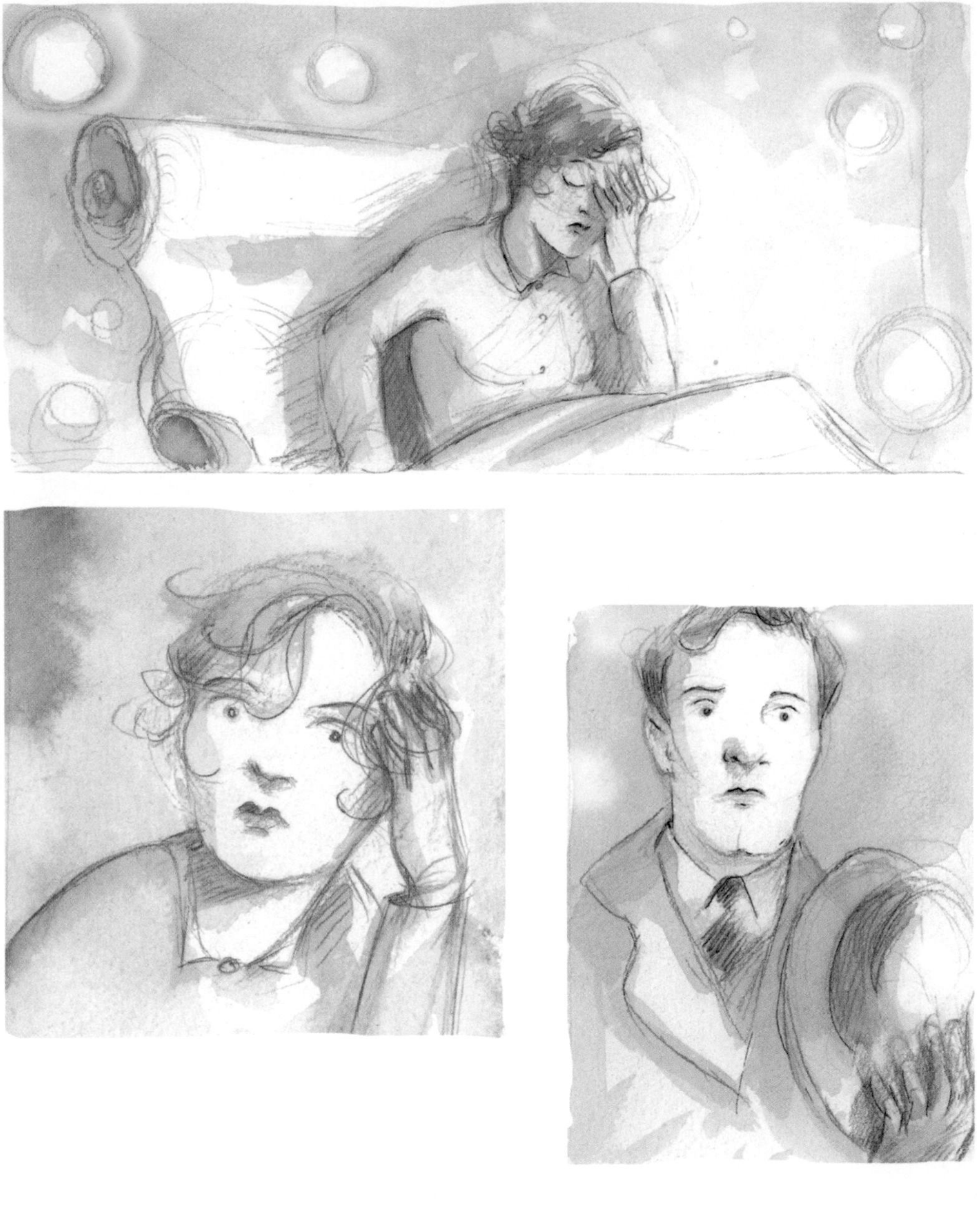

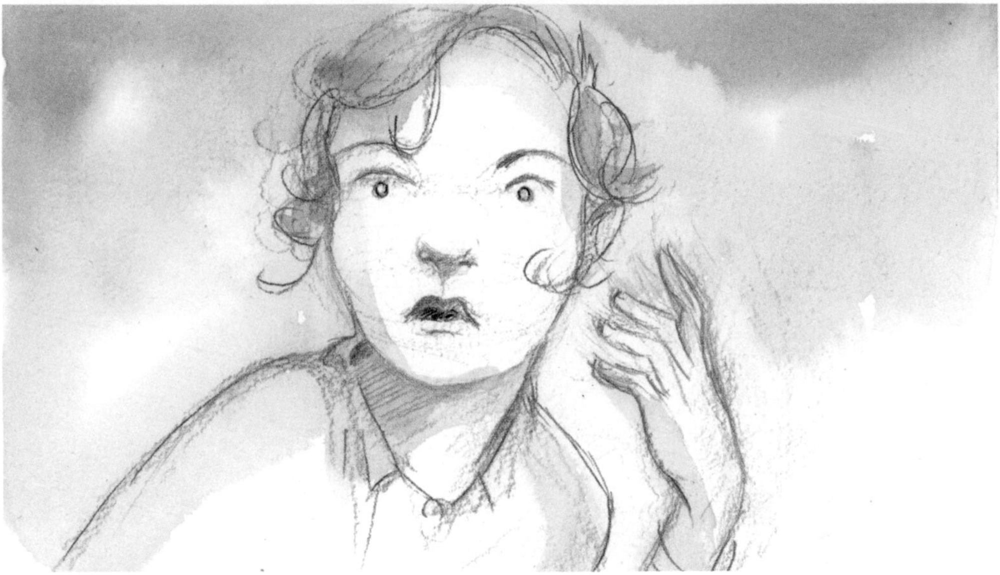

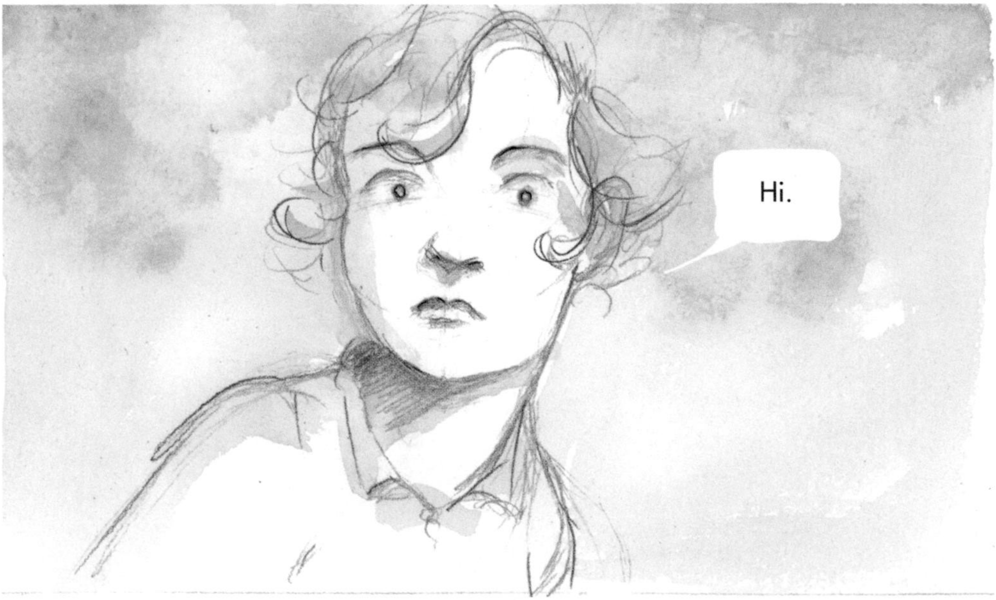
Hi.

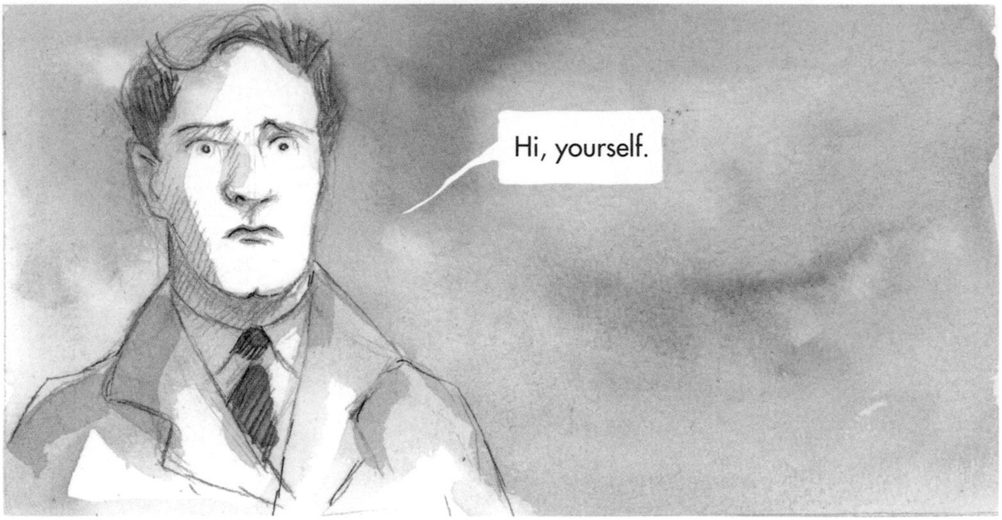
Hi, yourself.

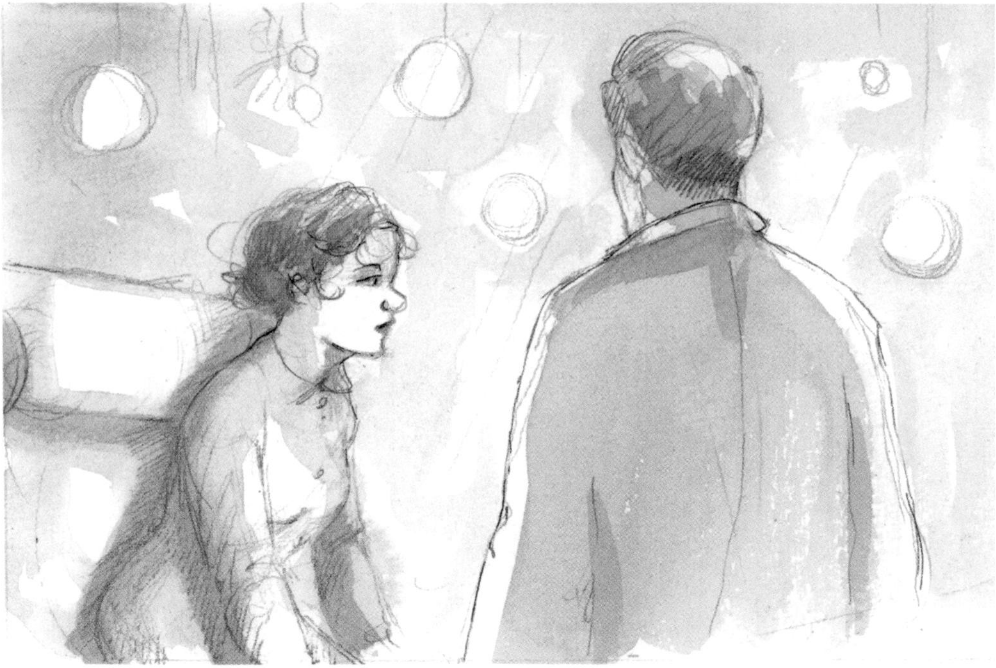

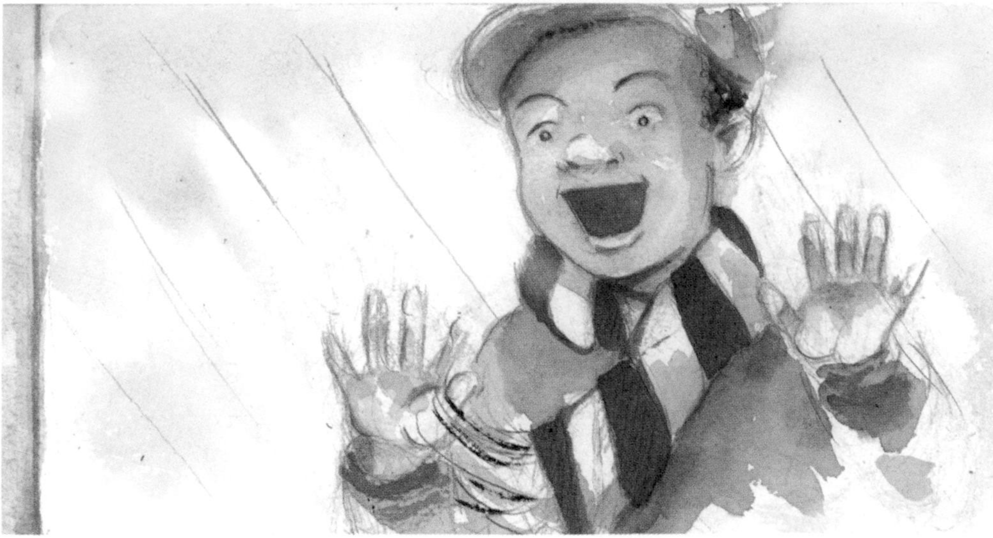

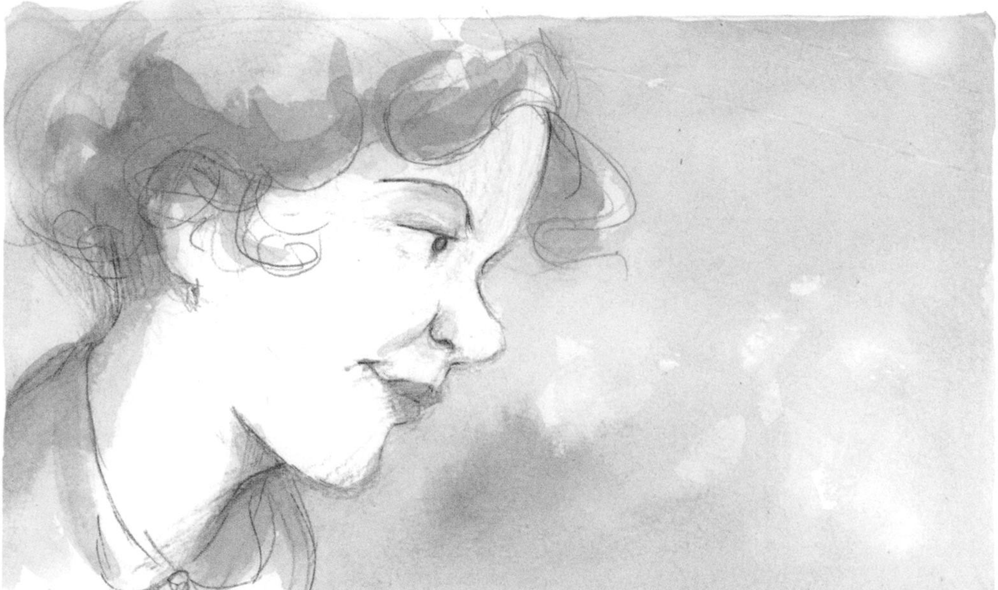

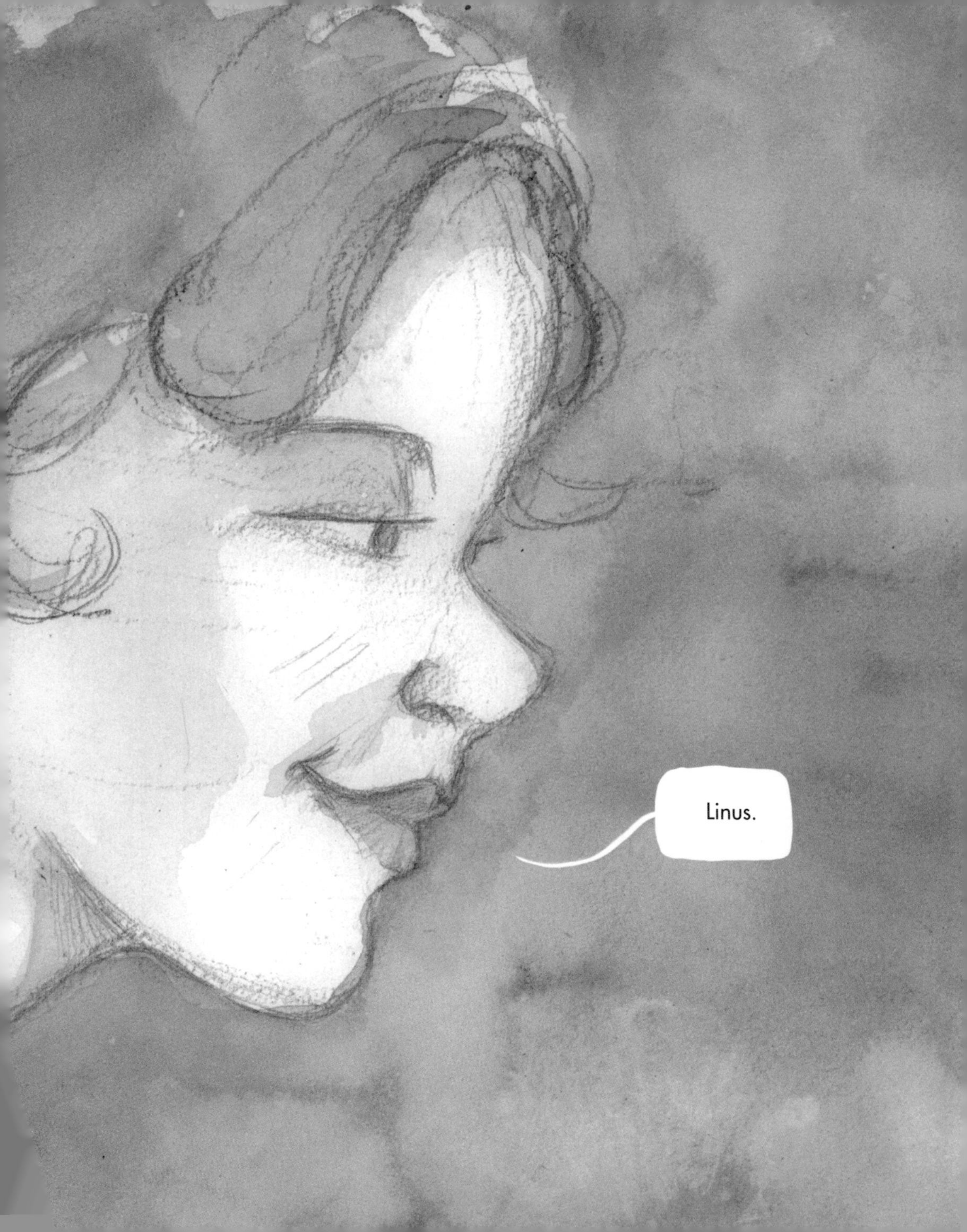
Linus.

AND THEY
LIVED . . .

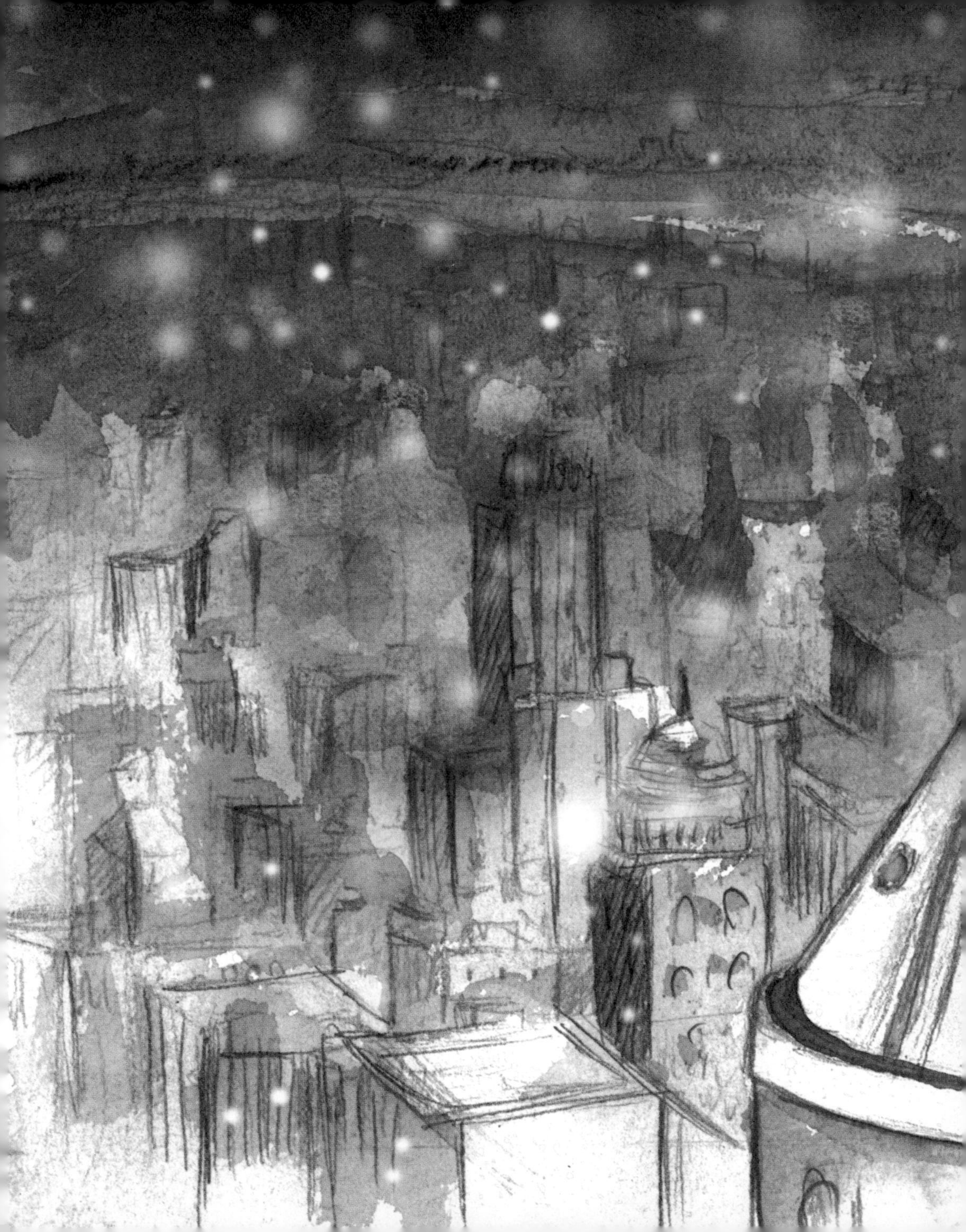

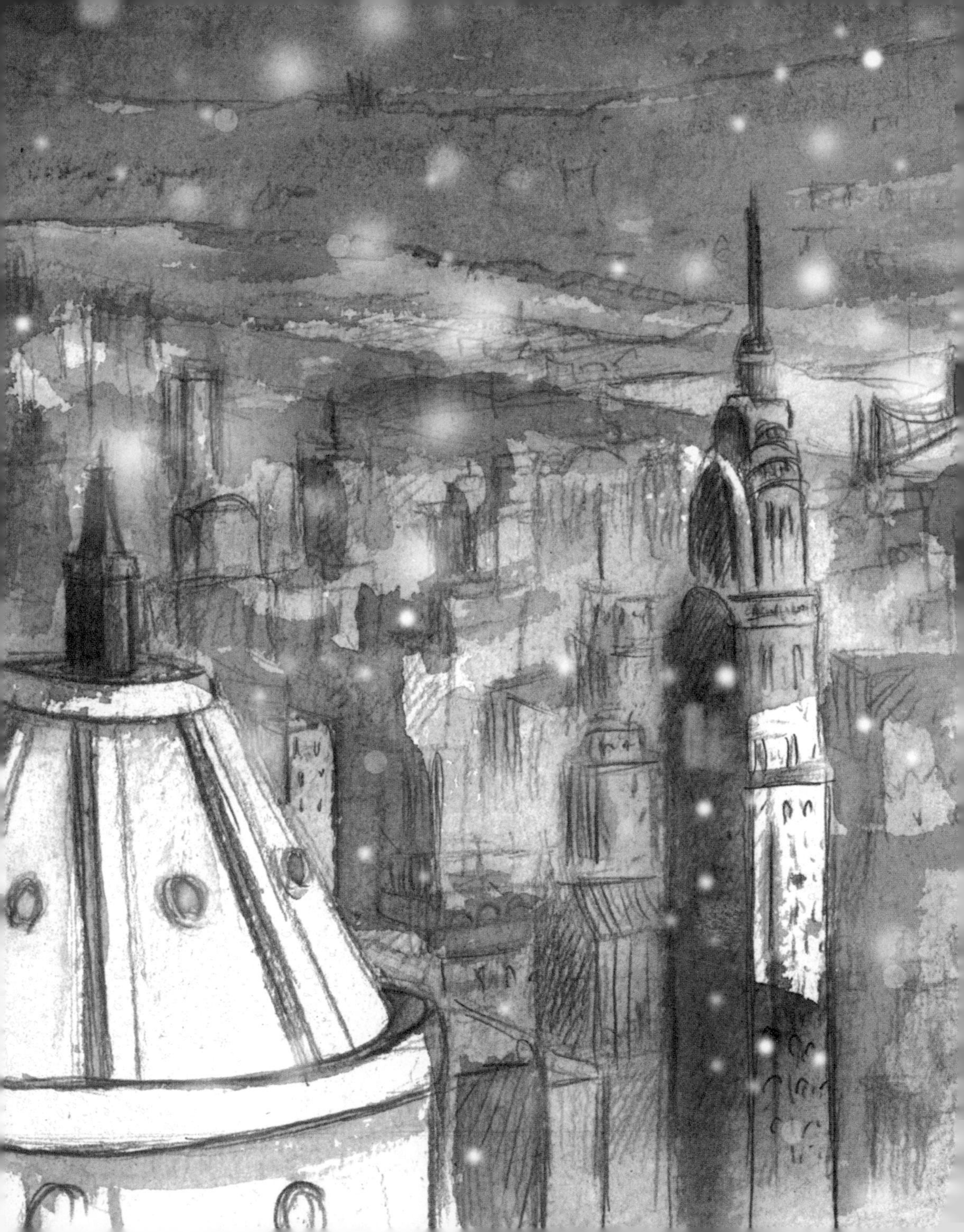

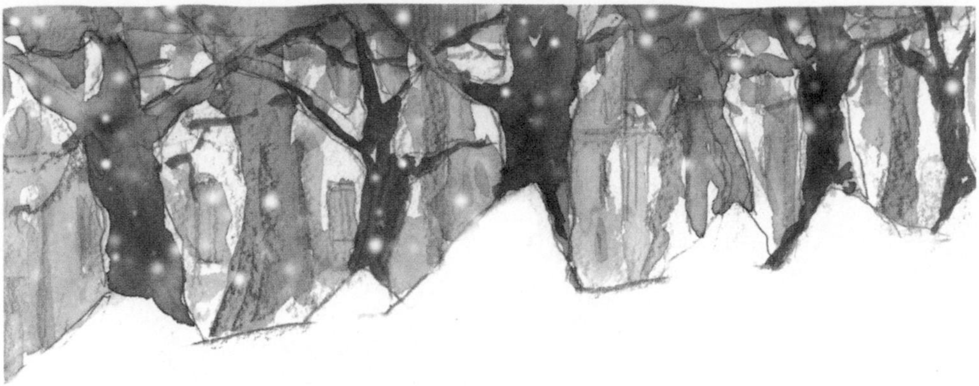

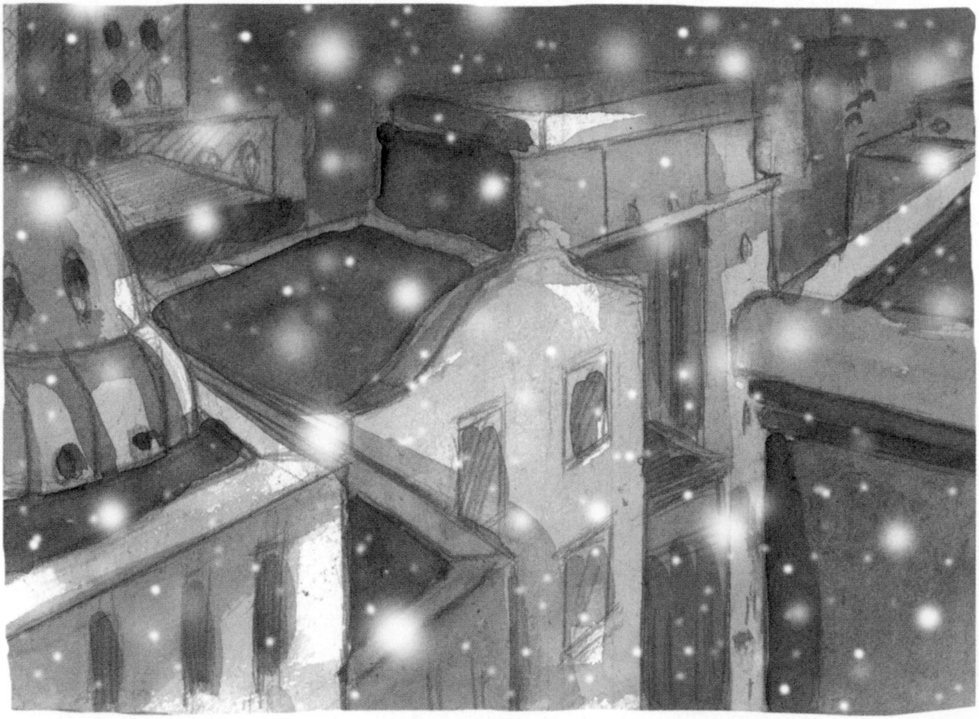

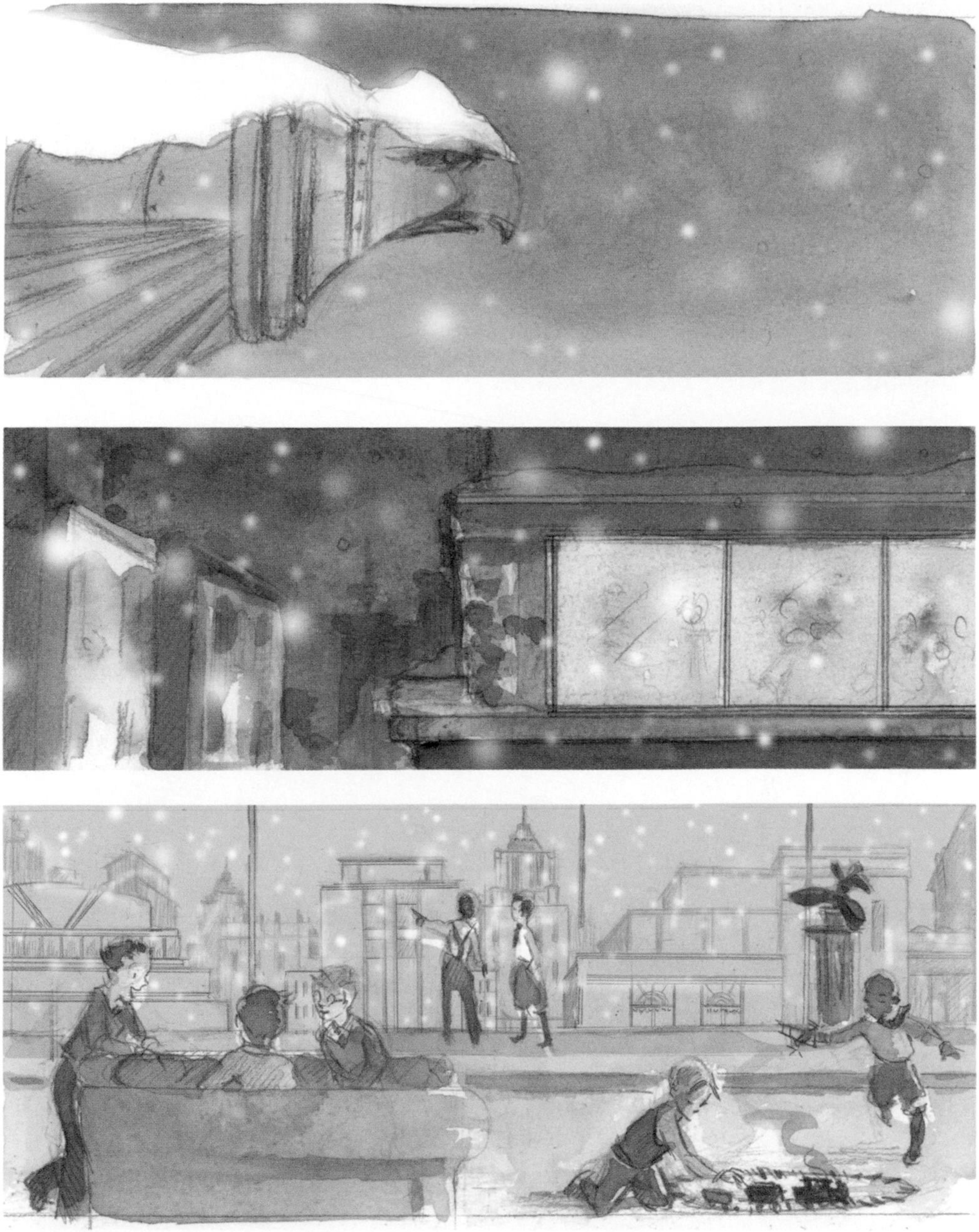

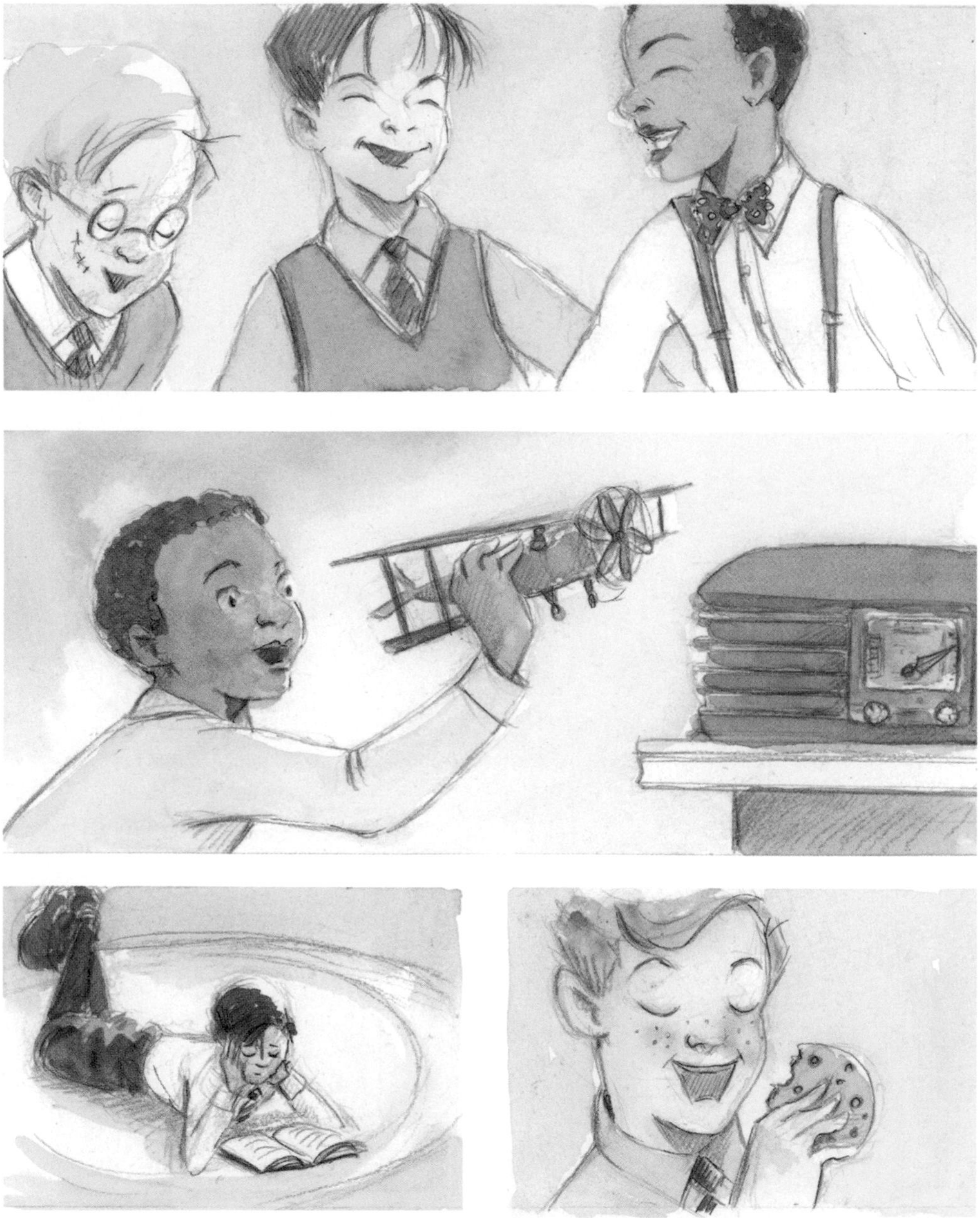

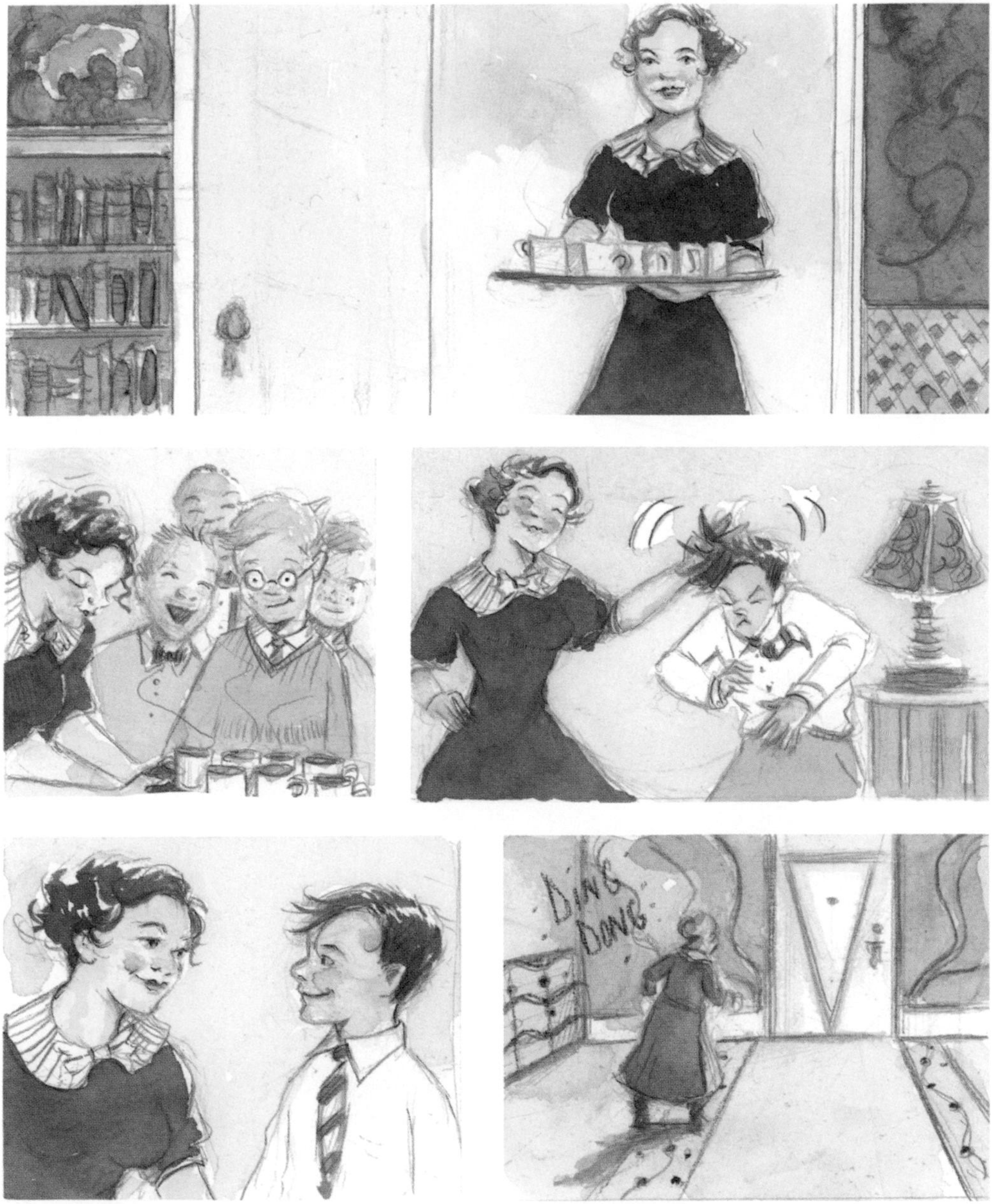
DING
DONG

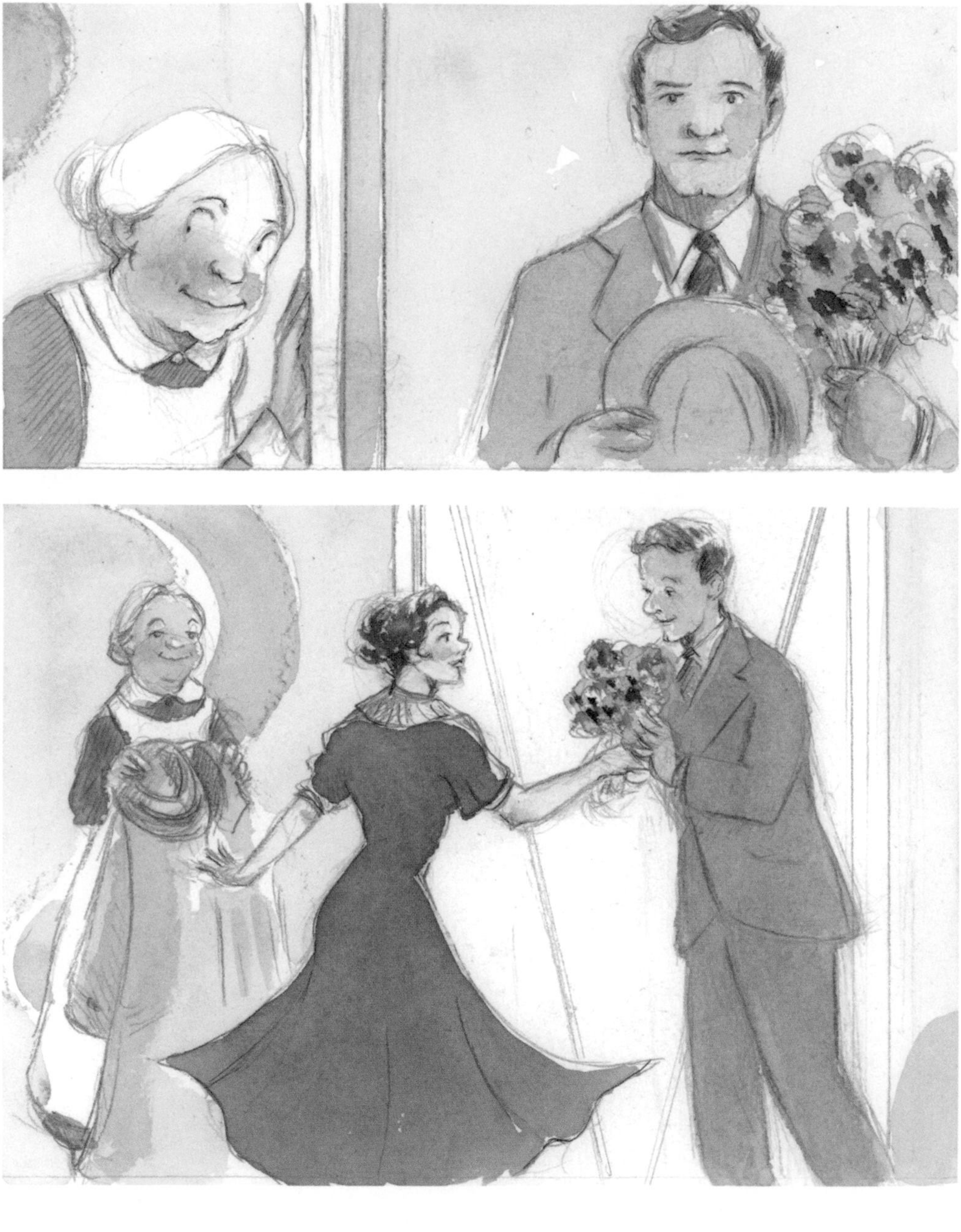

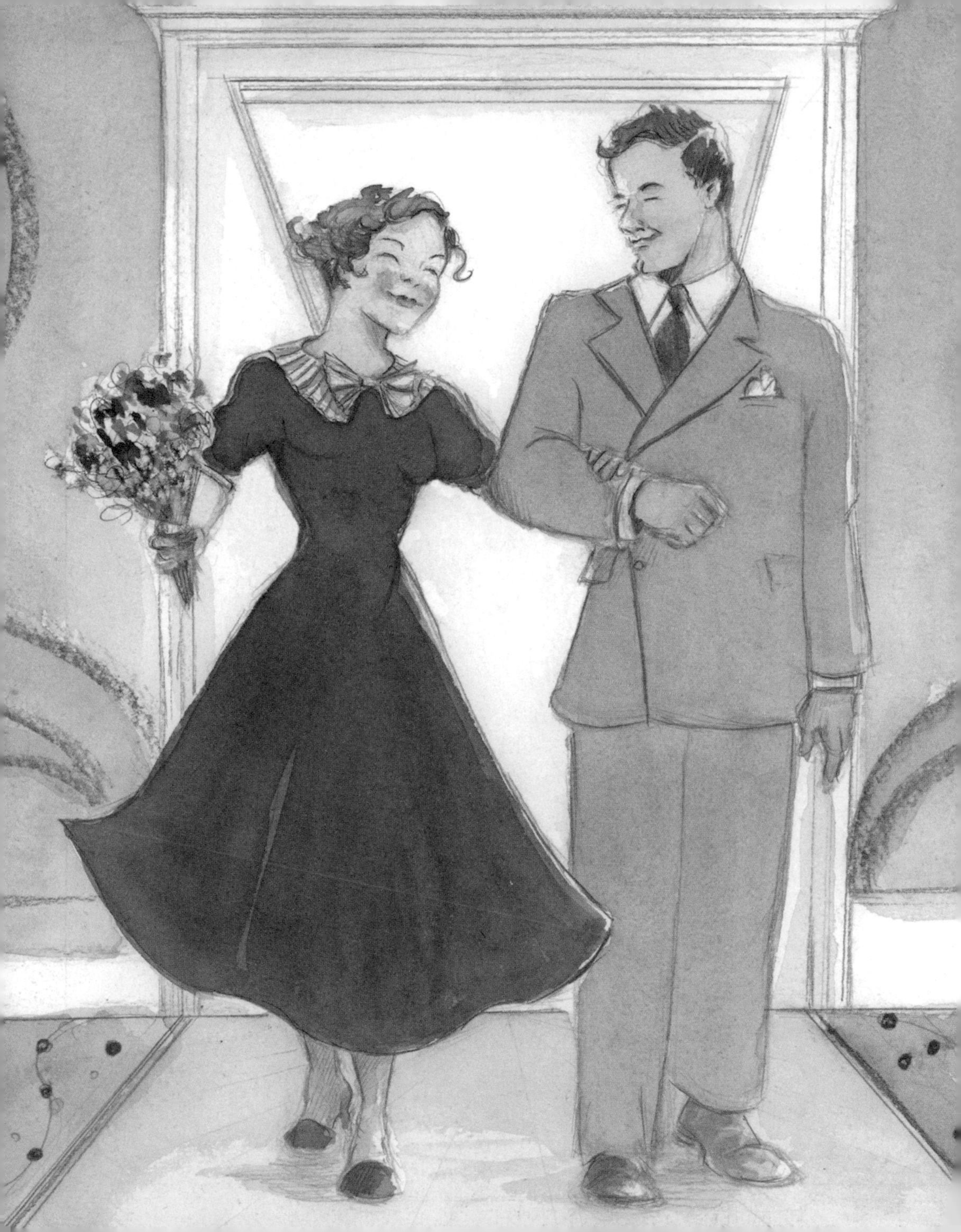

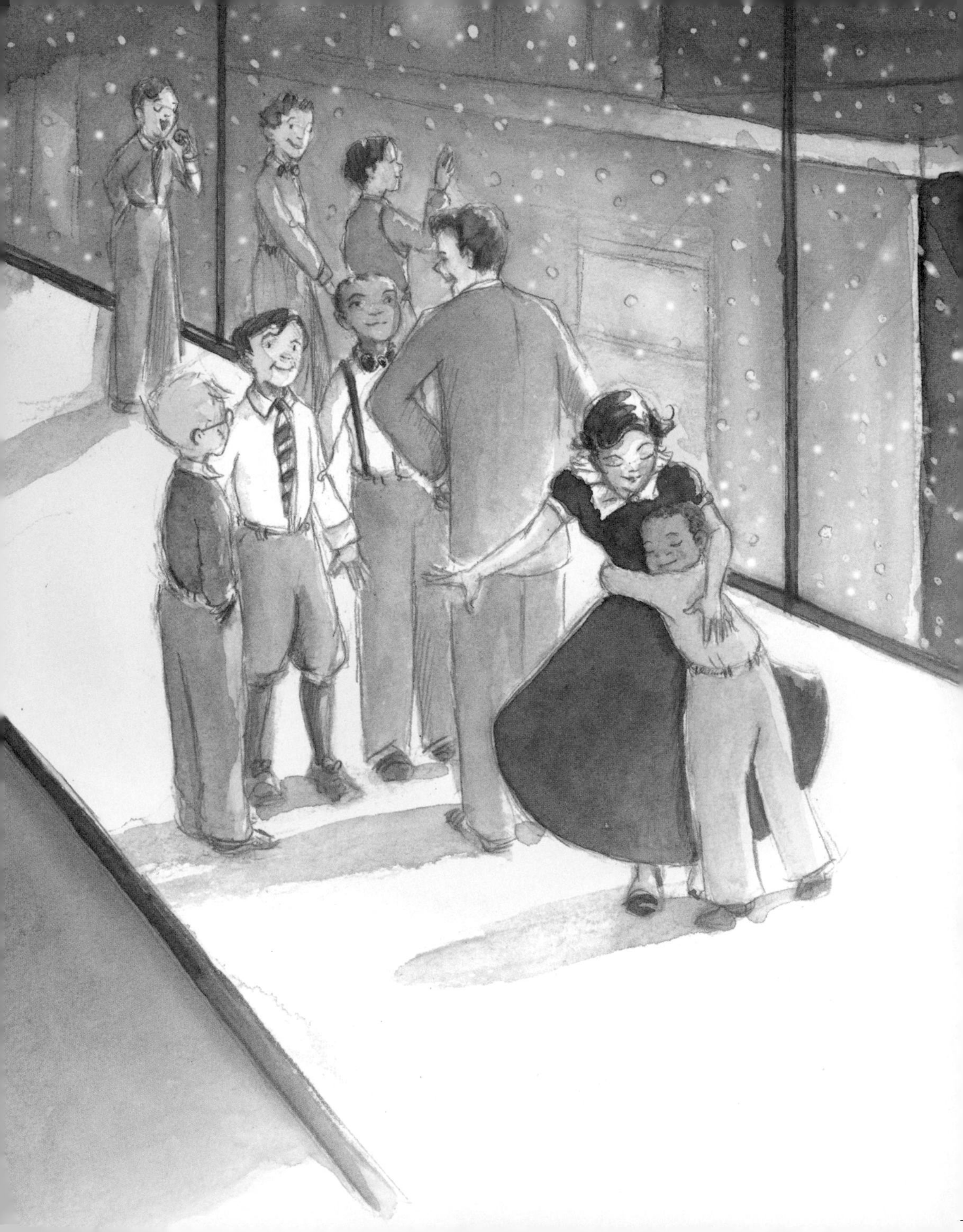

MATT PHELAN is the author-illustrator of three previous graphic novels: *The Storm in the Barn*, winner of a Scott O'Dell Award; *Around the World*; and *Bluffton*, which was nominated for three Will Eisner Comic Industry Awards. He is the author-illustrator of *Druthers* and the illustrator of *Marilyn's Monster* by Michelle Knudsen and *The Higher Power of Lucky* by Susan Patron, winner of a Newbery Medal. Matt Phelan lives in Pennsylvania.

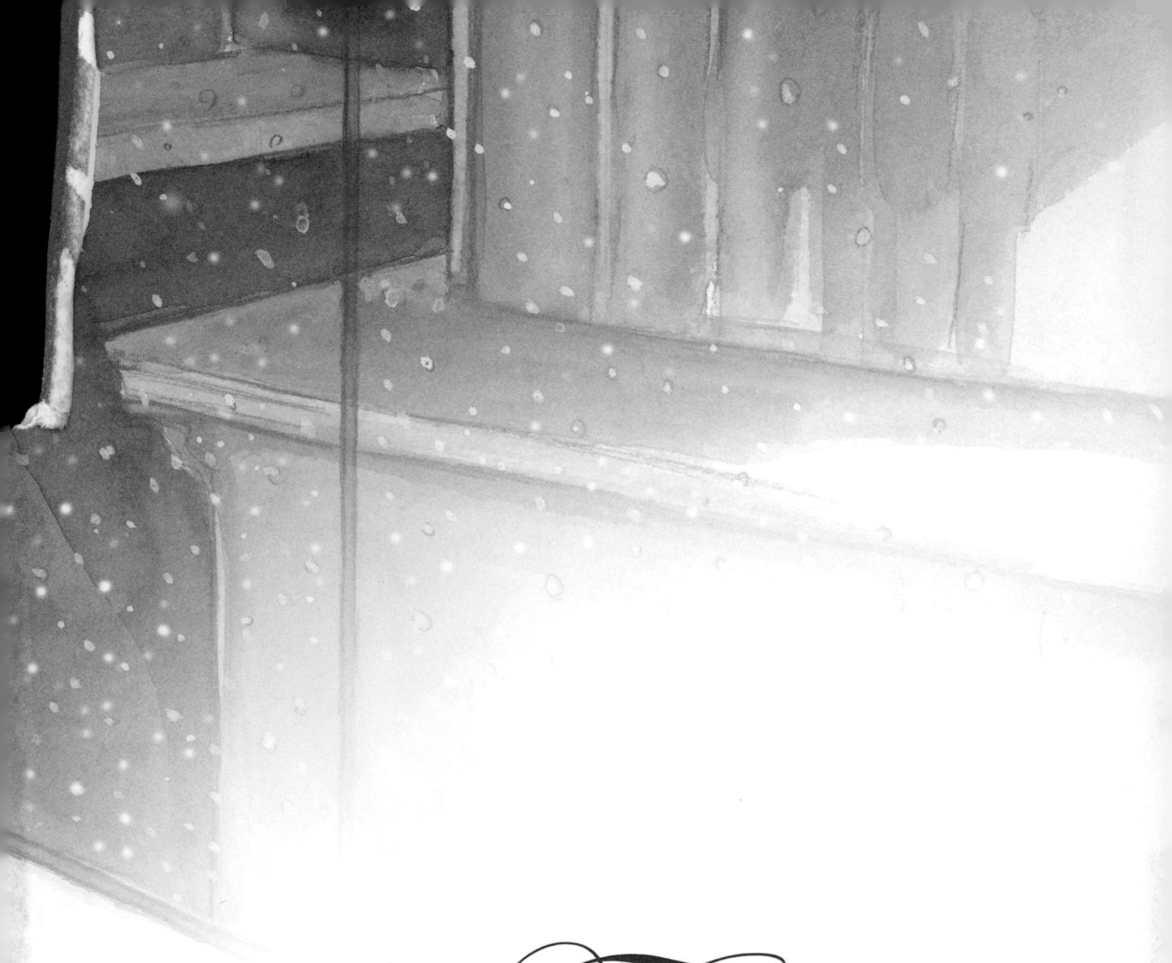

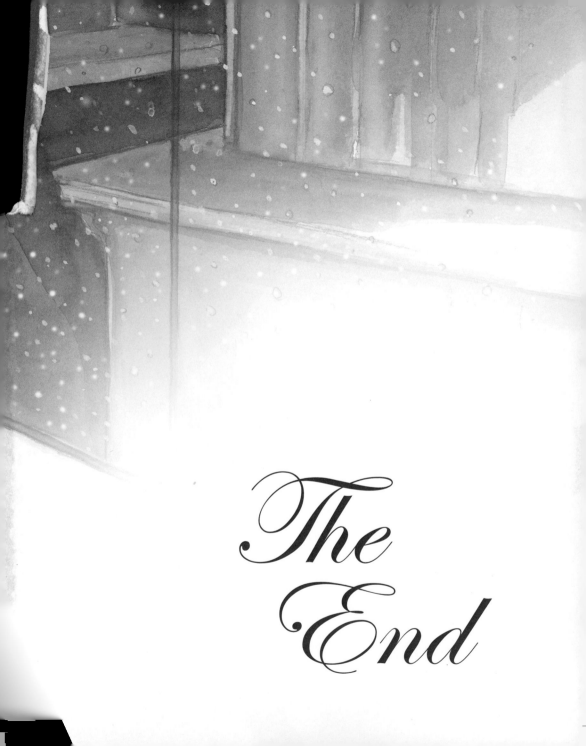

The End